The Silent Tempest

By

Michael G. Manning

Cover by Amalia Chitulescu
Editing by Grace Bryan Butler
© 2015 by Michael G. Manning
All rights reserved.
ISBN: 978-1512158809

For more information about the Mageborn series
check out the author's website:

www.magebornbooks.com

Or visit him on his Facebook page:

www.facebook.com/MagebornAuthor

The Silent Tempest

Prologue

"How about tonight?" asked Matthew.

"Tonight what?" I responded, although I already had a good idea what he was wanting.

"You can finish the story."

Moira walked up just then, "You've been putting us off for a week now."

"It isn't a very pleasant tale," I reminded them.

Matthew nodded, "I know, I've started having dreams."

That got my attention. I knew that being my first child, he would eventually face the same knowledge that I had been born with, but I had hoped it would be later. Much of it was depressing, and other parts were guaranteed to ruin the carefree innocence of his youth.

He saw the look on my face, "Dad, don't."

"Don't what?" I said, trying to cover my feelings.

"Don't give me that look. I'm not a kid anymore."

I did my best not to laugh. Every time I heard that line from one of them it provoked the same response, and I knew that it wouldn't be appreciated. Naturally, from my perspective they would always be children, at least until they were older than I was, which was unlikely to happen. But I knew that from their viewpoint it was an entirely different matter, they *weren't* the children they had once been. They weren't infants, or toddlers, or even pre-adolescents anymore, they were teenagers. "What sort of dreams?" I asked after a moment.

"About what you told us—about Daniel," he responded.

"Probably because the story sparked your recall," I said, nodding. "I shouldn't have told you all of that. It's started your mind down a path that would be better left until later."

"Well, it's too late now," he told me. "Besides, I think the story helps."

"How so?"

"The parts I remember, the parts you told us already, those don't seem as bad. It's like I'm thinking about something I've read, and less like something horrible that I actually lived. But I'm starting to remember more, and it really bothers me. If you tell me the rest, maybe it won't seem so real when I dream about it. Maybe it will be more like just a story…"

And less like your personal sin against an entire race, I thought, finishing his sentence silently. "That makes sense," I agreed. "Let's go sit at the table, this will take a while."

"Let me go find Lynarralla," said Moira. "She's going to want to hear the rest too."

Matthew and I waited for a quarter of an hour until she returned, bringing Tyrion and Lyralliantha's child with her. The serious young She'Har girl took a seat at the table with us. Once everyone was settled, I took a deep breath and began.

"Last time, I believe we stopped after Tyrion fought the krytek, and things had gotten rather peaceful. The years after that were pretty quiet for him, but despite Lyralliantha's presence and the lack of fighting, Tyrion was growing restless. At heart he was lonely, for the She'Har were not human, and despite her best efforts, Lyralliantha was not always the best company.

"I'll skip forward to the time when things began to happen again. Ten years had passed, and Tyrion had begun working on a stone house, a place he could call his own…"

The Silent Tempest

Chapter 1

Tyrion ran his hands down the stone, feeling its smooth edges. He had never had any training as a stone cutter, but his abilities gave him a considerable advantage. The stone itself was in ample supply, and Lyralliantha had no objection to allowing him to venture beyond the Illeniel Grove to obtain what he needed. Transporting it in large quantities from the hills was a lot of work, though.

His first real problem when he began constructing the house, was joining the stones. He knew absolutely nothing about mortar, and his first attempts at making it resulted in something that was less useful than plain mud. He considered trying to convince Lyralliantha to let him travel to Lincoln, in hopes of finding a stone-mason who would be willing to teach him what he needed to know. In the end, he decided it would be better if he did things his own way.

Tyrion's solution had been to craft an enchantment that would permanently bind the stones together. Since he could easily cut them to exactly the shape or size he required, he could fit them together without gaps and the final product was as strong as or stronger than if the entire structure had been built from a single stone.

'Enchantment' was the term he had started using for his new form of magic. Lyralliantha had been very firm in stating that what he did was *not* spell-weaving, although it bore many similarities. The basic geometry that his enchanting used was based on triangular shapes fitted together, each containing a rune identity that provided unique properties. Spell-weaving was based on smaller hexagons with a more complex geometry but simpler symbology.

Both magics produced similar effects, both were permanent, but enchanting made it possible for a human wizard to create long lasting effects through extensive planning and preparation, while spell-weaving was a product of the She'Har's innate seed-mind. Their magic was spontaneous, while enchanting was a labor of time and effort.

"I still don't understand why you insist on doing this," said a voice behind him. It didn't startle him, though. His mind had noted Lyralliantha's careful approach several minutes before.

Tyrion turned to regard her with his physical eyes. Magesight rendered her form and features, but it was a poor substitute for seeing her painted by the late afternoon sunlight. Her hair was a shimmering silver that seemed to capture the sun, even as it framed the vivid blue color of her eyes. "I explained this already," he responded. "I want a place of my own."

"I could have had one grown for you, and it would have been much easier."

"I wanted to design it myself."

"I could have accommodated any design you desired."

"And that's exactly what I *didn't* want," he explained. "I'm not a pet. I don't want you to provide for me. I want to do this for myself. Besides, I have specific ideas that would be difficult for you to produce."

"Enlighten me," she said.

Chapter 1

"Privacy," he answered. "I'm building something that your people, these trees…" he gestured to the massive god-trees surrounding them, "… won't be able to see into."

"Why is that so important to you?"

He stared at her, thinking. After living among the She'Har for more than a decade, he still found them alien. His relationship with Lyralliantha only served to highlight that fact for him on a daily basis. "I'm not sure how to explain it," he admitted. "Humans are social creatures, but not to the extent that your people are. We value our individuality, and part of that is reflected in a need to be apart from others, even others of our own kind."

"If you wish for me to stay with you, then you will not be alone," observed the She'Har woman.

"I don't need to be completely alone, and not all of the time," said Tyrion. "And besides, you don't count, you're my mate."

"I am *not* your mate," she stated firmly. "We will not produce offspring."

He sighed heavily. The She'Har had difficulty with emotional contexts; for them most words had rigid definitions. They had discussed procreation before, but since any child they produced together would be 'merely' human, and therefore a slave, he had told her he would rather remain childless. He had already had too many children, and he was a father to none of them.

"I don't mean mate in that sense," he explained. "We are partners and companions, like family."

"We have sex. You told me before that family members do not do such things."

7

"Not that sort of family," he told her. "Family can mean more than just people who are related to one another. In this case, I'm referring to love."

"That word is more problematic than any other."

"Just because you don't understand it, doesn't mean it doesn't apply to you."

She frowned, "Despite the brevity of your language, it is filled with ambiguity. Erollith is much more concise, the words do not have multiple or vague meanings."

Tyrion smiled, "Context is everything, and it allows us to convey emotions in our speech, something I find very lacking in Erollith. Do your people have a word for 'spouse', or life-partner? Surely in your race's extensive history you've had to create a word for such unions, even if it was just to describe them in one of your enslaved races."

The She'Har had a long history that went beyond the world that humanity lived on. Tyrion had learned from Thillmarius that the She'Har had come from another world, passing through different dimensions to colonize new places. The Krytek, their warrior minions were often constructed in the image of some of the bizarre creatures they had fought and enslaved during their long history. The She'Har children themselves were usually created in the form of whatever race was most appropriate to their current world. In this case, they had adopted the human race as their primary 'child' form, but their true adult form was that of the gigantic 'god-trees' that covered the world.

Chapter 1

"The most similar word in our language would be 'kianthi', but it has not been used since our most distant ancestors left the first-world," she answered.

"Kee-yan-thee," said Tyrion, enunciating carefully to make sure he had the sound of the word right.

Lyralliantha nodded, "The earliest of our people had partners to help them, acting cooperatively when moving to colonize a new region. Our first home had many enemies, and it was necessary for our survival."

"A male-female pair?"

"Male and female are misleading terms," she corrected. "The kianthi helped to seed a new grove. Many failed, but the most successful survived and flourished. Eventually we overcame all our natural enemies, and the first-world was filled, as this one is."

"And the two who had paired up, they would do anything for one another?" asked Tyrion.

"If a kianthi died, they could not create a new tree. They supported each other in every way possible," she explained.

"When I cut my collar off, you nearly killed yourself trying to save me," he noted. "Was that rational?"

"No," she admitted.

"But it was the sort of thing these 'kianthi' of yours would do for one another."

"It would be logical for them to do so. It did not involve any of the intangible concepts you humans ascribe to such things. It was not for love," she declared.

"How do you know?"

"Because my people do not function like that."

"They don't *now*," agreed Tyrion, "but you weren't there. You don't know what your ancient ancestors were like."

"Those who have eaten the loshti, the lore-wardens, they remember," she stated.

Certain select She'Har children were given a special fruit that passed on the collected knowledge of one of the god-trees, and every tree that had come before it, if it had also been a lore-warden. Some of the trees, and by extension some of the current lore-wardens, had memories that stretched back all the way to their original home, millennia before the present.

"You should ask one of them," suggested Tyrion. "The answer may be different than you expect."

Lyralliantha became still.

That, in itself, was nothing unusual, the She'Har were often notable for their lack of unnecessary movement, but it was the suddenness of it that caught his attention. Tyrion stopped working to give her his full attention, "What?"

"The elders have offered me the loshti," she said without preamble.

That surprised him, "But aren't you the youngest of the Illeniel Grove?" He wasn't sure how such things worked, but it didn't make much sense to him that the very youngest of their people would be given something considered to be one of their highest honors.

"Yes."

"Then why you? Aren't there many others with greater standing?"

"You misunderstand the purpose of the loshti and their reason for offering it," she told him.

His eyes narrowed, "You said it was to pass knowledge down, from generation to generation…"

Lyralliantha nodded, "That is correct, but the choice of to whom it is given is also guided by knowledge, or rather the acquisition of it. A child who displays great wisdom, who reveals new insights, or shows signs of innovation, those are the ones they seek, in order to add to the wealth of the loshti."

That made sense, now that he looked at it from that angle. Thillmarius was the first lore-warden he had met. His most notable characteristic was his clinical fascination with studying humans. Byovar, one of the Illeniel lore-wardens, had made a hobby of studying Barion, the human language.

Tyrion stared at Lyralliantha, "But what have you done?" The question would have been rude, if he had been speaking to a human, but her people were blunt and direct. She would take no offense at such a remark.

She returned his gaze without blinking. "You often tell me that humans learn from their mistakes. The She'Har do not make many mistakes, but when we do, we also try to learn as much as we can from the experience."

"Do you want this?"

She blinked, momentarily confused, "Please explain your question more clearly."

He stood and stepped closer, putting his hands on her shoulders to physically remind her of their relationship, "Do you want to take the Loshti? What effect will it have on *us*?"

Lyralliantha pulled away from him, "It will have no effect on *us*, or whatever your vague plural pronoun implies. I will change, you will not. My goals and priorities will likely change as well, as I assimilate the knowledge of ages. I doubt I will still be the person you are familiar with."

"What about love?"

"What about it?"

He winced at her cool tone, reminded again of her all too inhuman upbringing. "Will you still feel the same for me?"

"I feel pain when you are hurting, and my loyalties have become irrationally disordered where you are concerned, but I still do not know if that qualifies as love…"

"…but will you still have those feelings afterward?" he interrupted.

"I do not know. My guess is that I will not. My mind is but a drop in what will be an ocean of knowledge and experience." A feeling of uncertainty, or perhaps fear, emanated from her.

"Don't do it then," Tyrion told her.

"I am a child of the She'Har," she stated flatly.

Tyrion's hand snaked out with sudden speed, catching her by the hair and pulling her head close to his, "You are mine."

She didn't struggle, instead, meeting his gaze with languid eyes, "Technically, you belong to me, *slave.*"

He kissed her, before trailing his way along her jaw and then whispering in her ear, "Until I ask you to remove this collar." The statement was a bluff of course; while she had previously agreed to his terms, removal of his slave collar would make him a target of every one of the She'Har.

"Unless I decided to refuse," she purred back, a rising heat in her voice.

His teeth found her throat, nipping lightly at the tender flesh there. "In that case, we will die together."

"Would you really prefer that?" she asked.

"If the only other option were losing you—I might," he admitted.

Her eyes softened ever so slightly. The change in expression was so subtle it might have been missed by someone else, but he had had years of practice reading her quiet face. "You have a year and a half to decide. The loshti takes time to mature."

A sense of relief passed through him, but he hid it. Stepping back, he told her, "Oh good, then I have time to complete this house."

Lyralliantha growled at his seeming dismissal, and spellwoven vines began to grow around them, trapping him together with her in a small bower. "You have something else to finish first."

"Oh really?" he asked innocently. "What would that be?"

She graced him with a rare smile, "Me."

The Silent Tempest

Chapter 2

"Wake up."

His first impression in the dim morning gloom was of green eyes, sparkling as they somehow caught the first tentative light of dawn. Catherine Sayer was staring intently at him, urgency in her features. Something important was happening.

"She needs you."

"Kate?" he asked, confused. How could she be here? Kate was in Colne with her husband and teenage son.

"Wake up, Tyrion. You will want to hear this."

It was Lyralliantha's voice. His eyes opened once more, to find silver hair and blue eyes waiting for him. He blinked, struggling to separate his dreaming and waking thoughts from one another. "What did you say?"

"I said, 'you will want to hear this'. They have brought in another from your village," she told him.

A jolt of adrenaline brought him more fully awake. "Who is they?"

"The Mordan. It was one of their wardens who found her."

His dream was still fresh, and it connected with her words immediately. "Her?" *Surely Kate wouldn't be so foolish as to come here.* If she had come, if she had been claimed by another grove—the consequences were too terrible to consider.

"A girl."

"How old?"

She frowned. Lyralliantha wasn't good at judging human ages. She'Har children didn't age. They were created in what would be a fully adult form for a human, and they remained the same apparent age until the day they were allowed to transition to their true adulthood. All that aside, she hadn't seen the child with her own eyes. "I was told she is young, but not small, almost my height."

That could indicate anything from twelve to twenty, but it was almost certain the girl was a teenager. Whoever she was, she was probably terrified. Memories of the wardens and their red whips flashed through Tyrion's mind. "I need to see her," he said firmly. He was already sitting up and struggling to get his trousers on.

"It will not be easy. They are unlikely to welcome us."

While the She'Har were particular about their 'property rights' when it came to humans, they usually weren't overly territorial unless there were special circumstances. Over the past fifteen years Tyrion had been allowed to visit any of the human slave camps he wished, so long as he behaved himself. It was even possible the Mordan might allow Lyralliantha to buy the rights to their new find. "There's something else isn't there?"

"She is like you."

"Wait…" He had assumed that someone from Colne had foolishly come too close to the borders of the grove, but that didn't make sense. It was the Illeniel Grove that most closely approached Colne and the valley it was located in. The girl wouldn't have been taken by the Mordan in that case, which meant that it had been a patrol. The patrols ignored the people of the valley, unless they exhibited signs… "She's a mage."

Lyralliantha nodded.

"And she's from Colne."

"She's a wildling, like you," she confirmed.

The She'Har patrols were primarily to make sure that the traits that they had imbued their children with, didn't migrate into the small remainder of the free human population. Their magical slave collars were marvelously effective at preventing their human property from breeding without permission, but it had happened in the past. When Tyrion had first been captured, they had assumed he was the result of such an event. It was only later that they had discovered that his 'gift' was the result of a purely random mutation.

It was extremely unlikely that such a thing had happened by chance. *Don't think about it,* he told himself. "What about Thillmarius?"

"What of him?"

Thillmarius was the only She'Har trainer he had any real personal experience with. A child and lore-warden of the Prathion Grove, Thillmarius had been the one originally entrusted with Tyrion's care and training. Thoughts of the torture he had endured made a cold sweat break out whenever he thought of the black-skinned She'Har, but Thillmarius was his best hope.

The Mordan would be highly protective of their new find if the girl was a true wildling mage. Tyrion had upset the balance of power within the She'Har groves after he had been found, allowing the Prathion and Illeniel groves to gain greater status. His winning streak in the arena had brought a large amount of 'shuthsi', a sort of currency, to the Illeniel Grove, and Thillmarius had taken strategic advantage of his wins to improve the standing of the Prathion Grove as well.

"He's a trainer, and he's helped us before. If anyone could convince the Mordan trainer to let me see their new prize, it would be him," explained Tyrion.

After a somewhat hasty breakfast, the two of them went to Ellentrea. It was the most likely place to find Thillmarius, who spent most of his days training the Prathion slaves there. It took most of an hour to reach it, but the Prathion lore-warden was easily found.

Thillmarius smiled at their approach, an expression that never failed to chill Tyrion's blood. It was part of the She'Har's continuing attempts to communicate more effectively with humans, but there was no true feeling behind the smile. The Prathion trainer could kill or torture as easily as heal one of his baratti, and none of it seemed to truly affect him.

"I had a suspicion you might finally come to visit," said the She'Har, looking at them with golden eyes that perfectly matched his shining hair.

"I'm surprised you haven't already gone to see the new arrival," said Tyrion, keeping his tone cool. He had learned long ago that no good came of becoming emotional while dealing with Thillmarius, or any other She'Har for that matter.

"Actually, I would have sought you out first, if you hadn't come to find me. The Mordan are unlikely to welcome excessive interest in their new prize, until they have had a chance to test her abilities for themselves. "You will provide an excellent incentive for them to allow us into Sabortrea."

Chapter 2

"Trading favors?"

Lyralliantha spoke then, "You understand our people well, Tyrion."

"What will they want?" asked Tyrion.

"Nothing more than a blood sample," answered the Prathion. "They will want to confirm your relation to the girl and see if there are any pertinent genetic differences."

Tyrion winced. "Then they already suspect she is my daughter."

Thillmarius smiled once more. "I doubt you are aware of it, but the groves have been sending more frequent patrols since your arrival. They all would like to obtain the same advantage that the Illeniels enjoyed for so long."

Tyrion had long ago told them that he had no offspring, but he had known deep down that his lie was in vain. *I should have known this would happen,* he thought. *I just didn't want to face the possibility.* Now the girl, whoever she might be, would suffer for his refusal to face the inevitable. "What will they do with her?"

"You remember what it was like when you first came here," stated Thillmarius. "Sabortrea is much the same, and their methods are nearly identical."

***

The world below them was a vista dominated by the vast forest that stretched away to the horizon in every direction. The trees covered the world as far as the eye could see, broken only by the occasional river, or in the distance, a range of mountains. The ride to

19

Sabortrea was several days on horseback, so Thillmarius had summoned a 'dormon', one of the flying plant-like creatures that he had once previously used to show Tyrion the remnant of an old human city.

The flight made a trip of days into a few meagre hours. They had already passed the borders of the Mordan Grove and were now descending toward an open area that represented Sabortrea and its arena.

Upon landing they were met by two wardens, humans with the same hardened, indifferent faces that Tyrion had become accustomed to during his time among the She'Har. Raised in the pits and trained to constant violence, their hearts were stunted by cruelty and barely capable of the subtler emotions. Standing between them was one of the Mordan She'Har, recognizable by his light blue skin and ebon hair. The She'Har's eyes were a vivid blue, notably darker than the icy blue that the Illeniel She'Har exhibited.

"Thillmarius," said their greeter, inclining his head toward the dark skinned She'Har who rode in front of Tyrion and Lyralliantha. After a second he turned his eyes to Lyralliantha, skipping over Tyrion as an object to be considered later. 'People' took precedence over animals. "Lyralliantha, I see you brought your pet to visit our new prize."

She nodded, responding to the greeting with one word, "Dalleth."

Tyrion knew her response had been for his benefit. The Mordan She'Har might have taken offense if she had gone so far as to formally introduce them, slaves didn't merit such an honor. Instead, she had answered with the newcomer's name, knowing Tyrion's quick ears would not fail to take notice.

"Unfortunately, I am afraid you have wasted your time coming here," said Dalleth. "Our new baratt is still adjusting to her place here. I feel it would interfere with her training to expose her to uncertain influences at this juncture." His eyes flicked toward Tyrion as he spoke.

Lyralliantha touched Thillmarius' arm, a gesture indicating he should speak on her behalf. They had agreed on her response beforehand, but Thillmarius was a lore-warden as well as a respected trainer. He would do the negotiating.

"I'm sure you are interested in your animal's lineage. Since she comes from the same region as Lyralliantha's slave, you must have your suspicions," began the Prathion She'Har.

"The Illeniels have thus far refused to share the information gleaned from Tyrion's testing," commented Dalleth. "Are you able to offer something?"

Thillmarius glanced at Lyralliantha, waiting on her nod before answering, "A sample of his blood, in return for a like sample…"

Lyralliantha coughed, interrupting Thillmarius. His eyes met hers for a moment before continuing, "Correction, in return for permission to allow her baratt to visit with yours for a short period of time."

Dalleth snorted, "I thought you bargained for the Illeniels, Thillmarius, but it sounds as if you represent the baratt."

The Prathion showed no sign of offense, "You are mistaken, Dalleth."

"How so?"

"The wildlings are different from our domestic baratti. Tyrion's successes were a result of something beyond normal training regimen. We will learn more about your new animal by letting him speak to her," answered Thillmarius.

"That is of little concern to the Mordan Grove," answered the cerulean-skinned She'Har trainer.

Thillmarius lowered his head slightly, conceding the point, "No, but what is of concern to your grove, is the fact that your new animal may benefit greatly from even a brief interaction with Tyrion."

Dalleth sighed, "I find that highly unlikely. I would refuse your offer, but I will consult Gwaeri first. The lore-warden's opinion may differ from mine."

That surprised Tyrion. Since the only trainer he had had much experience with was Thillmarius, he had assumed that all She'Har trainers were also lore-wardens. Obviously, that was not the case here.

Dalleth left, and they waited for more than an hour before he returned. Tyrion was filled with a feeling of impatience, but he kept it firmly under control. He had spent years imprisoned in a tiny room. He had learned to wait, but he had never come to like it.

The Mordan She'Har returned alone. "Gwaeri's thoughts differed from my own. He has convinced me to accept your offer, though my own preference would be to reject it."

"Then we should discuss the details of our terms," offered Thillmarius.

The two She'Har trainers spoke at length before eventually settling on the specifics. Tyrion would be allowed to spend twenty-four hours with the Mordan Grove's new slave in exchange for a sample of his blood. Dalleth led them to the slave quarters within Sabortrea immediately after drawing his precious sample.

As they walked, Tyrion scanned the dwellings around them. The structure and layout of Sabortrea was very similar to Ellentrea, but he couldn't be sure which of the small huts contained his daughter.

No, that must be her.

They had gotten closer and he now sensed a dwelling with a noticeably different occupant. A girl was within, and he could tell at a glance that she must be at or near the age of fifteen. What really stood out though, was her aythar. Unlike the other human slaves, hers was far brighter; she shone in his magesight like a star among candles. Her strength was far greater than anything he had seen before, among either the She'Har or their human property.

And someone was in the small hut with her.

He could feel her pain well before they reached the door, and his rage, long dormant over the past years, began to rise once again.

Lyralliantha's hand was on his arm. "Remember, this is not our place. I cannot shield you if you make a mistake here."

His eyes were stony, staring ahead as he responded. "I know."

Dalleth watched him, a faint smile on his lips. At his touch, the living wood of the doorway drew apart. "You may enter."

Tyrion stepped inside without hesitation, although he could sense Lyralliantha's hand behind him. She had tried to catch his arm again, to urge caution. Within, his eyes saw what his other senses had already shown him. A man in brown leathers stood over the girl, the red whip so often used by the wardens in his hand.

The girl at his feet was young, her body still soft and her features still rounded with the fat that gradually disappears in adulthood. She was naked, like all slaves of the She'Har, and her skin was marked with dirt and bruises. Dried blood stained her thigh.

His eyes took these things in instantly, with a clarity wrought from adrenaline. The red whip was descending toward her, and he reached out, catching it with his left hand, feeling the old, familiar agony as it wrapped itself around his wrist.

A shield would have saved him from the pain, but to raise one in the presence of the She'Har was a declaration of hostility. Instead, he caught it without protection, gritting his teeth while the magic of the whip sent fire through his nerves and tore at his sanity.

It was something he would never have dreamed of before. His first year among the She'Har had instilled a fear of the red whips that went so deep as to be engraved in his soul, but that was the fear of another man. He wasn't Daniel Tennick anymore. He was Tyrion, and his anger, like a silent tempest, had scoured his soul clean of its old frailties.

"We need to step outside," he told the warden, his lips twitching involuntarily as he spoke.

The warden's eyes widened as he stared at the man holding the other end of his whip. The pain should have sent him to the ground, screaming and twitching, but rather than collapsing, Tyrion continued to hold it, a grimace on his face and sweat forming on his brow.

Chapter 2

"Tyrion no!" barked Lyralliantha. She knew him well enough to see that he was almost beyond reason now.

The warden's eyes flicked to the doorway, noting the presence of the three She'Har, including his own master, Dalleth. They returned to Tyrion's face, and then he released his will, letting the red whip vanish. "My lord," he said, dipping his head in deference to the She'Har.

"Outside," repeated Tyrion slowly.

The girl watched them in confusion, not knowing any of them. She hadn't seen Tyrion since she was a small child, and it was highly unlikely she would recognize him. She scrambled back from them across the dirt floor, pressing her back against the far wall.

"If he damages my property, there will be consequences," said Dalleth coolly, speaking to Thillmarius and Lyralliantha.

Tyrion glanced at Lyralliantha, noting the fear in her eyes. It was not something he had ever seen before. *She's afraid of losing me.* He knew his next actions would likely result in a swift demise, but he no longer cared.

"Actually," said Thillmarius, his voice sudden and unexpected, "I have an idea. Would you consider selling me a couple of your wardens, Dalleth? I promise you'll find it entertaining."

The Silent Tempest

Chapter 3

The evening air was cool as he stepped into the arena. He felt it more acutely now, since he had been forced to remove his clothing and leathers. It had been many years since the last time he had crossed into such a space.

"What are those strange markings?" asked Dalleth from behind him. The question, naturally enough, was addressed toward Lyralliantha rather than her slave. The Mordan She'Har was puzzled by the tattoos that covered Tyrion's body. Most of them had been added in the years since he had been released from the arena.

"A new magic, but I doubt we will get to see it," she answered smoothly.

"Why is that?" said Dalleth.

"This fight won't require it." She glanced down at the girl standing in front of her. The young human was trembling, which was understandable considering the cold air, but Lyralliantha could also sense her fear. In the human tongue she added, "Relax child, no further harm will come to you today."

Dalleth coughed, then commented to her in Erollith, "Child? The rumors must be true."

Lyralliantha raised a brow in an unspoken question.

"That you've gone soft on the baratti," he stated.

Thillmarius broke in, "The Illeniels have never been in favor of keeping the baratti as slaves."

"Yet she keeps one," noted Dalleth. "He is more of a pet to you, though, isn't he? Or do you have more perverse 'emotional' ties?"

She ignored the question. "They are about to begin." Touching the girl's shoulder she added in Barion, "Pay attention, child, you may learn something that will help you survive."

Tyrion was staring across the field, watching the two men who had just entered from the other side. One was the warden he had just met, the other was new to him. As far as he knew they were both Mordan, meaning they would be able to teleport. It was a troublesome talent, and one that made it hard to predict where they would be from moment to moment.

In the past he had dealt with that problem by turning large regions of the arena into an uninhabitable hell, either with wind or fire. It was a brute force approach that would end the match too soon, however. Now that he was in the arena once more, he found himself not wanting to end it too quickly.

The two wardens across from him stepped apart from each other, exchanging a few quiet words. Then, the first one raised his voice, "No shield, Tyrion?" The Mordan vanished after his first words, reappearing twenty feet closer before vanishing again. He was advancing toward Tyrion by teleporting unpredictably, always closer but never following a straight line. The second warden remained where he had entered the arena.

"It wouldn't be interesting if you didn't have a chance," answered Tyrion. As soon as he spoke, the second warden vanished.

It was an old tactic. The one who was advancing was meant to hold his attention, while the second would appear behind him at the moment he seemed most distracted.

Chapter 3

The second warden appeared and then flew backward, struck by a wave of pure force so powerful that his shield collapsed. The man's body hit the outer barrier that surrounded the arena with lethal speed. He was dead before he finished falling to the ground.

Tyrion hadn't even turned. Still watching the first warden he cursed, "Damn. I had hoped this would last a little longer." Focusing his will on his hand, he batted aside the deadly lance that the first warden had sent surging toward his midsection. His return attack blasted the warden's shield with a powerful strike calculated to almost overwhelm his foe's defense, without actually doing so.

The other man staggered and then teleported to avoid the second attack. He knew he wouldn't survive a second strike. He began teleporting at random, hoping time would offer him a chance, but the warden already knew it was hopeless.

Tyrion began to raise a fog, one that went beyond the merely physical; a strange mixture of aythar and water vapor that rendered the area within it difficult to sense. He had long ago named it 'mind fog'. Its practical result was that it obscured magesight just as effectively as it blocked eyesight. It had originally been one of his solutions for dealing with the invisibility of Prathion mages, but it had interesting applications in many other situations.

In this case it prompted the warden to panic. Unable to sense his surroundings, the Mordan mage would be teleporting blind. Sooner or later he would make a fatal mistake.

The one unbending rule of combat was movement. Everyone who had survived more than a few matches knew that. If you stayed in one place for too long, you were dead. The warden knew that Tyrion's first action after raising the fog would have been to move. The wildling could be almost anywhere by now. The only place he *wouldn't* be was the spot he started. It was also the one place he wouldn't expect the warden to teleport to.

The rule of movement went hand in hand with another important rule of survival. Be unpredictable. The warden teleported to the position where he had last seen Tyrion standing before he had raised the fog. He would wait there, conserving his aythar and preparing a powerful counterstrike. When the wildling wandered close enough for him to sense, he would be ready.

Unfortunately for him, Tyrion was still standing there.

Aythar flared at the speed of thought as the tattoos on Tyrion's arm lit with sudden power, sheathing his arm in a razor sharp blade of magical energy. The warden's shield utterly failed to stop it and the blade took his right arm off at the elbow before continuing to cut a deep gash through his belly. He stared at Tyrion in horror before slowly dropping to his knees.

Tyrion sealed the stump of the warden's arm before blood loss could rob the man of consciousness.

"Why?" asked the warden weakly, looking up at the man who had slain him.

"Do you know how many Mordan mages I have killed?" asked Tyrion.

"No," whispered the warden.

"Neither do I," responded Tyrion, "but you will answer my questions before you join them." The fog continued to swirl through the arena, blocking the view of any spectators.

"I will answer nothing," said the warden, looking down at his ruined midsection. "I am already dead."

Tyrion smiled, "I can keep you alive for quite some time. The manner of your death could be painless, or…" He reached down to push his hand through the gash in the man's stomach, wrenching the wound wider, and starting to pull out his entrails. "…it could be very unpleasant."

***

A long scream pierced the fog before being replaced by empty silence. Dalleth stood beside the other two She'Har and waited in frustration. The fog had spoiled his enjoyment of the match.

"You should have forbidden him to do this," complained the Mordan She'Har. "We can't tell what's happening in there."

Lyralliantha's lips quirked into a half-smile for a moment, "It won't last too long."

In contradiction to her words, the silence, as well as the fog, lasted for several interminable minutes, before finally dissipating. When the air cleared they could see Tyrion kneeling over the warden he had encountered in the hut. It appeared to be over, except for the final blow.

Tyrion's arm lit up with focused power once more as he stared down at his fallen opponent. "My final gift to you…" he said, in a voice just loud enough to be heard. "…freedom." His arm moved, and the blade touched the warden's throat in a motion that was almost delicate. The spellwoven slave collar there vanished, disintegrating at the touch of the blade.

The She'Har slave collars were linked to their slaves in such a way that their proper owners could order their death at any time. They were also designed to kill the wearer if they were destroyed. The warden lost consciousness almost instantly, even though Tyrion's blade barely nicked the skin of his throat. He was dead within seconds.

Tyrion watched the entire process with intense focus, waiting until the warden was completely gone before standing up and walking back toward Lyralliantha and the other She'Har.

The girl, his daughter, watched his approach with barely suppressed fear.

Dalleth wasn't paying attention. The moment the collar had been destroyed he had turned to Lyralliantha, "How did he do that? I had heard rumors, but…"

"That information was not part of our agreement," she responded lightly. "Perhaps we can discuss it when I return to collect Tyrion tomorrow."

***

The girl huddled at the far end of the room. She was still cold, still naked, and most definitely still afraid. It didn't help much that the man who had, until just recently, been torturing her was now replaced by a different man, one who had killed her previous tormentor. She knew nothing of his motivations, but the events of the past few days had made her wary of trusting anyone.

He watched her with cold eyes, studying her intently, but he said nothing.

Eventually she could stand it no longer, and anxiety overcame her fear. "What do you want?" she asked.

"Who was your mother?" asked the stranger.

That was the last question she expected, but she answered quickly. Her captors had been quick to punish any hesitation. "Emily Banks."

The man sighed, "Then you are Haley, correct?"

She nodded, wondering how he had known. Until now, no one had seemed to care what her name was. Looking at the man's intense gaze, she became even more aware of her nakedness. Hunching forward she hugged herself with her arms, hiding her chest.

"Stop that," he ordered.

Haley flinched, but ignored his command. A sinking feeling came over her. She knew what he must want. Her previous tormentor, the one he had slain, had already violated her once, though he had used only his fingers.

"You're broadcasting your vulnerability. Keep your head up and your shoulders back," said the stranger. "Forget about being naked, that means nothing here. Showing strength, or weakness, that is all that matters."

She glanced at him in surprise. The man hadn't come any closer. *Who is he? Why does he look familiar?* "I'm cold," she replied. "It's hard not to cover myself."

"I brought a blanket, but after I'm done you won't need it. Let me show you how to warm yourself first."

She gave him a puzzled look.

"Close your eyes. It will help you focus. Then imagine yourself with a thin layer of warm air around you. You will need to visualize it carefully before you put your will into it. Go slowly or you might burn yourself. I frequently put a shield around the air, to make it easier to maintain, but if you do that around the She'Har, they'll take exception to it," he explained.

"Shield? She'Har?" she responded. The words confused her almost as much as the strange descriptions.

He waved her questions away. "Forget those things, I'll explain them afterward. For now, focus on creating a layer of warm air around yourself."

She tried, and the room began to heat up.

"No. Stop," he commanded. "Your effort is unfocused. While it may be nice to heat the entire room, it's a waste of energy. It will also be far too inefficient when you go outside. Watch me."

She opened her eyes to stare at him intently.

"Not like that. Close your eyes. Use your magesight to watch what I do. Your eyes will only distract you," he told her.

Magesight? She guessed he was referring to the strange new visions she had recently been afflicted with. Rather than ask, she did as he said, watching him only with her mind. After a minute, she understood what he had intended, although her own effort at replicating it was much sloppier and diffuse.

"I think you're getting the hang of it," he noted.

Haley nodded, "I thought I'd never be warm again. They took my clothes several days ago."

He was staring at her again, studying her face carefully. "You have your mother's hair, but your eyes…"

She looked down, hooking her hair up over one ear self-consciously. "People always say that."

He seemed curious, "What do they say, Haley?"

The stranger's continuing use of her name was disconcerting, but she couldn't help the feeling that he wasn't really a stranger. He knew too much about her home, though she wasn't sure how. "They say I have my mother's looks, but the demon's eyes."

She looked up again, and her blue eyes locked on his.

He smiled, "That's a sad way of putting it. I would have said you have your grandparent's eyes; both Alan and Helen have blue eyes like yours."

Haley was certain then. The stranger's eyes were so much like her own, and now he had given the names of her grandparents—the people who had raised her. He might be—no he had to be her father, Daniel Tennick, the gods-cursed man who had raped her mother and driven her to suicide. The monster who had fathered over a dozen children before being chased from Colne by the forest gods themselves, but not before he had set fire to the town itself.

At least, that's what the townsfolk said.

Her grandparents had told her different things about their son—about her father. They had told her of a young man frightened by a gift he hadn't understood. A man who had made mistakes before being enslaved by cruel beings who were not fit to be called gods at all. And now she was trapped with him.

"You're him, aren't you?" she began, "You're Daniel, my…" She let the sentence trail away. It was just too strange to say aloud.

He nodded, "That used to be my name, but I don't deserve to be called a father. My name is Tyrion now."

Haley couldn't speak. She opened her mouth, but no words would come forth. It closed while her mind struggled to present something to her other than a blank void. There were a million questions, but she could not give utterance to any of them. Fear and surprise, had robbed her of the ability to communicate.

Tyrion waited patiently, wondering if she would curse him when the shock wore off. Eventually her lips moved again, and a few halting words emerged.

"Did you really…? Why did you do…?" She stopped, afraid to accuse him. After a moment she started with a simple statement, "I have a lot of half-siblings."

"You're afraid to ask me if I raped her, or the others? You want to know how much is true?" he asked bluntly.

Haley nodded without looking at him. His answer was not what she had expected.

"I did. I can make no excuse for that."

"Why did you want to hurt them?"

Tyrion stared up at the ceiling. "I didn't. I can't excuse what I did, but I didn't consider the fact that I was hurting them. Deep down I think I knew, but I wasn't fully conscious of it. They weren't either, at least not until later."

His answer confused her. "How could they not know? Are you saying you didn't force them?"

"No," he responded. "I coerced them. I used magic to alter their feelings, overwhelming them with a passion that they thought was of their own making."

"Then you seduced them, but you didn't actually rape them," said Haley.

He could see her youth and naiveté trying to put a more positive light on his past actions, but Tyrion had come too far to try and cover his sin with such a thin veil. "It was rape, Haley. I didn't hurt them physically, but the lack of a choice is not the same as choosing. I am certain that if they had been in control of themselves, none of them would have lain with me. I regret it now, but I cannot pretend it was not an evil act."

She paused for a minute, absorbing his words before speaking again, "They said she was—that my mother, Emily, that she was in love with you. That she killed herself, not for shame, but because of a broken heart."

His chest tightened. "That's the sort of thing people tell a child to paint things in a better light. She was obsessed with me, Haley, because of what I did to her. We were friends before that, but afterward—I'm sure shame had as much to do with it as any affection she may have felt for me."

"Why am I here?" she asked, giving vent to the building, hopeless frustration that the fear and terror of the last few days had instilled in her. "Why is this happening? I never did anything terrible like that. I didn't hurt anyone. What did I do to deserve this?"

"It's going to get worse," he cautioned.

"Why?! This isn't fair," angry tears began to slip down her cheeks. "I'm not like you!"

"Because of your power—the power you inherited from me. This world isn't fair. It's full of evil and suffering. The creatures who own you now have no understanding of kindness or compassion. The other humans here, their slaves, are worse than animals. They have been raised on cruelty and torture."

She looked at him with wet eyes, but a tiny spark of hope remained in them. "Are you going to help me escape? Will you take me home?"

He shook his head, "I cannot." Touching the spell-woven collar at his neck he then motioned to her own throat. "These prevent our escape. If you go too far without their permission, you will die. If they decide you are being disobedient, they can simply order your death."

"Can't you use magic to remove it?"

"I can, but it would still kill me. Nothing you can do yet will even damage it."

"Then what is the point of this? You should just kill me," she returned.

"No. I cannot stop them, but I can help you. I can give you what I never had when I first came here."

"What?"

"Knowledge." He stepped toward her, moved by the surge of emotions in his heart.

She shrank back and he stopped, reminded of her fear of him.

"When I was first taken, I was alone, frightened, and ignorant. No one talked to me. I knew nothing, and I barely survived that first year. Now I have some small amount of hope. I have bargained for twenty-four hours, to teach you what I can. With luck it will be enough to keep you alive. I will show you…"

"Why only twenty-four hours?" she interrupted.

"The Grove that owns you is different than the one that owns me. They are competitors. They are reluctant to let me have much time with you, for fear I will weaken or kill you," he explained.

"But why? You're my father, why would you hurt me?" she said, aghast.

"The She'Har, the forest-gods, they don't think like us. They don't understand familial bonds, just loyalty to the Grove. The Mordan have claimed you, while the Illeniel Grove owns me. That is enough to make them cautious," he explained.

"None of this makes sense," she exclaimed.

"I will teach you as much as I can. They will force you to fight. I will show you how to make a shield, how to defend yourself, how to kill…"

"No! I won't fight, I won't kill for them. They can't make…"

"You will!" he interrupted. "You will kill, or you will die."

"I can't do it. I'm not a fighter. I wouldn't hurt anyone," she argued stubbornly.

Seeing her, listening to her, Tyrion felt his anger growing. His years struggling to survive, and the torture that had gone with it, had taught him otherwise. He wanted to help her. The girl standing before him now was his own flesh and blood. She had even been raised by his own parents. He cared for her, yet the words coming from her now were nothing but weak complaints. She might as well beg for death.

His hand itched, and he felt his shoulders tense. He wanted to strike the words from her mouth. *Teach her pain, teach her anger, before they teach her fear and death.*

It took an act of willpower to restrain himself. *That was not how I was raised. Why would I hit her?* Those thoughts were not enough. He was no longer Daniel Tennick. That person was too soft, he couldn't help her. But Tyrion could.

"Say what you like," he said after a moment. "I will teach, and you will learn. First you must learn to create a shield around yourself."

"I'm not going to—ow!" her sentence ended in a sudden shout.

"A shield will prevent me from doing that. You will learn, or I will continue and the pain will grow more intense and powerful each time," he said through gritted teeth. "Do you understand me?"

Haley stared at him, her face suddenly pale. Sweat was starting from her brow, and her eyes had changed. Where there had been defiance, now there was fear. She nodded.

"Good. Your mind," he tapped his temple, "is the most effective defense, as well as weapon, that you have. You must train your imagination. To create a shield, you have to visualize a barrier between you and the rest of the world. It can be any shape or form, close against the skin or farther away, like a bubble. Try to create one, close your eyes…"

Chapter 4

Tyrion worked with her for hours, until one of the nameless appeared to bring food, a small tray with two bowls. The nameless were human slaves who had been deemed unworthy of fighting in the arena. The She'Har only granted a slave a name once they had been blooded, killing their first opponent.

The young man who entered was thin and awkward. Like all the humans living in Sabortrea he was a mage, but in Tyrion's magesight he appeared to be a very weak one. It was no wonder he had been relegated to his role as an errand boy. Tyrion stepped in front of him before he could withdraw after delivering the food.

"I need you to take a message for me," he told the man.

The nameless one kept his eyes on the ground, mumbling a response that was too soft to be heard.

Tyrion already knew what it would be. The slave wasn't supposed to interact with them, and he definitely wasn't supposed to be taking on extra tasks from other slaves. Tyrion also knew how the She'Har slave cities worked in the real world. There was always a hierarchy, and the slaves traded favors with one another.

The She'Har stood above all of them, but beneath them were the wardens, slaves who had fought long enough to be released from the endless killing of the arena. Wardens were allowed to wear clothing, and they commanded considerable respect amongst the other humans in the slave cities. They acted as trusted servants   for   the   She'Har.

Among the wardens would be one feared and respected more than the others, one with considerable ability to affect the treatment and consideration shown to a new slave such as Haley.

Tyrion didn't respond with words, instead his power lashed out, enclosing the nameless one and pinning him to the wall. "You will find the one called 'Gwaeri' and tell him that I wish to see him." He had learned the name while interrogating his opponent in the arena. "Yes?"

The nameless one nodded fearfully, but not with the same terror someone from Colne might have shown. Fear and intimidation were part of daily life in Sabortrea.

Tyrion released him, stepping aside so he could pass through the door. "If he doesn't visit before the next feeding time, I will find you," he added.

Haley had shrunk back, terrified by the violent exchange.

"Stop that," said Tyrion calmly. "Straighten your back. Keep your head up. I told you before, do not show fear or weakness. You will wind up like that one otherwise." He jerked his thumb in the direction of the doorway the nameless one had left through.

She nodded, sitting straighter and trying to look calm. The effort wasn't enough to disguise her timidity, though.

"You saw the difference in strength, didn't you?" continued Tyrion. "You could see how weak he was. I cannot see my own aythar, but I am guessing he looked like a candle beside a bonfire. Is that right?"

Chapter 4

"Y—yes," she stuttered.

"You are the same," he responded. "Your aythar shines like the sun, even compared to one of the wardens."

"Wardens?"

"The ones who are allowed to wear clothes."

"Oh."

"You must wear your strength with pride. You are a hunter, a predator. They can see your power; act like you know it, and they will fear you," he told her.

"I d—don't want p—people to fear me," she struggled to say.

"Your old life is gone," said Tyrion mercilessly. "These people are animals. The only thing they understand is fear and power. Strength is everything here; without it, you will be abused, but with it, your lot will be much less unpleasant."

His words had the opposite effect of what he intended. Instead, Haley began to cry.

The sight of her tears was so different from the reactions he was used to from the slaves of the She'Har that it made his mind reel for a moment. It reminded him of his old life. The emotions that followed threatened to destabilize him. He wanted to hold her. He wanted to cry with her, for what he had lost as much as for what she had lost.

But he had not survived among the She'Har for the past fifteen years by giving in to such feelings. Viciously, he suppressed the sorrow that rose within him, shoving it back down, pushing it into the darkness where it must forever hide. Anger replaced it, and reaching out with his mind he touched her skin, sending a jolt of burning pain through her.

Haley gasped, choking on her tears.

"Put your shield back up. We aren't finished," he informed her.

***

The man who entered was not what Tyrion had expected. He was short and stout, neither of which was particularly unusual. What was strange, was his hair.

It was gray.

Tyrion stared at him for a long moment. In all of his years among the She'Har, he had not seen anyone with gray hair. People simply didn't live that long in the slave cities. The closest thing to gray was the shining silver hair possessed by the Illeniel She'Har, which was almost metallic in its hue.

The old man stared back at him, appraising him with cautious eyes, mentally assessing the danger that Tyrion represented.

Tyrion had already recovered from his shock and had made his own mental calculation. The Mordan warden was strong, his aythar far brighter than most of the Mordan mages he had seen before, but it was not strong enough to concern him. "You are Gwaeri?" he asked.

The old man nodded.

There was little reason to delay the point. "I want you to see that the girl gets good treatment."

Gwaeri listened but didn't respond.

"No one is to harm her or seek favors from her. I want her treated as if she were your 'friend'," continued Tyrion. Friend was a word with a different meaning among the slaves of the She'Har. In essence, he was asking Gwaeri to make sure that Haley was treated as well as if she were one of his sex partners.

"I care little for favors anymore, certainly not from one so scarred as you are," responded Gwaeri. "You have nothing to offer me." One of the few currencies in the slave cities was sex. There was little else for slaves to trade, since they were allowed almost no personal possessions.

Being from outside of Sabortrea, there was little Tyrion could offer the man. His influence was non-existent there, and since Gwaeri was already at the top of the limited slave hierarchy, his good will meant nothing to the old man. "Your continued well-being should be of some value, even to one as old as yourself," said Tyrion.

"I am Mordan."

A simple statement, meaning that he couldn't hope to threaten one who could be gone with a thought. The Mordan gift of teleportation made it difficult to threaten them.

Tyrion skirted the issue, "You think you could deny me?"

"I know your legend. I am not such a fool to think I could face you, but you have no way to keep me here. This is not the arena."

He had expected that line of reasoning, but what the old man didn't know was that he could render him helpless in less time than it would take the Mordan mage to teleport. He didn't want to offer that threat, though, for it would end their negotiations. "You know what happened to the other warden. I have some influence among the She'Har. You could be sent to the arena."

That was a complete fabrication. Tyrion had never discussed such a thing with Lyralliantha, nor did he know that the Mordan would even consider selling their most senior warden, but based on recent events, he judged it to be a credible threat.

Gwaeri laughed, an uncommon thing among the humans kept by the She'Har. Reaching up, he stroked the coarse gray hair that crowned his pate, "I have lived longer than most. I do not fear dying."

Tyrion stared at him. Torture was his next option, but he had hoped to find a more amicable solution.

Gwaeri spoke again, "You have given away the importance this girl has to you. Perhaps we should consider how you will appease me so that her condition does not become worse after you leave." The old man gave him a grin, showing a mouth full of rotten teeth. The glint in his eyes spoke of pure evil.

"You seek to extort *me*?" said Tyrion, surprised by the old warden's boldness.

The old man sensed the flicker in his aythar. Gwaeri was wily as a fox and had only survived to such an age by trusting his considerably well-honed instincts. The Mordan mage raised a shield and then turned his mind to escape. A half-second would be all he needed.

Tyrion didn't bother raising a shield himself. His first action was to lash out, crushing the warden against the wall with such sudden force that his shield collapsed. The backlash didn't quite render the other mage unconscious, but it ruined his effort to teleport. Tyrion's second attack was more precise, clamping down on the other mage's still reeling mind.

He held Gwaeri trapped, his aythar crushing the old man's will. He nearly missed the movement of the warden's hand. The warden had somehow hidden the moment he had drawn his wooden sword. *Eilen'tyral* was the material it was made of; a special heartwood grown by the She'Har father-trees to produce weapons that were as strong as steel and just as sharp. The blade shattered as Tyrion's rune-sheathed arm swept across, destroying the weapon.

Tyrion expanded his mental hold, paralyzing the warden's body as well as his aythar. "Now that we understand your situation better, perhaps we can have a more meaningful discussion."

Gwaeri's eyes rolled wildly as he stared back at Tyrion. He was unable to speak or even scream as he saw the younger man produce a long red line of power from his hand—the red whip used so often by wardens to discipline their victims. It struck his leg first and then his mid-section, sending burning pain tearing through his body.

The old man's body shook despite its paralysis, and tears ran from his eyes. The expected scream that filled the air though, came from Haley.

Tyrion had forgotten about her. The girl was frantic, with a look of stark terror in her eyes. She was frightened beyond reason, and not of the warden; she was afraid of her father.

If she only understood, thought Tyrion. "I am doing this for your benefit," he told her.

She stopped screaming, but her fear was no less. Haley continued to cower, her eyes searching the room, hoping against reason to find some way to escape the horror.

Sighing, Tyrion dismissed the red whip. Obviously, Haley had been treated to its use a few times already, and the sight of it would only make her state of mind worse. Instead, he loosened his control of the old man's throat, returning his power of speech.

"Please!" begged Gwaeri. "I'll do anything."

"Of course you will…" sneered Tyrion. "…now. But I have to make sure I can trust you after I have gone. You are obviously too sly to make a simple bargain."

"No! I was just testing you. I never meant to offend. I will make sure no harm comes to her…"

"Yes," interrupted Tyrion. "Yes, you will. After you awaken, I will explain precisely, why you will do anything and everything I ask of you." Reaching out with his aythar, he drove the older mage into unconsciousness, forcing his mind to sleep. Then he relaxed his hold.

Haley stood at the door. She had been trying to force it to open, and now she shivered when she saw her father's gaze fall on her.

"I need your help," he told her. "Carve a small sliver of wood from your bed, then burn it. I need black ash to mark him, and a bit of urine."

She stared at him uncomprehendingly, her mind in shock.

"Use your power to slice a small piece of wood off, then make a small flame to burn it. I've already shown you how to do both. Snap out of it!"

Startled, she jumped, but after a moment she moved to do as he told her. Her aythar was rough and untrained, but she managed to cut a small piece of wood as he had asked. She wasn't sure where to burn it however, "Where…?"

"Use the food bowl," he said, indicating the bowls they had recently emptied.

Haley dropped it in before producing a small flame and carefully burning the wood. She scorched the bowl as well, but that was of little consequence to Tyrion. After finishing, she held it out to her father.

"Mix a little urine in with it," he commanded, "but crush the charred wood first."

"Uri…" She stopped without completing the word.

"Piss in the bowl, or your hand, however you think best. Just a little bit mind you. I need it to be more fluid than a paste, but not much."

Haley went to the farthest corner of the room, but it took several long minutes before she managed to complete the task.

I should have done that myself, he thought. Haley had been scared, and her body ill-equipped for the job. Her hands were a mess and her face was red with shame. Hesitantly, she brought him the bowl, retreating as soon as he had taken it from her hands.

He mixed the blackened charcoal as thoroughly as possible, crushing the larger pieces with his mind and turning it into a thick slurry. Then he leaned over the unconscious warden.

"W—what are y—you going to do?" asked Haley.

He grinned, but immediately regretted it. The expression seemed to frighten her more. Looking back at Gwaeri, he answered, "I'm going to tattoo our friend here to ensure his loyalty." He pushed the man's gray hair and slave collar aside, studying the warden's neck as he chose the spot for his artwork.

***

When Gwaeri awoke sometime later, the first thing he noticed was a stinging burn at his throat. Instinctively, he tried to reach up, fearing a cut, but his arm refused to move.

"I'll release you in a moment," said the Illeniel warden looking down on him.

"What have you done?"

"I've given you a reason to cooperate," answered Tyrion. With a thought, he activated the tattoos along his right arm. He held the force blade up in front of his prisoner's eyes. "You know what this is?"

"Everyone has heard of your arm-blades." Gwaeri's attention was firmly on the deadly weapon.

"Does 'everyone' know that it is capable of severing She'Har spellweaving?" asked Tyrion.

"Your fight with the Krytek," said the warden. "Not everyone believes the story, but there's no other way…"

"I can sever a slave collar as well." He lowered the tip of the blade to the old man's throat. It made a shallow slice in the flesh as it slid close to the spellweave around Gwaeri's neck. Blood welled and dripped to the ground, but the warden didn't flinch or cry out. "Do you know what happens if the collar is broken?"

"Death." Sweat was beading on the older man's forehead, but he gave no other sign of fear.

Chapter 4

Tyrion dismissed his enchanted arm-blade and then presented the outer edge of his arm for Gwaeri's inspection. "See the runes there?" He waited for the other man to nod before continuing, "Those are the secret. They forge my aythar into a type of magic that is similar to She'Har spellweaving. I call it enchanting.

"If you refocus your magesight, you'll find something similar on your skin." He used a finger to push the slave collar up a bit, to make it easier for the warden to examine the symbols on his throat. They had been hidden by the collar.

Gwaeri frowned.

"I kept the marks as small as I could, so your masters won't see it, unless you deliberately show them. I wouldn't advise it, though."

"What purpose does it serve?"

"Mine," said Tyrion with steel in his voice, "just as you do now. If I decide you have been disloyal, I will activate the enchantment tattooed onto your skin, destroying your slave collar and ending your miserable life."

"I cannot disobey, Dalleth," said the warden.

"Then you should take care to make sure he never gives you an order that I will take exception to. If you displease me, if the girl comes to harm, or if you attempt to show your new decoration to anyone, the enchantment will activate," Tyrion stated calmly.

In truth, the enchantment would do none of those things, unless he deliberately activated it, and that would still require him to be within a few hundred yards of the tattoo. It was possible to create an enchantment that would do all those things, but Tyrion had yet to discover how to trigger one beyond the limit of his own power. Nor did he know how to set an enchantment to detect betrayal.

But of course, Gwaeri knew none of those things.

Chapter 5

Haley had fallen asleep exhausted, both emotionally and physically. She lay on the living wooden pallet that grew from the floor. The buildings in Sabortrea, like those in Ellentrea, were actually part of the roots of one of the nearby god-trees. The She'Har could control how they grew, forming them into buildings complete with furniture-like protrusions such as the 'bed' she now slept on.

She was shivering now, her concentration had lapsed when she fell asleep, and the pocket of warm air she had kept around herself had dissipated. Done properly, the spell that maintained the warmth around her would have lasted through the night, but she was still a novice, and her father had been pushing her hard.

Tyrion felt impatient. He only had twenty-four hours, and it bothered him that they were being forced to spend some of it sleeping, but he knew she wouldn't be able to learn without rest. She had already had far more help than he had received when he had first been taken.

He picked up the blanket he had brought, his only gift to her, and draped it over her gently, tucking the edges around her shoulders and feet. Haley seemed small under his hands.

Looking down on her, he couldn't help but examine her features. Her face was smooth, relaxed and calm with sleep. She was beautiful.

She'll probably die in the arena.

Tyrion shoved that thought aside and stretched out on the ground. He spoke a word and wrapped himself more firmly in a shell of warmth, outlining it vividly in his mind. It would last long past his descent into unconsciousness. Years and constant practice had given his imagination and will a strength that iron would envy.

He closed his eyes and tried not to think of his own parents. He didn't want to remember childhood, or his mother's kind hands tucking him in at night. *I am not a parent,* he told himself, but Haley's sleeping face returned to his mind before he drifted away.

He awoke sometime later. He felt hot, and his body was sweating. Something was covering his shoulders. He was disoriented for a moment until his senses sorted out what had happened.

He was covered by the blanket, and the warmth at his back was Haley, curled up soft behind him. Her body heat, combined with the extra insulation of the blanket, was the reason for his perspiration.

Dismissing the magical warmth was enough to allow his body to reach a more comfortable temperature. *We've probably slept enough. I should wake her and continue training her.*

He lay still, though, despite that thought, listening to his daughter's slow breathing. Tyrion was filled with an odd sense of peace, and he was loathe to ruin the moment, despite knowing that it was an illusion.

***

It was morning, and he knew they had little time left. Their food had been brought an hour earlier, and he had been pleased to see that it was much better than the previous meal. Gwaeri was already making good on his promises.

"Name the five groves," he commanded.

"Illeniel, Prathion, Centyr, Gaelyn, and Mordan," she recited dutifully.

"When facing their slaves, what special qualities do you expect from each?"

She answered promptly, "Prathions can make themselves invisible, and they have a knack for illusions. Centyr mages can create spellbeasts to aid them during battle. Gaelyn mages can transform their bodies at will, and the Mordan are able to teleport to any location they can see or remember. Illeniel…" Haley frowned. "What can Illeniel mages do?"

"There are none. The Illeniel Grove does not keep or breed slaves," he told her.

"But you're an Illeniel," she responded.

"I'm from Colne, the same as you," he reminded. "Their special abilities come from birth, not training. You and I have nothing of the She'Har in us. What is the weakness of the Prathion's invisibility?"

"To become completely invisible, even to magesight, they must forgo their own ability to see."

"How do you handle a Mordan mage?"

"Trust my defense and strike when they strike. They cannot teleport while doing something else," she said immediately. "I won't have to fight a Mordan, will I? Since they are the ones who—own me?"

"You may. The groves do trade slaves. Every grove has some fighters that come from other groves," he explained. "When is a Gaelyn mage weakest?"

"During a transformation their shield becomes weaker. Some of them cannot maintain a shield at all while transforming."

"When do you shield yourself?"

"Always, even while sleeping…"

"Except?"

"…Except when in the presence of the She'Har. They consider a shield to be an act of hostility," she replied promptly.

He continued drilling her with both questions and exercises until it was close to noon. Lyralliantha would be back for him soon. Their time was nearly at an end. Haley was far from being ready for the arena, but Tyrion comforted himself with the fact that she was much better prepared for it than he had been.

"You may have several days or even a week or two before they decide to blood you," he informed her. "Make sure you practice every day."

"There's nothing else to do here," she replied somewhat bitterly.

He could only agree with that, "The solitude will test your sanity."

"Is that what changed you?"

Tyrion stared at her, unsure how to answer.

Bolder than she had been in the past twenty-four hours, she elaborated on the question, "I can see Alan's features in your face. He talked about you a lot. Helen did too, but you seem very different than the son they described."

"I am not the son they raised." *Daniel is dead,* he told himself, uncomfortable with the direction the conversation was taking.

Chapter 5

Haley turned away, but her voice continued, "Listening to them while I was growing up, I often imagined you as an older brother. I knew you were my father, but they were my true parents. Hearing them talk, I couldn't help but feel like we were siblings, except I never got to know you."

"You were lucky…" he replied hoarsely, "…on both counts." The voice of the wind was whispering in his ear now, as it often seemed to do when his emotions grew stronger than he could bear. Beneath his feet the earth pounded like a distant drum.

"I am lucky," she said defiantly. "Despite everything else, they loved me, just like they loved you. Not everyone is given that much. Now that I have met you, I have one less regret."

"Here you will discover that no one even understands the word 'love'," he told her. "Don't think about the past, or the pain will undermine your will to survive."

"I don't intend to survive," she said in a quiet voice.

"What?"

Calmly she turned and looked him fully in the face, "I have been taken from my family, terrified, and abused. Until you arrived, I had no hope at all. I appreciate what you've tried to do, but I can't be like you. I can't kill. I would rather die remembering the life I had, than live by becoming a beast."

Tyrion's eyes turned hard, but he knew he had no more time. Beyond the walls of the hut he could sense Lyralliantha's approach. She would be at the door in a few minutes. *You stupid girl,* he thought, but his mouth found a better response, "Keep your defense up.

Don't let them kill you easily. You'll find your will to live before it's over."

"You're wrong."

He suppressed an urge to slap the impudent girl. Curbing the violent impulse only served to remind him further that he was no longer anything like the kind boy his parents had raised. He was a beast, just as Haley had implied. He survived, but violence had become ingrained at the center of his being. He stood without answering, his fist clenching. Despite his anger, he didn't want her to die.

A minute passed without a reply from him, so she asked another question, "What's your reason for surviving? Why do you keep living like this?"

Tyrion gave her a long stare before finally answering, "There is no reason to life."

She shook her head, "You have one, or you wouldn't still be alive after all these years."

The door opened behind him, and Lyralliantha's voice called to him, "Your time is done. We must leave."

He turned and moved toward the door, "Remember what I have shown you." Beneath the surface he was seething with anger, but he had no answer for Haley's question.

"What *is* your purpose?" said Haley, repeating her question as he walked out. She wanted to follow him, a sudden desperate urge filling her as the door began to close between them. She saw his eyes watching her as the gap closed. Then he was gone.

She was alone.

Her calm vanished, and a wave of anguish and loss rolled over her. She was alone. Sitting down on the bed, she picked up the blanket he had left her and wrapped it around herself, balling the extra material up in front of her and hugging it closely.

Haley fought against the urge to cry, but the tears came anyway. The walls closed in and the air in the room seemed to suffocate her.

She was alone.

The Silent Tempest

Chapter 6

Tyrion and Lyralliantha rode back atop a large dormon, but they didn't attempt to talk. The wind made conversation difficult, and he was in no mood to talk anyway. The world seemed to crawl by slowly beneath them as they drew ever closer to home. Thillmarius hadn't bothered to come for this trip, a fact that didn't make much of an impression on Tyrion until they had reached the Illeniel Grove.

"It seems Thillmarius wasn't interested in seeing if I made any impression on her," he noted as they descended the god-tree that the dormon had landed on.

Lyralliantha paused, giving him an odd look. "What?"

"We need to talk," she answered.

"So talk," he suggested.

"In private," she added.

Privacy was not something the She'Har valued, or even considered most of the time. Tyrion's interest was piqued. "Your platform is closest."

"No, more private," she replied. "Your house?"

Now he was definitely curious. She was referring, in a roundabout way, to the fact that he was building his enchanted stone house partly for the purpose of preventing eavesdropping, magical or otherwise. *She really wants to make sure we aren't overheard.* "One of the rooms is finished," he stated simply.

Half an hour later they stood within the front arch of his enchanted stone house. The outer walls were up, and the roof was in place, but there were no doors, and the interior was still unfinished. The building stood three stories in height, an oddity amid the massive trees at the edge of the Illeniel Grove.

"If you wanted it to be so tall, why not grow it?" she asked. "Stone is a crude medium for such a building."

"Stone endures," was his only reply before stepping through the empty doorway and leading her up the first flight of stairs. He had built the master bedroom on the third floor, and so far it was the only one that had an actual working door. *And the ability to shield us from any who might be curious about our conversation,* he added mentally.

Once they were inside the room and the door was closed he turned to face her squarely, "No one can hear us now."

Lyralliantha took a moment to test the enchantments herself, letting her magesight roam throughout the room, seeking any opening that might let a spy intrude upon them. Once again she marveled at her pet's cleverness. While his new magic was not so fine grained as the spellweavings of the She'Har, it was no less effective, and she was continually surprised at its versatility.

"Your people are in danger," she said without preamble.

Tyrion frowned, "What do you mean?"

"News of the new baratti found by the Mordan has spread rapidly…" she explained.

My daughter, he thought irritably, but he held his tongue. After fifteen years Lyralliantha had gotten better, she never referred to him as an 'animal', but she still used the term when she spoke of other humans.

"… and they will send wardens to search for more of your offspring," she finished.

His heart jumped. Haley had been hard enough. *What would I do if they had all of them? How could I watch them being forced to fight one another?* A hard lump formed in his stomach. He should have thought of this already. Haley's discovery would lead to a rush of wardens searching Colne, and probably Lincoln too, hoping to find another human with his wild talent. Every grove would want at least one—or more.

How many children do I have? He had no idea.

"I have to get there first," he stated firmly.

"Thillmarius has already sent a team to get there before the others. That is why he was too busy to come with me today," she informed him.

Tyrion clenched his fists, "How long ago, and how long before the others leave?"

"I am not sure," she admitted. "They probably left at dawn. The others will surely leave by dawn tomorrow."

"It will take them a lot longer, though," he noted. "None are as close as the Prathion Grove, besides us." The Illeniel Grove had the closest border to the stony foothills in which Colne was located, but the Prathion border met the edge of the Illeniel Grove not far from there.

Lyralliantha shook her head, "They will use the dormon and fly them to the foothills and proceed on foot from there. The distance will not delay them much."

"Shit," he said, growling in frustration. "Still, they can't carry horses with them, can they?" None of the dormon he had seen thus far were large enough to carry livestock.

"Some dormon are made large enough for such things, but I doubt they will bother," she answered. "They aren't worried about the speed of their return, for which horses would be useful, only the speed of their arrival. Once they capture a slave, the other teams will respect their claim."

"I have to go," he said firmly. "I can't let this happen."

"You cannot stop them, Tyrion," she told him. Her features hinted at sadness, though it was well hidden by her near lack of expression.

"Then help me!" he bit back, raising his voice. "Send wardens with me." An idea struck him then, "Yes! Send wardens, help me capture them for the Illeniel Grove." At least then they would all have the same owner. They wouldn't be forced to fight each other.

"We have no wardens, Tyrion. You know that. The Illeniel Grove doesn't keep slaves. You are the only one."

She was right, of course. He wasn't thinking clearly. "Then send me—alone. I can't let them take my children."

"No."

His eyes narrowed, "Then remove my collar."

Her calm exterior began to crumble, and her eyes widened, "No, Tyrion. If I do that, you know what will happen. They will kill you. All the She'Har would set themselves against you, to kill, or even to capture you for their own."

Chapter 6

"You swore you would," he pressed. "If I asked, either that or…" He held up his arm, flattening his hand into a blade, reminding her of the other side of their bargain.

"Maybe that would be better…" she said, a strange hesitancy in her voice.

"They're my family," he said firmly.

"They don't even know you."

Tyrion was unmoved, his determination clear. "Makes no difference, they're my family even if they hate me."

"You told me family was about love. You said I was your family." Lyralliantha's face was hidden by her hair now, her eyes cast down toward the floor.

He reached out, lifting her chin with his hand, "You are. Love and hate are not so different; both require that you identify someone or something as a part of yourself."

The skin around her eyes crinkled as her face tensed, "Then it's alright that I hate you now?"

He kissed her briefly. "Of course."

They stood together silently for a moment before she broke the silence, "So those are my only options, your freedom or death together?"

"Don't neglect the first option, sending me on your behalf," he reminded her.

"You will set the Illeniel Grove against the others if you kill their agents," she cautioned.

He snorted, "I'm glad you have faith in my abilities."

"I know you," she replied. "If you find they have already taken some of them, you must respect their claim."

"I can't do that."

"Then you must make certain none of them return to inform the elders of your betrayal," she added.

"I hope it won't come to that," he told her.

She clenched her jaw, resolving herself to the decision, "Go. You have three weeks. Do as you will." Lyralliantha stepped back, leaving his path to the door unobstructed.

He took several steps, then paused, "I'll need a horse."

"You are my agent, take whatever you need."

***

An hour later he rode for Colne, pushing his mount as hard as he dared. There was little in the way of underbrush beneath the massive god-trees, but once he reached the border the terrain became more difficult. The giant trees gave way to smaller oak and elm. Bushes and rocks crowded beneath them, forcing his horse to slow and pick her way more carefully.

The journey to Colne was just over six hours from the border of the Illeniel Grove. If the Prathion group had left at dawn, they would probably have arrived sometime after noon, perhaps a bit later since they had started from Ellentrea. Given those assumptions, the Prathion group would have had at least six hours to search before he got there.

Tyrion glanced at the sun where it hung low in the sky. It would be dark when he reached the town. *But there's a good chance they haven't taken anyone yet,* he told himself. None of his other children had awakened to their power yet, at least not as of a week ago when the Mordan warden had found Haley. If there had been others, they would probably have been detected.

Unless they were hiding their power like I did, he corrected mentally.

Still, the chances were that none of the others would appear as anything special yet, unless one of them had awakened very recently. That gave him a distinct advantage. While he might not know how many children he had, he did know which women he had slept with. He could approach each directly, and if they had a child of the right age, he would know it was almost certainly his.

And then you'll have to take them.

It wasn't a pleasant thought. He had brought nothing but misery to the women he had known back then. Now he was returning to do even worse, stealing their children, but the alternative was unthinkable. The She'Har would take them all, one by one, as they discovered their power. Slaves to various groves, his children would then be forced to murder one another in the arena.

Unless some of them don't inherit my curse.

If that were the case, then he would be dooming some of them to miserable lives, trying to prevent a disaster that might never come to them. He turned those thoughts over and over in his mind as he rode, but he found no satisfying answer.

Pragmatism dictated one response. He would take them all.

He bypassed the first few widely scattered farms. None of the women he had been with lived in them. It wasn't until he reached the Tolburn's house that he stopped. Brenda Sayer had given birth to his first child, and she had married Seth's father. It had been over a decade, but it was likely that she was still there, raising her daughter Brigid.

My daughter, Kate's half-sister, and Mr. Tolburn's step-daughter… it's a complicated world I've left behind. In his mind's eye he remembered the one time he had met her, a strange dark haired girl full of energy and whimsy. She had played with his parent's dog, Lacy, and afterward he had tried to teach her to play music on his cittern.

It was the only remotely parental memory he had.

As soon as the Tolburn house came into view he knew something was wrong. It was still beyond the range of his magesight, but he could see smoke rising from the main house, and it didn't appear to be coming from the chimney.

Tyrion felt a surge of anger, but he refused to give in to it. The horse felt his anxiousness and began to walk faster, but he reined her in, keeping the pace steady. Whatever had happened there was done. *I may need her strength later,* he thought, putting one hand on the mare's neck to reassure her. Despite his forced calm, his mind's eye envisioned them running down the men who had attacked the Tolburn home.

"Not now, not yet," he told himself.

Twenty minutes later he was riding into the yard in front of Owen and Brenda Tolburn's home. It was dark now, but his magesight had already located the one survivor. Owen sat in the front room of his home, cradling his wife's dead body. The fire that had burned the front of the house had gone out already, leaving the front wall of the house scorched and still smoking.

Either Owen had been lucky, or he had managed to put the flames out himself.

Tyrion stopped some twenty feet from the door and dismounted, tossing the reins over the mare's saddle and uttering a one word command in Erollith. The horses kept by the She'Har were well trained, he knew she would not move from the spot until he returned to her.

His shield deflected the crossbow quarrel that struck him as he stepped through the front door. Owen held the empty weapon in his hands. He still sat on the floor, his wife's limp body draped across his lap.

"Back to finish what you started!?" the farmer screamed. "Kill me! I don't care!" Owen's face was mottled, angry red blotches combining with smut and tears to render his visage an ugly testament to grief and despair.

A thousand things ran through Tyrion's mind. Memories of the man before him, his best friend's father. He had never felt particularly close to Seth's dad, but the man had always been fair to him. The years had made him a stranger, though. Owen showed no sign of recognition as he looked at him.

"I'm not here to kill you, Owen."

The older man's eyes focused on him more intently, trying to understand why the stranger had known his name. "Who are you?" he asked.

"Where is Brigid?" asked Tyrion, ignoring the question. His old name would only reopen wounds that were better left undisturbed.

Owen looked down, focusing on Brenda's face in his lap. "I won't tell you. Just kill me, so I can be with my wife."

"I'm not here to kill anyone," said Tyrion. "I want to protect Brigid from those who came here before me. Where is she? Is she with Seth?"

Owen looked up again, and recognition slowly dawned on him. "Daniel?"

The name sent a sliver of pain into his heart. "Something like that," he admitted. "Where is Brigid?" He wanted out, he wanted to be away. Owen's eyes held an image of him that he didn't want to remember. The expectations there belonged to another person, to another life.

"She didn't tell them," said the farmer. "That's why they killed her. She wouldn't betray her child."

Tyrion's eyes narrowed, "Then why are you alive?"

"I got here too late. They were already gone…"

"Then how do you know what she said?" said Tyrion harshly.

"She wouldn't. She loved Brigid dearly, more than her own life." Tears dripped from his nose to mingle with the blood covering his wife's bosom.

"People will say anything if you inflict enough pain. Where is Brigid? There's no time to waste if I'm to catch them."

"At Seth's," answered Owen Tolburn.

Tyrion turned away and began to walk out.

"Do you even care that she's dead?" asked the older man, confused by his abrupt dismissal.

He paused and glanced back, letting his eyes roam over the dead woman's body. Brenda Tolburn, no *Brenda Sayer,* was as dead as any of the other corpses he had seen before. He felt empty looking at her. She was the reason he had become what he was now.

Chapter 6

Once he had hated her. Hated her for destroying his dreams, hated her for raping him, but he could no longer feel even that for her. He had done far worse than what she had. Staring at the terrible wounds on her body, he wondered how long she had held out before she had given them the information they sought.

Even she loved. She loved her children.

He made his way out and reclaimed his horse without bothering to answer. It would take at least an hour to reach Seth and Kate's house. He already knew he was too late. Now it was just a matter of how long it would be before he caught up to those who had gotten there before him.

The darkness could not touch him as he rode, for he was darker inside than even a moonless night could hope to challenge.

The Silent Tempest

Chapter 7

He passed his old home without stopping. There was no light coming from it, and his magesight found no one within, which was just as well, he had no time to waste. He couldn't help but wonder where they were, though. Haley had told him that they weren't injured when she was taken.

Tyrion kept his pace steady. The wardens would have already been to Kate and Seth Tolburn's home. Even factoring in the time they had spent at Owen Tolburn's farm, they had to still be at least three or four hours ahead of him. By now they had taken Brigid and moved on. The only question was how many they had hurt or killed along the way.

He stroked the horse's neck as if to calm her, but it was his own tension that needed soothing. *Save your strength for the chase,* he thought.

Catherine and Seth Tolburn's house was well lit when it came into view, and as he drew closer Tyrion could detect several people within, two women, one man, and a boy. A moment later he had identified them. *Mother, Kate, Seth, and the boy must be their son, Aaron.*

His mother, Helen Tennick, appeared to be preparing a meal, standing over a stove in the kitchen. The boy was close by, sitting at the table, strangely quiet and still for a child of eleven years. He was either tired or…

"…in shock," said Tyrion as he rode.

Kate and Seth were arguing in the bedroom, and while his magesight didn't bring him their words, it showed him enough that he could see it was a serious squabble. Tyrion kept his mind clear, refusing to speculate. *Not my business...*

The boy, Aaron, fell out of his chair and began scrabbling across the floor when Tyrion opened the front door. His eyes were wide with fear. Helen was startled as well, but she recognized her son almost immediately and began shushing the boy.

"Aaron, it's alright. It's my son," she told him, wiping her hands on a towel.

The boy was having none of it, and fled into the back of the house. A door slammed as he sought sanctuary in his parent's bedroom.

"I have some bad news, Mother," said Tyrion.

Helen had been moving forward, picking up speed with each step. She caught him in her arms, crying. "Daniel! They took her. They took her, Daniel. There was nothing we could do!"

"I know," he muttered over her shoulder. It felt strange to be held. The smell of his mother's hair was familiar, even though it had been over ten years since he had last seen her. She felt small, almost frail in his arms, but her grip was strong. She clung to him with the sort of desperate emotion he never felt from Lyralliantha.

"Why?" she cried. "Why would they do this? Why did they take Haley? We did nothing to them!"

"Because they're my children," he said flatly. His magesight showed him that the others were creeping out the back door. Trying to escape. They thought he was one of the wardens, back to inflict more pain and suffering.

Chapter 7

He put a hand over his mother's ear. "Pardon me," he told her, before raising his voice and shouting toward the back of the house, "Kate, Seth, it's me! I'm not here to hurt anyone. I need to find the ones who took Brigid!"

Helen pulled away, "It's Daniel. He's back!"

Tyrion flinched involuntarily at the sound of his old name. He hadn't been able to bring himself to say it.

A minute passed before the others stepped out from the hall, the boy clutching tightly to his mother while Seth carried a heavy crossbow. "What do you want?" asked Seth warily.

Tyrion didn't answer immediately; his mind was absorbing their images, remembering them, and readjusting to their new appearances. Seth was older, with gray showing in his hair and beard. His hairline was receding, and his body was heavier, thicker, with more muscle on his shoulders, and a bit of fat around his chin.

Aaron was the most changed, naturally; no longer an infant, the boy was a lanky adolescent with thin straight hair and a fearful gaze.

It was the third person who took most of Tyrion's attention, however. His eyes stopped moving when they reached Kate. She had somehow collected even more freckles, and her face showed lines around her eyes where time and sun had taken their toll on her fair skin. Her fiery hair was shorter now, and what there was of it was trapped behind her head, wound into a tight bun.

Even in the dim room, her eyes sparkled with emerald defiance. Her face was swollen and purpling on the left side. She took a step forward but jerked to a halt as her husband pulled her back.

"Daniel?" she said, when he failed to respond.

"Your mother is dead," he said finally, staring through her, refusing to let his eyes focus firmly on any of them. "I need to know which direction they took."

Kate flinched at the words, but only for a second. "There are too many, you can't fight them."

"How do you know he plans to fight?" asked Seth beside her. "He's one of them now."

"Because it's *Daniel!*" she snarled back, but her eyes never left the man in front of her.

"They headed toward town. Your father is following them," said Seth.

Kate turned then, glaring at her husband, "I thought you didn't trust him."

"The sooner he goes after them, the sooner we're rid of him."

She swung at him then, her hand flying up, but Seth caught her wrist, and his own fist clenched as he prepared to punish her.

"Don't." He said it quietly, but both of them froze at the sound of his voice. "How many of them are there?"

"At least ten," answered Kate. She pulled her arm free from Seth's grasp. "They wanted to kill us, but the black one wouldn't let them."

"Black one?" asked Tyrion.

Helen spoke then, "One of the forest gods, he had coal black skin and golden hair."

"Just one?"

She nodded.

"That will complicate things," he said, thinking aloud.

"Alan's going to get himself killed," said Helen. "He went after them. He still blames himself for Haley. He's gone mad with guilt." She looked at her son with a mixture of hope and shame. Hope that he might be able to put things right, and shame that she was willing to let her son put himself in danger. "Do you know what they did with Haley?"

"She's safe," said Tyrion. "But the ones who came here plan to find the others."

"Others?" said Helen.

"His bastards," answered Seth. "They had their names already. That's why they went to Colne. Most of them live in town, since that's where he did the majority of his whoring."

"Then I have less time than I thought," said Tyrion. *They had the names. Who told them? Brenda, or was it Owen, hoping to negotiate for their daughter's freedom?* He turned his back on them, heading for the door. The others began fighting as he left.

"Let me go!" came Kate's voice.

"Do you even care what he said? Your mother's dead, Kate! Does that mean nothing to you?" That was Seth.

"You know *nothing* about my mother," she growled back at him. "Give me the crossbow."

"You can't be serious!" said her husband. "He's a monster, and you want to chase after him?!"

Helen interrupted then, "He's my son."

Seth's voice was furious, "Well your *son* fucked half the women in Colne, including my wife!" He addressed Kate next, "Is that what you want Kate?

Once wasn't enough? You're just as much a whore as your mother!"

Tyrion was mounting his mare now, but despite himself, he kept his ears focused on the voices arguing stridently behind him. It appeared that Kate was about to follow him out the door. She was carrying the crossbow now, along with a quiver full of bolts.

"Don't you step out that door…"

"Or what?!" Kate shouted back. "You'll hit me again? Will that make you feel like more of a man?"

"You walk out that door, and it's over. You aren't coming back," said Seth menacingly.

The door flew open as if someone had kicked it, which of course, she had. Catherine walked through it with an expression that might have made even a warden flinch. There was murder in her eyes. She was halfway to the horse before a second, smaller form, ran after her.

"Momma! Don't go!" Aaron yelled.

She turned and caught him in her arms, dropping the crossbow as her features softened. She held the boy tightly, fighting back tears.

"Don't go," the boy sobbed into her hair.

She kissed the top of his head, "I want you to be a good boy. Mind your father, alright?"

"I want to come with you."

"I wish you could," she said softly, "but it isn't safe."

"You're leaving because of Dad aren't you?" asked her son.

Kate squeezed him again, "No. Your father is angry, but he loves you. I need you to take care of him for me. Can you do that?"

Chapter 7

"I don't want to."

"Do it for me, alright?" she told him.

"Why are you going?" asked her son.

"They've got my sister," she replied matter-of-factly. "I would do the same if it were you."

"You'll come back with Brigid, right?" said the boy.

Tyrion spoke then, "No."

Kate looked up at him, startled, "What?"

"The girl won't be coming back. Even if I recover her, they will send more," he explained.

"Then what do you plan?" she asked him.

Tyrion looked back toward the road. "I'm taking her with me. I'm taking all of them."

"Taking them? Daniel, these kids don't even know you. You can't just take them away from their families," she said, disbelief written clear on her face.

"I'm not asking," he said flatly. "You should stay here, with your family. There's nothing you can do to help."

"You're giving them to the forest gods? They'll be slaves! You can't mean that," she insisted.

He nudged the mare with his heels, and she began to walk.

She watched him, torn in two directions as a war raged within her. Hugging Aaron once more, she told him, "I love you. Go inside. Mind your father." Pushing him away, she started after the horse.

"Momma no," cried the boy, but he didn't move from where he stood.

"Take care of him, Aaron. He needs you," she said once more, catching up to the horse.

Tyrion kept moving, ignoring the woman walking beside him. After a hundred yards he stopped. "You're making a mistake."

"She's my sister, Daniel," she answered. Kate's face was streaked with tears, she could still hear her son's voice in her heart.

"It would be better if you forgot about her. She can't come back with you. None of them can."

"Then I'll go with them."

"You can't," he told her. "You have a son, a husband, you have a life. If you come with me they'll collar you."

"It isn't your choice," she insisted stubbornly. "I'm not letting you take my sister into slavery alone."

"I won't take you."

"Then I'll follow on my own," she replied flatly.

He considered kicking the horse into a gallop, but he couldn't bring himself to leave her alone on the road. Instead, he continued to feign indifference, riding without looking at her while he considered his options.

If he rendered her unconscious he could leave her back at the house, but she would probably follow again as soon as she woke up. *Unless Seth tied her up,* he thought. He might have considered it before, but the bruise on her face left him uneasy. The Seth he had grown up with would never have struck a woman, Kate least of all.

People change, he mused, glancing at the tattoos that lined his arms.

The violence she would encounter among the slaves of the She'Har would be far worse, though. In his mind's eye he imagined her being beaten by one of the wardens. His anger, never far from the surface, rose at the thought. *She won't go to Ellentrea. None of them will. Lyralliantha will take them. I'll make a new place for them.*

There were a lot of 'ifs' involved in that scenario. Not the least of which was the fact that he had no idea whether Lyralliantha would agree to such a thing, or if she could convince her elders to let her keep a dozen or more slaves.

An hour passed in silence. Tyrion alternated between scanning their surrounding with his magesight and surreptitiously studying the woman beside him.

She had changed. Her features were sharper, her face leaner. Life and hard work had put lines on her face while her hips had grown a bit wider. *Not that that's a bad thing,* he thought, *she was almost too skinny before.*

His mind saw a flash of aythar, and he stopped, holding up a hand. "They are ahead of us."

"How can you see? It's pitch black."

He tapped his temple. "Let me focus, they're at the limit of my range." He concentrated, trying to count their numbers. After a minute he spoke again, "You were right. There are more than ten. I count twelve wardens and one of the She'Har. They have a girl and an older man as well."

"She'Har," muttered Kate. "That's what you told me the forest-gods call themselves, right?"

He was impressed by her memory. That conversation had occurred over ten years ago. "Yes. It means 'the People' in their language."

"What does that make us?" she asked.

"Cattle."

She frowned at that, but another thought came to her, "If you can sense them, can they sense you?"

"Probably not. My range is longer than most, but they will definitely know we are coming long before we reach them."

"Then surprise isn't possible…"

"There's more than one sort of surprise," he told her, "but yes, I know of no way to keep them from sensing me at all. I could hide myself up to a certain point, but not enough to get within striking range." He thought of the Prathion gift with a bit of envy, but there was no help for it.

Kate stared off into the darkness, thinking carefully. "Would they negotiate with you?"

He smiled. "Now you're getting closer. No, they would not, but they would talk. They don't see me as an enemy, to them I'm more of a competitor."

"So you're planning to walk in amongst them and—what?" She was beginning to suspect the nature of his answer, but she wanted to hear him lay it out before she objected.

"Take what is mine," he responded.

"There are thirteen of them…," she began.

He held up his hand, "No, there's only one that I'm worried about, the Prathion."

"Are you daft? You think you can walk in there and just kill twelve or thirteen of them? They all have strange powers, like you. You didn't see them when they came into the house. There wasn't a thing we could do, we were helpless, Daniel. Helpless!" She stopped before her emotions got the better of her. Taking a deep breath, she spoke in a more reasonable tone, "And what about Brigid? What about your father? Do you think they won't use them against you?"

"Hostages are only useful against the just."

Kate glared at him, her eyes speaking volumes.

"You should go home, Kate. I'm not the man you think I am. I'm not any better than the ones I'm about to kill. They know it, and I know it. They won't bother trying to use Brigid as a hostage because she's just as valuable to them as she is to me. They won't bother with Alan either, because they don't even understand the meaning of the word 'father'." He looked away, unable to bear the accusation in her eyes. "All they know is blood, and all they know of me is that I've spilled more of it than all of them put together."

"Brigid or your father could still get hurt during the fight," she insisted, ignoring his declaration.

"So?" His eyes were dead when he met her gaze, it was an expression he had perfected during his years among the She'Har—complete indifference.

She suppressed an involuntary shiver. Daniel was changed. She had no doubt of that, but despite his improved acting skills, she knew there was still something more hidden behind the mask. *But not very much,* she suspected.

"A good man couldn't win this fight, Cat," he said, calling her by her childhood nickname. "Me? I'm willing to roll the bones."

Kate caught herself grinding her teeth and forced herself to stop. "Fine," she said at last. "What's your plan then?"

The look on his face unsettled her when he spoke again, "Did you get that bruise before or after they took

Brigid?" He used his hand to indicate the purpling around her eye and over one cheek.

"A—after," she said, uncertainly.

"Perfect, a new slave always has a few marks."

"Slave?" She gave him a hard stare.

"Get used to the word. It's what you are now." Reaching out, he gave in to his impulse and pulled her forward, kissing her roughly, then he added, "Just like me."

She pulled away as soon as his hand relaxed. Flustered, Kate searched for a response, "And what would you have done if I hadn't already been 'marked'?"

"Marked you," he said immediately, but even he didn't believe his words.

"Liar," she spat back, finding her balance. "You're a liar, Daniel. I haven't forgotten."

Her accusation brought back painful memories. "Hand me the crossbow," he said, pushing the past from his mind. Pulling one of the quarrels from the quiver she carried, he organized his thoughts.

The situation was hardly ideal for enchanting, but Tyrion had spent years honing his focus. His finger was far too large, so he used his imagination alone to envision the lines he wanted on the steel point. Carefully he released his will, burning them into the metal, linking small triangles and their interior runes one by one, until the head of the bolt was covered in tight magical lines. When he was finished it was sheathed in an impossibly sharp field of pure force, similar to the blades he often created around his arms.

Kate stared at it when he handed it back, noting the fine engravings, but the magical blade that capped it was impossible for her to see. "What will this do?" she asked.

"Penetrate a mage shield," he replied. *Even a spellwoven one,* he added mentally.

"There's only one," she noted.

"You'll only have time for one shot."

"There are thirteen of them."

"I only need you to shoot the Prathion," he answered.

Kate frowned, "The Prathion?"

"The forest-god."

"Oh," she said, holding the weapon in her hands. "Won't they be suspicious if I'm carrying a loaded crossbow?"

He snorted, "They won't even see it as a threat. Besides, I'll be carrying it. You're my prisoner, remember? When the time comes I'll hand it to you. Take careful aim, and put the bolt through the Prathion's chest."

"And what will you be doing?"

"Killing. Stay as far away from me as you can after you take the shot. If you get a chance, grab Brigid and run. If that isn't possible, just run," he said.

"And if I miss?"

"The Prathions can make themselves invisible. The She'Har will probably escape. If that happens we've lost, whether I kill the others or not," he told her.

"And you think you can handle all the others by yourself?" Kate didn't bother trying to hide the doubt in her voice.

In fact he wasn't sure of that at all. Killing them wasn't the issue, preventing them from escaping once they realized what he was capable of, that would be the real problem. Taking out the She'Har first would simplify things since he thought he could keep any Prathion wardens from escaping, but if the group included Mordan wardens he had no way to keep them from teleporting home. The chance of that was fairly small, but he knew from past experience that the Prathion Grove had several Mordan slaves. He could only hope none of them had been included in the party they were facing.

"I can kill them," he assured her.

Kate reached down, gathering her skirt and drawing it up. She pushed the excess material between her thighs before spreading it behind her and then pulling it around on either side of her hips. She tied the two ends in front of her.

Puzzled, Tyrion asked her, "What are you doing?"

She gave him a wry smile, "Girding my loins. You said to run after I shoot the forest-god."

"I haven't seen that before," he admitted.

"That's because you don't wear dresses," she told him. "If you have to wade a creek or run, this is a lifesaver."

He eyed her attire, "Technically, She'Har slaves are supposed to be naked, but I guess since you're newly captured they won't expect that. You'll have to give up your clothing once we reach the Grove."

She gaped at him, "They let *you* wear clothes."

"We can discuss that later," he added. "There's plenty that can go wrong in the next hour that would make this a moot point."

"I'll take that into consideration when I decide who to shoot," she said pointedly.

Chapter 8

All eyes were on the two of them as they stepped into the small clearing. The fire in the center cast strange shadows of the cruel men and women who had arrayed themselves around it. The wardens all wore their usual leathers, swords made of Eilen'tyral at their sides. Tyrion recognized all of them but one, including the She'Har who stood apart.

"Good evening," Tyrion greeted them in Erollith, dipping his head in deference to Branlyinti.

The Prathion She'Har accepted his gesture but watched him carefully as he replied, "Tyrion, I am surprised to see you so far from your mistress."

"I am here on her behalf."

None of the wardens had shields up, in deference to the presence of the She'Har trainer. Tyrion had made certain to follow their example as well, otherwise he and Kate would not have been allowed to approach. Brigid sat on the ground in front of the ebon skinned Prathion, her head bowed. Alan Tennick lay on the other side of the fire.

Tyrion's father was a miserable sight, stripped of his clothing, his body was a patchwork of bruises and small burns. The wardens had been using him for their amusement, since a human without any gift was worse than useless in their eyes. Alan Tennick wasn't even considered fit to be one of the nameless. Barely conscious, he watched his son with one eye, for the other was too swollen to see.

"Lyralliantha sent you?" said Branlyinti with some interest. Unlike his wardens, the She'Har was fully protected by a spellweaving, a defense that would be impenetrable to anything a human mage could produce. "Does this mean the Illeniel Grove has abandoned their long standing principles?"

"The Mordan discovery has forced them to reevaluate their priorities," answered Tyrion.

"And so they send you here alone," noted the She'Har. "How sad, or perhaps simply foolish."

"I am worth at least five of these," said Tyrion, lifting his chin with visible pride.

The She'Har's face became more animated, "Do not overestimate your worth, baratt. If I take offense, you will suffer the consequences."

"Forgive me," said Tyrion obsequiously, bowing his head. "I did not mean to be rude. I meant only that my abilities will be more than sufficient to deal with any resistance from the baratti. I do not mean to engender conflict between Prathion and Illeniel." His statement both reinforced his subservience to the She'Har and served to remind Branlyinti that any action against him might create problems with the Illeniel Grove.

"What is your purpose in coming to our camp?" asked the Prathion.

Kate spoke softly at almost the same time, "Daniel I can't under…"

"Silence, slave!" barked Tyrion. Lashing out suddenly he backhanded her, knocking her from her feet. The other wardens laughed as she fell. Shocked, she stared up at him from the ground, blood dripping from a split lip.

Damnitt, cursed Tyrion mentally. *She can't shoot from the ground.* Reaching down he gripped her by the hair and hauled her roughly to her feet, ignoring her cries of pain. "You stand in the presence of your betters, bitch. When I want you prone, you'll know it." Turning back to Branlyinti, he apologized, "Please forgive the interruption. I thought I might share the fire with your servants. I will make my own way in the morning, without seeking to interfere in your mission."

The Prathion watched him for several long seconds before speaking, "Very well. You may spend the night with us, so long as you respect my authority and the Prathion claim on the wildling." He gestured at Brigid.

"Of course," said Tyrion. "May I talk with your wardens?"

Branlyinti nodded, waving his hand in dismissal and then returned to the spellwoven chair he had apparently been sitting in before Tyrion's arrival.

Tyrion pulled at Kate's arm, dragging her along as he went to stand beside one of the wardens who was particularly well known to him. "Garlin," he said by way of greeting.

"Tyrion," responded the older man using the human tongue, Barion. "You've chosen a strange prize." His eyes indicated Kate.

Tyrion smiled, answering in the same language, "She is beautiful, isn't she?"

"She isn't even fit to be one of the nameless," noted the other warden, referring to Kate's complete lack of magical ability.

"That's not what I want her for."

"You think Lyralliantha will permit you such a toy?" said Garlin with some wonderment.

Tyrion shrugged, "She has proven to be very unusual for one of the She'Har."

Garlin glanced in the direction of his own master to make sure he hadn't taken an interest in listening. Reassured, he replied, "You are lucky in many ways."

Another warden leaned in, a woman with a face marked by a long scar that ran from one eye to her chin on the opposite side, "Are you suggesting his wins were nothing but luck?" She gave Tyrion a smile that was so poorly executed it came off as more of a lopsided leer.

"I think everyone knows better than that, Braya," said Garlin, glancing at her in annoyance. "No one defeats five at once with luck alone, and no one will ever forget his last fight."

Tyrion was making a mental list as he looked from face to face. Braya was a Prathion, as were most of the others, except for Garlin who had the Mordan gift, and one of the others, a tall man named Laori whose talent came from the Gaelyn Grove. There was one final warden he didn't recognize at all, a woman with blonde hair and skin with deep pockmarks.

"Did you really defeat one of the Krytek, wildling?" asked the stranger.

"I'm standing here," he answered. *What gift does she have?* If she was Mordan his plan might fail. She would have to die second, unless he could discover her origin.

"They say a freak storm stunned your opponent; that you would have lost otherwise," she added in a challenging tone.

Kate listened with interest, questions on her tongue, but she dared not ask them.

Chapter 8

Garlin spoke up then, "That's what they *say*, Trina, but most of us believe that storm was no mere chance."

Tyrion looked at the woman, "Where are you from, Trina?" It was an unusual question to be asked among the slaves of the She'Har.

Garlin had known him longest. He was one of the first wardens Tyrion had met, and the only one to ever call him friend, though that was something they kept secret. He looked at Tyrion with sudden interest, "Why would you ask that?"

"Just curious," said Tyrion, keeping his face smooth. "You've known me long enough to know I'm a little different than those who grew up among the She'Har."

Garlin's eyes moved rapidly, studying his face, shoulders, and legs. Tyrion feigned being at ease, but his body was taut with hidden tension. Garlin had been on the wrong side of Tyrion's anger a few times in the past, when he had had to guard the man he now called friend. Returning his gaze to Tyrion's face, he spoke calmly, "You can't be serious."

"I'm sorry, Garlin," said Tyrion, his tone somber. He shifted the crossbow he still carried and he could almost feel the other warden's attention being drawn to the enchantment on the tip of the bolt it was still loaded with.

"Just relax, old friend. It isn't as bad as you think," added Tyrion.

The older warden's eyes stared into his for a second, "I should have known it would come to this…"

Trina had latched onto Tyrion's last statement with shock, "Did he just say the two of you were *friends*?!" Her question ended in rising laughter. Among the slaves of the She'Har, the term 'friends' generally meant sex partners. It was also a thing no warden would reveal, being synonymous with foolishness.

Garlin was probably the only human raised in the slave pens who truly understood the meaning of the word. He was the only friend Tyrion had, other than Lyralliantha. Blinking, he responded quickly, "Yes, Trina, Tyrion and I have been friends for years now, but then that's something someone from the Centyr Grove probably wouldn't understand."

Tyrion knew the last part of his friend's statement had been a gift. He wished there was another way, but his path was already set. He knew Garlin would understand that as well. *Centyr will be last, for she is the least likely to evade me,* he thought to himself. The other wardens were laughing amongst themselves now, finding the new revelation to be humorous.

"Thank you, Tyrion, for the music," said Garlin.

He ignored the mockery of the wardens around them. "I wish I could play for you again, my friend, but I have only one trick left to show you." Over Garlin's shoulder he could see that Branlyinti was approaching, drawn by the raucous laughter around them. The She'Har stared at them, wondering what had his slaves so worked up. Tyrion handed the crossbow to Kate.

She lifted the weapon, fitting it against her shoulder smoothly and without hesitation, sighting along it to line it up with the Prathion She'Har's chest.

Everything happened quickly after that, although the moment seemed to draw out into a long timeless second. The She'Har stared at her in amusement, for he knew such a weapon offered him no real threat, and then his attention shifted as Garlin's head exploded.

They all stared in shock at Tyrion, who had slain his oldest friend without warning. Reflexively, the other wardens raised their shields, while the harsh crack of the crossbow firing rang out. Branlyinti looked in shock at the quarrel standing out from his chest before collapsing silently to the ground.

"No one move!" shouted Tyrion.

The air was tense with uncertainty. "You won't leave here alive," said Laori Gaelyn.

"Hear me out and you might," responded Tyrion.

"He doesn't even have his shield up yet," noted Trina. "He can't win. There're twelve of us." Then she remembered Garlin, "Well, eleven…"

Kate stood warily beside him, the empty crossbow feeling heavy and useless in her hands. Brigid and Alan Tennick stared at her from across the fire.

Tyrion's voice was resonant, "Listen to me, and I will let you live." Meanwhile, his heart was whispering to the wind, and a sense of chaotic detachment fell over him.

"Without a shield you'll die if we all attack at once," suggested Laori.

"I will kill the first one who tries to use his aythar before they can do a thing," he responded with dead eyes.

"You'll still be dead," said Trina.

The sky rumbled and then a flash lit the night. A second later, a cracking boom rolled over them from a lightning strike in the distance.

"Looks like there's a freak storm tonight," said Tyrion, looking into Trina's eyes. "I'm feeling lucky."

"Wait," said Laori. "Tell us what you want."

"Let the prisoners go," he told them.

"They'll kill us if we do that," said one of the men.

"Not necessarily," said Tyrion.

"The collars will force us to return. There's no other option," reminded Laori.

"I can remove them."

They glared at him, disbelief warring with fear and hope in their features. "Human magic can't affect a spellweaving," said Trina.

"It can't pierce a spellwoven shield either, or kill one of the Krytek," replied Tyrion confidently.

"I don't believe you," she responded.

He smiled, "Then I'll have to kill you."

"Most of us are Prathions," noted one of the others. "Even if you tried, you couldn't catch us all."

"I could get most of you," said Tyrion with resignation. Focusing on the one who had spoken, he added, "I'll make sure you're one of them."

"Alright," said Laori commandingly. "Let them go."

The others stood silent, none of them arguing the decision. Tyrion nodded at Kate, and she moved to help Alan Tennick to his feet before taking Brigid by the hand.

"Take them to Colne," said Tyrion. "I'll meet you there when I'm finished here."

"How do we know you'll keep your promise?" asked Trina as their former prisoners began to walk away.

"Because if I don't, you'll kill me," answered Tyrion. He motioned for Kate, Brigid, and Alan to keep moving.

Chapter 8

"Take them off now," challenged Trina. "If you fail, those of us who survive will hunt them down."

"Fair enough," said Tyrion, "but let me take care of the storm first."

"Then the rumors are true?" said Laori. "You can control the sky?"

Tyrion walked to the edge of the camp and extending one finger he sent a thin beam of force into the ground, etching a line there. He made his way around the fire in a wide circle that was at least fifteen yards across, surrounding them in its circumference.

"How will that change the storm?" questioned Trina.

Tyrion gave her a feral grin, "It won't." He spoke another word, and the tattoos on his body flared, covering him with hard translucent planes of magical force. "It's just to make sure you don't escape."

Lines of power struck him from all sides as he lifted his arms, raising a spherical shield around the campsite, enclosing the wardens within it. Several of the Prathions made themselves invisible but they had nowhere to run now. They were trapped. Laori sent a hastily made spellbeast at Tyrion but he cut it neatly in two with one stroke.

Tyrion's arms were sheathed in blades of magical force, and the enchanted shield around his body allowed him to ignore their attacks as he began to dance around the campfire. Laughing, he cut them apart; arms, legs, and torsos falling away as blood filled the air. Sanguine fluids sprayed everything but failed to touch him; the enchanted shield keeping his skin and clothing pristine while the ground around him turned red.

Kate watched in horror from beyond the edge of the circle, and Brigid began to retch. Alan Tennick remained silent, his one good eye closed as he tried not to see the butchery his son was committing. He could not stop his ears from hearing it, though.

Screams and Tyrion's haunting laughter filled the night.

Chapter 9

The battle, if it could be called that, was over. The camp was silent now but for the sound of the fire and the soft moans of those who had yet to finish dying. Tyrion stood near the fire, his heart still pounding and his skin flushed from exertion. He felt more alive than he had in years and he licked his lips as he looked around him.

I forgot how much I missed it, he thought. The guilt he had once felt after his bouts in the arena was a faint shadow of what it had once been. In its place was something more akin to excitement.

Glancing over his shoulder, he saw the look of revulsion on Kate's face. She held Brigid close against her, shielding the child's face from view. Alan Tennick sat facing away, holding his hands over his ears.

It must have sounded pretty awful, too, thought Tyrion, suppressing a sudden chuckle. *They don't understand. They couldn't possibly understand. The only people who could understand this feeling are the ones I just slew.* Looking down, he studied the mangled bodies that lay scattered around him.

Three were still alive, if only barely. Two men, one with a deep cut passing through his abdomen and another who had somehow managed to seal the arteries in his legs after Tyrion had cut them off. The third was Trina, part of her head and skull had been shorn away, yet somehow she still breathed, lying wide-eyed and silent on the bloody earth. Of the three, only the man who had lost his legs looked to have any chance of living more than a short time.

Bending down, he examined Trina. Her injury reminded him somehow of the way a chicken might survive for a while after losing its head. Her heart beat, her lungs continued to fill with air, but her mind was gone. She was unlikely to last more than a few minutes.

The slave collar around her neck drew his attention. Focusing his magesight until he could make out the finer details of the spellweaving it was composed of, he spent half a minute before reaching out and cutting through it. Trina's blood began to boil within her as the collar disintegrated, and moments later she was dead.

Hmmm.

Turning to the man who was dying from a gut wound he saw the fellow was still conscious. "What are you going to do?" the warden asked.

"What I promised," said Tyrion. "I'm going to remove your collar." Repeating the process he had followed with Trina, he deliberated carefully before cutting through the collar in a different location. The warden died seconds later, his death no less gruesome.

The last man was silent, he had blacked out from loss of blood while Tyrion attended to the others.

"Lucky you," he told the unconscious man. After studying him for a minute he cut the last warden's collar as well. The man's heart stopped, and he died almost instantly.

But his blood didn't boil, noted Tyrion clinically.

The aythar faded from the last man, and now Tyrion was truly alone. At his feet was a headless corpse, a man with a name tattooed on his hand, 'Garlin'.

His adrenaline gone, Tyrion's stomach tightened at the sight. A sense of vertigo washed over him. He could still hear Garlin's last words, *'Thank you, Tyrion, for the music'*. He couldn't remember ever hearing the man say 'thank you' before. It was probably one of the least used phrases among the people kept by the She'Har, almost as rare as the word 'love'.

A dark ache crept through him until his body felt consumed by a cold phantom pain radiating from the center of his being. He wanted to cry, but tears refused to come, and his eyes remained stubbornly dry.

He understood. He knew I had to do it, he told himself. The words were true, but they did nothing for him. Instead he changed the words he told himself, *I feel nothing. I feel nothing. I am empty.*

The pain faded but did not disappear.

With an errant gesture and a thought he released the shield enclosing the bloody campground. A second later he dismissed the shield enchantment that encased his body. It had worked well, though it was the first time he had ever tested it. With his enemies dead it would remain a surprise for his next opponent.

"Bring the girl," he said, turning toward Colne. His voice sounded different in his ears, rougher.

I feel nothing.

"Where are you going?" asked his father, finding his voice at last.

"To collect the rest of my children," he replied. "Can you walk?"

Alan nodded, "I think so."

"Then go home." He looked at Kate, "Come on, we don't have forever."

"Let me come with you, Daniel," said his father, a faint tremor in his voice. He was afraid, but not yet ready to abandon his son.

"So you can see more of what your son has become?" said Tyrion bitterly. "Go home."

"Let me take Brigid back with me," suggested Alan.

"It isn't over, Father," said Tyrion. "They will keep coming until they have every child I sired. She will never be safe here."

"What about Haley? Is she safe with you? Do you know where they took her?"

The hope in Alan's voice tore at him, but he answered with an honest cruelty that made him hate himself even more, "No. She isn't safe. A different grove has her. I did what I could. That's why I'm here. The best I can do is to make sure that they don't get any others."

"But—you're going to take them to the forest gods anyway?" Alan was still very unclear on the distinctions between the different groves of the She'Har.

"My…" he paused for a second, searching for the right word, "…owner, is different, less cruel. If she has them I will have some control over what happens to them. They won't be forced to fight each other."

Meanwhile, Brigid was pulling away from Kate. "I don't want to go," she whispered to her half-sister.

Kate glanced somewhat fearfully at Tyrion, hoping he hadn't heard the girl's words. She wasn't sure how stable he was anymore. The last thing she wanted was for him to turn his psychotic rage loose on Brigid. "Shhh," she replied. "It's alright. He's going to do his best for us. You have to trust him."

"I'm scared, Kate," admitted Brigid tremulously.

"Let's go," said Tyrion, ignoring his father's gaze as he walked away. Kate pulled her sister along in his wake.

"You won't leave me will you?" Brigid asked her.

Kate shook her head, "No, sweetheart. I won't. I'm coming with you. I'll be there."

***

Tom Hayes stood behind the door to his store. Tyrion had knocked loudly several times, which had awoken the store owner, but the hour was late. They had arrived in Colne close to midnight, and everyone had already been long abed.

"Mr. Hayes, open the door," said Tyrion. "I know you're standing there."

"Who is it?" asked Tom Hayes uncertainly.

Tyrion's patience was running out, and his brow furrowed as he struggled with his temper.

"Tom, this is Kate Tolburn. I'm outside with Brigid and Daniel Tennick. Please open up, it's late."

Tyrion's magesight easily picked up the flare in Tom Hayes' emotional state at the sound of his name. Fear. The last time he had been in the town of Colne it hadn't been pretty. He had threatened, maimed, and even branded some of the townsfolk.

They had deserved it, though.

"My wife is sick," said Tom hesitantly.

"She's standing three feet behind you, and she seems fine to me," said Tyrion angrily. "Open the door, or you won't have a store for much longer."

"Daniel, you can't threaten everyone you meet…" began Kate.

Cold eyes burned into her like ice, "This isn't a social call. I'm here to take every child I fathered and hand them over into slavery. You think I should pretend to be a kindly guest?"

A fire kindled inside her, and her old spirit began to assert itself, "You have a good cause, don't paint yourself worse than…"

"I'm the lesser of two evils, Kate," he interrupted, "That doesn't make me good."

The door opened in front of him, and Tom Hayes peeked around the edge, "What do you want?"

Tyrion molded his will and pushed the door open even as he wrapped Tom in a bubble of force, driving him aside and trapping him on one side of the room. The man's wife, Alice, stared at him in horror as he entered the room. "Tell your son, Thaddeus, to come downstairs."

"Y—you k—knew I had a son?" stammered Alice.

Kate stepped forward, claiming the space between them, "The forest gods know as well, Alice. They're coming to take all of them. It will be much worse if they get Tad. Daniel is trying to protect them."

"You can't have my son," declared Alice, mustering her courage.

Tyrion stepped forward, prompting Tom to shout from the side where he was still imprisoned, "Please, don't hurt her!"

Chapter 9

He stopped, frustrated—tired. It had been a long day, and he was surrounded by nothing but resistance. He had expected that. Tyrion knew he was the villain of his own private story, but he was tired of arguing at every turn, tired of being hated.

"We'll sleep here," he announced, surprising everyone. "I'm taking your bedroom for the night, Alice. Kate, Brigid, and Thaddeus will stay in the room with me. You and your husband can sleep wherever else you like, but don't leave the building."

"What?" said Alice, somewhat alarmed.

"You heard me."

"Are you taking us prisoner?" asked Tom.

"You can think of it like that if you prefer," he answered. "Stay here and behave yourself, and we will be gone tomorrow. Leave, talk to anyone, or try to warn the rest of the town, and you'll regret it. Don't forget your son will be sleeping in the room with me." He motioned at Kate to head for the stairs while at the same time releasing the shield imprisoning Tom.

Once upstairs they woke Thaddeus and forced the confused teenager to relocate to what had been his parent's bedroom. When they were all inside Tyrion sealed the door and window to make certain no one could leave. Removing his boots, he lay down on the bed. He didn't bother giving any instructions to the others. They could sleep on the floor or stand all night, either way he didn't care. He closed his eyes.

***

The warmth of someone beside him was comforting, the touch of another's skin. The tight ache

103

that seemed to constantly clutch at his heart eased a bit. Tyrion was surprised, he hadn't expected Kate would be willing to chance getting near him after what she had seen the day before.

Stretching out his hand, he felt the gentle curve of her hip. He traced her leg down to the knee, which had been thrown over his own leg. She was close against him and her warm breath fluttered against his neck. He could feel her arm across his bare chest.

He didn't remember taking off his clothes, but he was glad they were gone. Opening his eyes, he found soft morning sunlight filtering into the room. The others were gone, but he didn't mind, he was alone with Kate. He pulled a lock of her hair across his face, enjoying the soft feel of it accompanied by the scent of summer flowers.

He closed his eyes again. This was a moment not to be disturbed. It needed to go on, but he felt her move and seconds later the soft touch of her lips on his.

He returned the kiss, but the taste of iron brought with it a feeling of guilt. Her lip had been split when he struck her. *I'm so sorry,* he thought. *It was necessary, or they'd have seen through our deception.*

He was considering how to apologize when she pulled away. Studying her face clearly in the morning light, he noted that today it was even more bruised and swollen. Kate's eyes held a look of sadness and resignation.

"Thank you, Tyrion, for the music." The words came from her lips, but the voice was Garlin's.

He stared at her in horror, and a feeling of immense dread swept over him. "No!" he shouted, wanting to deny what he knew was coming. Her head vanished, exploding into a red mess of gore and blood. He screamed again, searching the room with all his senses, trying to find the source of her death, but he knew it had been him.

Tyrion thrust himself out of the bed, his hand flailing to find his sword.

Kate sat in the corner holding her sister while Tad was close beside her. All three of them were staring at him with frightened expressions.

It was a dream.

Glancing down, he saw that he still wore his leathers from the day before. His sword was still belted at his side, and Kate's crossbow lay on the floor. He had fallen asleep from sheer exhaustion, and the others had been too fearful to approach him. The other pillows were still on the bed.

They slept on the floor, without pillows or blankets.

As the world sorted itself out, falling into place within his head, he searched for words to reassure them. "Are you hungry?" was the best he could manage.

The boy nodded, and Brigid whispered in her sister's ear. "They have to pee," said Kate in a neutral tone.

That made sense. He felt the urge as well. Casting his senses outward, he located Alice and Tom Hayes. They were still downstairs. Tom sat nervously at a table while Alice was in the kitchen.

Tyrion unsealed the door and gestured toward it, "Let's go down. We can take care of our bladders and bellies…" The words sounded stupid in his ears, but he had no gift of eloquence.

Kate ushered the two teens in front of her, and they went down.

Tom greeted them with a nervous look, making room at the table but keeping his mouth shut. After they had taken turns visiting the outhouse they sat with him, and a few minutes later Alice brought out several heavy clay bowls filled with warm porridge.

"Thank you," said Tyrion quietly, the words awkward from long disuse.

They ate in silence.

When they had finished Tyrion glanced around the table, "I need to know their names."

Alice, Tom, and Kate shared several glances between them, but none of them spoke. An awkward pause grew until at last Kate took up the challenge, "We aren't entirely sure which ones are yours. Some may not be yours, even if…"

"…Even if they are the right age?" he finished for her. "I'll list the women for you. You tell me which ones have children the same age as Brigid and Thaddeus. Fiona Brown, Emily Banks, Jennifer Wilson, Greta Baker, Rachel Moore, Wilma Carter, Sally Phillips, Peggy…," he stopped for a moment. "What was her last name?"

"Do you mean Mrs. Morris?" asked Alice.

"I think that's her," he affirmed.

"Let me get some paper," she suggested. Rising she found one of the old ledgers and returned with it and a small bottle of ink. It took her a moment to prepare the pen, but a few minutes later she was penning the names he had given in the margin of one of the pages.

"Laura Collins, Mrs. Price—I don't remember her first name…," he admitted.

"Selma," provided Kate.

He nodded, "Greta Baker…"

"You said that one already," said Alice.

He continued until he ran out of names and had begun to repeat himself.

"What about Laura Collins?" suggested Kate, "She has a son the right age."

"I forgot her," he agreed.

"Vicky Jenkins?" added Alice. "Her daughter Piper is fifteen now as well."

Tyrion nodded, the name jogged another memory, "Darla Long too, she lived next door to Vicky."

"Did you just go door to door?" asked Kate in a tone of disgust, daylight and his calm mood had erased much of her earlier anxiety.

He ignored the question, and after Alice finished her tally they had a list of names that was longer than he had expected. He had lain with twenty-seven women and there were sixteen children who showed every likelihood of being his bastards. With Haley already taken, and Brigid and Tad being there with them, there were thirteen others whom he needed to collect before returning.

Tyrion stood, he had been thinking while they discussed his transgressions, "I'll be back soon. Gather the children here while I am gone. I want them here before noon."

Tom finally found his voice, "You expect us to be your accomplices?"

He returned the older man's angry stare with a face devoid of expression, "The other wardens are already moving. They weren't far behind. They will probably be here by nightfall. You will have my offspring here for me before then, otherwise I will resort to more drastic means to make certain that they don't fall into the hands of the other groves."

Tom Hayes ground his teeth, flinching under the younger man's wilting gaze, but apparently he had found his spine once more. Refusing to give up he continued, "Drastic means? I don't believe it. I watched you grow up, Daniel Tennick. You might be sick enough to threaten us, but I don't believe for a second that you'd hurt your own children."

"Really?" said Tyrion, his eyes falling on Tad Hayes. "Stretch your arm out on the table, boy," he commanded.

Tad stared up at him, his lip beginning to tremble, but he didn't move.

"Wait!" shouted Alice. "We'll do as you say. Please, don't hurt him."

Tyrion relented, "Fine." Moving for the door, he addressed Tom once more, "I know what you're thinking, Tom, and if you run it will be worse. You'd best hope that I'm the one who finds you first then. You don't want to know what they'll do with your son."

He left, closing the door behind him and walked behind the building, taking the most direct path out of Colne rather than walking down the main street. He kept going until he was far beyond the edges and then circled around to follow their path from the night before. Once he was out of sight, he stopped and sat on the side of the trail that led back toward the house that belonged to Seth and Kate Tolburn.

His hands were shaking.

Closing his eyes, he took a long deep breath, *I feel nothing.*

Kate's green eyes flashed accusingly at him from the shadows in the back of his mind, and he opened his eyes again to dispel the vision.

His parents, Kate, Seth, Tom and Alice Hayes… and the children as well, they all held so much emotion. He could feel it, he could see it. Fear, hope, expectation, it was in their eyes when they looked at him. Things he had grown accustomed to not finding among the She'Har.

The people here, their hearts were shouting at him, projecting emotions that he was no longer capable of dealing with. Most of it was fear, and with it came the inevitable—hatred. Even Kate, she was the worst. Affection mingled with fear and anxiety, flashes of hope, and then the final result, hate.

I feel nothing.

He took to his feet again and made his way back to the small stall where he had left his horse. Saddling the mare he rode back to the camp where he had slaughtered the wardens and their leader, Branlyinti. He hadn't been thinking clearly the night before. He should have erased the evidence, but he had been overwrought.

He found Branlyinti's body first. The bolt had entered the body cleanly, slipping between two ribs and skewering the She'Har's heart. It might have shattered if it had struck bone, but it was still intact. Tyrion carefully removed it, cleaning away the gore on the shaft and wiping it on the dead man's clothing. He tucked it away. It might come in handy later.

Using the same circle he had the evening before, he surrounded the grisly camp in a hemisphere before filling it with flames. After a short time the air exhausted itself, and the visible flames died away, but he kept his will on the area, driving the temperature even higher until the dead air glowed with strange gases, and everything else was reduced to flickering ash. The heat became so intense that he was forced to step back in spite of the shield, until he was more than ten yards distant.

Satisfied at last he stopped heating the area and then did his best to cool it down to a tolerable level before releasing the shield around it.

The bodies were gone. Only white ash and blackened, glassy soil remained. It would be immediately apparent to anyone who happened upon the site that something unusual had occurred there.

"That won't do," he told himself.

The simplest thing to do would be to bury the ashes and glass, but that would still leave an unusual area of freshly turned soil. He wanted the site to look old and undisturbed, preferably with grass growing over it. He could achieve such a look by spending considerable time moving the scorched parts lower and redistributing the plants and other flora at the margins, but it would take a lot of time and painstaking effort.

He decided to take a risk and turned his attention over to the voice of the earth echoing slowly beneath him. It was something he had done only rarely since his fight against the Krytek in the arena some ten years before. He feared the She'Har discovering his hidden talent, but even more, he feared the talent itself. His mind changed when he opened it to the earth, or to the sky, as he had done the night before. He became less himself, and more *other.* He had no easy way to describe it, even in the privacy of his heart.

Crystalline calm came over him as his mind shifted to match the heart of the world under his feet. Rocks, soil, those things lay close to the surface, but deeper still were different things, greater stones that went on for vast distances, and beneath those an ocean of liquid fire. For a moment he was almost swept away, carried into the unending depths, but he drew back, holding onto himself.

The memory of his desire returned to him and he moved his earthen body in response to it. Soil moved and rocks shifted, churned, and then smoothed again. Contracting he made himself small again, until his consciousness was once again bounded by flesh and bone. It was an uncomfortable sensation, packing himself into such a tiny shell.

This must be what dying is like. The words echoed through him, but he wasn't sure of their meaning at first. Slowly his awareness returned, and the babbling sounds within began to make sense once more.

Tyrion blinked, his eyes feeling dry. He must have forgotten to do that while he was listening to the earth.

The ground was smooth and undisturbed. The grass was thinner and the soil rockier, but it didn't look as if it had been touched in a long time. Nothing remained of the incinerated campsite. "I have to learn to do that without completely losing my mind," he told himself.

Last night had been better. The situation, the tension and hostility, those things had served to anchor his mind more firmly. So firmly that he had almost been unable to sense the voice of the wind. Today he had nearly lost himself completely.

He wondered what would happen if he forgot himself.

His actions had only cost him an hour or so, and he had more to do before he returned to Colne. Continuing along the path, he made his way back toward the house that Seth and Kate had shared. There were things that needed to be said, and debts repaid.

Chapter 10

Seth was coming out of the barn when Tyrion arrived. The barn itself was new, at least in Tyrion's mind. When he and Kate had been children there had been no barn, but after Seth married her he had built it to house some of his tools and keep his livestock from freezing in the winter.

Tyrion stopped the mare by the barn and tied her reins to a small post there. Then he made his way directly to where Seth stood waiting with a look of disapproval on his face.

"Where are Kate and Brigid?" asked his childhood friend with an expression of genuine concern on his face.

"In Colne," said Tyrion, "gathering my children. They don't know I'm here."

"Oh," said Seth, watching him cautiously.

"You said something the other night that I thought needed to be corrected."

Seth shifted nervously, "Listen Daniel, I was really worked up, and I know I might have said some things that I shouldn't have. It had only been a few hours since they took Kate's sister, and I felt ten kinds of useless after they humiliated us."

Tyrion ignored the statement, "I never had sex with Kate."

His old friend went still, remembering his accusation. It was the sort of motionless that one might find in a forest creature, when it knows the hunter is about to strike.

The fear annoyed Tyrion. "I'm not here to kill you. I know you think I'm a crazed murderer, and—well maybe I am to some extent. I'm not like I was, I'm not like you anymore, but I'm not going to turn rabid on you. I'm just here to talk."

"I didn't believe her," said Seth, staring uncomfortably off to one side. "When she came back that day, after you left—she said nothing happened, but I knew that couldn't be true."

"I kissed her," said Tyrion, "that's all, and she wasn't pleased with that either." The last part was a lie. She had kissed him, and there had been nothing innocent about it. He pointed at the collar around his neck, "This thing, it prevents me from doing much else in that regard." He glanced downward, to emphasize his point. "Only my owner can grant permission for me to—well, you get what I'm saying."

Seth waved his hands, "Alright! I believe you. I don't want to talk about this."

"Too bad," said Tyrion. "'Cause I'm not done. I want to know if that's why you started hitting her."

"Hitting? No. You're mistaken there. That was just once, yesterday. We started fighting after they took Brigid, and she wouldn't leave me be. Kept shouting for me to go after them, but I knew it was hopeless. I couldn't stop them, but I was ashamed of myself for not going anyway." Seth looked down, clenching his jaw. "Then she called me a coward and—I just snapped."

Tyrion nodded understandingly, "I know just exactly how that can be."

Seth glanced up at him, surprised at his friend's sympathetic response. He saw Tyrion's shoulder tense, but the motion was so swift that he could barely twitch before a fist smashed into his jaw. Reeling, he stepped back, tripped and fell hard to the ground. Tyrion stood over him.

Seth closed his eyes, *Damn, he's going to kill me anyway.* Nothing happened for several moments, so he opened his eyes again. His friend was offering him his hand.

"Take it," said Tyrion. "We're even now."

Seth took his hand and stood shakily. His vision seemed slightly blurry, and it felt like one of his teeth was loose. "You really pack a punch, Daniel."

"Violence is about all I'm good for anymore," he responded.

"Kate seems to feel differently," said Seth somewhat bitterly.

"Did you mean what you said, about her not coming back?" asked Tyrion seriously.

"No," admitted Seth. "I was out of control, but I knew I was lying even as I said it. Doesn't matter though, she's not planning on coming back anyway."

"It's really a bad idea for her to come with me," said Tyrion.

Seth squinted at him, "I agree."

"Last night I showed her a sample of what my life is like..." began Tyrion, "...and I'm pretty sure she didn't like what she saw. In fact, I think she's afraid of me now, if she doesn't hate me outright."

Spitting a mouthful of blood to the ground, Seth worked his sore jaw, which was beginning to swell. "You do tend to have that effect on people," he gave a half-hearted laugh as he said it, but then stopped. He looked at Tyrion worriedly.

Tyrion laughed, and Seth joined him, but it was an uneasy laughter.

"I'll do my best to convince her not to come with me," he told his friend. "When she comes back, be kind, and try to remember that some of what she describes about me, will have been for your benefit."

"Are you saying you're going to pretend to be a frightening, murderous, asshole, just to convince her to come back home?" asked Seth.

Tyrion shook his head, "No. I'm just not going to hide the fact that that is exactly what I am." He turned away and began walking toward the house. He could sense his father and mother inside, and he had some words for them as well.

Seth didn't move to follow, but he raised his voice for one more question, "Are you sure you can't just let Brigid come home too?"

He looked back at his friend sadly, "I wish I could, but the She'Har will send more wardens. There won't be any peace until they have all of them."

Passing through the back door of the house, he found his mother, Helen, waiting there for him. He almost flinched when she opened her arms, but after a moment he relaxed. Her embrace felt good, too good; it threatened to undo the walls he had built around his weakness.

I feel nothing, he chanted mentally, but he knew it was a lie. "Mother," he said aloud.

"I'm glad you're back," she said immediately. "Last night you seemed…" she stopped. "When your father returned—I just couldn't believe it."

He pushed her out to arm's length. "It's true, Mother. I'm not who I was, and it doesn't do any good

116

to pretend otherwise. I'm not safe for civilized society."

Helen frowned, "Don't say that, Daniel."

Hearing his old name fall so naturally from his mother's lips sent another shiver of pain through him. "Stop," he told her. "I need to see Dad, then I'll go."

His words hurt her, that was obvious, but she stood aside and let him enter the small bedroom where his father lay. Alan Tennick was bruised and swollen, his features almost unrecognizable. The old man lay with his head turned away, staring out the window with his one good eye.

"Father."

"You shouldn't have come," said the old man hoarsely.

Tyrion nodded, "I just wanted to check your wounds before I leave." His magesight was already searching, checking Alan's battered body for fractures or more serious wounds. He found none, though. The wardens were good at what they did. They knew how to beat a man senseless without doing permanent injury. They had been careful. It was a matter of practice, refraining from inflicting deadly wounds until you knew you were done with your prey.

Finished, he waited, staring at the man whom he had admired for so much of his younger life. Silence filled the room, until at last he started to leave.

"You enjoyed it, didn't you?" Alan's voice broke the silence without warning.

Tyrion paused, bowing his head, "I did."

"I thought maybe, after you left last time—I thought maybe it was a fluke. Maybe you were just angry, or too worked up, but last night, you proved me wrong. I've been a failure as a father."

"No…"

"If I had known," continued Alan, "back then, what you would become." The older man's voice faltered. "Forgive me son, I should never have become a father."

Tyrion turned back, surprised. "It isn't your fault. You did the best you could."

Alan was looking at him now, tears running down his swollen cheek, "When I see you, I can see your pain, son. And that hurts, but what hurts most, is that I wish…," his voice broke.

Unable to help himself, Tyrion took his father's shaking hand and then let the old man pull him into a painful hug. "What do you wish, Dad?" he asked, wrinkling his nose at the smell of alcohol on Alan's breath.

The words were almost incoherent, but he heard them anyway, "I wish you'd never been born, Daniel." The old man was sobbing now, "I'm so sorry."

His stomach twisted as he heard the words, but he did his best to keep his body still. *I feel nothing.*

He had to get away. Untangling himself from Alan's arms, he stood up again. He could sense his mother's presence, listening on the other side of the door, so he wasn't surprised when he found her standing there as he opened it.

"He's been drinking whiskey for the pain, Daniel. He's not himself," she began.

"I know," he agreed, letting her hug him one more time. Then he pushed her away and went back out the same door he had entered. *The truth is still the truth, though.*

He nodded at Seth and began walking back toward the small road that led to Colne.

"What about your horse?" asked Seth.

"Keep her," he replied. "I won't be able to make much use of her with a bunch of kids in tow."

"You sure? She's a valuable animal."

So am I, Tyrion thought with a sense of irony. "Yeah, keep her, trade her, whatever suits your needs." He kept walking.

Seth followed for a short distance, "You really think she'll come home?"

Tyrion didn't look back, but he ground his teeth, "I'll make sure of it."

***

Colne was buzzing with activity when he returned. The tension in the air made him think of a hive of angry bees. Some of the people who were in the streets went inside when they saw him coming. Faces stared at him from windows.

There was a small crowd in front of the Hayes' store. It was composed of familiar faces, particularly the women. For the most part, they were the ones who had borne his children, along with quite a few unhappy spouses and some other assorted family members. The teenagers among them all held a certain resemblance to one another.

None of them looked particularly pleased to see him.

"What's he doing here?!" said Brad Wilson with a certain amount of alarm. Gasps went up from the others as they recognized him. The quicker thinking among them began to scatter, heading as rapidly as they could away from the area without actually running.

They came up abruptly against an invisible wall. Tyrion was taking no chances.

"The children stay, the rest of you can go," he announced.

"What's the meaning of this, Tom?" shouted Greta Baker, directing her words at Mr. Hayes. "You said you had a way to hide them."

Tom's eyes were on the ground now.

"Don't blame him," said Tyrion. "He knew if he didn't get you here I'd make sure there wasn't enough left of him or his family to bury."

"The forest gods are coming for them. Daniel is here to take them to safety, to hide them. There isn't a better option," said Kate, raising her voice to be heard above the crowd.

Dalton Brown spoke then, "I wouldn't trust my David with him. He's a monster."

At that point someone near the back threw a stone, arcing it over the crowd to bounce off of Tyrion's personal shield. A scuffle ensued as the wiser heads near the stone-thrower wrestled the man to the ground.

Tyrion laughed, "I'm not here to kill anyone today, not even stupid people."

"Then you should leave, 'cause you're not taking my daughter!" shouted Rachel Moore.

Showing his teeth he strode forward, until he stood directly in front of Rachel. The woman almost collapsed, but he gripped the front of her dress before she could fall. Her daughter, Abigail, cried fearfully as she stood behind her mother.

"That doesn't mean I won't stoop to other forms of persuasion," he growled into the frightened mother's face. His nose picked up the scent of urine, and his magesight confirmed his suspicion, Rachel Moore had lost control of her bladder. He released her, letting her fall backward.

"Let the devil have them. They're demon-cursed anyway," muttered someone from the crowd.

"Children to the right," commanded Tyrion, "the rest of you over on the left."

Some moved to obey, others stood dumbly. He nudged and herded those who were in shock, using invisible planes of force to separate them. *Like sheep for the shearing,* he thought silently. Many of the teens cried, while others glared angrily at him. Some cursed, but he ignored them.

"Why are you doing it like this?" asked Kate. "You're making it worse. They might understand if you just talked to them."

He gave her a warm smile, "There's no time. My way is faster."

Kate looked away, unnerved by his bizarre expression, "This isn't right."

Tyrion was counting the youths he had winnowed away from their parents... *thirteen, fourteen...*

He should have fifteen. Their tally earlier had been sixteen, counting Haley who was in Sabortrea. There was one missing. "Who isn't here?" he asked.

"Gabriel Evans," said Kate. "We were sorting that out before you got here. He and his mother hadn't shown up yet.

Evans... The name seemed vaguely familiar, but he couldn't remember the woman.

Kate sighed, "Mona Evans. She lives at the end of the road, past the Price house. Her husband left her after he found out she was pregnant. She's been raising Gabriel by herself."

The name "Mona" he remembered, but he still couldn't think of what she had looked like. "Well, we had best send someone to fetch him then." He looked over the crowd of upset men and women he had separated from the teens. Pointing at five men he called out, "You, you, you, you, and you... go find Gabriel Evans and bring him here. I don't really care if Mona comes along or not."

They looked at him uncertainly, then one of them spoke up. "She won't listen to us."

"I'm not asking you to talk to her, Mr. Baker," said Tyrion.

One of the others, Gary Carter, protested, "You don't expect us to drag him from his home?"

Tyrion gave him a cold stare before gesturing at Wilma Carter, "Do you like your wife, Mr. Carter? If you do, I suggest you make certain you return with Gabriel as swiftly as possible. That goes for the rest of you as well." He opened the shield behind them.

They shuffled for a moment until he shouted at them, "Go!"

The men began running, and he looked at the others, "The rest of you can leave."

People scattered.

The crying of the teens left behind grew louder. The sound annoyed him, and his stomach was rumbling. "I'm going inside to eat," he told Kate. "Shut them up, so they don't disturb my appetite."

Her anger flared again, "Or what?!"

Leaning in close to her ear he whispered, "Or I'll burn their tongues out." He turned away and ushered Alice and Tom Hayes back into the store, leaving Kate and the children in the street. He enclosed them in a new shield to make sure none of them ran.

Kate spat into the dirt behind him as he left, and he heard her mutter something almost inaudibly.

It sounded as if she had said, "Liar", but he let it go. "Alice, I'll expect a better lunch. No more of that pig-swill you called porridge this morning…"

The Silent Tempest

Chapter 11

The men returned while he was still eating the ham Alice Hayes had brought out. They brought Gabriel Evans in through the front door of the store while his mother, Mona, screamed at them from the street.

It was enough to ruin his appetite. *I feel nothing.*

He kept eating, hoping none of them would realize his heart was no longer in it. His hold over them would be weakened if they knew his stomach was churning. Years among the She'Har had taught him the deepest secrets of intimidation. They must never suspect that anything remained of the person he had once been.

I feel nothing.

"Leave the boy and escort his mother home," he commanded without looking up from his plate.

He made a point of taking his time with the rest of the food. When he had finished, he addressed Tom Hayes who sat awkwardly at one end of the table, "I'll need a wagon, a sturdy mule, and provisions to last at least a week. Make sure you include blankets, water, food, and the rest of that delicious ham."

Tom's eyes bugged a little, "I only have the one mule. I need it for the store or else…"

"Seth Tolburn has a new mare," suggested Tyrion, interrupting. "He might trade it to you if you need a replacement."

"But the wagon, and the rest, I can't…"

"Have it ready within an hour. Those kids out there will need it. Make sure they aren't left wanting. Understand?"

Tom Hayes closed his mouth, unhappy but afraid to protest further.

Tyrion smiled. "I *will* be back again. If I feel that your packing and provisions were lackluster, I will make certain to visit you."

The store owner left, and Alice spoke up, "Is there anything else you...?"

"Pack up the rest of this pig and go help him. Make sure the cheap bastard doesn't let his stingy nature get the best of him," he ordered.

Gabriel Evans still stood in the corner, watching him silently with wide eyes. The boy was afraid, but he kept his fear under control. Tyrion couldn't help but be impressed with the teen's composure. Rising from the table, he walked over to inspect the youth.

Long limbs and wild hair were the first things that stood out. Gabriel's hair was brown, a gift from his mother no doubt, most of Tyrion's other children had dark hair. He was still thin, but he would probably fill out with time. His bones indicated he might be quite tall when he had finished growing.

"You seem calm," he told the boy. "Are you always so cool, child?"

"N—no, sir," answered Gabriel.

"You're worried, then," said Tyrion, nodding. "It must feel something like facing a mad dog, eh lad? Stand still, don't run, no sudden moves, otherwise the beast will be on you." He leaned in, until his face was only an inch from Gabriel's nose. "Is that what you're feeling?"

The boy nodded, his head bobbing almost imperceptibly. "Yes, sir," he almost whispered.

Tyrion straightened up, "You could have run. When they left, while I was eating. Nothing held you here. Your mother was still calling for you outside, but you didn't move. Were you too afraid to move?"

Gabriel swallowed, "No, sir. I was thinking about my mom. I didn't want…" His words trailed off as the teen realized his words might offend the man in front of him.

"You didn't want me to hurt her, did you boy? Is that right?"

Gabriel nodded.

"At least you're honest," said Tyrion approvingly. "I can appreciate that, so I'll give you some advice. Fear isn't always bad, but it isn't always good either, it's a tool. Master it and you can use it to become stronger, faster—sharper. Let it rule you, and it will make you a slave in a way that no chain could ever do. Do you hate me, Gabriel?"

The teen shook his head, "N—no, sir."

"Then you're either a fool, or that was your first lie. You should hate me; I expect you to. You can use that as well."

Emboldened by Tyrion's seeming rationality, the boy spoke up, "What are you planning to do with me, with all of us?"

Tyrion started to answer but then paused, "Let me get the others, so I don't have to repeat myself."

He went outside and released the shield around the other teens, thinking to order them inside, but as soon as the invisible wall vanished, one of the males started running.

"Damnitt all!" muttered Tyrion. He sent his will outward, forming a long rope-like line of force to wrap itself firmly around the youth's ankles. The boy fell, slamming his chin on the hard packed dirt surface of the road.

The boy screamed as his captor dragged him back toward the others, flailing his arms and crying for someone to help him. The few windows facing the main street that weren't already closed were shuttered as people sought to block out the view or perhaps the sound of the scene in the street.

Tyrion grabbed the boy by the collar of his shirt, causing the fabric to rip slightly as he hauled him to his feet.

Frantic the young man twisted in his grasp, turning to face the man who held him. One arm half raised to strike at Tyrion. He froze as he saw the look in his captor's eyes.

"Time to calm down, boy. Let's not do anything you'll regret."

The teen stared at him, wild-eyed, but he didn't move. Blood dripped to the ground from the split skin on his chin.

Tyrion placed one finger under the boy's chin, lifting it, and then sealing the wound. "You'll have a scar there. Next time could be worse. I expect you'll make better choices from here on."

The kid nodded, still fearful.

"What's your name, boy?" He knew the names on the list they had come up with, but he couldn't yet match the faces to them all.

"Blake," said the youth after a short pause.

"Blake what?"

"Blake Cruz."

That meant he was Samantha Cruz's son. Tyrion remembered her, thick hair and dark eyes, Samantha had been one of the more beautiful women he had wronged. She had been unmarried when he had beguiled her, and the pregnancy had probably ruined her chances of finding a husband.

"You don't look much like your mother," noted Tyrion. The boy was a tangle of skinny arms and legs. He looked healthy, but his bones were too prominent. Blake showed little of his mother's grace and poise.

"She said I look a lot like you did," admitted the youth.

Was I that ugly once? Tyrion wondered. "Go stand with the others."

Once they were all together again, Tyrion raised his voice, "We're going to be together for a long time, and there are some things you need to understand, so you don't make a similar mistake to young Blake here.

"The first thing you should know, is that I can see in the dark. I can even see through walls. There is no place you can hide. I can reach you from great distances, whether to paralyze or to punish. I have been tolerant so far, but my patience is in short supply.

"Most of you live here in town, so I expect you should know it well. Who can tell me what lies behind the Brown's house over there?"

No one spoke.

Tyrion sighed, then picked out one of the few he already knew on sight, "Thaddeus. What lies behind Mr. Brown's house?"

Tad swallowed, then answered, "A small shed, sir."

Tyrion nodded, "That's correct, but I'd rather not destroy Mr. Brown's shed. What else is back there?"

"They have an outhouse," volunteered Tad.

"Yes, they do," agreed Tyrion smiling as he focused. He sent invisible streamers of force outward, guiding them around the small home and past the shed. When they reached the outhouse he changed their nature, and with a sudden pulse of energy the wooden outbuilding burst into flames. Smoke rose from behind the Brown home. "Or I suppose we should say, 'they did'."

Shock registered on some of their faces, while others continued to stare dumbly at him. He supposed they'd had a lot of surprises for one day. Tyrion knew from the past that there was a point at which people simply couldn't register any more fear or surprise. At some point the mind would just go blank.

He glanced at Brigid, "Go look behind the Brown home, and then come tell the others what you see there."

She nodded and then began quick stepping in that direction, uncertain whether she would be allowed to run or not. They waited for a long minute until she returned. "The outhouse is on fire," she told them.

"Good," said Tyrion. "I think all of you should be able to learn from that. Now, let's go inside the store. I'd like to talk to you all a little further before we leave."

Brigid piped up then, "What about the fire?"

"I've already suppressed it," he reassured her. Dalton and Fiona Brown would have to endure the smell of smoke for a long while whenever they used it, but he had made sure the damage was mostly cosmetic. "Move along, we don't have all day."

Once they were inside, he had them all line up along one wall before asking them to name themselves. He did his utmost to memorize their faces, and when they were done he repeated them back to them. He forgot one or two, but after another repetition he was sure he had them all firmly in his memory.

"Today we will be taking a trip, away from Colne, away from your parents, away from everything you've ever known. We will be entering the deep woods, treading upon the domain of the forest gods. Do any of you know why?"

One of the girls raised her hand, "She told us that the forest gods are bad, that you're really trying to protect us from them." The girl's name was Sarah Wilson, and she was indicating Kate as she spoke.

Tyrion nodded once, "That's partly true. The reason they're coming is because you may have inherited the same powers that I have. That would make each of you very valuable to the She'Har, but not in the way you might think. They don't want you for a higher purpose. There are several different groups of them, called 'Groves'. They use humans with abilities like mine in their games.

"Games isn't really a good term either," he said, continuing. "They compete with one another, using human slaves as their proxies in arena combat. When they discovered that I had produced children before I was taken, it sparked a rush to find you. Each of the Groves is sending teams of wardens to come and try to claim some of you before the others do."

Sarah raised her hand again, and Tyrion nodded at her. "If we don't have any powers, like you do, can we go home?" she asked.

Tyrion grimaced. None of the teens in front of him showed any sign of special ability yet, but he suspected it was only a matter of time before some of them began to manifest their gift. Whether they would all develop magical ability, or whether none would, he had no way of knowing. "Once they put the collar on you…" he shook his head. "I don't know. If some of you turn out to be normal—it's just too hard to say. It's possible I could convince them to let you go, but I won't lie, they may just as well decide to keep you for breeding experiments."

"Experiments?" That was from Kate.

He nodded. "I cannot keep them from taking you, so instead I am claiming you for the one who owns me. What she will do with you, is not for me to decide. My only consolation will be that if you all share the same owner you won't be forced to fight one another."

Another boy, Ryan Carter, spoke up then, forgetting to raise his hand, "We don't have to fight, do we? I mean, those of us who don't want to—they can't make us, right?"

Tyrion gave him a flat stare, "If you manifest the same gift I have, then you will probably be forced to fight. If you refuse, they will kill you. If you don't manifest the gift, then you'll be used as a servant, unless I can somehow convince them to let you go." He glanced over them, studying their features. It was obvious that they still hadn't fully accepted the truth, but only time would help with that.

He lifted his hand to his throat, indicating the spellwoven collar there, "This is what they will put on you. It marks you as their property, it ensures your obedience. Once it is on, you cannot remove it without dying, you cannot run. You will be their slaves, just as surely as I already am." There was more he could have added, more that he wanted to say, but it would have only been false hope.

Whatever I plan, the reality is that I will probably fail. It's best they accept the truth sooner rather than later. Hope will only get them killed.

***

Tyrion drove the wagon up the small road from Colne, heading back toward the Tolburn house. They passed it after an hour, but he didn't stop there. The wagon was slow and, with so many walking they were making poor time.

The provisions filled most of the bed of the wagon, but there was still enough room for two or three of the teens to ride in the back. Rather than decide on favorites, though, he had forced them all to walk—including Kate. She had wanted to ride on the front seat beside him.

She was hurrying now, speeding up so that she could come abreast of him. Looking up at him, she spoke, "We could have stopped at my house."

He didn't bother to answer, keeping his eyes on the road ahead.

"I could have seen my son again," she added.

Tyrion looked down disdainfully, "You can go back now. I don't need you."

133

She looked back, uncertain. "What about them?"

"They aren't your concern," he told her. "Their future is going to be a hard one. The last thing they need is you there, reminding them of what they have lost."

"Are you sure you're talking about them, or about yourself?" she challenged.

He pulled on the reins, stopping the wagon. Climbing down he walked toward Kate purposefully. She took a step back, but he kept moving forward until he stood in front of her. Taking her hand, he pulled her along with him, walking until they were fifty yards away, hidden by trees and thick underbrush. He was half a head taller, which meant he had to look down at her from such a close distance. "Is that what you want? You think that coming with me will change the past? That we can have a second chance, or that you can change me?"

She turned her head away in denial, "No. I know there's no going back."

"Yet you think to abandon your son, and your husband, for what?"

"When you left the first time, fifteen years ago," she began, "I was devastated. It was years before I finally accepted it, and then you returned again. You agreed to a deal that you thought was certain death to return, and when you left you were certain you'd be dead in your next fight. Now you're taking my only sister, and the only thing I have left of you, back to that place. She's young, and she's scared, and you've already admitted she may have to fight for her life. You expect me to let you walk away a third time?"

Chapter 11

The look in her eyes pierced him, but he drew on his anger to shield him from the softer emotions that lay deeper, "What exactly do you think you'll be when you get there?"

"It won't matter," she said. "As long as I can help her, or them. They're only children."

"You'll be a slave, Kate, and once they put that collar on you, there's no going back. Believe me on that, for I've tried. Not only will you be a slave, but you'll be considered near worthless since you have no power. They call those the 'nameless' back in Ellentrea, and they are universally bullied and abused. The only thing you possess of value are your looks, and those will only bring you trouble. The only currency among the slaves of the She'Har is sex, but you won't be able to trade it, they'll simply take what they want from you."

Her face blanched as he spoke, but her stubbornness remained, "You said the collar prevented that."

He sneered, "Only the most common form of penetration, there are plenty of other ways to seek pleasure—or to violate someone."

"I saw how you were with them yesterday. They wouldn't dare…"

"I am the first one you should be afraid of," he growled. "Go home."

"Or what?" she said, scowling back at him.

In Ellentrea the only way to react to such defiance was with violence or submission. His self-control snapped, and his hand shot out, catching her by the hair at the back of her head. He wanted to hurt her, but rather than strike her, he channeled his rage in a different manner. Leaning forward, he twisted her head to one side and bit her ear, hard.

She yelled, pushing at him with her hands, but she was trapped. One knee came up, seeking to wound him where it would count most, but he had expected that, twisting to one side. He kicked her feet out from under her and let her fall to the ground.

Before she could rise he was on her, pressing her down. She was helpless. The beast within him rose, demanding he feed it. *Blood and ashes,* he thought. *Blood and ashes.* Emerald eyes stared up at him as she stopped fighting.

A single tear escaped, falling to the ground.

He went still. He was hurting Kate. He was hurting the only woman who had ever truly cared for him. *To make her go home,* he reminded himself, but he knew that was a lie. He wanted her. Forcing her to go home was just an excuse.

She pushed him off as she sensed his hesitation. "Is that it?" she demanded, "Don't you want to prove how evil you are? Can't you finish the job?"

He looked away, "I will hurt you far worse than this."

"What? You'll bite my other ear?! You'll pretend you're going to rape me? I'm not afraid of you!" She was as furious as he had ever seen her.

Somehow he had lost control of the situation. Fifteen years he had been among the She'Har, regularly inculcated with cruelty and indifference, and yet it had only taken Kate fifteen minutes to strip away the years and leave him feeling like the uncertain boy he had once been. For a moment it was Tyrion who was merely a memory. Daniel Tennick stared at the girl he had once loved beyond all hope, and the pain of everything he had done threatened to overwhelm him.

No, no, no, no—no! She had to go home.

Kate was watching his face intently, her anger vanishing as she saw the muscles around his lips begin to tremble. Daniel's face was twisting, shifting, as if a wave of grief had abruptly struck. The hard uncaring veneer was crumbling, and beneath it lay an ocean of suffering. *He's about to lose it,* she thought. The realization brought feelings of both triumph and fear. Her 'Daniel' was still in there, but she was also worried he might collapse, utterly broken.

Suddenly she was the one who was uncertain. Her intuition told her she had two courses. Take him in her arms, and he would dissolve. If there was one person his inner child looked to for forgiveness, it was her, and if she granted it—it might start an avalanche. He was vulnerable. The only way his soul could ever begin to heal was in her arms.

But it might also completely undo him. Would he fall apart?

The other course was obvious. Rebuff him. Hurt him. A sharp treatment with the sort of cold cruelty he had learned to expect would probably snap him back into what had become his normal mindset. Only hatred could summon the devil.

Daniel felt her eyes on him as his world crumbled. Everything was spinning out of control. He should never have come back. His father's words echoed in his mind, *I wish you had never been born.* What was he doing? Kidnapping his own children. It seemed like the grandest folly he had ever committed. They hated him. Everyone hated him. His legs felt weak, and a moment later he found himself on the ground.

The logic he had relied upon no longer made sense, and then he felt *them.*

Several points of brilliant aythar, approaching from the direction of Colne. Somehow they had gone around, probably during the night, searching the outlying regions around the town. Now they were advancing from the town itself. The wardens were coming.

They would try to take the children. He was sure of that. They were un-collared and he had no She'Har with him to make a claim for the Illeniel. *How many will die if I fight them with all of these children present?* He couldn't fight. He didn't want to fight.

Everyone hated him, except possibly the woman who was studying him now, staring at him with a shocked expression. *She has to go home. She can't be here when they come.*

"They're coming, Kate," he told her sadly. "Please, you have to go. They don't want you. You'll be safe if you aren't here." Staring up at her, he could see her aura wavering, uncertain, as if she was making a decision. "Please, go home."

Panic struck her at his words. *They're coming.* Kate made her choice. She spat on him, "Get up you fucking coward. Did you think I'd forgive you if you *cried?* I don't give two shits about your *feelings.* You're pathetic. Seeing you like this makes me sick!"

"You don't understand, Kate…" he began, but she kicked him then, and he quickly realized he had let his shield lapse.

The pain in his side, combined with the look of disgust on her face, sent a wave of coldness through him. She was looking down on him, just like the She'Har, just like the wardens.

The bitch was looking down—*on him.*

Fury burned, and Tyrion stood again.

For a brief second he considered giving in to the impulse to kill her. That would be satisfying, but something stopped him. No, he would punish her. Let her learn the lessons he had. "You will regret that, *slave,*" he told her coldly.

Her demeanor changed, disdain replaced by fear. Tears started in her eyes, and this time they pleased him. She cast her eyes downward, letting her hair hide her features.

"Get back to the wagon," he ordered. "We have to prepare for guests."

The Silent Tempest

Chapter 12

Fifteen teens, two adults, and one wagon; there was no way they could move quickly enough to stay out of range. Tyrion could dampen his aythar as much as possible, but it would only delay the inevitable. The She'Har scouting party would find them.

He could probably close his mind completely, totally hiding his aythar, but they would still note the presence of seventeen people. Once they approached to investigate, it would only seem more suspicious when they realized he had been attempting to hide from them.

He scanned the youths once more. If any of them had begun to show signs of power, he might be able to use them, but there was still nothing. Gabriel Evans had flickering signs in his aura, but they were so weak he probably wasn't even aware of them yet.

Tyrion's saddlebag rested on the driver's seat. He reached into it and took out the quarrel he had recovered from Branlyinti's body and then handed it to Kate. "Load it and hope you don't have to use it."

She nodded, avoiding eye contact.

"There are riders approaching," he said, raising his voice for everyone to hear. "I can count eight. They will probably be mostly wardens like myself, but they may have one of the She'Har with them, the ones you call 'forest-gods'. They will seek to take you from me, by force if necessary.

He paused then, gathering his thoughts, and Gabriel Evans spoke up, "What are you going to do?"

Tyrion was surprised at the boy's temerity. "I am going to persuade them otherwise. Quite possibly that will mean I have to kill them."

Brigid piped up, "What if you can't?"

He smiled, "Then I will see you all dead before I let them take you."

Their faces blanched, many turning white.

"If that sounds cruel to you, that is because it is, but you have no idea of the sort of torments you will find at the hands of the She'Har and their servants. I consider it a mercy," he told them. Searching their faces he went on, "None of you are ready to fight, nor do I need you to, but there is a risk that you may be injured or killed during this—discussion. Therefore I need you all to listen carefully and follow my instructions exactly. Can you do that?"

Some of them nodded, while others just stared at him dumbly.

That will have to be good enough, he thought. "I will draw a ring around the wagon, to create a strong shield. It should be enough to protect you. Those who are coming want to take you alive, so I doubt they will try to penetrate it. If they do, it will be in the hope that they can spook you into running. If we become separated, I cannot protect you. If one of them lays hands on you, don't fight, but do not cooperate; feign unconsciousness, make yourself dead weight, force them to carry you. Otherwise, stay by the wagon, and if the circle is broken do not run."

He turned away then and began etching a line in the dirt, forming a circle around the wagon. He kept it as small as possible, to minimize the drain on his strength, for he would have to keep some of his power focused on it during the fight that was to come. When he finished it was fifteen feet in diameter; just enough to encircle the wagon, the mule, the children, and Kate.

The party that was approaching had sped up, sensing his presence now. They were less than a mile distant and covering ground at an almost unbelievable pace. Tyrion had thought at first that they rode horses, but he could tell now that they did not. They had taken the shape of wolves, lupine bodies and long legs eating up the ground between them far faster than would be possible for a horse and rider in such rough terrain.

The Gaelyn Grove then, thought Tyrion. That explained the ease with which they had gone around the town and searched the countryside while remaining outside of his detection range. Taking the form of wolves or even birds had enabled them to travel far faster than other wardens. *At least I know for certain what grove they all come from,* he noted. Their tactic would have been unusable if they had included wardens with other gifts.

He walked roughly thirty yards from the circle and the wagon it would guard—once he empowered it. *No shields yet, or I'm considered hostile by default.* That meant he had to leave himself unprotected as well, even though he knew what the outcome would be. The difference now was not that he hoped to surprise them, but that he knew some would escape. He was in a defensive position this time, which would make eliminating all of them virtually impossible.

That was fine, though. This was a fight he could justify—so long as he could give an accounting that absolved him of initiating the conflict. That meant he couldn't defend himself until his opponents had declared their intentions.

Eight massive wolves emerged from the underbrush and spread out before him. Seven of them sat back on their haunches, letting their long tongues hang out as they panted, while the eighth shifted, taking human form. Seconds later a human figure stood where the wolf had been.

Tyrion recognized the strange looking man who stood before him. *Charlanum.* The brown-skinned, red-eyed She'Har of the Gaelyn Grove had been present at many of his fights in the arena.

He dipped his head respectfully toward the She'Har trainer.

"Tyrion," said the She'Har. "I see you have found a rich harvest. I assume these are the ones whom we seek."

"I have already claimed them on behalf of my mistress, Lyralliantha," he answered. There was no point in wasting time getting to the point.

The She'Har raised one eyebrow, "If that is so, then we will respect the Illeniel claim…" His eyes roved over the teens, "… but I see no collars on them."

"They will be collared as soon as we return."

"Then Lyralliantha is not here with you?" asked the Gaelyn She'Har in mock surprise.

Tyrion tensed, "No."

"Do you expect me to take your word then?" continued the trainer. "A slave cannot make claim to them unless he is following the orders of his master."

"I have been so ordered."

"I see no proof of that."

Tyrion's eyes narrowed, "I could not be here without her permission. She made her wishes very plain to me before I left. I have taken these, and they will be delivered to her."

"She is not here," insisted Charlanum. "Stand aside. When we return I will speak with her and verify your claim. If you speak the truth, she will forgive you for obeying my command and I will give her my apology for transgressing against the Illeniel Grove."

"But you will already have collared them for the Gaelyn Grove…" said Tyrion, letting his words trail away.

Charlanum smiled, "Of course. I cannot allow slaves to be left unrestricted."

"I will have to decline your generous offer," responded Tyrion. "Killing me would incur a serious debt for the Gaelyn Grove." His last hope of dissuading the She'Har was to remind him that Tyrion's death would result in a heavy penalty of shuthsi, the honor currency that was traded between groves.

Tyrion was currently the most valuable slave in all the groves, but the prospect of fifteen others who might have similar potential made the risk small in comparison to the possible reward. Charlanum would not be deterred.

"I will regret killing you," said the She'Har, and his aythar flashed as he began a powerful spellweaving.

Spellweaving was fast, compared to enchanting, but it was slightly slower than the ultimately spontaneous nature of human magic. Ordinarily the difference in speed was insignificant, for human attacks couldn't penetrate a spellwoven shield, nor could human shields stop a spellwoven attack.

Fortunately, Tyrion didn't have to produce his enchantments from scratch. The tattoos on his body were complete, they needed only his will and an investment of aythar to activate the enchantments they represented. His prepared shields expanded near instantaneously, with almost a half a second to spare before the Gaelyn She'Har's attack struck.

Two of the 'wolves' sent blasts of force at him. Neither attack had any hope of penetrating his special protection, but they nevertheless sent him tumbling from the sheer force of the blows.

"Two of you secure the baratti young, the rest of you assist me in handling the warden," ordered Charlanum.

Tyrion snarled, rolling with the momentum granted by his enemies' assault, even as he focused his will and raised a shield around the wagon. Somewhere beneath his anger his mind was calculating still, and it didn't like the odds. Unlike his previous battle, he was now contending with one of 'the People', as the term 'She'Har' meant when translated into the human language.

The She'Har's attacks could potentially penetrate his defense, particularly if he grew tired and weakened. One on one that probably wouldn't be an issue, since he possessed nearly twice the raw aythar that the Gaelyn trainer did, but he still had to factor in the seven human wardens. Keeping a shield around the wagon and dealing with the human mages at the same time would almost certainly exhaust him long before he could finish the She'Har.

Tyrion moved, leaping forward to threaten one of the wolves and then sidestepping to avoid a sudden trap as another removed the earth in front of him, creating a pit. Seconds stretched out like hours as he twisted and turned, avoiding attacks and trying to keep his opponents from organizing against him. As he fought he could feel the first serious attacks on the shield he kept around the wagon beginning to put a strain on his strength.

Unlike his last battle, his enemies now had an unlimited area to move in; that fact, combined with their lupine bodies gave them a clear advantage in mobility. The unrestricted airspace also made certain tactics he had used in the past almost worthless. Desperate, he began to create the aythar laced fog he had used so often before to conceal his movements, but three of the other wardens worked to keep the air moving, destroying his fog before it could become effective.

Similarly, he was unable to create a windstorm, for the same three fought with him for control of the air currents, all while the other two sought to ensnare him, using the earth to create pits or using lines of force to try and slow him down. Charlanum was able to conserve his energy, saving it for focused attacks on Tyrion's enchanted shield, attacks that Tyrion was becoming less and less able to avoid.

Tyrion was beginning to face an unsettling realization—he was losing.

He had faced long odds before, but rarely had he felt the fight slipping away from him. Even in his fight with the Krytek, he had kept control of the battlefield until the very end. This time he was being forced to fight defensively, reacting rather than taking the initiative.

Without the She'Har's presence, he could have taken them, or if there were fewer human mages to support the She'Har, but the deck was stacked against him now. His opponents moved in tandem to restrict his movements while their own mobility made most of his attacks ineffective. They had planned for this.

Something had to give soon, and it wasn't going to end well for him.

Another heavy blow to the shield around the wagon staggered him, and he almost lost it then. If the shield collapsed while he was still supporting it, he would potentially lose consciousness. Tentacles of force shot out from three of the wardens and tangled around him. They couldn't penetrate his enchanted personal shield, but they slowed him down. He slashed at them with his arm blades, but he couldn't cut them apart as fast as they sent new ones at him.

Charlanum was lining up for his next attack as a nasty looking spellweave formed in the air before him. Tyrion had no doubt about where it would be aimed.

Fuck this.

Two wardens were working together to keep him from wresting control of the air or the soil. Those were common things that mages used against one another in the arena. He would have to do something the wolves didn't expect.

Wolves, he thought suddenly, and then he lit on an idea.

Using a small amount of aythar, he created a sudden burst of sound, pitching it high in the hope that it would disorient the Gaelyn mages. Their hearing

148

would be much more sensitive than his given their current forms. Then he released the shield around the wagon. Gathering his remaining aythar, he used some of it to expand his enchanted shield outward, clearing the air around him for several feet before releasing it as well.

The sudden emptiness around him gave him some leeway, and he leapt up and forward, focusing his strength on one arm blade, making it as long and sharp as possible.

Charlanum's attack was a focused spear of spellwoven power, meant to pierce the shield he had had around him. Tyrion's sudden shift in tactics threw his aim off, but the attack ripped through his left leg nonetheless, even as Tyrion's force-blade ripped through his own shield and cut through the She'Har's skull.

His sonic attack hadn't worked as well as he had hoped, however. It had shaken the wolves, but they had recovered quickly. Two of the wardens sent spear-like blasts out before he could restore his defense, impaling him through shoulder and abdomen. Tyrion fell, landing off balance and hitting the ground as he raised his enchanted shield once more.

Near the wagon he could see that Kate's crossbow had taken down one of the wolves that had been assigned to take them, the other was nowhere to be seen.

Bleeding and in pain, Tyrion struggled to stand on his one good leg. Five wolves circled him as he opened his mouth and laughed, "You missed my heart. You'll regret that."

One of the wolves stood, shifting into human form before speaking, "You're dying, Tyrion."

"You first," he answered, grinning. There was madness in his eyes.

"You're losing blood, growing weaker," said the Gaelyn warden. "You can't protect the children anymore either. You've lost. Drop your shield, and I will make it quick."

"I've got enough blood left in me to finish you off," said Tyrion. "That's all I need." The shield around the wagon reappeared as the words left his lips. Another mage stood within the circle, a powerful one by the feel of him.

Shit, thought Tyrion. One of the Gaelyn mages was inside. He had lost. *But I can still kill this one.*

A look of uncertainty was on the Gaelyn warden's face now, and he backed away. He turned to the wolves, "We return to Garoltrea. This fight is done." Shifting back into wolf shape, he and the other wolves retreated.

Confused, Tyrion watched them go, but he didn't waste the opportunity. Turning his attention inward, he began sealing blood vessels, stopping the bleeding that was rapidly killing him. *Punctured lung, clean hole through the liver, and the leg...* Any of the three would have been fatal on their own, but only without prompt attention. He closed the small arteries and veins that had been damaged and sealed the skin on the outside. There was more to be done, but it wasn't urgent, nor did he have the energy for it just then.

Tyrion slid slowly to the ground. He was bone tired—and thirsty. He still didn't understand their retreat, and his mind was too fuzzy to focus on the other mage, the one that still stood within the shield that protected the wagon and the others.

"I'll kill him later," he muttered to himself as his vision narrowed to a dark tunnel. His eyes closed, and he let oblivion take him.

The Silent Tempest

Chapter 13

"We should kill him now while we have the chance."

The voice was that of a girl, though he couldn't be sure which one.

A male voice responded, "He's dying anyway. Let's just go home."

"The wardens will come after us. Some of them are still alive," said another boy.

"He isn't dying." That was Kate. "And no one is going to 'finish' him, not while I'm here."

"We'll load him onto the wagon and keep going," said another. Tyrion recognized that one, it was Gabriel Evans. His voice held a certain confidence and a trace of authority, something it hadn't had before.

"Who died and made you king?" asked one of the girls.

"You'll do as I say," answered Gabriel. Tyrion felt a surge of aythar, and a brief flash of light made the inside of his eyelids turn orange.

"You don't even know how to use that yet," said the girl, still somewhat defiant, although her tone was quieter now. Tyrion was guessing that voice belonged to Brigid.

"Gabriel is right," said Kate. "Help me get him to the wagon."

He felt her hands sliding under his shoulders and other hands at his ankles. The pain that went through him as they began to lift was unbearable. "Stop!" he groaned, opening his eyes.

"He's awake," warned one of the girls watching from the side.

Looking up, he found himself staring into Kate's face. Her hair had come loose from the bun she had tied it in and was now a red tangle, falling around him. Her cheeks were red, and her eyes looked puffy. *She's been crying again,* he thought.

He addressed Gabriel, who stood near his feet, "There's a better way. Use your mind and try to imagine a flat plane, strong and hard, underneath me. Once you've got a good hold on the image, push your aythar into it, make it real, then you can use that to lift me and put me in the wagon bed."

"There's blood all over you," Kate informed him. Her voice sounded thick.

He met her eyes, but then let his gaze drift, noting the way her neckline gaped as she leaned over him. *Damn, she's grown since I left.* "Don't worry," he told her. "It's all mine." Looking back at Gabriel he asked, "Can you do it?"

The youth nodded, closing his eyes.

Several minutes and a few painful jolts later and Tyrion was lying in the back of the wagon. Kate sat beside him and Gabriel had climbed into the driver's seat.

"What happened?" asked Tyrion.

"When they came in..." she began before pausing and restarting. "There were two of them. I shot one, but I couldn't stop the other one, but then, Gabriel did something."

"His power awakened," said Tyrion.

Kate nodded, "Something happened, and then the other wolf fell over, its body was almost in two pieces."

Killed a warden, thought Tyrion. *Even I couldn't have managed that right after my power awoke.*

The sound of retching caught his attention. Gabriel was leaning away from the driver's seat, vomiting onto the ground.

"Get out of the driver's seat, fool," said Tyrion. "Let someone else drive." He turned his head toward Kate, "Tell Tad to drive. I'm sure his father must have taught him."

She gave the orders, and the teens moved to obey her, then she looked back at Tyrion, "What's wrong with Gabriel?"

"Nothing," he answered. "He's just got vertigo. The magesight does that when you first get it. His brain is struggling to deal with his new sense of aythar. Have him sit back here with us. Tad can drive, and the others can walk."

"I'm not going," said Piper Jenkins. "I'm going home."

Everyone froze for a moment. The other teens were considering her words. Tyrion felt Kate leaning back in the wagon, bracing against something, and pulling. He ignored that, focusing on his next threat.

"I'd regret that, girl," he told her. "I'll be very displeased if I have to sit up and waste my time and energy on…"

"Nobody leaves," said Kate, interrupting him as she stood, crossbow in hand. It was cocked and loaded.

"You wouldn't do it," said Anthony Long, challenging her.

Kate leveled the weapon at him, lifting it to her shoulder and sighting along it. "Run and we will find out."

"You can't be siding with him!" protested the boy. "He's a lunatic. He'll kill us all."

"No," she said calmly, "he's right, and what's more he just saved your ass. The wardens will be back, and there are others already on the way. If you go home you'll just be putting your families in danger. Lunatic or not, we're going with him."

"What's going to happen to us when we get there?" asked Piper uncertainly.

"I don't know," said Kate, "but if he thinks it's better than what will happen if the wardens catch you, then I believe him."

You'll probably wish you hadn't said that later, thought Tyrion.

The wagon began to roll, and the teens followed, unwilling to chance Kate's threat. After a mile or two, Tyrion figured the chance of one of them running had significantly diminished.

"Go home, Kate. You don't need to do this," he told her.

She patted the crossbow, "I think you're wrong."

"Someone else can hold that," he suggested, looking at Gabriel who seemed to have mostly recovered from his nausea.

The boy nodded, "I can hold the bow."

Kate gave him a doubtful glance, "Have you ever used one of these before?"

He shook his head, "No, but it doesn't look too complicated."

"I'll keep it," she said, addressing Tyrion again. "Besides, someone has to take care of you."

Tyrion closed his eyes again. He had failed, and he knew it. Now that he was injured he couldn't force her to go home. "Get me some more water then," he told her. "I've never felt so dry in my life."

He had learned from past experience that thirst was one of the most notable side effects of blood loss.

***

Haley stood in the arena, naked before a crowd of... well not thousands, but surely hundreds at least. She wasn't cold, for she had been practicing at Tyrion's technique for staying warm, but she shivered nonetheless. She was vulnerable, bare before spectators, and standing across from the boy who would kill her.

He had the look of a killer too, coarse faced and mean. The youth was probably close to her age, but being male he was larger. His nose was crooked and misshapen as though it had been broken in the past, which, according to what Tyrion had told her about the people of Sabortrea, was not unusual.

He grinned at her, exposing a mouth that was already missing several teeth. It was not a friendly expression.

A voice was speaking to the spectators, but she couldn't understand any of it. Her father had mentioned that listening for the name of her opponent's grove would provide valuable information, but she couldn't sort out the words well enough to pick out what grove they had said. Besides, she didn't plan on winning.

"I'm not going to live like this," she repeated quietly to herself. Today would be her first, and last fight.

Several blue lights stood atop pillars spaced around the edge of the arena. A chime sounded, and they shifted from blue to red. The match had begun.

In spite of herself, Haley created a shield, nervously pouring her strength into it. *I won't fight back,* she told herself, *but I can't help defending myself.* She would wait, letting him batter her until she lost control, and he killed her.

A light touch against the shield startled her, almost wringing a cry of alarm from her throat. Haley was nervous, her nerves wound so tight she felt as though she might explode. *That was just a test.*

The boy vanished, reappearing off to her right almost instantaneously.

So he's Mordan. Like most of the people here.

Another attack came, this one slightly stronger, but still ineffectual. She ignored it, closing her eyes, but her magesight still showed her the battlefield. She wanted to block that out too, but it would probably cause her to have to release the shield. Haley wasn't prepared to do that.

More attacks came, and her opponent became bolder, attacking more frequently and moving less. Gradually he was realizing that she had no intention of fighting. Still, nothing he did came remotely close to cracking her defense. Seconds wore on into minutes, and nothing changed.

Chapter 13

Cracking her eyes open, Haley could see the boy was breathing hard, as though he had been running. His aythar was flickering slightly, and it seemed dimmer.

He's getting tired, she thought, *but he hasn't done anything yet.*

The attacks had stopped, but she felt something new happening. The ground beneath her was shifting, soil and rocks sliding apart. Haley was sinking. Puzzled, she watched the earth move until she was standing six feet below ground level, then the excess moved to cover her.

She was being buried alive.

He couldn't break my shield, so now he's going to suffocate me, she realized. *That's probably better than the other ways I could die.*

She tried to believe that, but as the thin layer of air within her shield grew stale, her heart began to pound. It was dark, and her lungs were heaving. Claustrophobia set in, and she began to panic.

No, no, no, no!

Flailing with her aythar, she tore at the earth, pushing and ripping until the soil around her churned and moved like water. The teen who had buried her fought to keep her down, using his aythar and the weight of the soil already above her to press her down, but his strength was no match for hers. Haley's head emerged from the ground, and she gasped as fresh air filtered in through her shield.

He kept struggling, trying to force her down, but the boy had half sunk into the churning earth himself while they battled. His aythar flickered more now, and it was clear that he was tiring fast. It was almost sad how easily Haley had worn him down.

She tried relaxing, letting him win, but as soon as the darkness closed around her head, she panicked again. Fighting once more, she forced herself up, and then she wrapped her enemy within bands of her own aythar, squeezing tightly against his shield.

Haley didn't want to bury him, she didn't want to kill him. She just wanted it to stop.

Desperate, he thrashed about, throwing his strength into the shield around him, trying to force her back, but she wouldn't let go.

"Just stop!" she yelled, angry and frightened, but he refused to listen.

His aythar was squirming beneath hers, like a worm trying to escape a bird's vice-like beak. He wouldn't quit, and her fear was fading, being replace by irritation and annoyance. She just wanted him to quit, to stop fighting.

Mad, she squeezed harder, screaming at him, "Leave me alone!" Suddenly his shield collapsed with a strange popping sensation, followed by a wet crunch as his chest was enveloped by the crushing force of Haley's mind. With her magesight she could feel his ribs crack.

Horrified she stopped, releasing him, but it was too late. A single groaning shriek had issued from him, and he was unconscious now. Blood ran from his nose, but the broken ribs and bruised organs in his chest were what made Haley sick.

"I'm so sorry," she said, though there was no one to listen. "I didn't mean to do that!"

Chapter 13

She looked up, staring into the crowds gathered at the edge of the arena, overwhelmed with guilt. Everything she had ever learned growing up indicated that she had just made a terrible mistake. Hurting people was wrong. She had been sent into the arena to fight to the death, but her mind just couldn't accept it.

"I didn't mean to kill him!" she shouted.

The spectators remained silent, watching her. Several had strange smirks on their faces, and one even laughed. Dalleth stepped into the arena, a look of mild annoyance on his face. Walking closer, he loomed over her, "What are you doing?"

"I'm sorry," she answered, bowing her head as tears ran down her cheeks and nose. "I didn't mean to do it."

"He's still alive," the Mordan She'Har told her.

Her magesight had told her that much, but she knew the boy was dying. His heart had been bruised, his lungs were barely working, and he was bleeding internally. "He's dying!" she insisted, hoping the She'Har would help him.

"Yes," said Dalleth, "but it could take hours. I would rather not wait around here that long."

Haley gaped at him, "But, I—I—I won. It's over. He can't fight. Can't you help him?"

"The match is over when one of you is dead," said the trainer.

The boy groaned, his eyes fluttering open as he coughed, trying to clear his lungs.

"Please!" cried Haley. "You've got to help him!"

"He seems to be in considerable pain," said Dalleth with a detached look. "As sensitive as you seem to be,

I would think you would want to end this quickly." The trainer turned his back and left the arena.

Haley watched the She'Har go, but her mind was on the boy dying a few feet away. He tried to sit up, but the movement drove one of his cracked ribs in deeper, damaging his lung even further. A gurgling cry escaped his lips.

The spectators were beginning to disperse, bored with the lack of activity, but the shield around the arena remained up. Haley would remain until her opponent was dead.

Haley sensed a movement, a flash of aythar. One of the teen's ribs, the one threatening his lung, moved back, fusing with another piece of bone and giving his heart and lungs some much needed space. He hissed, air coming painfully from between clenched teeth as he set the rib back in place.

Her eyes widened as she watched, realizing he was healing himself. If his strength didn't give out, he might manage enough to keep himself from dying. She could see an artery sealing itself now, stopping the majority of the bleeding within his chest. The boy's eyes glared daggers at her as he worked, as though he blamed her for each painful moment.

"I'm going to kill you," he growled.

"Why?" she said. Tears were trickling from her eyes once more. "Why do you want to kill me? I never did anything to you."

The youth sneered, "Because you're stupid. You don't deserve to live." Most of his ribs were whole now, but his aythar was so weak it flickered in her magesight. "I'm going to kill you, and then they'll give me my name."

Chapter 13

Haley knew it was futile. She couldn't kill him, but she couldn't let him heal himself either. It would be easier if he just finished dying. Without thinking she lashed out, using her aythar to stop him from closing the last leaking blood vessel. It was a medium sized vein that had been leaking blood slowly into his chest.

He fought her, opposing her will with his own, and the two of them struggled silently for several seconds, he to hold the flesh of the vessel together, and she to keep it open—to let the blood flow. His strength failed almost immediately, and in the absence of his resistance she ripped the vein further, causing it to bleed faster. It had been unintentional, but her stomach twisted as she felt the damage she had done.

Hate-filled eyes stared accusingly at her. As soon as she released him he began to try to close the vein once more.

"Just die!" she shouted. With desperate strength she drove her power into his chest and *pulled.* Skin, ribs, and sternum ruptured, sending a gout of flesh and blood upward as she wrenched his chest open. He couldn't even scream.

Haley watched him die, his aythar fading and his eyes glazing over. Something warm dripped from her nose, leaving a sticky trail across her lips. Some of his blood had gotten on her.

Her heart was pounding, and her knees felt weak, but she still felt a sense of relief. He was dead, and she was alive. The shield around the arena faded, and she knew it was over. Raising a hand she tried to wipe the blood away from her lips, but the more she wiped the more she tasted the sharp tang of iron.

A hand fell on her shoulder. Dalleth stood beside her.

"A grisly victory, but a victory still. You will receive a name tomorrow," said the She'Har trainer.

Haley wanted to argue. She already had a name, but Tyrion had warned her. *"Just accept it,"* he had said.

Gwaeri was close by as well. Dalleth turned to him and gave one more instruction, "Take her back to her cell. Have her whipped until she loses consciousness."

"What?!" exclaimed Haley. "I did what you wanted!"

Dalleth gave her a cold glance, "You will learn not to *play* in the arena. Pain is a valuable teaching tool."

Chapter 14

The wagon rolled on down the trail, following it ever lower until it reached the river that ran through the rugged foothills where Colne was situated. The river continued on, eventually passing beyond the rugged land and into the ever growing forest before finally crossing into the Illeniel Grove.

The wagon couldn't take such a direct course, though. It would have to cross the river and follow the level ground on the other side. The trail would lead up and away from the river again before paralleling it on its journey to the deep woods.

The ford where the trail met the river was shallow, but the jumbled rocks that lay under the water made a difficult crossing for wagons. Kate and Gabriel got off there and helped the other teens push and pull, aiding the horses as they struggled to make the crossing. One of the wheels slipped into a deep hole that had been hidden among the rocks, but with numerous hands lifting they got it free and made it across.

Tyrion slept through the entire process, his fatigue too great for even the jolting movements to rouse him.

Hours passed, and they reached the edge of the forest without further problems. The land flattened there, still rocky, it held numerous oaks and elms, along with a scattering of ash trees. A mile farther and the ground became softer and more fertile, and there the god trees began, visible even from their current position, the massive forms loomed over the smaller oaks.

Gabriel put a hand on Kate's shoulder, "There's someone out there."

She looked at him worriedly, "Where?"

"Straight ahead," said the boy. "There are a bunch of them, too far to see from here. I think they're like him." Gabriel scrunched his face as he spoke, as if trying to bring something into focus without knowing quite how to do so. Squinting obviously wasn't working for him. "It's hard to tell exactly how many, and I'm not sure how far away either. I'm not used to this."

"They could be friendly," observed Kate. "This is the direction he wanted us to go." The words brought her no comfort, though. Daniel's comments in the past had made it clear that the term 'friendly' was a poor adjective to apply to any of the She'Har.

"I want to go home," suggested Ashley Morris. She had been listening from her position behind the wagon. "Who knows what will happen if we go in there?"

Gabriel opened his mouth, unsure what to say.

Kate knew better than to hesitate, "We will wait. Daniel will know what to do when he wakes."

"Stop calling me that," said Tyrion quietly. The sudden stillness of the wagon had woken him when the movement and jostling could not.

"You're awake," she responded with obvious relief.

"There are some people ahead of us," said Gabriel leaning close to Tyrion's head anxiously. "We don't know how many exactly or whether…"

"There are twelve," said Tyrion impatiently. "Eight women, four men, and one She'Har trainer from the Centyr Grove." He started to sit up, but a wave of pain and nausea made him think better of the idea.

"I think they're coming toward us now," added Gabriel.

"Yeah," agreed Tyrion. "One of their scouts got closer, and now they know we're here." He looked over at Kate, "And no, to answer your question, they are *not* friendly."

Jack Baker, another of the boys who was paying close attention to the conversation, began to groan in fear.

"Somebody shut that kid up before I kill him," growled Tyrion.

Jack began to groan even louder, but before Kate could say a word one of the girls, Sarah Wilson, struck him hard, slapping the boy with her open palm. "Shut up, Jack!"

Jack didn't take well to being slapped. He started to react by punching Sarah, but a second boy, Ryan Carter, drove his fist into Jack's stomach. "Dammitt, Jack," said Ryan in a hoarse whisper. "Be quiet. This ain't the time to be fighting or crying."

Jack was on his knees now, gasping for air, but doing so as quietly as possible.

"So what are we going to do?" asked Kate, drawing everyone's attention back to Tyrion before they could do further violence to one another.

"Not much," said Tyrion. "There are three possibilities. One, you run, they capture you, and within an hour you'll be collared, naked, and whipped into submission. The second option is waiting here, fighting, being captured, and then within an hour you'll be collared, stripped, and then whipped into submission..."

"What about the third option?" asked Tad anxiously.

"I'm too injured to fight," Tyrion informed him, "but I can try something else."

"What's your plan?" prompted Tad.

"There's a storm coming," said Tyrion. The wind had picked up a little over the past minute, becoming a brisk breeze.

"What's the plan?" said Gabriel, adding his voice to Tad's.

Tyrion said a word, but Tad couldn't understand him. The horses shifted, their heads lowering and their eyes drawing closed as they fell suddenly asleep. Tyrion looked at Tad, "Get the rope out that your father put in the wagon. Cut it into lengths and have everyone tie themselves to the wagon. If anyone else can fit in the bed, they should climb in as well. The extra weight might help."

"Help what?" said Kate.

"Help keep the wagon from blowing away," responded Tyrion. His eyes were distant now, staring up toward the sky.

Tad was staring at Tyrion uncertainly. Kate punched his arm.

"Move!" she barked at him. "Get the rope! We need to tie ourselves down quickly." The wind was beginning to whistle as it moved through the trees around them now, making a high pitched keening sound.

Chapter 14

"I don't understand," announced Gabriel. "He isn't doing anything. Where is the wind coming from?"

Tyrion didn't answer, his eyes were glassy, unfocused.

Kate looked at Gabriel, curious. "Are you saying he isn't controlling the wind?"

Gabriel nodded.

When the wind had first come up, she had felt hope, but now fear touched her heart. She looked around her, watching as the teens awkwardly tied themselves to the wagon. *Ropes might not be enough,* she thought. In the distance there was a roaring sound.

Kate looked back at Gabriel, "Can you make another of those shield things? Like you did during the fight earlier?"

"M—maybe," answered the boy.

"Then do it," she told him. Her hair was standing out from the side of her head, parallel to the ground. The air was rushing about them, plucking at their clothes. A limb broke away from a tree and flew past.

Gabriel wasn't sure if it was necessary or not, but taking a heavy wooden spoon from the wagon he began tracing a circle in the ground around the group. It took him half a minute to finish it, and by then the gale was threatening to lift him from the ground. Repeating what he had done before, he poured his strength into it, creating a rough hemisphere above them. The wind cut off abruptly, but he could feel it battering the invisible dome.

Kate was alarmed to see Tyrion's body rising from the wagon, floating as if he weighed nothing. His features were limp, and his limbs seemed loose. She grabbed hold and pushed him down, pinning him with her own body. There was no wind inside Gabriel's shield, but Tyrion felt light, as though he had been hollowed out and stuffed with feathers.

"Wake up, Daniel!" she shouted at him, but there was no sign that he heard her.

The roar of the wind was deafening now, a solid wall of sound that devoured all hearing. The trees around them were bending and starting to break. Heavy limbs flew through the air, striking their protective dome and bouncing away. Entire trees began to come free from the ground, ripped skyward, roots and all.

A deep shuddering vibration passed through Kate's stomach as a massive elm slammed into the shield. Gabriel fell to one knee, but he retained consciousness and somehow his shield held. The tree began to slide away, but then Brigid Tolburn stood.

The girl's eyes were on the tree, and it stopped moving, as though she held it pinned there. Her arms were outstretched, fingers grasping at the space around her, as though she was gripping something invisible. Another tree struck the shield and then stopped, its branches tangling with the first elm that was still there.

Kate could see the others crying, covering their heads, shouting, or attempting to climb underneath the wagon itself. She could hear none of it, of course, for the roaring outside the shield was so great that no other sound could overcome it.

Gabriel was kneeling, hands held against his ears while blood dripped from his nose. More trees struck the shield, but each one seemed to catch, twining its branches with the other trees already there. A great wooden palisade of fallen and tangled oaks and elms was forming around them.

Brigid stood in the center, mouth open, and Kate knew that if the roaring stopped she would hear the girl screaming. The dark headed girl's blue eyes were wide, and her hair flew around her, carried by a wind that seemed to touch only her.

Is she the one binding the trees together like that? wondered Kate. She had no way of knowing, since she couldn't sense aythar, but it seemed unlikely that Gabriel was doing it. He seemed to have his hands full just maintaining the shield, and the others were clearly in a state of panic.

She looked at Daniel. His body was no longer just light, it felt *wrong,* as if he were becoming insubstantial. The light was fading as trees covered the dome above them, but it appeared as if his arms were fading.

"Daniel!" she shouted, hoping she could wake him, but she couldn't even hear her own voice. Leaning close, she tried yelling again, this time directly into his ear. Again there was no response. He continued staring blankly into space.

It might have been an illusion in the darkness that was now enveloping them, but she could no longer see his legs.

Something is wrong, she thought. *This can't be what he intended to happen.*

Her arm felt as though it was about to pass through him. The only thing still solid about him now was his face. Not knowing what else to do, she took his left ear lobe into her mouth and bit down.

He never flinched.

She bit him again, harder this time, until the taste of blood found her tongue. "Wake up, damn you!" she shouted. "Wake up, or I'll bite this ear off to make it match the other one!" Years before he had lost most of his outer right ear when a warden had cut it off.

His eyes blinked, and his chest seemed to grow more substantial.

Unwilling to bite him again she kissed his ear instead, something she had once dreamed of doing. *Once,* she thought, *before you became a monster.*

He shivered and cold silver eyes turned to regard her, alien eyes. They were grey now, as if they were made of swirling mist, with no whites, or even pupils or irises.

A feeling of revulsion swept over her. She knew then, whatever she was touching, whatever she had kissed—it wasn't human. It stared at her with no sense of feeling or humanity. Kate drew back, and the eyes moved away. Tyrion began to fade again.

"Damn you!" she cursed. Grabbing his head she nipped his ear once more, before kissing it again. The eyes turned toward her, and steeling her stomach against the disgust she felt she drew his lips toward her own. They were cold and unresponsive.

It was like kissing the dead.

But the cold flesh around his mouth was growing warmer.

She clung to him and kissed him harder, fighting herself even as she did. Soon his arms were back, and he turned, pushing her onto her side, his tongue sliding between her lips. The noise outside the tangled barrier of trees faded, and the wind slowed.

One of his hands was searching now, making its way under her blouse, tracing cold lines along her stomach. Kate pushed down, trying to keep his hand away, but he growled and forced it up, grasping rudely at her flesh, clutching at her breast.

"Daniel, no! Let me go," she protested, trying to push him away.

Tyrion's mouth opened, but nothing like human words emerged. It was a bizarre sound, like the rustling of trees in the wind. Swirling silver eyes looked through Kate, but still he held her down. He forced her onto her back before blinking, his eyes shifting even as she watched.

Blinking again, the silver mist vanished, replaced by blue human eyes.

No, not human eyes, Kate realized, *more like the eyes of a beast.*

Tyrion was still groping with his hand, heedless of her protests.

"Stop, Daniel!" she shouted. "Not now, not like this!"

He froze then, looking deeply into her eyes. He seemed confused. "Who are you?" he asked suddenly, using the first human words to enter his mind.

She took the opportunity presented by his hesitation to disentangle herself. Gazing back at him, she studied his features. They seemed to present genuine puzzlement, but there were thoughts passing behind his eyes now. Whatever his transformation had been, it had apparently scrambled his mind just as it had altered his body.

He appeared to be fully physical, but there was something different.

His ear!

The lower half of his right ear was no longer missing. It perfectly matched the left one, with no visible sign of the wound that had once removed most of it. His eyes were locked onto hers now.

"Kate?" he said, questioning his own recognition even as he remembered her.

She moved farther away. *Is that even him—or is it something else, just pretending?*

Brigid still stood beside the wagon, her body locked into some sort of rictus. Her mouth was wide, as though she were screaming, but no sound came out. Tyrion became aware of her odd condition and climbed out of the wagon, walking over to stand next to her.

His thoughts felt strange, but they were clearer. The girl had come into her power, but the stress and newness of the situation had made her exert herself in a way she was not prepared for. She was killing herself, straining against something that was no longer there. Tendrils of aythar extended in every direction, winding and tangling themselves through the fallen trees above them. Brigid's lips were tinged blue.

He slapped her with enough force to send her tumbling from her feet.

Brigid stared up at him in shock, and then her chest heaved, drawing air in a desperate choking gasp. She had forgotten to breath.

The structure above their heads shifted. Without the young woman's power to hold it together, the trees were no longer stable. A massive oak slid sideways and then broke free, dropping rapidly toward the wagon. Other trees moved in its wake, falling in an avalanche toward the people beneath them.

Tyrion lifted his hand, swiping at the air as if brushing away a fly, his aythar followed suit, knocking the heavy trunks and limbs away so that they fell outward, rather than inward. He looked down at Gabriel Evans, who was unconscious at his feet. The feedback when his shield had given way was the most likely cause for his senseless condition.

"Put them in the wagon," Tyrion ordered, directing his words to the other teens who huddled beside and under the sides of the heavy cart.

Two of the boys, Jack and David, lifted Gabriel and carried him. Brigid didn't need to be carried, but Emma Philips helped her find her way since she still seemed dazed.

Through all of this, Kate watched Tyrion. *What happened to his injuries?*

***

Gwaeri led the young girl back toward the wooden cell that housed her. He was in a quandary. He had been ordered to whip her. Ordinarily that would have been a pleasant task, but his neck still burned in the place where Tyrion had placed his tattoo.

Will a simple whipping trigger it? he wondered.

He had never felt so impotent as he did then. Tyrion's abuse, and the mark he had left on Gwaeri, had wounded his pride, and pride was one of the few things the old warden prized. He had fought, brawled, and beaten his way to the top of Sabortrea's slave hierarchy over a period of decades. Now he was supposed to bow to the whims of one tender girl?

He stopped, motioning her to walk ahead of him, so that he could study her with his eyes as well as his magesight. The first thing that stood out was her skin, smooth and unbroken. She looked as though she had never been in a fight. A few freckles, a tiny scar or two, but nothing else.

Her hips were round too, swelling with the promise of her youth. Gwaeri's heart sped up a bit as he watched her walk, a reaction that surprised him. He was no celibate, but at his age he was not as commonly bothered by such urges as he had once been. The collar at his throat prevented him from engaging in any action that might lead to pregnancy, but there were many other ways to find pleasure.

He refocused his thoughts, pulling them back from that path. He was very sure that Tyrion's warning would include sexual coercion as well as physical abuse. That thought made him even angrier.

They stopped when they reached her hut, and Haley looked up at him, fear in her eyes. She had already been whipped a few times, but only briefly. She wasn't sure what the old warden would do now.

Gwaeri frowned and then made his choice. He would rather die than live like one of the nameless. His thoughts moved, and a glowing red whip appeared, stretching like a living thing between his hands.

"Remember what my father told you!" said Haley in a voice that was even higher pitched than normal. Her heart was leaping, causing her nerves to vibrate with its staccato beat.

"Fuck him," swore the warden. "I'd rather die. We'll see how far I can go before his damned mark kills me."

Chapter 14

Panic drove Haley to flight, but before she had gone two paces the red whip swept out, coiling around her left leg and sending a sensation like fire racing along her nerves, from her thigh to her spine. She collapsed with a shriek that ended in a croak as the ground knocked the wind from her lungs.

The pain vanished, and her vision cleared. Gwaeri stood above her now, looking down thoughtfully. "Looks like one stroke isn't enough to trigger this thing," he said, fingering the sore place at his throat before smiling. "Let's try again." The red whip leapt out, curling around her throat and trailing down her spine.

Haley knew she was screaming, but the agony was so great she couldn't hear herself. She writhed for what seemed an eternity, until at last the whip withdrew again, leaving her shaking on the hard packed earth. Gwaeri was licking his lips now, one hand on his groin, massaging himself through his trousers.

Not again, thought Haley, remembering what had happened before Tyrion had arrived. She felt sick thinking about it, and then relieved when she thought of the whip. That chain of thoughts led to an even greater sense of disgust and self-loathing.

The warden opened the door to her wooden prison. "You're learning," he said, reading the expressions that were passing across her face. "There's nothing as bad as the pain." The whip undulated in his hands, moving like a snake. "You should be grateful I'm offering you a lesser punishment. It's not something I do much these days."

She darted inside, hating herself for giving in to her fear so quickly, but the sight of the whip robbed her of all reason or thought of resistance. Gwaeri followed her in, closing the door behind himself before opening the front of his trousers. "Get on your knees, girl."

She knelt as he drew closer, displaying himself proudly. The dark musky smell made her want to gag before he had even touched her. For a second forgot the whip, and anger took the place of her fear. She had teeth, and she would make him pay—in blood.

Gwaeri saw the defiance in her eyes even as she opened her mouth, and he responded to her pretense at submission with a heavy fist.

Haley found herself on the floor, blinking away tears and unable to feel her cheek. There was pain, but the blow had left her stunned. Before she could recover her wits, he had her by the arm, dragging her up and twisting it behind her painfully before shoving her face down toward the raised pallet that served as her sleeping place.

"Obviously you need to be broken before you can be properly trained, girl," said the old man gleefully. "Now, straighten your legs and hold still, or I'll break this arm."

She did as she was told, closing her eyes as she felt his hands groping at her. Focusing on her magesight, she considered raising a shield. He hadn't used the whip and her mental balance was returning. She searched along his neck, trying to resolve the symbols beneath his collar, the strange pattern that Tyrion had tattooed onto the vile old man's skin.

In her mind she remembered the strange symbol that Tyrion had scratched into the dirt floor, a triangle enclosing an odd wavy line. *"This is the final line of the enchantment I put on him. The tattoo is designed to be activated only when complete. You have to visualize this symbol before pushing a small part of your energy into the tattoo itself. The enchantment will take care of the rest after that."* He had drawn the rest of it out then, showing her where the imagined symbol should connect to the ones he had inked on Gwaeri.

He was pressing against her now, pushing.

No! Haley's mind latched onto the tattoo, and in a moment of vivid clarity she completed the pattern, firing it with her aythar. A tiny blade of force surged outward from it, severing the collar around her tormentor's neck.

Gwaeri stepped back, his eyes bulging, and then quickly folded into himself. He twitched on the ground as the blood within his body bubbled and boiled. He lost consciousness almost instantly, and death followed after no more than a minute.

Two men dead in the space of a few hours, she thought. *And I don't feel sorry for either one.*

That wasn't entirely true. Killing the one in the arena had been awful, although she knew he was merely a younger, cruder version of the old man who lay at her feet now. She hadn't wanted to kill him, but now she thought perhaps she had done him a favor.

"If this is the sort of man you would have become, you're better off dead," she told herself, completing the thought.

The pain, terror, and adrenaline began to fade, replaced by a coldness, an empty relief. She was alive. In spite of her resolve to die rather than kill, she couldn't bring herself to regret what she had done. She had failed, but she was certain that when Dalleth discovered her murder, he would give her the death she wanted.

"I will not live like this," she said to the empty room, "but neither will I let them abuse me."

Chapter 15

The forest that had been around them was gone. Some of it remained, of course, broken and toppled trunks along with scattered limbs and heavy roots. All of it was horizontal, though, and much of it looked to be missing completely, carried away by the monstrous winds.

Everything had been flattened for nearly a mile in every direction. The gigantic god trees still stood in the distance, but a few of those at the edge were tilted at odd angles. Kate and the others stared out in awe at the destruction. One of the boys, David Brown, looked back at Tyrion, "How?"

"It was a freak storm," said Tyrion. "We got lucky."

The sky was clear, and sunshine beat down on them now that there was no tree cover, making them warm despite the chill winter breeze. Kate said nothing, although she knew very well that Tyrion was lying.

Ashley Morris spoke then, "Weren't you injured?"

"It was worse than it looked," responded Tyrion. "It was mostly fatigue. The nap has me feeling like a new man."

"But there was blood and…" she began.

He gave her a menacing look, "I was tired. Remember that when they question you."

Tyrion used his magic to clear the ground ahead of the wagon, moving tree trunks and other heavy debris so the horses could pick their way through. Another hour and they had reached the edge of the god-trees, the border of the Illeniel Grove. A large party waited to greet them there.

Party might have been a poor description, however, several hundred of the strangest looking She'Har that Tyrion had ever seen were standing, crawling, and climbing just within the edge of the tree line. *Krytek,* he noted.

The krytek were the warriors of the She'Har, soldiers produced by the father-trees. They were born with all the knowledge the She'Har possessed about fighting, giving them battle-wisdom far beyond their short lives. The krytek were sterile, unable to grow into trees, and they lived only a few months. In his fifteen years among the She'Har, Tyrion had seen them only rarely, most notably when he had been forced to fight one in the arena.

Someone's worried.

"Halt," said one of them, riding out to meet the small group of humans before they had approached within fifty yards of the trees. On closer inspection he saw that it wasn't riding, this krytek had a quadrupedal body connected to a humanoid torso and arms above it. It spoke in Erollith, the language of the She'Har. "You will come no closer until the baratti have been secured."

"Where is Lyralliantha?" asked Tyrion.

"Listrius is in command here," said the krytek. "He will collar them."

"Lyralliantha is my owner," stated Tyrion. "No one will approach us until I have spoken with her." He didn't bother with threats, regular She'Har were largely unemotional, but the krytek took that trait to an entirely new level. Most of them were inhuman in their 'design', and their short lifespans insured they had little fear of dying.

"My orders are to keep the grove safe and to secure the baratti whom you have with you. Listrius approaches now to collar them," said the krytek.

Tyrion could see a silver haired man approaching and recognized Listrius, one of the She'Har lore-wardens. The Illeniel She'Har was still thirty yards distant, so Tyrion raised his voice to make certain both he and the krytek could hear his answer, "The baratti I have brought with me are valuable. Any one of the five groves would be pleased to have them, and I will gladly surrender them to you, but *not* until I have spoken with Lyralliantha."

"You will submit to my authority," insisted the soldier.

Tyrion sighed, one misstep and everything would be over, but he refused to give up. If a conflict started now, he and his children would wind up dead—or worse, but he would take that possibility over the alternative. "I will gladly submit, once Lyralliantha is here. You will endanger the well-being of the grove if you are impatient."

He hoped that couching the refusal in neutral language while calling upon the soldier's greater duty would accomplish what an outright threat could not.

The soldier looked back, and Listrius nodded at him.

"Very well, your mistress will be brought here. Until she arrives you are to remain still," ordered the She'Har warrior.

Tyrion bowed his head in acquiescence, but otherwise remained motionless. "As you command."

Lyralliantha appeared in somewhat less than half an hour, walking across the ripped and torn ground with grace and serenity. The long dress she wore hid her legs, but it never seemed to snag on the many limbs and roots that stood up from the ground. It made her movement look as though she were gliding, weightless, across the damaged earth.

That was quick, thought Tyrion.

The silver haired woman looked at him with a placid face that might have been cut from stone. Her gaze drifted across the children in and around the wagon, pausing only a moment longer when it reached Catherine Tolburn. She had seen that face often enough, in the visions that Tyrion had shared with her.

"You have been busy, my pet," she said quietly. "It was unwise of you to resist the authority of Listrius, however."

"I apologize mistress," responded Tyrion, filling his voice with the closest approximation of honest contrition that he could manage. "I only sought to please you."

"The krytek were called to defend the Grove," she added. "It seemed that we were under attack." Her eyes held a silent warning.

"A freak storm, mistress," lied Tyrion. "I had nothing to do with it, although the timing was fortunate. The Centyr were waiting at the border to claim your prizes."

"I am glad you and your offspring weren't damaged," responded Lyralliantha. "Now you must submit and allow them to be collared, or your efforts will have been for naught."

Tyrion leaned closer, pitching his voice so low it was almost inaudible, "Only you may collar them."

She gave him a startled glance, but the look in his eyes warned her. Reacting with her usual mental agility, she responded without hesitation, "Stand aside that I may inspect what you have brought me." She moved to examine the first of his children, and without waiting immediately began the spellweave that would produce a collar.

Without looking back he raised his voice, speaking now in Barion, the human tongue, "When she comes to you, accept the necklace that she offers you. Keep your thoughts submissive, and if you can feel the magic, do not resist it."

The spellweaving that produced a slave collar was peculiar in that it required the initial acceptance of whomever it was placed upon. In individual cases if the human tried to resist, it was futile, the red whips would rapidly assure submission, but today, with a small army staring at them, any defiance could result in a disaster.

Listrius called out from where he stood, some thirty yards distant, "Lyralliantha, what are you doing?"

"Claiming what is mine," she replied without stopping. She had completed three collars already and was now moving to place a fourth around Abigail Moore's neck.

"The elders ordered *me* to secure them," insisted the lore-warden.

Lyralliantha ignored his protest, moving to collar Brigid next. When that was done she replied, "We are both children of the same grove, Listrius, the end result is the same, but it was *my* servant who brought us this prize, and I will be the one to claim it." Then she whispered in Brigid's ear before moving to the next of the teens from Colne, "Wake the boy, I cannot put the collar on him unless he is conscious."

Brigid was still unsteady from her recent ordeal, but she knew that shouting or shaking wouldn't be sufficient to rouse Gabriel. She went to the water barrel at the front of the wagon and drew a ladle full of the icy liquid. The shock of the cold water on his face brought Gabriel to a semblance of being awake. His eyes rolled in his head while his eyelids fluttered.

Lyralliantha finished the collar for Ryan Carter and then went to Gabriel. Working quickly she produced another spellweave, but the semi-conscious boy resisted when she tried to join the ends. She sighed in frustration.

Gabriel was groaning, his eyes not quite able to focus. Brigid spoke directly into his ear, "Say 'yes'. When you feel it again, just say yes, with your mind. Please, Gabriel... there's no time."

Lyralliantha tried again, and this time the spellweave fused properly. Gabriel's eyes closed almost immediately as his awareness faded. Brigid lowered his head to the wagon bed, then sat down. She was finding it hard to remain awake too. Nausea threatened to overwhelm her, and the world was pulsing with new energies and new visions. She could barely understand what her mind was sensing now.

Kate looked down on her half-sister, "Just relax, Brigid. He said it was normal to feel sick after your power comes. You've done enough."

Chapter 15

Tyrion kept his attention firmly on the krytek and the She'Har lore-warden standing yards behind him. Listrius was positively anxious, pacing back and forth as Lyralliantha worked to collar the human children. The She'Har knew he had been outmaneuvered, but he couldn't see a better option.

The last to accept the collar was Kate. The alien seeming silver-haired woman who approached her was a stranger, but she knew, with the deeper intuition that women often have, that this was *the* woman. The one who had stolen her Daniel away. The one who had chained him, the one who loved him in some bizarre fashion. She was her enemy and her ally, the woman who had taken him and yet who had also kept him alive.

Kate's blazing green eyes met Lyralliantha's icy blue, and the two stared at one another, communicating on some level that lay beneath consciousness, or even magic. Neither blinked for a moment, and then without warning the She'Har woman leaned forward and softly brushed her lips across Kate's cheek.

Straightening Lyralliantha began to produce the spellweave that would create a new slave collar.

"What was that for?" asked Kate.

"I am not sure," responded the Illeniel She'Har. "I think it is because you are a part of him."

"Ordinarily that creates a different feeling between women," said Kate.

Lyralliantha spread her hands apart and stretched the necklace's ends wide while Kate ducked her head forward. She said a few words in Erollith, and Kate felt a straining within herself, a tension. *Yes,* she told herself mentally, and the strain eased. The two ends of the collar clicked into place, and it was done.

On sudden impulse Kate spoke up, "Thank you."

Lyralliantha raised one brow before answering in perfect Barion, "What for?"

"For keeping him alive."

"Do not thank me too soon," said the She'Har. "He may have pushed things too far this time. I cannot shield him from the elders."

"The elders?"

Lyralliantha turned, raising her arm in a sweeping gesture to indicate the massive trees that stood some fifty yards distant. The god trees at the edge were torn, limbs damaged and trunks canted slightly. They had been on the edge of the storm, but some of them had come close to being uprooted.

"That wasn't him," insisted Kate.

"Let us hope they believe that."

Listrius stepped forward, gesturing behind him. The krytek along the forest edge moved as one, encircling the group of humans. Two moved to either side of Tyrion. "Chain him," commanded the lore-warden.

"The collar isn't enough?" asked Tyrion with a wry smile.

"Not any longer," said Listrius. The two krytek began spellweaving, creating long vine-like extrusions of magic that wrapped themselves around their captive's arms, legs and torso. When they finished, Tyrion could no longer move, his limbs were bound, physically and at a deeper level. His body had become rigid, locked into a straight stance; he might have fallen but the magic lifted him above the ground as well, maintaining his position.

The spellweave reached into the heart of his being as well, caging the source of his aythar, the font of consciousness, and for a mage, power. It was an effort to speak, even though that freedom had been explicitly left to him.

"Take the humans to Ellentrea," ordered Listrius.

"No!" argued Tyrion. "They don't belong to the Prathions."

"It is not your decision, baratt. Do not test my patience, or I will have you punished," said the lore-warden.

Lyralliantha stepped forward, "It is my right to decide on their housing."

Listrius gave her a hard glare. "You are to be brought before the elders as well. They will decide your fate. Until then Thillmarius has offered to handle the humans for us."

"But..." she began.

"I trust you will not force me to have you chained as well," warned Listrius.

Lyralliantha closed her mouth, bowing her head before answering, "No, lore-warden."

***

Dalleth entered the small hut, glancing down at the cold form of Gwaeri. To his experienced eyes the body had probably been dead for less than five or six hours. *She must have killed him not long after he brought her back,* thought the She'Har trainer.

Haley stared at him from across the room, fear and something else showing in her features.

Is that defiance? wondered Dalleth. The thought almost made him smile.

"Did you do this?" he asked flatly.

Haley turned her chin up at his question, "Yes." There was no use in denying it.

"It appears you have learned your lesson then," said the trainer. "Remember it when you enter the arena again—tomorrow." He stepped back outside, and then two wardens entered, moving to take Gwaeri's body away. They gave Haley several curious glances before leaving, but said nothing.

Chapter 16

Tyrion floated in an empty abyss. The world was gone, along with his body. He was alone in the darkness, naked and vulnerable in a way that only an empty soul, bereft of flesh, could understand.

It isn't possible for this one to have done what was observed.

The voice was purely mental, but it wasn't his own. It was alien. The pattern and cadence of the thought was utterly foreign. *It must have been one of the elders,* thought Tyrion. He was surprised at himself for thinking. His own mind had been silent for an unknowable period. He had begun to wonder, in a nonverbal way, whether he still had thoughts, if that were possible.

This was a place replete with contradictions.

He is stronger than any of the children, or any one of us. That voice belonged to a different elder, but somehow Tyrion knew it was a Prathion.

Tyrion was aware of a great number of them now, numbers beyond counting. They had stripped him bare and were examining him—dissecting and discussing him in some metaphysical realm where their minds met. What might have happened to his body he could only wonder, in this place it wasn't important. This was a realm beyond bodies, or places, or perhaps even time.

But he is not 'that' strong. No individual agent could have created such a storm, nor was any movement of aythar observed. That observation was from a Mordan elder.

The fact still remains that it has occurred twice now, said an elder of Gaelyn.

The Prathion elder spoke again, *Three times if we include the volcanic disruptions that occurred in the Grove of Mordan.*

He was nowhere near that event. The latest voice was from a Centyr elder.

But he dreamed of it, insisted another.

The first voice spoke again. *That only indicates the possibility of precognition. Such gifts have been seen before,* responded the Centyr elder.

In a technical sense all of the events could be explained with precognition. This came from a new voice, but Tyrion knew it was one of the Illeniels. How he could recognize them amongst the vast array of others, he was unsure.

You do not seriously propose that the events were purely natural and he was merely timing his actions to match them? argued the Mordan elder.

The Illeniel voice responded, *We have no better explanation.*

His memory of the latest windstorm indicates deliberation. The human made a decision to enter a different state of mind before the storm occurred, said the Gaelyn elder.

It is likely that the mental change occurred as a result of information passing from the present into the past. His mind may have folded, meeting itself at other points in his continuum as is consistent with our current theories regarding precognition, responded the Illeniel elder.

The Prathion elder scoffed, *Passing information to the past, such that he could time his arrival. The very idea is a paradox.*

Everything known about precognition is paradoxical, noted one of the Centyr.

None of this negates the danger the baratt presents, whether these events were merely his taking advantage of future knowledge, or whether he is able to manipulate the environment via some unknown mechanism. We must decide how to proceed. The Gaelyn elder gave the impression of extreme practicality.

The Illeniel elder spoke, *He should be studied further. There is much we do not understand, which is in itself a rare occurrence. We might gain knowledge that could allow for a better defense against the great enemy.*

Our current defense is sufficient, said the Mordan elder. *The risk he presents is too great.*

No defense is perfect, replied the Gaelyn elder. *The Kionthara might become corrupted. We cannot know how they will endure, and we have not found a new refuge to harbor us if they fail.*

The gate-guardians are flawless, there is no weakness in our creations, said the Centyr elder with a sense of indignation.

He must be destroyed, reiterated the Mordan elder.

Tyrion could feel a wave of assent coming from many of the elders. Their decision seemed inevitable.

No!

He recognized that mind immediately. It was Lyralliantha and now that he had heard her, he could almost feel her presence beside him.

Silence, daughter, it is not your place to comment here, remonstrated the most senior of the Illeniel elders.

One of the Centyr spoke, *The examination has shown her to be suspect as well. Her memories reveal complicity. She has hidden things that should have been reported.*

She is one of the people, said the Gaelyn elder.

You just suggested the gate guardians could be corrupted, yet you would ignore the possibility in our children? questioned the Centyr.

We alone will decide the disposition of our children, said the Illeniel elder with authority.

But you cannot extend such a provision to the animal, insisted the Mordan elder. *He presents a threat to all of us. He will be destroyed.*

A feeling of agreement came from the others, including the Illeniel elders.

No, if he dies, then I die as well, came Lyralliantha's thought. *Your decision to kill him will end my life also.*

Tyrion could feel the weight of the collected minds of the elder She'Har shifting, bearing down on her.

The child is defective.

She should be terminated as well.

She was chosen to become a lore-warden.

Dispose of the child.

The chorus of voices came from different groves, but the Illeniel elders raised a mutual feeling of opposition. The most senior of them gave it voice, *Stop. Let us analyze this. The child is valuable to us.* The next message was directed purely at her, *Why have you said this, child?*

Because it is the truth, she answered.

There is no logic in your words, said the Illeniel elder. *We have honored your eccentricities in the past in order to grow from whatever knowledge you may have gained. The human will be terminated, and you will remain. Do not embarrass us further by arguing against your own survival.*

He is my kianthi.

A shocked silence ensued. *That is not possible, daughter.*

It is the truth, Lyralliantha replied firmly.

He is not one of the She'Har, not one of the people—he is a baratt. You have become deranged, said the Illeniel elder.

Kianthi are chosen, said another of the Illeniels, *and we have not chosen him. Kianthi are no longer useful or necessary.*

Tyrion could feel the power of her determination as she responded, *I chose him.*

Ridiculous, children do not choose. Kianthi are chosen by the elders.

I chose him, she said again.

He is not She'Har. He cannot produce children. Baratti cannot be kianthi, insisted another of the Illeniel elders.

She must be terminated, said one of the others.

Kill me if you must, but do not harm her or my children, said Tyrion, raising his inner voice for the first time, shouting at the void.

Chaos was the result.

It was listening? Impossible!

How could he be aware? His mind was fully suppressed.

A deluge of similar thoughts flew around Tyrion, giving him the sense of being battered mentally. Eventually they slowed and resolved into a single question.

Why would a baratt give itself for our child? said one of the Illeniels.

He is the one! said another. *Her words and his actions have proven it.*

He is my kianthi, said Lyralliantha once more. *Neither of us can exist without the other.*

The voices of the Illeniel elders rose in a tumult as they argued over her words, battering at Tyrion's mind. He fought to maintain his balance, but it was no use. The weight of their thoughts fell on him, and he found oblivion creeping over him, smothering his awareness.

Silence it...

***

Tyrion awoke to bird song. Sunlight filtered through the canopy in patterns that were already familiar to him. He lay in Lyralliantha's bed, high up in the tree that served as her home. He had slept there many times, though not as often in recent months. He had begun sleeping in the more traditional bed in his stone house once the bedroom had been finished.

He turned his head, but he already knew he was alone. Lyralliantha wasn't there.

"What happened?" he said aloud.

A quick assessment told him that his body was whole and sound. Better than he remembered, even his scars were gone; the only marks remaining on his body were the tattoos he had placed there deliberately. It was a relief to see those still there. He would have felt naked without them. Clothes he could live without, but the enchantments he had engraved on his skin were both armor and weapon to him.

A She'Har male was approaching, walking up the trunk of the great tree in the languid casual fashion that was normal for them.

Byovar, he noted, recognizing the Illeniel lore-warden almost immediately.

Sitting up, he greeted the lore-warden with a nod while reaching for his trousers. His clothes had been removed at some point while he was unconscious. "Good afternoon, Byovar."

"Tyrion," said the silver-haired She'Har.

"I seem to be missing some time," noted Tyrion. "It was turning dark when I arrived."

"That is why I have come," said Byovar. "The elders felt you would need a guide when you awoke."

The word "elders" brought flashes of memory back to Tyrion, and with them uncomfortable thoughts. "Where is Lyralliantha?" he asked with some concern.

"She is still conversing with the elders," informed Byovar. "You should not expect to see her for some time."

"But she is unharmed?"

Byovar nodded.

"Where are my children, and the woman I returned with?"

"Thillmarius is caring for them in Ellentrea," said the She'Har.

Tyrion finished with his trousers and hurriedly pulled on his boots before grabbing his shirt and leather jerkin. "I don't think the term "caring" should be applied to anyone kept in the slave camps." He stood and made his way to the trunk, preparing to descend.

Byovar looked amused at his statement but didn't bother to argue the point. He contented himself with following the human. "Perhaps you should let me fill you in on the present before you leave," he said wryly.

"I would prefer to move while we talk," said Tyrion.

"Are you not hungry?"

In fact, now that he was on his feet again, Tyrion had noticed a terrible void in his belly. He doubted he had ever been so famished in his entire life. There was also another pressing urgency. He gave Byovar an uncomfortable glance, "If you'll pardon me for a few minutes…"

The male She'Har nodded politely and waited while Tyrion moved back out along the platform to the special area set aside for such needs. The limbs and leaves moved around to provide a modicum of privacy as soon as he was within, a change that Lyralliantha had made years ago to accommodate his odd need for seclusion while managing his bodily needs.

Tyrion's urine was the color of dark cider. *That doesn't seem warranted,* he thought. Some injuries had done similar things to him in the past, but normally only when his kidneys had been bruised, or he had been unconscious for long periods.

"I need some water," he admitted to Byovar when he returned.

The She'Har had already poured a cup from the pitcher Lyralliantha kept on a small table near the bed.

He handed it to Tyrion. "Come with me, I have food waiting at my platform."

Tyrion drank the water in gulps, surprised at his thirst once his lips had tasted it. Pausing, he replied, "I really need to check on the others…"

"A few more hours, or even another day won't make much difference," advised the lore-warden.

Tyrion frowned, "How long has it been?"

"A little over a month—five weeks to be exact," answered Byovar.

He was aghast, and his face showed it.

"Time moves differently for the elders," explained the She'Har. "To converse with them, your thoughts must be slowed to a pace that will enable communication. A discussion of a few hours for us can take weeks when you speak to them."

"Wouldn't it make more sense for them to speed up to our pace? What if there were an emergency?"

Byovar smiled, "Few things are truly an emergency for the elders. Most small matters are left to us, or to the krytek. If something truly disastrous occurred they might do as you say, but it hasn't happened for ages."

A few things made sense now. Lyralliantha had spoken to the elders before, and it had often been days before she returned. If what Byovar said was true, then those had been extremely short exchanges. Considering that the She'Har almost never found a good reason to lie, he had no doubt about the truthfulness of the lore-warden's revelation.

Thinking about it, something else occurred to him, "It could be a while before Lyralliantha's conversation is done then."

Byovar nodded.

"I guess I should eat. Then I would like to visit Ellentrea," said Tyrion with some resignation. He hadn't wanted Kate or his children to wind up in the slave camp, but a few more hours wouldn't make much difference, and he was starving after all. Without Lyralliantha's presence he wasn't certain if there would be any way for him to get them out in any case.

Byovar gave him a sidelong glance as they walked, "You have changed, Tyrion."

"How so?" asked Tyrion, hoping he wouldn't have to explain his missing scars or his regrown ear. He didn't have answers for those questions.

"Your patience has grown," said the lore-warden. "When you first came to us you would not have accepted such delays so easily."

"It isn't patience as much as pragmatism," said Tyrion. Remembering his actions in Colne, he wouldn't have described them as the decisions of a patient man. He had become practical to a fault. Patience, violence, negotiation, extortion, or even sexual persuasion, all of these were merely tools to an end.

"You have become like us in many ways," said Byovar.

More than I would like, and enough that I will make the She'Har regret it, thought Tyrion.

Chapter 17

The food was delicious, consisting of a variety of vegetables, some fruit, and, of course, the ever present "calmuth". Calmuth was the fruit produced by the god trees, light-gold in color it was mildly sweet and moderately juicy, with a taste that was reminiscent of a pear but less distinctive. The fruit of the god trees was unique in that it could serve as the sole source of sustenance for their children, although they usually combined it with other foods to avoid boredom.

It also contained a substance that suppressed the growth of the 'seed-mind'. The children of the She'Har were human in a purely physical sense, but they were born fully developed and containing an extra organ within their bodies, the seed-mind. The seed was the true product of their species, the human body was merely a vessel, somewhat like the flesh of a more ordinary fruit which existed purely to protect the seeds within it.

In fact, in times past, on other worlds, the She'Har children had been born with bodies that were not human at all. The She'Har could tailor the bodies of their offspring to match their environment. The Krytek were an excellent example of that, for the father-trees often used varied forms from their history on other worlds to produce the short-lived soldiers that protected them.

Calmuth served as the primary sustenance of the children of the trees, and it also kept their inner 'seed' from germinating. If calmuth became scarce, presumably from a lack of elder She'Har, or an overabundance of their children, then the seeds would begin to mature, the children would take root, and new elders would spring forth.

As far as Tyrion knew, the calmuth had no ill effects on normal humans. He had been eating it for many years with no trouble, but he still yearned for a meatier diet. When he had the time to spare, he often hunted to satisfy his tastes.

An odd question occurred to him, "How does this compare to the taste of the loshti?"

Byovar's brows shot up.

"Lyralliantha told me that she was chosen to become a lore-warden," he explained, to give his question some context.

The lore-warden nodded in understanding, "I see, however I cannot remember the taste."

"But you had to eat it, correct, in order to become a lore-warden?"

"Of course," said Byovar, "but the experience that came immediately afterward drove trivial details, such as the taste of the loshti itself, from my mind."

"What was it like?" asked Tyrion.

Byovar spread his hands wide, as if he were trying to encompass the world around them, "My world expanded. No, it exploded. The knowledge I gained was so much greater than that which I possessed before, that it shattered my previous self-conception, and when the process was over I felt as though I had been reborn."

"Because it filled your seed-mind with the information of the past?"

"Not the seed directly," corrected Byovar. "The loshti is designed to alter the working mind. Our seed-minds are passive, merely recording our experiences until the day that they germinate. The seed remains quiescent in our daily lives, except for the purpose of spell-weaving."

Tyrion frowned, "What would the loshti do in an ordinary human then?"

Byovar's nose wrinkled in disgust. "What you describe would be an abomination, a dead end."

"Dead end?"

"The knowledge would die with the host, rather than passing to a new generation…" Byovar paused, searching for the words in Barion that would convey his meaning. "It would be like the burning of one of your libraries."

That was a new word for Tyrion. He might have thought the term originated in Erollith if it hadn't been for the way Byovar had used it. "I'm not familiar with that word."

"Library?" asked Byovar, but then he understood. "I should have known better. Your kind have not had them since the great war between our races. It was a place of knowledge, where humans stored their collected wisdom. A much cruder method of preserving information than ours, but effective nonetheless. Humankind had thousands of years of history, science, and philosophy stored within them."

"And your people burned them?"

"Yes and no," said Byovar. "We did destroy many of them during the war, but when it was over, we preserved as much of the information that they contained as was possible. The She'Har learn from their enemies. The last remaining libraries were studied, and their useful knowledge recorded before they were demolished."

"That sounds like a simple 'yes' to me," observed Tyrion.

"Well the phrase 'burning libraries' is one I borrowed from your history. Humans regarded it as a great sin, but they made war upon each other in the past, before we came, and sometimes the conquerors would burn the library of the defeated as a means of destroying their past. What we did was different," said Byovar.

"In what way?"

"We preserved the knowledge," said Byovar, tapping his temple, "the parts we could understand at least."

"I thought your race was far superior," said Tyrion sardonically.

"In most respects, yes," agreed Byovar, missing the sarcasm completely, "but your species was mechanistic in their search for understanding. While our science is superior, your race's way of thinking was very foreign, making it difficult for us to grasp the finer points of many of your conceptual models."

"If you weren't careful, Byovar, I might think you meant to compliment my kind."

The lore-warden ran his hand through his hair, smoothing it after a sudden breeze, "The war for this world was the hardest we ever won. We came close to losing, despite the fact that your kind was crippled by its inability to manipulate aythar. Humans were our second greatest enemy."

"Second greatest?" said Tyrion. "If we were the *second* greatest, how could this have been the hardest war you ever fought?"

"Not *fought*, Tyrion," corrected Byovar. "The war for your world was the hardest that we *won.*"

"So the She'Har lost one?" That was the first he had ever heard of something like that.

The lore-warden's voice became more serious, "Almost."

Tyrion chuffed, "How do you *almost* lose a war?"

"We are still alive, and we believe the great enemy cannot threaten us here. Someday we will find the means to defeat them and take back what was lost," stated the She'Har with the utmost gravity in his tone.

"It's hardly a war if you aren't fighting," said Tyrion. "When was the last time you encountered this enemy?"

"When we abandoned our last home, millennia ago, before we came here."

"That was a long time ago. Maybe they've forgotten your people."

Byovar's cold eyes stared into the empty sky, "They do not forget."

***

Thillmarius smiled when he saw Tyrion enter the room. It was the same room he had once used to forcibly take samples from Lyralliantha's wild human slave, and the sight of it still sent shivers down Tyrion's spine.

"I have looked forward to your visit," said the Prathion She'Har. "I was pleased to hear that the

elders had decided to continue your experiment."
Something approaching a genuine smile took shape on
his lips.

"My experiment?"

"You are still alive," said the lore-warden. "I
regard that as a great success."

The Prathion trainer's positive attitude irritated
him. "Would you have me believe your opinion is part
of the reason for my continued survival?" asked
Tyrion.

Thillmarius shook his head, "Not at all, it was
Lyralliantha's brilliance that saved you. What she did
has changed everything. I am not even sure how to
address you now." The She'Har was practically
bubbling with enthusiasm, or at least with the closest
She'Har equivalent.

"Baratt or wildling usually sufficed before now,"
said Tyrion dryly.

"You cannot be a baratt if you are Lyralliantha's
kianthi," stated Thillmarius firmly, "nor can you be
She'Har, since you cannot spellweave. You have
become a delicious paradox." The Prathion actually
licked his lips as he said the last.

"Semantics," said Tyrion. "It doesn't change the
fact of my biology at all."

"True," replied Thillmarius, "but it is far more than
semantics. Never before has a sentient creature
disrupted the boundaries of our definitions. In the past
the most basic categorization for my people has been
that of She'Har and baratti. You no longer fit in the
second category, but we cannot admit you to the first."

"Sounds like a problem for the elders," stated Tyrion. "I could care less what your people think of me. I am here to claim my family."

"Your family?"

"The woman and the children I brought here."

Thillmarius nodded, "Yes, I understood the 'who' of it, it was the use of the term "family" that confused me. The young ones are your offspring, but the woman—she is no relation to you."

"Don't try to distract me, Thillmarius. I wish to take them back to the Illeniel Grove."

"They have no place to keep them, no wardens to mind them," said the Prathion She'Har. "I am housing them here as a favor to the Illeniel Grove."

Tyrion didn't budge, "That is no longer your problem. I will have them regardless."

"As a warden, as a slave, you have no standing to make such a demand," explained Thillmarius. "On what authority do you make such a claim?" Something in the Prathion's expression hinted at some sort of anticipation on his part.

Tyrion glared at him for a moment before answering, "On Lyralliantha's authority…"

"She is not here, nor has she been away from the elders to order any such thing," said Thillmarius immediately. He moistened his lips before repeating himself, as if anxious for something, "On *what* authority do you make this request, Tyrion? Lyralliantha is not here, and we both know your owner has given you no instruction on this matter. Be specific, *where* does your right to demand them come from?"

Tyrion was confused. *He wants me to say something. But what?* His blue eyes locked onto the Prathion's red ones as he thought furiously.

"It's just semantics, Tyrion," hinted Thillmarius.

It clicked then, "As Lyralliantha's kianthi, I demand you release her property to me now." He felt uncomfortable using the term, but he couldn't think of anything else the She'Har trainer would want him to say.

"Since you put it that way, I have no choice," agreed Thillmarius, smiling slyly. "Follow me, I will show you where they have been kept." He stood and made for the door, but he said one more thing as he walked. "Don't forget this lesson."

Tyrion had spent years under the Prathion trainer's control, tortured at times until his sanity had left him. Even now, a decade later, just the sound of the She'Har's voice evoked a primal fear response that made his stomach twist. He had learned to deal with the fear, but he had never succeeded in banishing it. It was too deeply embedded in his psyche.

That fact made it hard for him to understand the Prathion lore-warden's true intentions. Paranoia and anxiety clouded his thoughts. Yet he still wondered, *Why is he helping me? Is he helping me? What is his purpose in this?*

At one point he had been convinced that Thillmarius was evil incarnate, and then the She'Har had helped save his and Lyralliantha's lives after his last arena battle, hiding them until they could recover, and she could replace his slave collar. Now the Prathion was giving thinly veiled hints and helping him to remove his prized acquisitions from the control of the Prathion Grove.

Nothing he does makes sense.

"Five of them have awakened their gifts since coming here," Thillmarius mentioned as they left the large central building in Ellentrea.

"Which ones?"

"Three of the males and two of the females."

He had expected the answer to be phrased like that, but another realization came with the statement. *They haven't been blooded, otherwise he'd have names for them.* "You haven't fought any of them yet?"

"My orders have been strict. Nothing has been done with your offspring, Tyrion, aside from feeding them."

Tyrion stopped, staring at the trainer's back suspiciously, "Why?"

Thillmarius turned, "I am not your enemy, Tyrion. I only wish to learn from you."

He gaped at the ebon-skinned She'Har. "Learn what?"

"Since you came here wildling, you have been a mystery. You have been nothing like our own baratti, and I have seen in you the same spark that made your ancestors such a formidable foe. Yet we do not understand why. Why are you so different from the others? At every turn you have insisted that we know nothing about properly rearing and training your kind, but it is hard for my people to believe that such large differences are the product of something so small as the methodology of your upbringing.

"Did you know that your other child, the one taken by the Mordan, has already begun fighting in the arena? Gravenna has won five matches," finished the lore-warden.

Tyrion had known none of that. "Gravenna? That's the name they chose for her?"

Thillmarius nodded.

"Your people have terrible taste in names."

"The point," continued Thillmarius, "is that she has already defied the odds. The question is, whether it is purely because of your genetics or whether it is due to your short visit with her?"

"It probably has a lot more to do with her life before she was captured," observed Tyrion.

"Eventually I hope to tease out those factors as well," said the She'Har trainer. "I have begun a small project within the slave pens here in Ellentrea. I've had some of the younglings kept in a separate area, to be reared by their mothers after weaning, rather than putting them in the general pen."

He knew that Thillmarius had always been deeply interested in the subject of human beings, that was why the She'Har had become a trainer, and why he had been elevated to lore-warden, but he hadn't expected to hear something like that. "How is that going then?" he asked.

The Prathion grimaced, "Several of the younglings died, killed by their mothers, but the remaining five are doing quite well."

The She'Har's words hardly bothered Tyrion anymore, though they sounded callous, there was no true malice behind them. Thillmarius talked about people in much the same way his father had once spoken of sheep. *He hopes to improve his herd.*

Chapter 17

Thillmarius sent the first two wardens that he encountered to begin collecting the Illeniel slaves while they waited in a small open courtyard. The two men returned a few minutes later with fifteen very pale and shaky looking teenagers. Some of them looked as though they had lost weight, and none of them looked like they had been enjoying their stay in Ellentrea. Squinting and blinking at the sun, they stared at Tyrion with recognition and perhaps some hope.

"Have they been outside at all?" he asked the She'Har trainer.

"Yes, of course," said Thillmarius. "I've had them out to be exercised and make sure they got some sun on their skin."

Two of the boys, Ryan and Ian, looked positively ill and Abigail Moore was almost skeletal. "Have they been eating?"

"Some of them have," said Thillmarius, "but one of the females has been refusing to eat for the past few days. I have to admit, Tyrion, I don't think they're doing well. I've had them all checked to make sure they really are your offspring, but they don't seem to be as hardy as you were."

"I nearly died of a fever when I first came here," reminded Tyrion.

The lore-warden nodded, "Yes, but you improved after Lyralliantha remanded you into my care. Your children have gotten worse. I have begun to doubt my choices. The wardens have suggested that their soft treatment may be the problem. Do you think whipping would stimulate their appetites?"

"No," said Tyrion immediately. *Except in the case of complete refusal to eat,* he thought, looking at

Abigail. *Of course, I think I can come up with better solutions than that.* "Where is the woman?" he asked, noting Kate's absence.

"Do you really want that one back?" asked Thillmarius. "It may take a while to find her. She was put in with the nameless servants. I could easily replace her with one or two others if you just need labor to help care for them."

Dread filled him. The nameless were the lowest of the low in Ellentrea, those without enough ability to be considered for the arena, to win a name. Technically, his children were still counted as 'nameless', but they had been segregated and marked for special treatment. He could only imagine what Kate might have gone through.

"Allow me to find her," suggested Tyrion. "I know her aythar well enough to spot her at a distance, and I'm very familiar with Ellentrea."

"There's no need," said Thillmarius. "I can send the wardens."

"I will be quicker."

"Very well," agreed the lore-warden. "I will have them keep the children here while you search. I have other things that need attending to. If you have any difficulty finding her, or if something has happened, please feel free to take two others to repay Lyralliantha."

"You are too kind," said Tyrion, suppressing his budding anger. Letting his emotions get the better of him would be counterproductive as well as pointless. He opened his mind to its fullest, scanning the auras of the hundreds within range of him. His legs were moving already, taking him in the direction of the large communal huts that housed the nameless.

That proved to be a dead end. Kate was not there, so he was forced to begin a long circuitous walk around Ellentrea. It was half an hour before he found her. She was in one of the private huts of the wardens. That alone would have upset him. Other than cleaning, there was only one reason one of the nameless would be in one of the wardens' homes.

One of them had decided they needed a new toy.

Unwanted visions entered his mind, of Kate, beaten and forced into… *No, I'm not going to think about that. I just have to get her out.* He had picked up speed as soon as he had spotted her and was drawing closer at a jog.

She was with someone, someone with a strong aythar, most likely the warden who lived there.

Another quarter mile and he would be there, but his mind was so focused on Kate he could hardly maintain enough awareness to keep from stumbling as he ran. The warden was holding her, their heads close together. With a flash, he realized that the warden was a woman, and it was someone he knew, Layla.

Layla was almost a friend. She and Garlin had been frequent playmates, although neither of them would have used a word as strong as 'friend' to describe their relationship. Tyrion knew better though, Layla and Garlin had been as close as wardens could be. She would mourn Garlin's death.

He was close enough now to see exactly what they were doing, and talking had little to do with it. During his time in Ellentrea he had seen many things, and the 'favors' that were traded amongst its inhabitants were frequently between members of the same sex, perhaps not quite as often as between opposite genders, but it was by no means unusual.

But, the transactions between wardens and the nameless were rarely consensual. It was a matter of power, and the lack thereof. While Tyrion himself had once had a relationship with one of them, Amarah, he had not abused her. He had been seeking love, something the wardens simply couldn't understand.

Now one of them had made a toy of Kate.

He hadn't really let the possibility enter his mind, and now that he was suddenly faced with, it he found his anger burning white hot.

The door wouldn't open at his touch since it wasn't his dwelling. Inside the two women had paused, pulling apart. Layla could just as easily see that he was outside as he could sense her within.

Tyrion's aythar flared as he activated one of his arm-blades and destroyed the door, its frame, and some of the wall. Layla's shield came up as he strode into the room. She was standing in front of Kate. She was also naked and flushed. While nudity was required for most slaves of the She'Har, it was optional for the wardens, and they rarely removed the outward sign of their elevated status.

"Tyrion!" she exclaimed. "This isn't what…"

He swept his arm to one side, gesturing as he used his aythar to slam her toward the wall, making sure she wouldn't crash into Kate. The force of the blow stunned her for a moment, but her shield held. Tyrion raised a shield of his own, one that encircled the room enclosing the two of them but excluding Kate. Layla was a Prathion and he expected her to use her gift to try to escape.

It was the only way she could hope to avoid death, after all.

The warden remained visible, but she strengthened her shield. "Tyrion please, listen to me."

He growled and his next strike was more controlled, using just enough strength to shatter her shield without causing her too much physical harm. Layla sagged against the wall as the feedback threatened to rob her of her consciousness. "You should have known better, Layla," he replied coldly. Stretching his hands apart he formed the red whip that was so often favored by the wardens.

Killing her wouldn't be enough. He wanted to prolong the moment.

"Daniel stop!" shouted Kate.

"You're too soft, Kate," he responded. "They have to know what will happen to anyone who hurts one of mine." He stepped forward, preparing to bring the whip down on the senseless warden.

"She didn't hurt me, you idiot!"

"I lived in this place for years, Kate. I know exactly how things work. Whatever happened, whatever she's done to you, it wasn't your fault. If you don't want to see this, wait outside." He readjusted the shield to allow Kate to reach the door.

She didn't move. "Let her go, Daniel. She protected me."

"I know how 'protection' works here," said Daniel. "And Layla should have known enough to know how I would react if she expected you to pay for such a thing."

"That's not what was going on," insisted Kate.

"I could see what was happening."

Kate glared at him, "I kissed her! Stop being a fool!"

He lost his concentration for a moment, letting the whip vanish. Blinking, he looked at Kate, uncertain. "Wait... what?"

"You heard me." Now that she had his attention, she made no effort to hide how angry she was.

"I don't understand."

"Maybe if your first reaction to every problem wasn't trying to kill someone, you'd discover that the world is more complicated than you imagine," she told him. She was pressing against the shield now. "Will you take this down so I can get to her?"

He glared at her.

"Please?!" she said with some exasperation.

Tyrion dismissed the shield and watched as she crossed over to Layla. Kate lifted the other woman's head, brushing back her hair and stroking her cheek gently. The warden's eyes rolled as she tried to focus on her.

"What did you do to her?" asked Kate worriedly.

"Nothing," he grumbled. "I broke her shield. It's the feedback, she'll be fine in a little while."

"You're a bully, Daniel."

His frustration returned, rekindling his anger, "I was trying to protect you."

"From what? Being kissed to death? There was no need to be so violent," argued his childhood friend.

"I don't think you really comprehend what these people are like," said Tyrion. "They aren't like the people of Colne. They're raised like animals. It does something to their minds. They behave like savages. They do things you wouldn't believe."

"Like what? Women kissing?"

"That isn't what I meant, but it's an example. That doesn't happen in Colne…"

"Yes it does," declared Kate. "You're just too stupid to know about it."

For the first time in a very long time, Tyrion's cheeks colored, and he found himself on the defensive. "Who then?" he asked confronting her head on.

"Me," shot back Kate.

"You and who?"

"Darla Long," she announced brusquely, naming the mother of one of Tyrion's children, Anthony Long.

"When was this?!" he demanded.

"After you left—the first time," she replied. "Before I married Seth…" She grew hesitant then, pausing, "…and then again a few years ago."

"Did Seth know that?!"

"No!" she answered, balling up her fists. "Things got difficult between us, not that it's any of your business. He never asked, and I never told him."

"So you were cheating on him, with a woman?" He was having trouble thinking clearly. All his assumptions about Kate seemed to be wrong.

Kate marched forward, planting her finger in the middle of his chest. "You…!" she declared with emphasis, "…have no business judging me, not after all the things you've done."

Unable to think of a better response he glared at her, and she stared back, boldly. Her green eyes were never more attractive than when she was furious. Then his mind registered the gathering crowd of wardens in the street outside. "We need to leave," he told her.

Kate went to Layla and began helping her to her feet.

"Leave her," said Tyrion.

"She's coming with us."

"She belongs to the Prathion Grove," he answered. "She stays."

"Then I'm staying too," replied Kate.

He considered killing her. No, killing both of them. Then he would destroy the room, the street, and burn Ellentrea to the ground. *I wonder how far I could get, before they managed to stop me.* Taking a deep breath he finally replied, "Fine. Bring her. I'll think of something."

Turning, he left the room.

Chapter 18

The wardens minding the teens watched him with puzzled faces when he returned with both Kate and Layla. They found other directions to gaze once they saw the look in his eyes, however.

"Tell your master I'll be taking this one as well," he said, gesturing at Layla. "We can discuss the terms later." A warden was considerably more valuable than any of the other slaves within one of the camps, but he hoped the strangely helpful Thillmarius would prove amenable in this regard as well.

Glancing at the others, he told them, "Let's go."

"They took our clothes," said Emma Phillips. The girl was trying to cover herself with two skinny arms and failing awkwardly. The gooseflesh on her arms told Tyrion she must be cold. He hadn't noticed the cold air until then.

"You don't have clothes anymore, not here," he stated flatly, starting to walk.

Most of them followed, but Emma held back, hesitating. Apparently they hadn't been outside much since arriving, at least not enough to make them lose their self-consciousness regarding nudity.

"You can stay here if you like," called Tyrion, "but they won't give you your clothes back."

Emma followed.

Most of them were cold he realized, even those whose powers had awakened. No one had shown them how to keep themselves warm. Kate seemed fine, though. Layla was keeping a layer of warm air around both of them. The observation colored his temples, and his ears grew hot. His temper was rising again.

"Where have you been?" asked Gabriel, walking closer to him than the others.

"The She'Har felt the need to interrogate me."

"We thought you were dead," added Brigid. "It looked bad when they took you away."

He said nothing, though he could feel Kate's eyes upon him.

"Where are you going to keep them?" asked Layla.

"At my house, for now," he replied. He had been thinking of that for a while, and it was the best solution he could come up with. There wasn't enough room there, of course, and it wasn't finished, except for his bedroom, but at least there was a roof.

"The white-stone?" said Layla.

"The what?" asked Tyrion.

"The white-stone place you have been building," clarified the warden.

The people of Ellentrea and the other slave cities lived in buildings grown from the roots of the god trees, so it was understandable that she didn't really know what to make of his stone construction.

"Yes," he nodded. *White stone,* the phrase gave him an idea. "I prefer to call it 'Albamarl'," he added, using the words in Erollith for white and stone.

They took the long way, following the edges of the Prathion border and skirting the edges of Illeniel territory. He didn't want to be forced to answer any awkward questions. Albamarl was at the edge of the foothills, where they bumped up against the beginnings of the Illeniel Grove, just a few miles south of where he had had his recent confrontation.

Chapter 18

Many of the young men and women breathed a sigh of relief when they entered the building. The air was warm, maintained at a comfortable temperature by the enchantments he had worked into the stone walls.

He made a quick walk through, reassuring himself that everything was still as he had left it. The wagon they had brought was parked behind the building, still loaded with supplies. The fresh goods had spoiled, but most of the dry goods were still usable. Beans, salt, and salt pork, onions, and some apples, much of it consisted of things that Tyrion had had little access to while living among the She'Har.

There's flour! he noted with some excitement as his mind explored the contents once more. Flour meant gravy, or maybe even bread, if anyone knew how to bake. *Some of them do,* he said to himself, even as he mentally avoided thinking about Kate. One of the boys, Jack, had been raised in a bakery.

Tyrion thought for a moment. If he was going to manage fifteen people, he was going to need more room, more supplies. The ones whose powers had awakened would need to be trained. There was much to be done.

He called his fifteen young charges together, pointing for them to line up in the large front room that was set to one side of the entry hall. Eventually, he planned for it to be a kitchen, but currently it was just a large empty space.

He eyed them, noting which ones had visibly wakened their abilities and refreshing his memory of their names. "David, Sarah, Jack, Abigail, Ryan, Brigid, and Gabriel," he named them aloud, pointing for them to move to the other side of the room as he did. "I want you seven over here. The rest of you will go outside and unload the wagon. Sort through the goods and wares. Some of it has spoiled while it sat out there in the elements. Discard the bad and bring the rest inside."

Ian Collins voiced what several of them were probably thinking, "What makes you think you can order us around?" He was probably the largest of the boys, but perhaps not the brightest of them. At fifteen he was already as tall as Tyrion and possibly wider, an impressive thing considering Tyrion's not insubstantial physique.

Tyrion graced him with a wicked smile, walking forward to stand nose to nose with the large teen. "You think you're a match for me already, boy?"

The others had already moved away, and Ian was sweating as he attempted to keep his eyes on Tyrion's. He knew he had made a mistake. "I—I d—don't have any m—magic yet, but…"

"…but what?" interrupted Tyrion. "Were you going to say that, if it weren't for that, you'd teach me a lesson? Is that it?"

"N—no, 'course not," blurted the younger man.

"Go ahead," challenged Tyrion. "I'll give you three free shots, if you think you can land one. After that I'll fight you without my power if that's what you want."

Ian stared at him, clenching his jaw. He considered the offer for a long moment and then without warning, he struck, launching a sharp blow from the waist, aiming for Tyrion's midsection.

The boy was fast, and the move surprised Tyrion. Given the short distance and the teen's speed, he wasn't able to avoid it, but he did manage to turn his body and tense in time to avoid having the wind knocked out of him. He felt the impact in his ribs. *That's going to leave a bruise.*

Ian hadn't waited for him to recover, the other hand had come up and swung wide, aiming to catch him in the side of the head as he naturally tried to avoid the body shot.

It wasn't quick enough, however. Tyrion had expected that and ducked his head forward and to the side, flexing his knees as he stepped in and to the right. Before the teen could make his third attack, he reached up and put his hand out, shoving backward on the boy's chest. Ian was still slightly off balance from his missed swing, and he stumbled backward.

Tyrion kicked his leg, sending him to the hard stone floor. When the boy started to rise, he kicked again, catching him in the stomach and leaving him gasping. "You've got good instincts, boy, even if your balls are too big for your brain. I bet you were in a lot of fights back home, weren't you?"

Ian coughed, gasping for air.

"Ever broken a rib?" asked Tyrion

"Daniel! That's enough!" shouted Kate, starting forward, but Layla grabbed her arm, cautioning her to silence.

Tyrion watched the boy carefully, waiting until he had almost gotten his air, then kicked again, sending the hard part of his shin into the boy's ribs with an audible crack. Ian fell away to the side with a heavy, gasping croak. He was clutching at his side, struggling to draw breath.

"Hurts doesn't it?" said Tyrion. "The pain is so intense you can't draw breath. It'll go on until you fear that you're about to die, but not to worry. Usually your body will let you start to get small breaths before you pass out, but they hurt like the devil. It's not something you forget."

He looked around at the rest of the room. The others had scattered to the far corners, each of them trying to put as much distance between the sadistic older man and his victim as possible. Only Layla had stayed in her original position, watching him calmly. She held Kate tightly by one arm.

Tyrion waved at the seven he named before, "I want you seven to come closer. I was going to begin with teaching you how to stay warm, but today is your lucky day. We'll begin with learning how to mend a broken rib. The rest of you..." he eyed the others, "...go unload the wagon. Bring the sacks of beans in here. We can use them to prop this idiot up, to help him breathe until we get this bone fixed."

He took his time with the bones, making sure they had time to understand what he was doing. He also tried to keep it as painless as possible, although he wasn't entirely as successful at that as he might have hoped. Tyrion was beginning to feel a bit of guilt now that his temper had cooled.

Kate was watching him with an expression that told him exactly what she thought of his methods. *Did my anger with her make me more cruel than necessary?* It was not the sort of thought he was used to anymore.

The past ten years had been neat and simple. Once he had been allowed to leave the arena for good, he had lived peacefully, no children, no family, and almost no friends. He had been isolated within a bubble. Now he was being forced to emerge into an environment fraught with annoyances and complications, and the only social tools he understood involved blood and threats.

But I have to make them ready, he told himself. *There's every chance that the Illeniel Grove will force them into the arena.*

But if they didn't? In that case, he had made an ass of himself for nothing, alienating the only other truly human people he had any hope of interacting with. The slaves of the She'Har had proven to be very poor company, with a few exceptions.

One of those exceptions was standing beside Kate now, talking quietly to her. He might have classified Layla as an acquaintance before this, which was actually pretty high praise for one of the people raised in the pens. Other than Amarah, and Garlin, he doubted he would have considered any of the others even remotely familiar.

She was very close to Garlin, he reminded himself, *as close as wardens get anyway.* He wondered if she would hate him once she knew the circumstances of her friend's death. She had been friends with Garlin in what her people considered the 'normal' usage of the word friend, meaning acquaintances with benefits. *And now she has Kate to fill the tiny void in whatever it is she uses for a heart,* he thought bitterly.

He wondered how she would react once he told her that he had killed her lover. Layla looked at him then, glancing up as if she knew his thoughts had been about her. Leaving his students and his newly mended patient, he walked over to the two women.

"I need to talk to you," he began.

"I'm not really in the mood for conversation," said Kate angrily.

"Not you," he corrected, focusing more directly on the tall dark haired woman standing beside her. "You."

"Haven't you done enough already?!" said Kate spitefully. "I think you made yourself clear enough earlier. If you hurt…"

"It's about Garlin," he said, interrupting the beginning of what sounded like might be a spectacular tirade.

Layla's eyes grew slightly wider, and Kate paused, unsure who he was referring to at first. Unfortunately her memory was uncanny sometimes, especially regarding names and people. Kate's face lit with recognition, "Wait, was that the warden we met? The first one, I think you said his name when we…"

"Kate," he said, giving her a serious stare.

"I know he is dead," announced Layla. "None of them returned."

Kate was watching them closely, understanding dawning on her rapidly as a look of concern swept over her features. Layla glanced at her before returning her attention to Tyrion.

"Branlyinti had claimed one of my children, as well as my father," he began. "He stood in my path. I was forced to eliminate him in order to reclaim them."

"You killed all of them?" asked Layla, her features smooth, like stone.

Tyrion nodded.

"Except the She'Har," added Kate. "I shot him with the crossbow."

Chapter 18

Layla looked back and forth between them, "That was a large group, a trainer and a dozen wardens…"

Tyrion looked down, "Garlin helped me; not directly, but he told me the groves of the others before the fight began."

"And you killed him?" she asked.

"He was first."

Layla blinked and her cheek twitched for a moment. "He was a fool for you."

'Fool' was the word the slaves of the She'Har used to describe friends, lovers, or people who were simply too emotional. Tyrion nodded, "He was a fool for you too, Layla."

The warden blinked again, and a tear made its way down one cheek. She turned her back on them, hiding her face, and her voice was thick when she spoke again, "You will play tonight? I have not heard your music in years." It was as much a demand as a request.

He had left his cittern in his bedroom when he left to capture his children, and he hadn't thought of it since returning. It had been a long time since he had played for anyone other than Lyralliantha. He had become rather reclusive over the past decade.

"I will play for you," he told her, "and for Garlin."

Layla nodded.

***

The rest of the afternoon went smoothly. None of the children felt like arguing after what had happened to Ian. He split them up into several groups. The mundanes he split into two details, one charged with preparing something edible for everyone that evening, and the other with cleaning the stone dust and other detritus from the interior of his house to make it suitable for them to sleep in that night.

Once he had them working, he spent the rest of his time with the ones who had already awakened their mage abilities, teaching them the rudiments of shielding and a few practical tricks, such as how to keep themselves warm. Once he had accomplished that, he took them outside and marked the outlines for a new building a short distance from his house.

"What will that be?" asked Jack, noting the size of the rectangle he had marked.

"A place for you and your brothers and sisters to live," answered Tyrion.

Ryan pointed at the lines he had marked on the ground, "Are those supposed to be the interior walls?"

Tyrion nodded.

"What's this large area here then?" asked the boy.

"That's a common room."

"And that?" said Ryan, pointing to a square he had marked with cross marks.

"That will lead to the storage cellar."

"Where are the bedrooms?" observed Ryan, squinting as he thought about the layout.

Ordinarily such questions might have annoyed him, but he could tell the boy was thinking, and he appreciated that. "They'll be on the two floors above."

"Where's all the wood going to come from?" asked Ryan, looking askance at the small pile of lumber that Tyrion had set aside near his mostly completed home.

"The extra will come from the oaks over that way," said Tyrion, pointing toward the hills, away from the Illeniel Grove, "but the building will be primarily stone, so you won't need as much as you're thinking. The wood will be for bracing and framing."

"Stone?" asked Sarah suddenly. "How are we supposed to build out of stone?"

Tyrion tapped his temple, "With this. Your aythar will be your tools, it will be your carts, it will cut stone, and it will carry materials. Everything will be done with it."

"But I don't know anything about building," she protested.

"You'll learn," he replied. "The task will help you hone your concentration and strengthen your will."

Ryan spoke again, "If you're going to build this out of stone, it won't work. That space is too large, the weight of the upper floors will cause it to collapse without more interior support."

Tyrion focused on him now, "Do you know something about building, boy?"

Ryan looked uncomfortable now that the attention was firmly on him, but he held his ground. "A little, I was apprenticed to a carpenter, but I got to see the masons working too."

"Think you can come up with a better design?" challenged Tyrion.

"W—well, maybe just some suggestions…"

"You're in charge of the building and its design, then," he ordered the boy, then he pointed at Gabriel, "You'll be in command of everyone in general, but I'll expect you to make sure everyone cooperates with Ryan's plan."

Gabriel nodded calmly, but Ryan's face was a picture of shock, "Wait, I don't know that much. What if it falls in? I'm just an apprentice I don't kn…"

"You know more than I do about construction," admitted Tyrion. "If it falls down, you'll just have to rebuild it. The sooner you get it right, the sooner all of you have private rooms to sleep in."

"What about the stone?" asked Brigid, speaking for the first time in hours.

Tyrion smiled, "It's in a pit, about a quarter mile in that direction." He gestured toward the foothills.

She frowned, "There's no way we can get enough here to build this gigantic house."

"See that house over there?" said Tyrion, waiting for their eyes to focus on what he had just recently named 'Albamarl'. "I built that with nothing but this." He tapped his forehead. "I knew nothing about stonework, and very little about carpentry. I had no tools and no assistance. Each of you is strong, and once you've matured and exercised your abilities, you will probably be as strong as I am, or close to it. Some of you might become even stronger. You'll build it."

Chapter 19

The meal that evening was—interesting. The different assignments had given the teens something to occupy themselves, and they had begun to subtly compete. One of the girls, Emma Phillips, had been adamantly confident in her cooking skills and had consequently taken charge of the cooking detail.

What they had produced was edible, but it left a lot to be desired. There were beans, but they had been cooked into a flavorless paste. Roasted turnips were there for variety, but they were scorched black in places and yet still raw in the middle. The oatcakes were passable, but somehow they had been salted until they were more of a savory item than sweet.

The complaints by the others were loud and lengthy, particularly by the others who had been overruled by Emma's decisions while on the cooking detail. All fingers were pointing in her direction, and she seemed to be on the verge of tears now, tears or a tantrum. It was hard to tell.

They sat in the open yard in front of the house, where two of them had built a large fire, and a couple of others had brought heavy logs to use as benches. It was chillier outside, but the fire made it tolerable even for those without magic.

They ate their food there, or as David put it, they "…choked down the remains of what was once known as food." Laughter was the only spice that made the food taste better, although it drove Emma to eat inside the house rather than listen to their jibes.

Tyrion had taken a seat on one of the large logs before most of the others, and as they all came to sit and eat, it was noticeable that no one sat beside him. The log bench was nearly eight feet in length, but it remained empty while the teens, Kate, and Layla crowded onto the three other logs.

He preferred it that way.

Finishing the last of his bean-paste, he rose and walked toward the house. Sleep would be welcome.

Layla rose quickly and caught up to him before he could reach the door. "Have you forgotten your promise?"

He stared at her blankly for a moment before his memory clicked and provided the answer, "Music?"

She nodded.

"It has been over a month since I played," he told her, thinking of his time with the elders and his week traveling before that. "I may not be at my best."

"It has been even longer since my ears have heard it," she reminded him. "No one will criticize your playing."

"Fine." He went into the house and found his cittern. Emerging again a few minutes later he returned to his place by the fire.

All eyes were on him now. The conversation died away as he began to tune the strings. The children of Colne were used to music, unlike the slaves of the She'Har, but although a musical instrument wasn't a rarity for them, it was still a welcome change from their bleak day.

He played 'The Merry Widow' first, hoping to lighten the mood, but the notes grated on his nerves, and his heart wasn't in it. The light gaiety of the song didn't suit his mood. He considered playing 'Dana's Lament', but one glance at Kate sitting beside Layla across the fire dismissed that notion from his mind. It was a sad, sorrowful melody, but the romantic connotations were too much for him. He still remembered the first time he had played it for her, over fifteen years ago.

Instead, he started an unnamed tune, one he had created himself over many long evenings of playing with the strings. It had no words, and because he had crafted it himself, it was wont to change at times to suit his mood. He began softly, letting his fingers find their rhythm before increasing the intensity of the sounds.

The faces staring at him around the fire bothered him, so he closed his eyes, turning his mind inward. People were the source of his suffering. The young people he had stolen away from Colne were the result of his prior sins, and now they suffered at his hands. He hurt because of them, and they hurt because of him, an endless cycle of pain. Whenever he looked into their eyes, he saw his own failing, and he could feel the condemnation that he fully deserved.

His music was angry at first, filled with the frustration that had been his daily companion since discovering that Haley had been taken by the Mordan Grove, but as he closed his mind to the outside world the melody softened. *I am not playing for them.*

He played to the silence, the empty place that was within himself. The void there was cold, but it was also free of pain, free of all the things that tore at him. His music was a thing of gossamer and moonlight, but it spoke now of solitude, quiet reflection, peace— perhaps it even spoke of forgiveness.

Tyrion's thoughts were free now, relaxed, for the music had taken the emotion. His fingers expressed the feelings that he no longer wanted, leaving his heart and mind lighter. Garlin's face appeared in his imagination, staring at him with the same strange curiosity that it always had when Tyrion played the cittern.

The warden had been his captor, even his tormentor once, but had later become a friend—his only friend among the cruel people tainted and twisted by the She'Har. *"Thank you, Tyrion, for the music,"* said Garlin once more, as his mind replayed their last meeting.

The scene that followed was grotesque, but he didn't shy from it, letting the music rise from a sad farewell to a discordant crescendo. His hands were full of fire, but his heart was empty. *I feel nothing.* The words floated through his mind above the chaos of his playing. They passed on, and the music continued, carrying him forward, to his parents.

Helen and Alan Tennick were there, hidden in the undertones, waiting for their chance, and once the violence of Garlin's death had passed, they moved forward to fill the foreground with his mother's sad eyes and his father's tears. *"I wish you'd never been born, Daniel,"* said Alan once more.

The music was lost then, falling and dying abruptly, leaving a rude silence behind full of hurtful things. *That's not me,* he thought. *Daniel isn't my name anymore.* But the fire had left his hands, and now it was at his center, burning through his chest and running like cold cinders down his cheeks.

Tyrion opened his eyes.

The young people around the fire stared at him with dismay on their faces, or simple shock. Their short lives had not yet given them the experience to interpret what they had just heard, instead the trauma in his music had left them stunned. The only ears that had understood had been the ones hidden by a soft fall of coppery hair.

Green eyes stared at him, wet and swollen, while beside her Layla sat with her head bowed, afraid to show her pain openly. Perhaps the warden had understood as well.

Kate's lips parted, as if she might speak, but Tyrion rose and tucked his cittern under one arm before the moment could complete itself.

"That's enough music," he said, turning away.

I feel nothing, he told himself, but wishing wouldn't stop the pain. Returning to his room, he shut the door and activated the enchantment that sealed the room. No one would interrupt his slumber.

***

Morning brought a new day and with it new changes. In particular the cooking crew rebelled and deposed Emma Phillips as the head cook. Anthony Long emerged as the next in the chain, and he supervised a much better batch of oatcakes for breakfast. He also asked Tyrion for permission to send some of the others out to hunt.

"We'll send some of the ones on the building crew," responded Tyrion. "It will be a good experience for them using their abilities."

Byovar showed up not long after that, walking carefully along the worn path that led out from the edge of the Illeniel Grove and across the field to Albamarl. Tyrion sensed him coming and was waiting outside before he arrived.

"Morning, lore-warden."

"Good morning, Tyrion," returned the She'Har. "I have news for you."

"Will Lyralliantha be back soon?"

Byovar shook his head, "I don't know. My news is about something different."

"Let's walk then," said Tyrion. "I need to stretch my legs." He took a circuitous route, leading Byovar out around the edge of his stone house and through the lightly wooded areas beyond.

"The elders have sent word that they will support your decision," said the lore-warden.

"My decision?"

"To capture your offspring, to bring them here."

Tyrion coughed, "Don't you mean Lyralliantha's decision?"

"My people do not deal in falsehoods, Tyrion. One of the details that became clear during your examination by the elders, was that you are indeed making decisions. Lyralliantha has chosen to support them, but the choices have often been yours. In fact, bringing the younglings back here, instead of leaving them with Thillmarius is a prime example."

"Do you disapprove of my bringing them back?" asked Tyrion.

Byovar sighed, "No, but that is not the point. Thillmarius informed me of your taking them after you had already done so. He also told me that the Prathions have decided to respect your bond with Lyralliantha."

Tyrion nodded, but remained silent, unsure what to say.

"Word came from the elders last night that you will be treated as a child of the grove," added Byovar. "The other groves will respect their decision as well."

He stared at the lore-warden, uncertain if he properly understood what the other man had said. "Are you trying to say I've been made an honorary She'Har?"

Byovar frowned, "You cannot become an elder, but they will treat you as a child until your death."

"A child—like…"

"Like myself, or more particularly, like Lyralliantha," clarified the lore-warden. "You are not a baratt any longer. You are like the krytek, a child that cannot grow and will someday die."

"What about this?" he asked, pointing at the slave collar.

"As part of the Illeniel Grove, we no longer require it, but it will be Lyralliantha's decision whether to remove it or not."

"And my children?" pressed Tyrion.

"Are still baratti," replied the She'Har. "Your new status does not affect them at all. In fact, that is the other matter I have come to talk to you about."

"They belong to me," warned Tyrion. "If I am no longer a baratt, then they are mine, or at least Lyralliantha's."

"You are a child of the grove, you are Illeniel. They belong to the Illeniel Grove," corrected the lore-warden. "If you wish to remain as you are, you will submit to the will of the elders."

"What do they want?"

"Your recent fighting, with the wardens and some of the children of the other groves, has been costly. We have given much shuthsi to balance the debt you created."

Tyrion's brow shot up, "The grove paid for the wardens I killed?"

Byovar nodded, "The wardens, three children of the groves, and the warden you took yesterday. Your actions have greatly weakened the Illeniel Grove's standing."

He narrowed his eyes, "The elders didn't have to do that. It would have been simpler to disavow me, even if that included Lyralliantha. Why would they…?" His mind followed the thought to its logical conclusion. "No!"

"They will fight in the arena, for the greater good of the Illeniel Grove," said Byovar coolly.

The words chilled him. He had been afraid of this outcome, but he had hoped that by keeping them under the Illeniel Grove's control he could avoid it. It was somewhat ironic that it was his fighting to make it so that resulted in them being forced to fight. Tyrion's knuckles had gone white. He was clenching his fists too hard. He took a deep breath and forced himself to relax his hands and arms.

"You understand?" asked Byovar, watching him with some concern. "They will fight," repeated the lore-warden.

"If they will just let me talk to…"

"There will be no negotiation, Tyrion. They were clear in their message. Your children will fight, or you and Lyralliantha will become nutrients for the elders. There is no other way, and your offspring will fight, whether you train them or whether someone else is forced to the task." Byovar's face was empty of all expression.

"Nutrients for the elders" was a phrase used by the She'Har that referred to their method of using bodies as compost to feed the god trees. Byovar's words weren't a threat. The She'Har didn't threaten, they 'informed'.

Tyrion could feel his anger building once more, but he held it in check. Instead he bowed his head, acknowledging the command.

"Much has changed since you came to us, Tyrion," said the She'Har. "You are the first sentient being outside of our own species to be considered a child of the grove."

"Change isn't always good, Byovar," said Tyrion. "I was also the first Illeniel slave. Now they are planning to use my children in their games."

The Illeniel Grove had historically been opposed to keeping humans as slaves or pets. Lyralliantha had broken that prohibition when she had collared him to save his life. His success in the arena had given them a taste of competitive victory again. Now the debt he had created had forced them to go even further.

"I know this isn't what you want, wildling," said Byovar, "but my people change slowly. There is a great debate among them now, a debate that you created. Do not give up hope. Someday we may find a common cause between us."

Byovar was one of the most understanding of his kind. He had originally been chosen to become a lore-warden because of his interest in humanity and his research about them and their language. That was why he had been chosen to tutor Tyrion in Erollith. If there were any among the children of the She'Har whom Tyrion thought might have a chance of understanding his emotions, aside from Lyralliantha, it was Byovar.

Tyrion glared at him now. It was a look that would have filled a human with fear, for there was death in his eyes, but it hardly fazed the She'Har. "I would like to be alone now, Byovar," he told the lore-warden.

The She'Har nodded and turned, walking away without the need for a farewell.

"How long do I have?" Tyrion asked his back.

"A week."

The wind picked up as he stood there watching the lore-warden walk back to the edge of the god-trees. The skies had been clear before, but now they darkened, as if the sky were brooding. Heavy clouds passed overhead, and Tyrion struggled to control his anger.

Breathing deeply he chanted silently to himself, *I feel nothing.*

Chapter 20

When Tyrion walked back to his white-stone house, it was with a heavy heart. The simmering hatred he felt for the She'Har had returned, coloring everything he saw and filling him with bitterness. Brigid, Jack, and Sarah were returning from the opposite direction, bringing a pair of does with them, levitating the bodies of the deer in front of them. Their faces were cheerful, almost bright, more so than he had seen from them since he had taken them from their homes.

They were beginning to see that perhaps living here wouldn't be as terrible as they had feared. Good food and a semblance of some self-determination could go a long way in making someone believe that, even when they were being held as slaves.

He had wanted to do even more. He had hoped the Illeniel Grove wouldn't make them fight.

The day before, with Ian, his actions had been cruel and excessive. He had felt guilty, but now he knew he had been right. He could not afford kindness, not now, not yet. Someday perhaps, but by then their hatred would be fully ingrained, etched into their hearts like a scar that would never fully heal.

And he would be the knife that carved it.

What kindness they seek, it must not come from me, he told himself. Kate emerged from the house even as he thought it, and when his eyes fell on her, he knew the role she would be forced to play. *You will be their mother, Kate. You will love them where I cannot. I will break them down, but you will keep them sane.*

She walked toward him purposefully, as though she had words for him. The music from the night before had told her more than it should. She had caught a fresh glimpse of his suffering.

She wants to forgive me, if I will just give her some small sign that I am not insane. Even now, after everything, she wants to believe.

"Daniel, I've been thinking…" she began.

"Stop," he ordered.

Kate frowned, "But I…"

"I don't care," he told her harshly. With his magesight he double checked their surroundings, making sure no one was within earshot. "I need to address everyone. I will explain how things will work."

She closed her mouth, looking at him with eyes that seemed to bore into him.

"You aren't going to like it. You're going to want to argue about it with me, and you'll probably be right, but you will need to keep your tongue," he warned.

"What's going on?" she asked.

He ignored her question. "Later you'll be angry. They will too," he said, waving his arm to indicate everyone else, even though they weren't nearby. "They're going to want to talk, and they'll need someone to listen. I don't care what you say, so long as it's not within my hearing."

She gave him a confused look. "You really have lost your mind. Have you been having a conversation by yourself? Because it sounds as though you're talking to someone who knows what the hell you're thinking."

He nodded, "I probably have lost my mind, and that's a good way for you to think about it. There are just two rules you need to remember. Never talk about the madman where he can hear you, and never argue with him in front of the others."

"Or what?"

He leaned in closer, "Or you'll wind up like Ian."

Kate's eyes narrowed. She wasn't particularly good at being threatened. Straightening, she took a firm stance. "Alright, if that's how you want to act, fine, but don't expect me to play along. I'm sick of your bullying, and I don't care what you do to me."

"Get the others together, I need to talk to them. You have fifteen minutes." He brushed past her, ignoring her bravado.

Burned out ashes remained from the fire the night before. Stepping around them, he took a seat on the same log he had used then. He didn't have to wait fifteen minutes, within five everyone was in the yard. Some of them started to sit at the other logs, but he stood and waved them away from the log benches.

"This isn't a 'sit down and chat' kind of discussion," he told them seriously.

"Is this a meeting?" asked Abigail.

Tyrion glared at her, "From now on, when I call everyone together, you do not speak to me. Only two people will speak to me at one of these gatherings, the warden Layla, or Gabriel Evans. The rest of you will only speak to me if I address you first."

The girl swallowed and nodded, afraid to reply.

He looked over the rest of them, "Next week, those of you whose powers have awakened will begin fighting in the arena."

Everyone grew still, and even the small sounds that had been filtering through the group disappeared.

"The arena is a place wherein mercy does not exist, and therefore you will not give it. Nor will you find any mercy here at my hands. Before I brought you here, you had something that the slaves growing up in the pens have never had—a family. You had parents. Your mothers, and your fathers, or whoever the hell raised you, those people loved you. Those people nourished you. They fed you with kindness and love and helped you become the strong, vital, intelligent, young men and women whom I see here today.

"But love will not keep you alive. Kindness will not keep a violent death at bay. That is why I am here. I will teach you the things your parents never wanted you to learn. I will teach you the art of violence. I will teach you to kill, and I will give you the cruelty to make you enjoy doing it. I will teach you to hate your enemy with a burning passion, a passion that can only be quenched in blood.

"You will be the disciples of my hatred. I will teach you to hate me, and when you step into the arena, it will be my face you see before you as you annihilate your enemy. You will cry yourselves to sleep at night with no greater desire than to see me dead at your hands, and when you enter the arena you will turn that anger loose upon your foes.

"Your parents' love has made you strong; now my hatred will take that strength and make you powerful. Your hearts will become weapons which will destroy anyone who stands before you." *And someday I will turn those weapons against those who have done this to us...*

***

"You wanted to see me," said Layla, staring evenly into his eyes. She was a tall woman, big boned, she stood almost eye to eye with him. It was easy to see why Garlin had been so obsessed with her. She personified strength, although it was tempered with the native cruelty of her upbringing.

"Thillmarius has sold you to the Illeniel Grove," he answered. "From today forward you are my slave, *my* warden. Do you understand?"

She frowned, "But you are a warden…" She left off the ending, "…like me". But he was sure she was thinking it.

"No, not any longer. The She'Har have chosen to elevate me. I am one of their children now, and *you,* along with the others, belong to me."

"How could such a thing be possible?" she said, her mouth gaping.

"The 'how' of it is not your concern, Layla. Obeying my orders *is.*"

The tall woman lowered her head in submission, and he could see her wetting her lips as she did. Her heart rate was quickening as well. "What orders would you give me, Tyrion?"

"It's about Kate," he began.

Her eyes lit up with understanding, "She is yours also. You wish me to stay away from…"

"No, Layla," he said with some frustration. "I'm not trying to keep you away from her. I want you to protect her from the others. She's the only person here who will never have the ability to manipulate aythar.

Eventually the young ones will realize how powerless she is, especially once I begin teaching them."

"We shall be yours alone, if that is what you wish, my lord," the warden answered dutifully.

"That isn't what I mean," he replied with exasperation. "I just want you to protect her. What the two of you do otherwise is not my concern."

The female warden was confused, but she held her questions. She could sense his frustration, and long experience had taught her the danger of questions when they were not wanted. "It will be as you say, Tyrion."

"There's one other thing," he continued.

Layla smiled then, she had expected this. Stepping forward, she pressed herself closely against him, "I have seen your eyes on me. I will do whatever you command."

He shoved her roughly back, "No, damn you! That's not what I'm after."

Layla colored with embarrassment, an unusual thing for a warden.

"I want you to help me train them," said Tyrion. "As a warden you have a lot of experience in the arena. It will be useful to have someone else to assist me in their education."

She sniffed, "You have shown them enough. I did not understand your speech before. Why waste your time on this?"

"I don't think of it as a waste. The more prepared they are, the better they will be able to survive the matches."

"You shouldn't coddle them," insisted the warden. "Let the weak die. What remains will be those who deserve to live."

He shook his head, once again reminded of the difference in their worldviews. Training, even cruel brutal training, was an expenditure of time and energy on people who might not deserve it in her eyes. To her, that was coddling. "Pay attention, Layla. Even the meekest child out there will become a terror in the arena when I am done with them."

***

Emma Phillips had her awakening that evening, so the next morning there were eight young faces lined up for the first lesson. Of course she was nauseous and ill from the onslaught of new sensory information, but Tyrion ignored her discomfort.

He worked with them on shields first, having them practice close personal defense. Gabriel and Brigid, having had more time and some practical experience, did best, but the others improved quickly. Emma's effort was sloppy, but that was to be expected given her discomfort.

After two hours he called a stop. "Alright, that's enough for a while. Some of you were barely passable, but the rest of you were pathetic, particularly you, Abigail," he focused his attention squarely on the girl. "That brings us to our next lesson."

Stretching out his hands, he created a bright red whip between them. Most of them had seen it before in Ellentrea, although thanks to Thillmarius none of them had experienced it personally.

"B—but Emma did worse than I did!" shouted Abigail, realizing what was about to happen.

"It was Emma's first day," said Tyrion. "I expected her to do poorly." The red whip licked out and wrapped itself around the girl's ankle, causing her to fall as her body convulsed. She screamed for ten seconds before he withdrew it.

"Get up, Abby," he told her coolly. "It's time for lunch."

She looked up at him with red eyes filled with fear. Her legs shook when she stood, but she found her place quickly.

"We will start again after lunch. Until then you are free to do as you please," turning quickly, he marched away, heading for the house, for his room. It was the one place he could be alone, without eyes on him.

Shutting the door behind him, he shivered, fighting the urge to vomit. *I feel nothing.*

He hadn't expected it to be that hard. He had used the whip before, of course, but only when he was truly angry, and only on those whom he felt deserved it. His mind replayed Abby's screams in his ears.

"They need it," he told himself, but he couldn't fully make himself believe it. "They have to learn the fear. From the fear comes hate, and from that will come the desire to kill. Without that they'll hesitate, and if they hesitate they'll die."

Liar. You just want to torture them, his inner observer accused him, using Kate's voice.

"Shut up," he shouted at the air. After a moment he sat down, trying to force himself to relax. *Maybe I am going insane,* he thought. This time his inner voice sounded like his own.

Chapter 20

Twenty minutes later he reemerged. He knew he needed to eat before resuming the training. Kate was standing in the kitchen area with Piper and Blake, and her eyes found him the moment he stepped out.

"You!" she growled.

Not now, please, not now, he thought.

"Do you feel better now? Was it fun torturing that poor girl?!" barked Kate. She looked ready to launch into a full tirade as she advanced on him menacingly.

He had warned her, but the last thing he wanted just then was another confrontation. *Not Kate, I can't.* As soon as she drew close enough, his hand darted out, slipping past her head to catch her by the hair. Twisting her head around painfully, he dragged her toward the bedroom. "I'll feel better after I've taught you a lesson," he said, trying to fill his voice with more conviction than he felt.

"Let me go!" she shouted, twisting, trying to free herself.

"Not until you've learned your place, *slave,*" he replied, kicking the door open and shoving her through as he released his grip on her hair. Closing the door behind him, he leaned against it, taking a deep breath and shutting his eyes.

Kate attacked, nearly breaking her hand when she slapped his shield with all the might in her slender frame. "Ow!" she yelped loudly.

Tyrion erected a shield within the room, this one meant to prevent sound from leaving, then he released his personal defense. "Try again," he said, offering his cheek.

She eyed him suspiciously, "That shield hurts."

"I took it down…"

Before he could finish, her other hand swung out, stinging his right cheek with a hard slap. Reflexively he rolled with it, robbing the blow of some of its momentum, but it still hurt. Kate hadn't been holding back.

He caught her other wrist as she twisted her body to pummel him with her dominant hand. She had made a fist with that one, more confident now that she knew his shield was down. He then shifted his weight, partially deflecting her knee as she attempted to do even greater harm.

She glared angrily at him as he held her at bay, "I thought you were going to let me have a couple of good shots."

"No," he replied. "I brought you in here so they would think the opposite."

"But you aren't going to really hurt me?" she responded sarcastically. "Is that because you're secretly not as bad as I think, or as they think? In reality, inside that murderous, sadistic exterior, lies a gentle soul crying to be understood—is that what you want to tell me?"

It hadn't sounded so ridiculous in his own mind. Nor would he have described himself as gentle, but the heart of his message was something like that. "As cruel as I am, even I don't enjoy hurting my own children," he told her. "Nor do I like hurting you, but if you take a stand against me in public again, I won't hesitate to do whatever is necessary to maintain the illusion."

He had relaxed his hold on her wrists, and she took the opportunity to jerk her arms back before spitting on the ground at his feet, "What illusion?! It wasn't an illusion when you broke Ian's ribs. It wasn't an illusion when you nearly killed Layla, and it *certainly* wasn't an illusion when you tortured poor Abby!"

He took a step toward her, "Look, I..."

She stepped back, keeping the distance between them, "No, *you* look! I left my son—I *helped* you bring those poor kids here. I kept them from running off or killing you when you were down. I *believed* in you, at least I thought what you were doing was a necessary evil, but this—this is sick Daniel! You're sick!"

"You don't have to agree with me," he told her. "In fact, it helps that you don't, but if..."

"Why does it help?" she interrupted, her eyes darting back and forth across his features, studying his face. Sudden realization dawned on her then, "Oh. You want me to be the kind one, don't you? The mother figure to bandage their bruised pride and wounded bodies—is that it? You want me to give them some kind of false hope to keep their spirits up, so you can push them harder, so you can hurt them more!"

"What I'm doing is necessary."

"Fuck you. There's absolutely nothing necessary about this. You can train them without torturing them. You can teach them to fight. If you showed them the least amount of kindness, you'd get far more from them. You're wrong! You don't have to play evil to get what you want. You could do far better by being their mentor. Don't you understand that?"

Tyrion closed his mouth, thinking. Deep down, he wanted to agree with her. He believed in the strength of the human spirit, of cooperation, of love, and family. He had spent years considering the reasons he had survived the arena, and in the end, he had decided his greatest advantage over the slaves of the She'Har had been his upbringing. But he also knew how hard it was to kill.

His first kill had been born of desperation and luck. It was afterward, when he learned to truly hate the She'Har and their wardens, that he had found the will to destroy his opponents without hesitation, without compunction or mercy.

And he knew the teens he had brought back from Colne were far from understanding that sort of brutal reality. They hadn't been tortured the way he had. They hadn't experienced what he had, and while some of them might survive their first fights in the arena, some most definitely would not.

But he had no way to convince Kate of that.

"When we leave this room, you'll keep your eyes on the ground and give every appearance that I've done something terrible to you..."

"No. I won't cooperate with your sick plan. If you want me to look like I've been beaten, or raped, or whatever... then you're going to have to do it." Kate raised her chin defiantly.

For a moment he was tempted, but he was too heartsick to go through with it. Instead he had another idea. "You have two choices then," he told her. "You can walk out of here and show me for a fraud, and I'll double the number of painful lessons I give them. Or, you can lower your head and pretend you've been beaten, and I'll limit myself to one object lesson a day."

"Coward," was her reply. Turning, she walked to the door, but she came up short when she found herself unable to open it. "Let me out."

With a word, he released the enchantment that sealed the room.

Kate threw the door open and ran out, head down and sobbing. She seemed entirely convincing. If he had not known the truth for himself, he would never had disbelieved her performance. Even her aura was in turmoil. She was an actress down to her very soul.

"What happened Kate?" came a worried voice. "What did he do to you?" It took Tyrion a moment to identify the speaker. *David.*

The young man hurried with her, trying to soothe her as she quickly left the house.

He won't have trouble finding reasons to hate me, thought Tyrion, but it gave him no satisfaction.

The Silent Tempest

Chapter 21

The days passed in a painful parade of training and misery. Things weren't completely dark for Tyrion's children, though. They had one another. They had meals together and a growing sense of comradery. They had Kate, a reminder of home and now something of a surrogate mother, but most of all, they had a common enemy.

His lessons were hard. He gave them new tasks and then pushed them until they failed. Sometimes the failures were bad enough to be a punishment in and of themselves, such as when he drove them until their shields collapsed, and they experienced first-hand the shock of feedback. Other times the punishment came at an unexpected time, when he determined that someone had performed too poorly.

In between lessons they watched him. He could feel their eyes on him whenever he was outside of his room. Fearful glances and occasionally hate-filled stares had become the norm. As he had predicted, their fear was blossoming into a bumper crop of anger and antipathy, except for Gabriel Evans anyway.

Gabriel had taken his new authority seriously, and even though Tyrion made a point of putting him under the red whip at least once, the boy had remained serious, perhaps even loyal to him. He excelled at the exercises they were put to, and he exhibited a strong focus, but he still worried Tyrion.

"He wants to please you," said Layla as they talked one evening.

Tyrion nodded, "That's what worries me."

"He is strong, and the first matches are against younglings from the pens," reminded Layla. "Most of them are weak, he will probably win."

"Probably isn't good enough," said Tyrion. "I want to be sure that all of them make it."

"Why are you so obsessed with making sure all of them win?" she asked.

"They are my children," he told her.

The warden shrugged, "You have many, one, more or less, won't make much of a difference."

"If you had children, you might understand better."

"I have given birth twice already," she answered.

Tyrion gave her a look of surprise. "I never knew that. How long did they let you keep them?"

"An hour," she replied. "Once they've had their first-milk, they are taken to be nursed by the nameless."

"Are they still alive?"

Layla looked down, poking at the ground with her finger, "I don't know. Once they enter the pens, only the trainers know where they go, or whether they even survive to adulthood."

"I'm sorry," said Tyrion.

"Don't be," said the warden. "I disliked their fathers."

He knew that the pregnancies had been deliberate. The She'Har slave collars prevented anything like normal intercourse, to prevent their stock from breeding unsupervised. If Layla had gotten pregnant twice, it meant she had been chosen for breeding. From what Tyrion had heard, the process was unimaginative; the mother to be was simply ordered to lean over a rail and the chosen sire, frequently a warden or occasionally one of the She'Har males, would then provide his contribution.

"Were they wardens?"

"She'Har," she replied.

Tyrion left the conversation alone after that, unsure how to continue.

***

The week was almost over, and Kate stood at a table, chopping vegetables, preparing for the evening meal, even though they hadn't eaten lunch yet. Lunch was finished, except for the eating, and there was much yet to do before supper, so she had gotten started early.

The window before her showed the yard in front of the house, and she could see the teens practicing, their faces intent. The level of concentration they displayed was hard to believe, unless one knew what sort of punishment awaited anyone deemed unsatisfactory. Her gaze fell on the man circling them, and her eyes narrowed.

How did it come to be like this? she wondered.

Daniel had been the gentlest of boys, a kind soul— once. He had been her inspiration when they were young. The way he had handled young lambs, his care with the sheep, the way he had handled dogs, all of it had shown her a man possessed of uncommon compassion. That was why she had loved him, his music had only been a wonderful extra.

When he had returned the first time, after years away, he had been different, but his heart had still been there, tightly bound and well hidden. What he had endured had changed him, but despite it, his kindness had still been there. He had worn his anger like a cloak, something that had covered his weaknesses, but without consuming him.

Now it's more the opposite, his occasional kindness is like a thin veil, hiding the rage of his inner self.

A sound made her turn, Layla stood not far away. "Shouldn't you be out helping?" asked Kate.

"My turn will come after lunch," said the tall woman, moving closer. She ran her hand down Kate's hair before tracing a line down her shoulder.

Kate felt a mild thrill at the touch. "That's something then," she observed. "At least you don't torture them."

Layla shrugged, "I prefer not to get worked up. I save my energy for—other things." Leaning in, she nuzzled the smaller woman's neck, inhaling deeply.

"Stop," said Kate. "I have too much to do, and besides, I'm not in the mood."

The female warden let out an uncharacteristic whine, "but I'm *horny.*"

"I smell like onions."

The other woman wrinkled her nose but didn't give up immediately, "Onions smell much better once you simmer them over the fire."

Kate pushed her away, "I'm serious. I have other things to do. Find something else to occupy you."

Layla sighed, "But no one else will play with me."

Kate had no illusions regarding what the warden meant by 'play', but the statement gave her pause. She knew the warden had had many 'playmates' before, but she hadn't considered the possibility that the woman might continue her polyamory now that she lived under Tyrion's roof.

"Who else would you play with?" she asked curiously.

Layla pursed her lips, thinking about the question seriously. Looking out the window, she smiled, "Hmm, Gabriel looks like he would be fun to train."

Kate was a bit shocked, "He's a child."

"Tell that to his shoulders," retorted Layla. "My people don't pay attention to such things anyway."

Kate still didn't approve, "Whether they do or not, it's still wrong." She had never forgotten what her own mother had done to Daniel once, long ago. She was also already aware that she was unlikely to change the other woman's opinions on pretty much anything. Layla was stubborn, nor was she given to reflection or deeper thinking.

"It doesn't matter," said the warden. "I'm pretty sure Tyrion would kill me if I took to playing with his offspring. He's almost as strange as you are when it comes to such things."

Uncomfortable with the subject, Kate tried to shift the topic, "I thought you preferred women anyway."

"I get bored easily," said Layla. "Women usually entertain me longer."

Kate considered her marriage and then her infrequent trysts with Darla Long, and she had to admit that Layla had a point, but her experience was too limited to really judge. She hadn't felt the thrill with Seth that she had once felt for Daniel, but then she had never really fallen in love again. Darla had been lonely, and a kindred spirit in many respects; her marriage had been dull and lifeless, much like Kate's.

"Tyrion seems like he would be interesting," continued the female warden. "I like the dangerous ones, but I wonder if he prefers men."

Kate was startled, "What?"

Layla gave her a look usually reserved for slow children, "Some men prefer only men."

"Why would you think that about him?"

"Well, over the years he rarely came to Ellentrea anymore, but when he did it was exclusively to visit Garlin, and he has already told me that they were friends. Since coming here, I have yet to see him show any favor to any of the girls, or you," explained Layla. "He even turned me down when I offered myself to him," she added.

"You what?!"

"Like this," said Layla slyly, pressing her full body languidly against Kate's. She ran her nails lightly down her back.

Kate pushed her away, frowning angrily.

Layla sighed, "That's exactly what he did, no reaction at all. How did he get so many children? Did the women of your village force him?"

Exasperated, Kate picked the knife up again and turned away, "Let me do my work."

"You're so dull. I may have to start punishing the students to entertain myself," teased the warden.

Kate pointed the blade at her, "You wouldn't dare!"

Layla laughed, "Relax, I like breathing more than that."

"Huh?"

"Tyrion," explained the other woman. "He hasn't forbidden it, but I can feel it. If anyone else were to touch one of them, they wouldn't live long. I certainly wouldn't risk it, not after what happened in Sabortrea."

Kate had heard enough to know the name of the camp that Haley had been taken to, but she hadn't learned much else about it. "What happened?"

"He killed two of the wardens there. The story is that he attacked one of them in the presence of the She'Har. They should have killed him for that, but his owner paid to preserve him, and then paid to buy the ones he wanted to kill," said Layla.

He really is going insane, thought Kate. "What set him off?"

Layla shrugged, "Who knows? They say he came across them taking favors from the girl."

"From Haley?" asked Kate.

"If that is what they called her. I have never understood your custom for giving names to unblooded children," said the warden.

Kate could understand his reaction, even if it seemed alien to Layla. Every day was making it plainer to her just how different the thinking of the people who lived among the She'Har was. Things that should be abominations to them were commonplace, while things that should be normal were frowned upon.

She was questioning her perspective of Daniel when the screaming started. Glancing out the window she could see David on the ground, writhing in pain. Daniel stood above him, holding the red whip in one hand, while his face possessed the coldest, most impassive expression that she had ever seen.

Kate's hand slipped, nearly taking off the end of her finger. She stared at the blood welling from a shallow cut, but then Layla lifted it, putting it into her mouth.

"Mmm," said the female warden. "You should let me fix this for you."

She tried to jerk her hand back, but Layla held it tightly. Withdrawing the finger she took her other hand and traced the cut, sealing the skin so that only a small silver scar remained.

From the yard David's scream trailed off, ending in a soft whimper. His punishment was finished. Kate pulled again, and this time Layla released her hand.

"I can't understand how that *doesn't* bother you," she noted.

"In Ellentrea such sounds are as common as birdsong in the forest."

Chapter 22

"Stay here," said Tyrion as Kate automatically started to follow them.

"I want to see this," she responded.

He shook his head, "No, you don't."

He was standing next to Byovar. The eight teens whose powers had already manifested stood behind him. Today was the day they would be blooded.

"I would like to come as well," put in Layla.

Tyrion glanced at her. "You have to stay here…," his eyes passed over Kate briefly, "…to keep an eye on things."

Kate frowned, "So I need a babysitter now?"

"I just want to be sure no one disturbs things around here. The She'Har have very loose concepts when it comes to property."

"They seem to have slavery down to a fine art," she retorted.

He nodded, "Slavery yes, livestock yes, but inanimate objects are a different matter. They don't really understand the owning of 'things' as well as they do people."

"Everyone will be at the arena today," observed Byovar. "No one will molest your stone building."

"I am bored. Let us come see the fights," said Layla.

Kate nodded in agreement.

Tyrion shook his head, "Nameless servants aren't allowed to attend…"

"You can bring whoever you wish, Tyrion," corrected the lore-warden.

"I'm coming," said Kate before leaning in to whisper in his ear. "Unless you want to discipline me here and now, and I don't think you're up for that, are you?"

"Very well," he relented. "It will do you good to learn the truth." Inwardly he seethed at her impertinence, but once again he found himself reluctant to call her bluff.

An hour later they were at the Ellentrea arena, a place that Tyrion knew intimately since the majority of his matches had been there. Thillmarius greeted them with a smile.

"The holding cells for your participants are over here," he said genially.

"I would prefer to let them watch," answered Tyrion.

"I'm afraid that's against the rules," replied Thillmarius. "It gives the watchers a potential advantage."

Tyrion dipped his head in acknowledgement. He had known that was the most likely response, but he still had hoped it wasn't something set in stone. He led them over to the wooden outcroppings that rose from the earth near the edge of the arena. Each one was a knobby part of the root from one of the neighboring god trees. They each contained a small room and a door. The walls were covered with a spellweave that blocked magesight.

Gesturing at them, he ushered each of his eight children who were to fight into a room of their own. He stopped then.

"What of the others? Their powers have not awakened yet. Will they be permitted to watch?" he asked, indicating his remaining children and Kate.

Thillmarius smiled again, "The rules only state that participants may not watch. Nameless without ability are not regulated. If they are with you, then they may observe."

Tyrion nodded. Much of what happened in the arena would be invisible to them without magesight, but they would see enough to understand. He wasn't sure whether it would help or hurt them in the future, though. Seeing a fight to the death might help them find their resolve, or it could fill them with a paralyzing dread of the future. He hoped it would be the former.

The She'Har who was overseeing the arena came over, a male by the name of Koralltis. He spoke directly to Tyrion, something he had never done previously, "You have eight to be blooded today, which of them is your strongest?"

He hadn't expected that question, or even to be spoken to. Koralltis was treating him as an equal, or at least as a trainer. Still, he wasn't sure of the purpose of the question, and he glanced at Byovar for guidance. The Illeniel lore-warden simply shrugged.

Thinking for a moment, he considered his reply. He could easily choose either Brigid or Gabriel, both had shown more progress than the others, and both were strong. Hesitating for only a second, he pointed to the cell which contained Gabriel, "That one."

Koralltis nodded, "Then that will be the first of them."

Tyrion felt a moment of relief. His paranoia had been aroused by the question. If it had only been to choose the first to enter the arena, then he could relax a bit.

A half an hour passed while the other trainers brought their nameless combatants in and settled each within their private cells. Tyrion watched the process with interest. In the past he had been kept within a cell himself, unable to observe. He was surprised when he saw Dalleth bring his nameless in, for one of them was Haley, who wasn't nameless at all, she was now known to the She'Har as Gravenna.

"Why is she here?" he asked Thillmarius. "I thought these were only going to be first-blood fights."

The Prathion gave him a curious look, "I do not know either. This is the first I have heard of her being brought today. Koralltis must have something interesting in mind."

Tyrion felt a stone settle in his stomach. 'Interesting' for the She'Har usually meant bloody.

Koralltis began projecting his voice, calling the trainers to bring out their first entrants. Tyrion's name was one of them. He walked over and touched the door to Gabriel's cell.

"It's time, boy."

Gabriel gave him a brave grin, "I know, old man."

His tone was entirely too familiar. "Are you angry?" he asked.

"Nope."

He glared at the young man. "You need to be. This isn't a joke. Look at me!"

Gabriel did, but his face was unrepentant, "I know what you're trying to do, but it's alright. I'll do what I have to do. I don't have to hate you to do that."

"You need your anger, boy. Find it and chain it. Keep it ready but your mind clear. Fight calm and when the moment comes, let the anger help you make the choice. Hesitation will get you killed," he said seriously as they walked to the edge.

"Relax, Father," said the boy. "I'm going to make you proud."

The words stunned Tyrion. He stood watching the young man's broad back as he walked onto the dry earth of the arena. *I'm not your father. I don't deserve that name. I'm just the man who brought you here to suffer. Your father is the man who loved you, who raised you, not me.*

Never me.

Half a minute later the starting chime sounded, and the lights changed. It had begun.

Gabriel was facing a boy from the Gaelyn Grove, a skinny, feral looking kid who was probably half his weight. Not that size mattered much, it was aythar that made the biggest difference, and Gabriel outshone his opponent by a large amount in that regard.

Focus on your shield, thought Tyrion. *Wait for him to make a mistake.*

The match began with a burst of activity. The Gaelyn boy went from still to moving in an instant. He sent a powerful bolt of force at Gabriel even as he ran to one side.

Ignore it, he's trying to distract you so he can...

The attack was strong enough to shake Gabriel, even though it didn't come close to penetrating his defense. Before Tyrion's son could refocus his attention on his opponent, the Gaelyn mage had transformed, taking the shape of a large falcon.

Tyrion cursed. The Gaelyn mage might be unblooded, but he was far from average. Few of them at that age could handle a bird form, but those that could were a lot more trouble. The Gaelyn boy would have unparalleled mobility now, and Gabriel had missed his best chance to take out his opponent, while he was shifting.

Gabriel began sending sharp, powerful bursts of force at the bird, but none of them came close to hitting.

Don't waste your strength, thought Tyrion. *That's what he wants.*

Kate put a hand on his arm, "What's happening?" From her perspective all she had seen was Gabriel acting oddly while his foe changed into a bird.

"The other boy is pretty skilled," said Tyrion tensely. "If I had fought one like him my first time, I probably wouldn't have survived."

She watched his features, reading the worry there. The cold impassive face was gone, replaced by that of a man riddled with anxiety, a man watching his child fight for his life. *Just when I think he's gone, beyond hope, I see this,* she thought. She hesitated a moment and then reached out, putting her hand over his. "He'll be fine. You didn't have anyone to teach you. He did."

The warmth of her hand surprised him, and Tyrion found himself blinking as he struggled to contain his emotions. The constant tension of the past week, along with his self-imposed isolation, had left him tired. His soul felt tattered and frayed, as though it might come apart, and the warmth radiating from her hand seemed to travel through him, eating away at his careful composure.

I feel nothi... He stopped in mid-thought, struggling with himself. Finally, he let himself relax and turned his hand over, enclosing her small fingers with his own.

He squeezed it tightly as the fight continued. Gabriel's attacks were growing wilder, less focused and noticeably weaker, even his shield was beginning to grow thin. The Gaelyn mage circled him at a distance, conserving his aythar, waiting for the moment his enemy would be vulnerable.

Tyrion's eyes narrowed. Even fighting wastefully, Gabriel shouldn't have been that weak. The boy had more strength than that. Then he understood.

Gabriel's shield flickered, and he began to run, until the earth rose in front of his feet, tripping him.

Kate's gasp was audible. "You have to do something, Daniel."

"I can't," he told her. "If I try to intervene they'll kill me, the boy, and who knows what would happen to the rest of you."

"But he's losing…"

"No," said Tyrion. "He knows to keep a firm grip on the ground around him. I beat that into them. He let that happen; watch what he does next."

The falcon stooped, diving at speed toward his fallen opponent. As he did, the he focused his aythar, forming it into an even more powerful shield and encasing his talons in wicked blades of force. He wasn't going to waste his strength on ranged attacks. He didn't have the aythar to waste on that. He would seize the opportunity, while his foe was tired, while he was down, and he would take the kill in one devastating attack.

Gabriel's aythar flared brightly a second before the Gaelyn mage struck, too late for his opponent to change course. His shield expanded powerfully, forming a wedge that sent the falcon to one side even as it ripped through part of it with its reinforced talons.

The bird landed awkwardly, off balance from the unexpected resistance, and then he caught Gabriel's return strike at close range, unable to dodge. Tyrion's son hit the falcon with a blow that landed like a battering ram, with predictable results.

The falcon's shield shattered, and the Gaelyn mage staggered, falling to the ground nearly senseless from the feedback.

Gabriel loomed over him.

Now! Don't waste time. Some of them recover more quickly than you'd expect. Tyrion found himself clenching his jaw.

A long pause ensued. Gabriel had gathered his will, but he held back, staring intently at the bird on the ground. It beat its wings, trying to regain its balance, to take flight, but it was still too uncoordinated to get off the ground.

Just when Tyrion thought he might have waited too long, the boy released a loud yell and sent a flat plane of aythar slicing downward. It neatly bisected the avian body, and the Gaelyn mage began to thrash about, flinging droplets of blood in every direction. The lower half stopped moving within seconds, but the upper half took almost a full minute before it sagged to the ground.

A wing flapped once more, and then it went still.

Chapter 22

The arena lights changed. The match was over. Gabriel stared down at his broken foe, trying to comprehend what he had done.

"You can go collect your charge now," said Thillmarius, nudging Tyrion.

Glancing at Kate, he saw that her eyes were wet. He gave her a soft pat on one shoulder. He remembered the first time he had killed a man, a warden who had been suffocating her. She had calmly tried to dash the man's brains out afterward, while he was helpless, but now she seemed softer, more vulnerable.

"It was just a chicken," he told her, referencing their conversation from that day.

"No," she said, shaking her head. "No, Daniel, that wasn't a chicken. That was a child—a poor, lost, motherless child." Unlike, fifteen years before, she was no longer a child herself. She was a woman, and a mother.

He hated the look on her face. It reminded him of everything he had given up, of who he had once been. His chest tightened. Stepping away he went to bring Gabriel back.

There are no winners in the arena…, he observed silently *…only the living and the dead. The only choice given is the choice of what to lose, your life or your conscience.*

Brigid Tolburn was next. Tyrion opened her door, and for a moment he was caught by her baleful gaze. Ice blue eyes framed by hair as black as his own; they burned into him with a malevolent resolve. She looked away quickly, knowing better than to challenge him, but he had already seen it. It filled him with conflicting emotions, of course the sting was only to be expected when you knew your child hated you, but he also felt relief.

She's ready to do someone a terrible harm.

"Remember what I taught you," he said as they walked to the edge.

Brigid nodded but didn't speak.

"Whoever you face, just imagine it's me," he told her. "Give them what you've been wanting to give me, and you'll do fine; just keep your head until the fight is almost won." He put a hand on her shoulder to propel her forward, but she flinched away at his touch.

She darted a glance at him from eyes shadowed by her hair, and he could see a touch of fear on her face.

"Win this, Brigid," he encouraged. "Win this and I won't have to punish you again."

A faint nod and she turned away, marching to face her opponent, another male, this time from the Centyr Grove. As the lights changed and the chime sounded she began running directly for him, wasting no time.

The boy had begun summoning a spellbeast from the moment the lights had changed, but he stopped and began running as well when he saw her charging toward him. Unable to focus, he ran full tilt, attempting to gain some distance, but Brigid never gave him a chance to collect his wits or focus.

She kept after him like a mad dog, her wild hair flying behind her. She was single minded in her determination to reach him, and despite his longer legs he failed to outpace her. He was obviously malnourished, while Brigid's limbs were strong and fresh with the power of youth. He ducked and dodged, changing course rapidly, but it only made the distance between them shorter.

At twenty feet she leveled a blast at his feet that sent him tumbling, and then she was on him. At close range she ignored his desperate attacks, and then she used her aythar to drive him into the ground, smashing his shield near instantly.

"Burn," said Brigid, with horrific results.

Kate turned her head, unable to watch, but Tyrion never looked away, even as the Centyr boy smoked and screamed.

Brigid walked back toward them even before the lights changed. She already knew she had won. When the shield around the arena went down, she walked past Tyrion, giving him a cold stare. Her lips moved, and she silently mouthed a word as she passed him, 'burn'.

He didn't reply, gracing her instead with a tight lipped look of approval and a nod. "She did well," he said to Kate.

"That was awful," she responded. "Couldn't she have chosen something less painful?"

Layla had moved closer, standing on the other side of Tyrion now. "There is no weakness in that one," she stated calmly. "You must be proud. We should celebrate tonight." The warden leaned in, letting her hand rest lightly on his shoulder. There was no mistaking what she meant by 'celebrate'.

Tyrion didn't comment, instead he moved from between the two women, going to fetch the next one to enter the arena.

Kate looked from Layla to Daniel, and quietly she was relieved. She had expected the female warden to be enthused by the victory, but it made her happier to see that he didn't revel in death in the same manner.

Jack was next, his body tense and anxious as he stepped into the arena. Having been in the cell, he hadn't seen either of the previous fights, but the sound of the crowd had made him nervous. He walked across the dry earth and stared at his opponent, a light haired girl from the Prathion Grove.

It reminded Tyrion of his first fight in the arena. He had faced a young redheaded girl then, but without understanding the rules, or knowing how to shield himself, he had nearly died. In the end he had gotten lucky and managed to choke the girl to death just before his own imminent demise. It was the healing skills of the She'Har that had kept him alive.

Jack had none of those disadvantages, though. While he was one of the newer ones to gain his mage abilities, he had been taught to shield himself, how to attack, and he had been drilled on the absolute rule of death in the arena: only one could emerge alive.

This girl was a bit stronger than the one Tyrion had faced however, and Jack was still a little unsure of himself when it came to trusting his magesight or using his other abilities. He was still stronger than his opponent in terms of absolute aythar, but of Tyrion's offspring he was the weakest so far.

The Prathion mage vanished as soon as the chime sounded.

Jack spun, looking behind himself and nearly lost his focus on his shield.

Damnitt, thought Tyrion. *He doesn't trust his senses, he's still relying on his eyes first. Even worse,*

Chapter 22

he's confused the Mordan and the Prathions. The boy had obviously thought the girl had teleported.

The girl reappeared in a new location, but a flicker in her aythar told Tyrion that all was not what it appeared to be. Even he couldn't be certain, but he would have guessed that she had gone invisible again, leaving an illusion of herself behind to throw off her opponent.

When the Prathion mage didn't move, Jack leveled a potent blast in her direction. Naturally it passed through her illusion without affecting it in the slightest. Jack gaped at it, unsure what to do next.

Move boy! screamed Tyrion mentally, wishing he could project himself to the teen. *She can't see you while she's invisible, but if you stay in one spot she'll ambush you for certain.*

"He was smarter than this during the training," noted Layla clinically, "but some can't keep their wits once the battle-fear strikes them."

"It doesn't look like anything is happening," complained Kate. To her eyes the only events to occur had been the girl's vanishing and sudden reappearance.

"The boy is about to die," announced Layla.

The girl appeared again, this time closer. As before, she vanished immediately after, leaving behind a second illusion of herself. Once again Jack took the bait, sending a powerful attack at her illusory self. Still confused, he spent his time looking back and forth between the two visible representations of his enemy.

"Damn his stupid ass!" swore Tyrion. "She's close now, and he still hasn't moved."

Layla shook her head, "Why doesn't he use that clever ground trick you taught them, to detect her feet against the ground?"

"He's forgotten," said Tyrion. "He's forgotten everything."

The next time the girl appeared, it was in four places, each of them in close proximity to Jack. One image appeared a split second before the others, focusing his attention in that direction. He sent a desperate attack in that direction, while letting his concentration on his own defense lapse slightly. His shield weakened just as the other three images appeared, one on either side of him and one directly behind.

Whipping to one side, he sent a second attack at the one on his right.

The Prathion mage was to his left, and her attack came at close range, a focused lance of power that tore through his neglected shield and went completely through his chest. A second and third attack struck before he could finish falling to the ground.

Jack was dead.

"That girl has promise," said Layla admiringly, but Tyrion wasn't listening. His world had narrowed, his vision spiraling into a small tunnel. All he could see was Jack's broken body lying on the dry earth.

Kate looked at him in alarm, she was upset as well, but she could feel a strange humming beside her. Staring at Daniel, she could see the air shimmering around him, like heat waves seen from a distance. Layla had backed away a step or two, alarmed by whatever her magesight was showing her.

Tyrion felt as though he was being smothered; he couldn't seem to draw enough air into his lungs. His heart was pounding out a furious rhythm in his chest. Death had never affected him like this before. Jack had been ill-suited to the arena, a sensitive child, and Tyrion had been reluctant to treat him as harshly as the others.

This is my fault.

Byovar was there now, saying something to him, but he couldn't seem to hear the words. Looking up, the sky was a deep blue, uncluttered by clouds. He could feel it calling to him. There was no pain there, only emptiness, a vast airy space devoid of the suffering that was inflicted on those who walked the earth.

Kate touched his arm again, and he looked into her eyes. She was suffering too, but there was more than just that. He could see worry there, an abiding concern, for him. Unlike Layla, unlike Lyralliantha, or any of the others, she could understand the turmoil in his heart.

Kate was afraid, not merely *of him,* but also *for him.*

Concentrating, he slowed his breathing, bringing his attention back to the here and now. *I feel nothing,* he told himself.

"I'm sorry, Byovar," he responded to the She'Har lore-warden. "I was lost in thought. Could you say that again?"

"Koralltis is calling for the next one, Tyrion," said the She'Har.

"Of course," he replied, automatically moving toward the holding cells. *Next will be Sarah…*

The Silent Tempest

Chapter 23

Sarah's fight went smoothly, as did David's, Abby's, Ryan's, and finally Emma's. Each of them faced their opponents and dispatched them without major incident, their training and superior strength being more than enough to make up for the random surprises they encountered.

With each fight, Tyrion found himself holding his breath. With each victory his dread increased. He knew they couldn't all win. The odds against that seemed greater with each successful kill. Surely one of them would make a mistake, it was impossible that he would escape the day without losing another one.

When Emma cut the head from her opponent, he felt as though a weight had been lifted from him. It was over. They had made it. No more of his children would die that day. With their first traumatic kills behind them, they would be even stronger in the future. Another week would see them better, more experienced, and more importantly, ready to kill.

They were past the most dangerous part of their arena careers, the uncertainty of the first fight.

Koralltis was back in the center of the arena, projecting his voice with magic and announcing the next fight, but Tyrion was hardly listening—until he heard the words, 'Gravenna Mordan'. That was Haley's new name.

The master of the arena was looking toward him now, calling for the Illeniel contestant to step forward.

Confused, Tyrion sought help from Thillmarius, "What did he just say? We've already finished our fights for the day."

"He said there would be an extra fight today. He has arranged an extra fight with the Mordan Grove—with one of your newly blooded fighters," the Prathion trainer informed him.

He gaped at Thillmarius, "That's hardly fair. She's had five or six fights now, while mine have barely recovered from their first kills." *And no matter what happens, I will lose another child.*

Byovar intervened, "I should have explained better before we arrived. The feeling is that since you have so many of the newly prized children from Colne, and because you have been training them personally, that Mordan should be given the opportunity to test one of them before your position of strength has been fully solidified."

"You mean they want a free kill," said Tyrion bitterly.

"That is far from certain, Tyrion," countered Byovar. "Your offspring are powerful, and your training has proven more effective than anyone thought possible. No one believed that so many of your entrants would survive their first-blood fights."

His temper was threatening to overwhelm his self-control. Scanning his immediate vicinity, he found himself unconsciously planning his killing spree, *Thillmarius first, then Koralltis. Byovar could wait, unless he tried to intervene. The krytek would appear soon after, unless I could create another windstorm like the last one. Maybe I wouldn't stop this time—how big would it become?*

Chapter 23

He closed his eyes, trying to clear his mind. Those thoughts weren't productive. No storm would be big enough to cleanse the world completely, and nothing else would satisfy him. He would only be killing the people he cared about, and the She'Har would remain. They could recover from any damage that didn't completely annihilate them.

"Should I bring him out, Tyrion? They are growing impatient," said Byovar, sounding concerned.

Not Gabriel, he thought, *he's the only one who doesn't really hate me.* He didn't think the boy could handle Haley either, nor was he sure he wanted him to. *She's almost like a sister to me, aside from being my daughter.*

Brigid was the best choice, if he wanted a chance to end this tragedy today, but he had already named Gabriel earlier. *And she's Kate's sister—how would she feel if I sent her only sister out and she died?* He looked at Kate, who was looking back with puzzlement in her eyes. She couldn't understand Erollith so she had no idea yet what decision he was considering.

Whoever he sent was likely to lose, but Brigid had the best chance. He knew that from watching the previous fights. "Send Br—no, get Gabriel," he answered, changing his mind. He couldn't do it, he couldn't send Kate's sister.

"What's happening?" asked Kate as Byovar walked to the holding cells.

"They're forcing an additional fight on me," he told her. "Haley against one of mine."

"But they're related," she protested. "They can't make siblings fight one another, surely?"

"The She'Har don't give a damn about us, or our relations," he replied.

Gabriel was passing by then, his features full of questions.

"Gabriel, they want you to fight Haley," said Tyrion, rushing to stay abreast of him. "Don't hesitate. I know it's hard, but she's been doing this for weeks. If you don't win, this will repeat itself, and she'll be forced to fight the others, one by one."

Although Haley had grown up in the countryside outside of town, she and Gabriel had known each other well enough, just as everyone did in the small community that revolved around Colne. The boy looked at Tyrion in a panic, "Haley? I can't fight her! We're friends. She's my sister!"

"No mercy, Gabriel. Kill her and end this. Do it for the others if you can't do it for yourself," said Tyrion, desperation filling his voice with urgency. There was no time to say anything else.

Gabriel stepped into the arena and looked across the field as he marched to his starting position. Haley stood in her place already, a look of disbelief on her features to match Gabriel's.

She looked behind her, asking questions of Dalleth. It was too far for them to hear what she said, but Gabriel could guess. She wanted to know why she was being forced to fight him. Haley was shaking her head, arguing with the answers she was given, when the chime sounded, and the lights changed.

Gabriel walked forward, moving slowly. He still hadn't raised a shield. His hands were out to his sides, palms forward and open, the universal sign of peaceful intentions. Haley was staring back at him with a horrified look on her face. She had a shield around herself, but she made no move to attack. She watched him approach in silence.

"What is he doing?!" said Layla, looking to Tyrion for answers. "She could kill him with a thought!"

Tyrion watched, unable to look away. "He's going to try to talk to her."

"But why?" asked Layla.

"Because he didn't grow up in the pens," he replied, "because he's still human. He's not like you…" *Or me.*

Kate was holding onto his arm, her fingers digging into his flesh painfully.

Layla tsk'ed in disapproval, "He certainly isn't like me. I prefer breathing."

On the field Gabriel was still approaching Haley slowly, they were a mere ten feet apart now, and tears were streaming down her face.

"We don't have to do this, Haley. They can't force us if we both refuse to fight," he told her sincerely.

She tried to answer, but her voice was thick with tears. It took several tries before she could get the words out, "You don't understand, Gabe. You don't understand at all."

"No," he argued, "*They* don't understand. We can make our own choices."

"I'm going to kill you, Gabe! Don't *you* get it? That's the only way out of here!" she yelled. "Why don't you have your shield up!?"

He watched her sadly, wishing he could convince her, but even he could see the resolve in her eyes. Gabriel lowered his head in acceptance. "Fine, we can start over, but I don't want to do this Haley. This wasn't my choice. I never wanted to hurt you." Turning, he started to walk away, to return to his starting position.

Haley's aythar surged violently, and a scything plane of deadly force shot forth, bisecting Gabriel's body diagonally, from shoulder to hip. He barely had a chance to register the attack before he was dead.

"Why didn't you have your shield up!?" she screamed hoarsely. "Why?! I told you I was going to kill you! Why?!" Haley's body sagged, and she fell to her knees still crying.

The crowed was silent. None of the She'Har had expected such a sudden ending, such an uncontested fight.

Thillmarius was as surprised as the rest. "I've never seen anything like that before. That was unprecedented. Why didn't he defend himself?"

"Because he wasn't a savage," ground out Tyrion. "He wasn't like your people."

Kate was still in shock. "She killed him while his back was turned," she mumbled.

She made the same choice I would have, thought Tyrion. *She knew the fight was inevitable, and she decided to end it right then and save herself the risk of a real battle.*

***

The return to Albamarl was a somber walk. Tyrion's students were silent. He knew from experience how traumatic the first kill could be. They were still fresh from that, along with the fact that they were walking back with two fewer than had started out.

Even Brigid, who had seemed the best adjusted to the situation, now seemed quiet and withdrawn. Her anger had faded, leaving an empty regret as she remembered the boy she had burned.

It was Sarah who spoke first, "What happened to Gabe and Jack?"

"Jack panicked, stopped thinking, and pretty soon after that stopped breathing," said Tyrion. "Gabriel did well on his first fight, but he wasn't prepared for the second one."

"He fought twice?" she asked.

Tyrion worried that telling them about Haley would demoralize them, but he couldn't hide the fact forever. One of them would have to face her, possibly more than one of them, until someone managed to kill her. There was no escaping that fact. "They wanted a special match, between him and Haley. He tried to talk, didn't defend himself. She killed him."

Brigid looked up, her interest piqued when she heard Haley's name. The two girls had been neighbors; much like Tyrion and Seth had once been, since Brigid had been raised by Seth's father and Kate's mother, while Haley had grown up with Tyrion's parents. "Was she—how did she look?" asked the dark hair girl.

He stopped, forcing everyone to come up short. "She looked very well, Brigid, until she saw Gabriel walk into the arena. She got pretty upset then. She screamed, she cried, and she cut him into two very dead pieces when he failed to take her seriously."

The look on her face was heartbreaking. Gone was the sullen malevolence that had marked her gaze earlier, replaced by the desperate look of a girl who needed some small hope to cling to. "But she didn't want to do it, right? They made her."

"They made her, and Gabriel is just as dead either way. Who do you think is next?"

Brigid was shaking her head, unable to accept what she was hearing, "No. No, no, no…" She started to back away, but Tyrion's hand darted out, catching her long black hair, pulling her to a halt.

"Who else do you think can do it, Brigid?" he asked her harshly, pointing at the others. "Do you think David can? He nearly pissed himself today. What about Emma? Do you think she has what it takes?" Twisting her head around, he brought her face close to his own. "You're their only hope. You're the strongest. You're the best killer among them. If you can't do it, she'll kill all of them, one by one. Is that what you want?"

"No! Let me go!" she shouted, pulling at his hand, trying to get him to release her hair. "I'm not going to do it."

"Then you've got two choices." Tyrion drew the razor sharp wooden sword from his belt, handing it to her before letting her go. "You can shove that through your heart, or you can let her do it for you.

She stared down at the deadly blade made from Eilen'tyral, the weapon-wood of the god-trees.

Tyrion's tone shifted then, becoming softer. "I wish I could do it, Brigid, but they won't let me. I want to protect you, I want to protect them. I even want to protect Haley, but I can't. The only one who can save you, who can save the others, is *you*. It's your choice." He turned then, and walked away, heading for the deeper parts of the Illeniel Grove.

"Where are you going?" called Layla.

"To think," he responded. "Take them back to Albamarl. I'll be there later."

He walked then, wandering without purpose until he found himself at the base of the tree that Lyralliantha lived in. She still hadn't returned, but it was the most familiar place in the grove to him. Walking up the trunk of the mighty tree he ascended until he found her living platform.

Once there he sat, pondering his life; the choices that had led him there, the mistakes that had created his misery. He could find no meaning in any of it. His only conclusion was that whatever happened, much of it was his own fault.

I should have died in the arena.

Death seemed to be the only escape available. He thought of the weapon he had given Brigid, and then he thought of the collar around his neck, the symbol of his slavery.

He wanted freedom, he wanted death, and he knew of one way that was guaranteed to provide one or the other. *They said I could have it removed.* He knew where to cut it now, or he thought he did. If he was wrong, he wouldn't live long enough to regret his mistake.

Both of his index fingers were tattooed, and a word brought the magic to life, razor sharp enchanted blades appearing around them. He rarely used the finger blades, but he wanted precision. *There are two places that must be severed simultaneously, or the collar's destruction will kill me,* he thought silently. One region of the spellweave was responsible for the boiling of the blood, the other would stop the heart, and both needed to be cut at the same time.

Unless there's a third trap in the spellweave, he reminded himself. He had intended to test that theory before ever trying it on himself, but he no longer cared. If he was wrong it would be as much a blessing as a mistake.

Lifting his hands to his neck, he positioned the two blades carefully with his magesight before letting out a slow breath, and then he cut the spellweave.

The collar fell apart, disintegrating as the minuscule She'Har symbols unraveled. Tyrion continued to breathe. "Damnitt." He had hoped he was wrong.

He slept for a time after that, lulled by the peaceful sound of the wind through the trees. After he woke he just lay there, letting his mind remain blank. He could almost imagine the terrible events of the morning hadn't happened.

But they had.

His face tensed, his eyes clenching as he tried to shut out the memory of Haley's face as she slew her half-brother. Restless now, he stood and began to descend the tree, keeping his body in motion to help prevent his mind from returning to that awful moment.

From there he made his way back to Albamarl, his magesight scanning the terrain ahead of him. Any number of She'Har made note of him as he passed quietly through the trees, but none approached him. They could see he wore no collar, but that rule no longer applied to him. Just a few weeks before it would have been a death sentence for him to walk uncollared through one of the She'Har groves.

Chapter 23

When he drew closer to his home he took note of the children. They were gathered in small groups, talking in quiet whispers, seeking comfort in each other's company, but neither Kate nor Layla were in evidence.

That meant they were alone inside the house, which was designed to block magesight.

It's been several hours, they've calmed down now, but Kate's just witnessed a number of violent events. He knew exactly what such events did to people, once the adrenaline wore off. He had thought he was beyond jealousy, but the thought of the two of them together made him angry.

He ignored the teens and went through the front door, closing it loudly behind him. The noise would surely alert them to his return. Even inside he couldn't sense them, which meant they were in the second bedroom. It had been finished over the course of the past week, and the two women had taken to sleeping there.

Tyrion stopped in the hall, wondering if they would come out. He had intended to go to his own room, but now he found himself irritated and indecisive. A strange longing filled him, but he wasn't sure what he wanted. He was alone. He was angry.

No one emerged from the other room. Obviously they were too busy to care or take note of his return. He knocked on the door. He could hear them scrambling within, startled by the sound.

Kate opened the door a moment later, leaning out, cheeks flushed with embarrassment. "I didn't realize you were back," she said.

Their eyes met, and he couldn't remember what he had meant to say. It seemed as if he was staring at her across an impossible gulf, a distance that could never be crossed. Kate might as well be back in Colne. He stood still, transfixed.

She watched his features, her gaze moving from one eye to the other. Kate could see that he was in turmoil. *No, he's worse than that.* She wondered if he was about to break down. Her heart leapt into her throat. She wanted to talk to him, to help him. Giving in to Layla's desires had been a mistake, borne of her own fear and desperate need for companionship. She should have waited.

Layla was waiting, she could feel the other woman's impatience. "Listen, Daniel, this isn't a good time. If you want to talk later…"

His face flinched, and his eyes hardened, "I don't want to talk."

Kate looked down, "I'm sorry. I know this is awkward. What happened today…"

"I came to fetch Layla," he interrupted. "I need her help with something."

She looked up at him, her green eyes filled with surprise, "But…"

Kate paused then, for Layla's hand was on her shoulder. She looked over the redhead's shoulder with an impish grin. She had no embarrassment over what she had been doing. "What do you need, my lord?"

"I need a little of your time," he replied, his face expressionless.

Her attention fell to his throat, and the warden's eyes widened, "What happened to your collar?"

"That's what I'd like to discuss with you."

Serious now, she looked back into the room, "Let me get my clothes." Being a warden, she almost never went out without wearing the symbols of her status, unlike nearly everyone else in the small camp who were required to be without clothes.

"You won't need them," he informed her. "Come with me."

Her face took on a sly expression, "Certainly."

He walked her across the hall and ushered her into his room, leaving Kate staring after him with a curious countenance. She was still trying to figure out what had just happened.

Closing the door behind himself, he muttered a word to seal the room, but he didn't bother to soundproof it.

"Did they remove your collar?" asked Layla immediately.

"No, I took it off myself," he told her, letting his eyes range down her body. Layla was tall and muscular, covered in scars, but lovely despite it. He could see why Garlin had favored her for so long.

She followed his eyes, sensing the change in his intentions from the day before. "What did you wish from me, *my lord?*" Her head was tilted slightly down, allowing her to look up at him as she spoke in a slow voice. She put special emphasis on the honorific.

"I think you're well aware of that already," he said as he removed his leather jerkin, dumping it on the floor before piling his shirt on top of it. He wasted no time unbuckling his belt. It had been months, and now that he had resolved himself, he found his desire driving him.

The Silent Tempest

Layla stepped close, kissing his neck and moving her lips upward to whisper in his ear, "What would you like me to do first?"

A grin spread across his face as he realized he was no longer bound by the traditional restrictions of the slave collar. In Ellentrea, sexual participants of opposite genders had to be careful, making certain to never bring the agencies of reproduction into direct contact. Experience and frequent practice had made them experts at alternate methods of pleasing themselves, but that was no longer necessary here.

Pushing her slightly away, he held her throat between his hands. With a word he activated the enchanted blades in his index fingers, "Hold very still."

Layla's eyes were wide with panic now, though she held perfectly still, "What are you doing?!"

With a moment's concentration he found the correct spots, and then his fingers dipped inward, slashing the spellwoven collar apart. The female warden yelped slightly, but then looked at him with astonishment when she failed to die. After she finally relaxed and caught her breath, she looked at him, "Was that alright to do? I am not allowed to go without a collar."

"You'll stay inside until Lyralliantha returns to give you a new one," he told her. He took the opportunity to sit down on the edge of the bed, removing his trousers.

Layla approached hesitantly, almost shyly.

"What's wrong?" he asked.

"I feel naked—without the collar," she told him.

She meant it in a different way, though. She was referring to the lack of imposed restrictions. She was

292

uncertain now how to proceed. The only times she had had normal intercourse were the two times she had been bred, and neither had been pleasant.

Tyrion chuckled, "Are you nervous, Layla? How unusual. There's nothing to be afraid of. Let me show you." Reaching up, he drew her down onto the bed with him, and then he let his hands roam while his lips met hers. "I see Kate's already warmed you up."

She nodded, moaning as they kissed.

"That's good. I didn't think I could restrain myself for long."

The first time was brief, and she screamed in fear as he began, a lifetime of conditioning was hard to ignore, but after that she relaxed. The second time was much more prolonged. He took his time, making sure to bring her to a loud and raucous conclusion.

He hoped Kate was paying attention.

The Silent Tempest

Chapter 24

The next morning things returned to normal. He felt better, more relaxed than he had since bringing his children back from Colne. Layla had slept beside him, but he had discovered that once the more active part of their evening was over she had had no interest in cuddling. In fact, she seemed positively repulsed by the thought.

He had forced the issue at first, she was his slave after all, but after several minutes of holding a tense and obviously uncomfortable woman, he had relented. Spooning with someone who clearly didn't want the attention felt like more of a violation than almost anything he had done in the past.

Layla was more than happy to repeat their performance that morning, eager in fact. She had no trouble with physical contact during sex, it was touching outside of that that bothered her.

Tyrion was strangely reluctant, though.

"What's the matter?" asked Layla, encouraging him in a rather direct fashion. "You obviously want to." She squeezed him once more.

"I need to get them started early," he told her. "In another week they have to fight again."

She stroked him again, using a lighter touch. "It can wait a few minutes. Would you change your mind if I asked Kate for permission?"

"What?!"

"Do you think I don't know exactly why you came to our room yesterday?" she replied. "You wanted your redhead, but for some reason you couldn't make yourself order her in here."

"That's ridiculous, she and I have never…" he paused before changing tactics. "If you thought that, why didn't you say something last night?"

"I do as I am told," she said, smiling slyly, "and besides, I was horny. It was clear you weren't going to allow us to continue on our own."

"I was irritated."

Layla laughed, "I'm sure she is very irritated too."

Tyrion sighed.

"You should have her come in here and take care of this, if you don't want my help," said Layla, sitting up.

"As you indicated, I think she's a bit too angry for that."

"So?" Layla raised one brow. "You are the master here. We live at your whim. Summon her, beat her if she is impudent. All of your problems stem from your strange reluctance to impose your will upon her."

He shook his head, "You don't understand. Kate is my friend. I have adapted to life here, but I could never do that to her."

"Your friend?" she scoffed. "I have seen no sign of that. You just said that you and she had never exchanged favors. Take her, *make* her your friend. It is entirely up to you."

"No," he told her. "I don't mean friend in the sense you do." He struggled to find the words for a moment. "I guess you would say that we have been *fools* together, since we were much younger."

"Oh," said Layla, staring at him thoughtfully for a moment. "As you were with Garlin?"

"Yes," he nodded. "Similar to that. There's never been any of *this* between us." He made a wide gesture encompassing Layla and the bed.

"You are an odd one, Tyrion," said the warden. "Just like she is. I have never seen two people so strange. I have watched you both, spying on each other constantly. She is just as obsessed as you are. I don't understand why you had sex with those other women and not her. Did they force you?"

"No," he corrected, "I forced them."

"But not her?"

"I could never hurt Kate," he replied. *I love her.*

"Perhaps you only like the ones who reject you."

He had no good response to that.

***

He and Kate remained in an uncomfortable silence the rest of the week. Tyrion resumed training his children, and three more of them awakened their latent abilities as the days passed, Ashely Morris, Ian Collins, and Violet Price. Thus far he had nine being trained while three still remained 'normal' without any obvious sign of magical talent, Anthony, Piper and Blake.

He wasn't sure if he hoped they would remain that way, or whether he would prefer for them to manifest the same power. The world of the She'Har was cruel, and it was far crueler to the weak.

But he could protect them.

If they remained powerless they wouldn't be forced to fight, and while in the slave camps the fate of the nameless was wretched, that didn't mean it had to be the case here. This was a new place, the beginning of a new city, one that would house the slaves of the Illeniel Grove.

They might be slaves in the eyes of the She'Har, but if I am in charge here, I can make their lives better.

He thought about those things constantly as he trained them. He was particularly harsh with the three who had yet to be blooded. They were sometimes punished with the red whip, while he refrained from using it on the others. He only needed to nourish the hate in those who had yet to learn to kill.

That was what he told himself anyway.

He spent the most time with Brigid. She would be his weapon, his salvation, and someday, very likely, his executioner. Her eyes burned when they were upon him. He no longer needed to punish her, that was clear. She hated him with a passion that rivaled his own hatred for the She'Har.

But she needed more. The black haired girl had to do more than slay a stranger, more than kill an acquaintance, she had to destroy her best friend. Her experience was inadequate, and her resolve was nowhere near what it would need to be to do that.

"Again," he told her. "Don't hold back."

Brigid showed her teeth, "Don't tempt me."

"That is precisely what I intend to do," he replied. "I want you to fight with everything you have. Try to kill me."

Her eyes lit with sudden inspiration. "Really, what if I succeed?"

"Then I will have made you into the deadliest mage in the world," he responded, "and you will have to spar with Layla for the rest of the week."

"She's too weak," observed the girl.

"You would have to be more careful with...," he was sent flying as a surprise attack struck his shield with unexpected ferocity.

She had distracted him, and when she had made her move, she had gathered her aythar so quickly that he hadn't had time to respond. *She's fast,* he thought as his body hurtled into a pile of quarried stone for the building project. His shield almost broke from the second impact, and the sudden stop had rattled his brain.

Another attack before he had recovered his composure might do the trick, and if he wound up stunned from feedback, the girl really would kill him. He started to roll and summoned an aythar filled mist, obscuring both normal vision and magesight. Then he stopped.

She will be expecting me to keep moving. He considered activating his tattoos, to create a shield she couldn't break, but the thrill of danger excited him. Brigid was strong, she was fast, she was a real threat. He wanted to beat her on even terms.

Or perhaps he truly did want to die; even he wasn't certain which was the truth.

The mist swirled as her will moved through it, her aythar reaching for something. Then the stone blocks began to fly, tearing through the mist with incredible velocity. There were too many to be dodged, that was the point. Several of them hit his shield, and he was sent tumbling once more.

Lying flat on the ground to minimize his chance of being struck again, he renewed his mist, and then he opened the ground beneath him, letting himself sink several feet before closing it over his head. He had barely gotten beneath the surface when he felt her aythar moving outward along the top of the ground forming a faint latticework.

He smiled inwardly, she was using his old trick, creating a thin pattern of aythar across the ground to detect an opponent she couldn't see or sense directly. He had been about to do the same, to track her position, but he held back. If he were to do so now she would find him.

Instead he turned his power inward, using it to heighten his hearing and slow his heart rate. He had taken a deep breath before the soil covered his head, but he would only be able to hold it for a limited amount of time. He intended to make the most of it. *She won't stand still, I just need to wait until she's close enough.*

He waited, listening to the slow beat of his heart and straining his ears for the sound of her steps. For a time there was nothing, and his lungs began to burn. He had been under for a few minutes already, and without air he would have to emerge soon. Doing so before he found her would be bad. She would know his location the instant he disturbed the surface, and she would be ready to attack as he made his way up and out.

Then he heard, or rather felt, her faint tread. *Which way?* In the darkness it was hard to be sure. Another step and he had the direction. She was approaching from his rear, but she was too far for him to ambush her as he had hoped. Trying to guess the distance from the sound of her footfalls was too hard. She might be ten feet or even thirty. That sort of accuracy was inadequate for a surprise attack.

An idea came to him then. Sending his aythar out through the earth, he punched a large hole in her lattice some twenty yards away in the direction he had heard her steps. He was guessing that that would be far enough to draw her attention in the other direction, away from his current position.

A split second after that, he exploded upward, using his magic to thrust himself skyward. A massive surge of aythar accompanied her attack on the location of his distraction. It also gave away her precise location as his thinning mist parted. He struck, quick as a viper, sending a focused pulse of power at the place she was standing, facing away from him now.

Adrenaline and excitement made his attack stronger than it needed to be. It was strong enough to break her shield, and it retained enough power to strike the back of her head with dangerous force. Brigid fell, her body completely limp.

He had won.

No! What have I done? In a panic he ran to the unconscious girl. Blood was trickling from her right ear. "No!" he yelled, unable to contain himself.

Some of the others had been watching their fight from a distance. As the mist cleared they saw him, and a cry of alarm went up among them. Abby ran toward him, while Ian and Violet ran to the house to find Kate and Layla. David and Emma remained where they were, watching in shock.

"What happened?" asked Abby, near panic herself.

"I went too far," he said, never taking his eyes off the dark haired child in his arms. Unbidden tears sprang from his eyes as he cradled her. His magesight was exploring, but his emotions made it difficult to concentrate.

Brigid's eyes were wide, unfocused. The pupils were huge despite the bright sun beating down on the two of them. Her heart still beat, but it was weak, unsteady. It skipped a beat as he watched. Seconds later it skipped again, and then it stopped.

"Is she breathing?" asked Kate urgently. She had just arrived and was kneeling beside them.

"What have I done?" he moaned, a keening note rising from the back of his throat. "Please no, no…" Then he felt her heart beat again, resuming its uncertain pace.

Looking up, he saw Layla standing nearby, a troubled look on her face. Kate had her hand under Brigid's nose, feeling for air.

"She's still breathing, Daniel," said Kate. "Can you tell where she's hurt?"

"It's her head," he said, his voice thick. "I did this. I did this." His body began to rock as his emotions swept reason from him.

Kate stared at him, worried. She had never seen Daniel like this. Once, when his dog Blue had been killed, he had been close, but he was beyond that now. He was distraught, as though he might dissolve into uncontrollable tears.

"Daniel, listen to me," she said, putting more calm into her voice than she felt. "She's still alive. I know you can heal some things, but not if you lose control of yourself. You have to focus. Take a deep breath. Is there anything you can do?"

Chapter 24

His vision was blurred beyond hope of seeing, but his eyes were useless for this anyway. He nodded, squeezing them shut. He let out a shuddering breath and then took a fresh one, filling his lungs completely. *Calm,* he thought.

Slowly he sent his awareness outward, refining his magesight to bring Brigid's body into sharp resolution. Her heart was still beating, it skipped now and then, but there was nothing wrong with it. Searching her skull, he found it was still intact, the bones were sound, but something wasn't right. The blood came from a ruptured artery on one side, but the blood leaking from her ear was the least of it. Farther in another artery was bleeding into the space between her brain and her skull. The blood was expanding, putting pressure on everything within her cranium.

He had lots of experience with blood vessels. Fresh hope brought renewed strength, and he found it easier to think, easier to focus. Quickly he repaired the artery, not merely sealing it off, but matching it up properly and restoring the proper flow. It was delicate work, but not difficult. He had dealt with far worse, in other parts of the body. After that he repaired the vessel in her ear canal, to stop the blood leaking there as well.

Tyrion paused then, thinking, observing. Brigid's breathing was still shallow, and her heartbeat was irregular. She hadn't improved. He had seen blood left in the body before. The body would absorb it slowly, but it would take days, weeks. That much blood would be there for a while, and meanwhile the pressure would remain for some time. What would that sort of bruising do to her brain?

I've got to let it out.

Clenching his jaw, he drew his will down to a fine point, using his aythar to create a small hole in her skull before opening the membrane beneath it. Blood began to run down her scalp, dripping into his lap.

Kate let out a soft gasp.

"It's alright," he told her. "I'm letting the excess out." His voice was much smoother now. Action had helped him regain his composure.

Once the blood had drained, he closed the skin but left the small hole in the skull open. Any additional blood could drain into the area beneath her scalp, to prevent any more pressure from building up. Brigid's heart rate seemed to have returned to normal, and her breathing was deeper now.

"She's going to be alright, isn't she?" asked Abby, still standing close by.

Looking around Tyrion could see that all of them were gathered nearby now. He met Kate's eyes, uncertain how to reply.

She read his look and spoke for him, "She's alright. We'll take her inside and let her rest. I think she will recover."

After a short discussion, Abby used her power to gently lift Brigid's limp form, levitating her sister a few feet above the ground before guiding her toward the house. They placed her in Tyrion's bed. The entire household was crowded into that one room for several minutes before Emma took the initiative and began ushering them out.

Abby was the last to leave. "I want to stay with her," she announced.

Emma looked to Kate for support.

Chapter 24

"We should probably take turns with her until she wakes up," said Kate, suggesting a compromise.

Tyrion broke in, "Kate can stay, everyone else out."

Abby refused to give up that easily, "She's my sister. You may think we're all just puppets for your games, but we aren't. We're human beings. I want to make sure she's alright. Let me keep watch over her." She stopped for a second, her eyes welling with tears but her face determined. "Please," she added.

Emma opened her mouth, thought for a second, and then closed it again. Finally she turned to Kate and Tyrion, "Actually, I agree with Abby. I want to stay too. Could we take turns?"

Kate glanced at Tyrion, unsure of his mental stability. He had shown a poor record for negotiation in the past. She worried he might explode at the girls' resistance, but his response surprised her.

"Fine," he told them. "I'll need to rest eventually. You can come and go, but only one of you at a time. If the others feel the same, you can share the duty with them. Everyone else will do as Kate says. I don't want to be bothered while I'm watching her. Understood?"

They nodded.

"Abby you stay first, Emma you come with me. You can help me organize the others. We still need to eat, so we need to get dinner started," said Kate.

The two of them left the room, while Abby sat on a small stool beside the bed, on the opposite side from Tyrion. He was kneeling on the floor, his eyes on the dark haired girl. Looking up, he met her gaze once before closing his eyes and focusing on his other senses.

Silently, he watched Brigid's heart and followed the movement of her lungs. It would be a long day.

Chapter 25

"You saw what happened to her," said Ian. He and most of the other teens were gathered outside. They were supposed to be practicing, but Layla wasn't with them at the moment, and Tyrion was preoccupied, so they had fallen to talking amongst themselves.

"He's been different since we went to the arena," replied Abby. "Less cruel."

"Less cruel?" responded Ian in disbelief. "He tried to kill Brigid yesterday!"

"That was an accident," she answered.

"Were my ribs an accident?" said Ian.

Ashley spoke up then, "Nobody's saying he's nice, Ian, but he seemed pretty upset over what happened. I still think he's a terrible person, but Abby's right, he isn't evil."

"He used that whip on you just two days ago," pointed out Ian. "Were you thinking, 'oh he isn't evil', while you were screaming in pain? Only a sick bastard tortures his own children."

"I hate him as much as you do Ian, but you haven't been in the arena yet," said Abby.

"You mean the arena that Jack and Gabriel didn't come back from? The arena they died in, that arena?!" he shot back.

"Yes, exactly, Ian! How many of us do you think would have died if he hadn't been so hard on us?" she said, rebuking him. "Do you think it was easy for me to *kill* someone? It made me sick!"

Sarah moved closer, putting a hand on Abby's shoulder in a gesture of sympathy.

Ryan broke in then, "Listen Ian, nobody here loves him, but I don't think he's doing this because he wants to. I think he's trying to keep us alive."

"Shut up," growled Ian. "Nobody wants to hear from you. You're just his little toady. You think you're special because he put you in charge of building our crappy house."

"If he had put a moron like you in charge of it, it would just be a pile of rocks with a shit-hole cave for us to sleep in," said Ryan.

"Why don't you say that to my face?"

"I just did, dumbass! Are you trying to prove my point?" responded Ryan with a sarcastic sneer.

Ian took a swing at him, which Ryan didn't bother trying to dodge. Ian was much larger, but bare knuckles didn't mean much when you had a shield up.

A moment later, Ian was swearing and holding his injured hand, but then he fell backward. Ryan had shifted the ground beneath his feet. Ryan brought his hand downward in a purely symbolic gesture as he hammered the other boy hard in the chest with his aythar.

Ian gasped for air and struggled to get his wind back.

"The rules have changed, Ian. You just got your power a few days ago, so you need to learn. It's not about *this* anymore," Ryan pointed at his bicep for a second before moving to point at his own temple, "It's about *this*. You haven't been in the arena yet, but I have. I've killed. If you keep thinking like that, you're going to die when they toss you in there next week."

Ian sat up, but didn't reply. Violet helped him back to his feet before turning to Ryan. "How did it feel?" she asked.

"What?" said Ryan.

"How did it feel to kill somebody? How did you do it?" clarified Violet.

He looked at the red headed girl for a moment. Of all of Tyrion's children, she looked the most like Kate, despite the fact that the two women were unrelated. "I hated it, but I did just what he said," answered Ryan. "I fought carefully, and when I had my chance, I pretended it was him."

Abby nodded at his comment, "Me too."

David had been listening, but at that point he spoke, "You can all say what you want, but he didn't just hurt us. He's hurt Mrs. Tolburn too. What kind of man abuses a woman like that?"

"That's why she's in love with him?" said Sarah. "Come on, David. He's never really hurt her."

"She is not! I was there," said the boy. "I saw him drag her into his room, and I saw her face when she came out. She was crying."

"You think that's why she's always watching him?" asked Sarah.

David nodded, "Of course. If you see a snake, you don't take your eyes off of it."

Sarah's eyes grew sly, "Why don't you ask her then?"

***

Tyrion woke feeling stiff and groggy. He had been sitting by the edge of the bed, and in his fatigue, he had leaned over and placed his head and arms on the mattress. From the soreness in his back, he must have stayed in that position for some time.

Emma sat across from him on the other side of the bed. "It was my turn, so I swapped with Abby. I didn't know whether to wake you or not," she said in response to his unspoken question.

"Has she woken?" he asked.

Emma shook her head, "No. Nothing has changed yet."

Turning his attention to the raven haired girl in the bed, he watched her heart beat for a long minute. It was different now. It had been regular before, but it seemed steadier now, and her breathing was more regular as well.

"You should go lie down," suggested Emma. "I doubt anyone is using the other bed."

"I'll stay here," he replied. *Besides, I doubt Kate would take kindly to me commandeering her bed.*

They sat in silence for a while, but it was not an uncomfortable one. Emma watched him as much as her sister, and eventually she could restrain herself no longer, "Why did you do it?"

"It was an accident," he said automatically.

"No," she said, "I know that, I meant something else. Back then, before I was born..."

"Oh," he said, unsure how to respond now that he understood. "You mean when I raped your mother."

"That's not what she told me," returned Emma, her soft brown eyes were uncertain as she spoke.

Tyrion sighed, "Look, no matter what she told you, it was worse than she might have thought. If you're looking for some reason to forgive me, to try to understand, or just to reconcile yourself with it—don't. I'm not your father. I'm just the man who forced himself on your mother. Fathers love their children. I've never done anything but bring pain to you, or any of the others."

Emma looked away, her mousy brown hair falling over one eye as her head moved. "Mother said it was like a fairy tale. She never expected it, but that when she saw you, she knew she…"

"It was a mistake."

"She said I was her best mistake," insisted Emma.

The implicit forgiveness in her tone made him angry, but he had shown enough of that lately. Taking a deep breath, he answered, "No. It wasn't a mistake on her part, Emma. Your mother had *no* choice. I took that from her, and I did it so completely that she wasn't even aware of it. I used my power to manipulate her mind, her feelings. I made her think she wanted me. It was still rape, no matter how you sugar coat it."

They lapsed into silence again, though this time it was not so comfortable. Even so, Tyrion preferred it to the questions. He hoped that the girl would surrender the topic, but she eventually found her courage again.

"You still didn't answer the question," she said at last.

"What was the question?"

"Why? Why did you do it?"

"I was horny," he said bluntly.

She didn't say anything to that, but her eyes were sullen.

"What?" he said, irritated. "What did you expect?"

"The truth," she said softly.

"That was the truth."

"That was *part* of the truth," she corrected.

Where does this stubbornness come from? he wondered. *Her mother was an easy going girl.* "If you ask too many questions I might lose my temper," he suggested. "Aren't you worried what I might do?" He kept his voice gruff, hoping to frighten her.

"No."

"Why not?" he asked, somewhat exasperated.

"You've spent the last day and a half sitting by this bed worried about Brigid," noted Emma. "I don't really believe you want to hurt me anymore."

"I did that to her."

"It was an accident," said Emma, repeating his earlier response.

He blew out a lungful of air in frustration. "What will it take to shut you up?"

"Just tell me the rest," she insisted.

Looking at her, he was struck by the sudden urge to hug the girl. She was so earnest, so young, and far too stubborn. More than anything he wanted her acceptance, but he knew he would never deserve it, no matter what she herself believed. *This is a mistake,* he thought, but then he opened his mouth anyway.

"I was broken. When I was fifteen someone hurt me so badly that I knew I could never be worthy of the girl I loved," he admitted.

"You were in love with her?"

"Not your mother," said Tyrion sadly. "Kate."

Emma frowned, "But Brigid is Kate's sister... If you loved her, why would you...?"

"An older woman took that decision from me."

"Oh," said Emma, but it was clear that she didn't understand. She stared at Brigid for a moment while her mind worked, then she sat straighter, "Oh!"

He nodded, "Brigid was the first, and because of that I deserted Kate."

"Was it your fault?"

"I thought so then," he told her. "But it really wasn't my choice."

Emma looked toward the door, "Does she know?"

"Yeah, she figured it out on her own."

"Is that why she hates you?" asked the girl.

"No," he admitted. "She is an exceptional woman. She forgave me for that. She has her own reasons for hating me. After I—after what happened with her mother, I told her I didn't love her. I pushed her away. Then I began hunting the women of Colne. I was empty, lonely, and horny. I knew it was wrong, but somehow I convinced myself it wasn't rape. It was much later before I finally faced the truth about myself."

"And that's why she hates you?"

Tyrion laughed, "No. She forgave me for that too. She's angry because I hurt *you.* She is angry because I hurt the others. She doesn't agree with my training methods."

Emma nodded, "It was pretty awful. Last week was the worst week of my life, until the day in the arena."

"It isn't over," he said quietly. "You'll have to do it again."

"Killing was the worst thing I've ever felt, even worse than the red whip. It felt like my soul was dying," she paused. "But I'm still alive."

The world seemed to darken as she spoke. Tyrion put his head in his hands. He kept his magesight on Brigid's heart, letting its steady rhythm swallow his other perceptions. He didn't want to face the world anymore.

"So how do you feel about Kate now?" asked Emma curiously.

"I still love her," he said frankly. "I always have. She was the one bright moment in my life, before everything went to shit."

"Maybe you should tell her," suggested Emma seriously. "It isn't too late."

"It's better this way. Brigid is a perfect example of what happens to people close to me. She's safer hating me." Tyrion stopped then, realizing the girl was baiting him. His awareness expanded to its normal range, and he found an eavesdropper just outside the room. He had left the door open so that they could come and go. Kate stood in the hall.

He gave Emma a hard look, "How long has she been standing there?"

"Since at least, 'does she know?', but that was just when I noticed. It could have been longer," said Emma.

Standing, he stepped around the bed and took her by the elbow, pulling her to her feet and ushering her unceremoniously to the door. Emma didn't resist. Kate started to step inside just as he pushed the girl out. He held up a hand to stop her from entering. "No."

Then he shut the door, and this time he sealed it. There would be no more intrusions.

I should never have let her get me to talking.

Chapter 25

***

Brigid was nauseated.

It wasn't something she was aware of at first. Her eyes were closed, and the world was dark, but gradually it was coming into focus. Her magesight was showing her the room whether she wanted to see it or not, but now that her awareness had returned, she began to focus on things.

That was the mistake; as soon as she attempted to guide her perception, to resolve something in better detail, the nausea pounced on her. A groan escaped the lips that she was just beginning to feel, and her eyes opened. Perhaps she would have better luck using her actual eyes to see.

The room wheeled around her in a colorful blur while her head was filled with pain. She closed her eyes again. *Let's not do that,* she told herself.

Her thoughts came as a surprise. She was alive. Brigid's memory was fuzzy, but she was pretty sure that she wasn't supposed to be alive. *I died. He killed me.*

The brilliant aythar that radiated from the man next to her belonged to Tyrion, her father—her murderer. *Why is he here?* She still couldn't resolve him very well with her magesight, so she risked opening her left eye a fraction of an inch.

He was beside the bed, his arms folded on the mattress to form a rest for his head.

Several facts made themselves known to her then. First, she was definitely alive, second, she was lying in Tyrion's bed, and third, none of it was fair. *I thought it was over. I didn't want this. Why am I still here?*

There might be an upside to her situation, however.

Fighting past the nausea and pain, she forced her magesight to show her Tyrion in better detail. He was definitely asleep. He had no shield. There was really only one thing she wanted still, and that was to kill him. Her last hope had been that she could accomplish that, before he had nearly killed her instead.

Apparently he failed, she noted.

Where was the sword? He had given her his magical wooden sword, with instructions to kill herself if she was unable to face her duty in the next arena battle. She was certain she couldn't muster enough aythar yet to take advantage of Tyrion's current vulnerability, but if she had something sharp, she could possibly manage to inflict a mortal wound before he could wake up.

She found it.

It was lying on the floor a few feet from the bed against one of the walls. Someone must have brought it in with her and left it there. That was problematic. She couldn't see herself using magic to pull it to herself, not in her current state, anyway. Maybe she could slip out of bed and walk to it?

She scooted sideways. Her body responded perfectly, but shooting pains echoed through her skull. It was an intense agony that made her hiss through her teeth. She stopped before she cried out. The pain faded, leaving an uncomfortable nausea in its wake.

Tears of frustration leaked from the corners of her eyes. There was no way she could make it. A golden opportunity was being wasted, and there was little she could do about it. She lay still and opened her eyes more fully, giving herself time to adjust to the light.

Chapter 25

It was painful, but after a while her headache faded. Movement was still out, but at least she could look around. Brigid studied the man leaning on the bed next to her.

Tyrion's hair was dark, as dark as hers, almost a raven black, though it was beginning to show a few gray hairs here and there. There was no denying the resemblance between them. In coloring, she had taken entirely after him. Brigid's features were fine boned and delicate, like her mother's, like her sister Kate's, but her hair, eyes, and skin, were entirely his. Kate's skin was fair but sprinkled with freckles, while Brigid's was unblemished, white in the winter and darkening to a smooth olive in the summer months.

A shade identical to his bronzed shoulders now.

It made her sick. She had never hated her own body more than she did then. If she could have chosen, she would have looked like Violet, who somehow had been born looking more like Kate and her mother than Brigid herself, even though they were unrelated.

The scars that had marked him when she first met him were gone. They had vanished after the freak storm when they had just arrived at the Illeniel Grove, but his body was still covered in strange tattoos. The symbols were tools, and she knew that when he used them, he was invincible. She had seen it often enough already. The shields the tattoos created were far superior to anything she could make, or anything that he could make without them, for that matter.

If I just had a knife.

As if in response to her thought, his head rose from his arms. Ice blue eyes stared into her own. They were like twins, male and female images mirrored against one another. Tyrion smiled.

"You're awake."

She clenched her jaw, and her eyes darted once more to the sword lying on the floor across the room.

He followed her gaze, "Have you been watching me sleep?"

Brigid didn't answer.

A flicker of something passed across his face, like a cold breeze across an autumn lake. For a moment she saw something. *Pain?* It vanished as quickly as it came, replaced by a satisfied expression.

"Were you thinking about killing me in my sleep?" he said teasingly.

She looked away.

A hand reached out, stroking her hair, sending waves of nausea through her as the motion jostled her skull. "You really are my daughter, heart and soul."

Standing, he walked across the room to retrieve the sword and brought it back. He drew it from its sheath and reversed it, putting the hilt in her hand. "Does that feel better?" he asked, and then he sat down again, bringing his bare chest within reach.

Brigid's baleful gaze burned into him as her hand closed around the weapon. Clenching her fingers sent shivers of agony down her spine, but she ignored them. Her arm shook as she lifted the blade, pointing it toward his heart.

"That's the spirit," said Tyrion, encouraging her and leaning closer. "It must be terribly difficult to coordinate your movements right now. You took a bad blow to the head. I can appreciate your determination. All you need to do now is thrust. This is your chance."

Her anger pulsed, white-hot. Surging up from the bed, she drove her arm forward with all the strength she could manage, ignoring the blinding pain. Darkness overwhelmed her, and she lost awareness of her surroundings for a moment. When it receded, she found herself still lying in the bed, her head throbbing. The hilt was still in her hand.

Opening her eyes again, she saw him holding the blade in his hand. Blood oozed from it, running slowly down the blade to gather on the quillons before dripping to the sheets.

Tyrion didn't release the sharp wood, instead he pulled it closer, using the razor edged tip to cut a bloody 'x' in the skin of his chest, over his heart. "There's what you want—right there. I've even marked it for you."

She tried once more to push it in, but his grip was like iron, the blade never moved. Brigid growled at him as more tears ran down her cheeks. The pain of her effort finally became too great, however, and she released the hilt, sagging back down into the bed.

Tyrion lifted the weapon, taking the hilt in his other hand before cleaning it on the sheets. Then he sheathed it and healed the cuts on his hand and chest, leaving thin silver lines where he had marked himself.

"I wish I could let you have what you want," he told her, "but I need you to do something for me first."

She gave him a tired stare.

"You have to kill Haley," he added.

"No," she answered, using her voice for the first time since she had awoken. Her tongue felt clumsy, and the sound sent more pain echoing through her skull.

"You must. If you don't, she will kill the others, one by one."

"She's my friend."

"She understands the arena. They'll put her in there, and she will cut you apart, just like she did with Gabriel," he explained.

"Then I would rather die," argued Brigid.

"It won't just be you. It will be all of them. Kill her and you can save them," he said, before pausing. Tyrion pointed at the 'x' on his chest, "Kill her and I'll give you what you want."

"You lie."

He pointed to the tattoos that lined his arms. "I will give you these. Use them and you can cut through my defenses, if you try hard enough."

"You won't let me."

Her father shook his head, "I will let you, but even if you don't believe me, you know that at the very least, it will give you a chance, even if I tried to renege."

"I hate you."

"Do we have a deal?" he asked, ignoring the statement.

She gave a single nod.

"I'll start the tattoos tomorrow, while you're recovering," he told her. "We only have a few more days before they call us back to the arena."

Chapter 26

Abby was waiting outside as he emerged. She immediately noticed the blood on his skin. "What happened?" She looked into the room, noting the stains on the sheets and the tears on her sister's face. "What did you do?!" She ran in to check on Brigid.

Tyrion ignored her, walking out past the others gathered in the front rooms on either side of the hallway.

Kate followed Abby inside the room, a question in her eyes as she passed him, though it went unsaid. He heard her gasp after she went inside. "There's blood all over the bed."

The others were giving him worried looks, but he blocked their path to the bedroom. "It's not hers," he said simply. "Get outside, we have work to do."

Anthony Long was already there, vomiting to one side of the front door. His aythar was flickering madly.

"Looks like someone else is awakening," said Tyrion. "Go lie down. You'll join the others tomorrow," he told the boy before looking around. "Where's Layla?"

"In the other bedroom," said Ryan.

"Tell her to come out," he ordered, but then he thought better of it. "Nevermind, I'll fetch her myself."

Going back inside, he found the female warden. "I need your assistance today."

"You said I couldn't be seen without the collar," she reminded him.

"I've changed my mind."

"And if one of the She'Har visits?"

"Get inside, hopefully before they notice."

She frowned, "And if they do notice? I could be killed."

Tyrion shrugged, "I'm willing to take that risk."

He got them started with new exercises, forcing them to stretch their imaginations, visualizing and creating shields in ever more complex shapes. Layla focused on Ashley, Ian, and Violet, since they were the newest to their powers and hadn't yet been blooded in the arena.

After a quarter of an hour he addressed them again, "Keep at this for another two hours, and then I want you to resume work on your dormitory, except for you three." He pointed at Layla's three charges. "I want you to keep them working on the basics until dinnertime," he told her. Then he turned and began to walk.

"Where are you going?" asked the warden.

"There are some things I need to take care of in the grove," he answered without looking back.

A half an hour later and he was deep within the Illeniel Grove. He walked without purpose, but his feet led him once more to Lyralliantha's home. Ascending the great trunk, he found her sleeping platform and lay down on the bed he had shared with her so many times. Only there did he ease the grip he had on his thoughts.

Visions of Brigid filled his mind, her vivid blue eyes burning into him once more; the same eyes that had once looked at him in awe while he played the cittern so many years before. A little girl then, she had played with his parent's dog and smiled with an innocence that was truly gone now.

Her hatred burned. It ate at him in a way that left his stomach cold and his body restless. His years with the She'Har had been largely devoid of strong emotions. Even when he had first been trained by Thillmarius, the lore-warden had punished him with passionless efficiency. The only hatred he had faced had been from some of his human opponents in the arena, and that never bothered him.

Even Kate's disdain, as painful as it was, didn't bother him as much. She didn't want him dead, but Brigid did. She stared at him from his memory with a face that might have been his own, if he had been born a woman, and in her heart he could see nothing greater than her desire to erase his existence.

I wanted them to hate me, he reminded himself.

But he had known Brigid and Haley better than the others. He had known of them before he returned to the She'Har, ten years ago. The other children he hadn't met until a few weeks past, but those two girls he had known about. He had met them, he had dreamed of them, and he had hoped for them for the past ten years.

Now he was about to force one to kill the other, and she hated him for it. She despised him even without that fact, and she wanted nothing more than to end his life.

His stomach twisted. *I feel nothing.*

He was exhausted from his long vigil at his daughter's bedside, yet it still took hours before he slept, and when the darkness finally claimed his consciousness, it did not offer much relief. His dreams were troubled with nightmares of what the future held.

***

It was midmorning the next day before Tyrion returned to Albamarl. He hadn't intended to spend the night away, but his body had had different ideas once he had lapsed into deeper slumber. His mind was clearer now, and his inner turmoil had faded somewhat.

He hadn't realized how exhausted he had been, but things seemed better now that he could face the world without a mental fog behind his brow. Thinking of his promise to Brigid brought a curious kind of peace with it now. He had done what he could. He would make her ready, he would give her the tools she needed to win. Once that was accomplished he could let her take his life with fewer regrets.

Once Haley was out of the way, the others would have much better chances of surviving. Some might die, but he couldn't take responsibility for everything the She'Har did. Most of them would live and eventually become wardens, no longer required to fight in the arena.

Most importantly he could lay down his burden. His hatred for the She'Har, for what they had done to humanity, to him, to his children, he could set it aside and let death erase his past, present, and future.

It wasn't that he wanted to die, but if that was what was required to get Brigid to play her part, then it was a worthy price to pay, and one that would release him from his personal suffering in the bargain. He was tired of anger, tired of driving the people he cared for away, and most of all, he was tired of remembering his sins whenever he looked in their faces.

The sun was halfway up now, brilliantly highlighting the world around him. The wind sang in the trees and whispered its secrets in his ears, while birdsong floated by, a friendly accompaniment to a world so beautiful that it made the soul ache. A world that lived and breathed to serve the She'Har.

"Go fuck yourself," he said, addressing the universe in general, and then he smiled.

"Good morning to you as well, my lord," responded Layla who had just come within earshot.

"That was for the rest of the world," he explained before adding, "but feel free to include yourself as well. I wouldn't want anyone to feel left out."

She gave a short laugh, sensing his good humor. Humor in itself was an unusual thing for Tyrion.

He began rattling off orders, "Keep them moving today, same routine as yesterday. Two or three hours practice for those that have already been blooded and all day for the new ones. Start working with Anthony as well, he will be unsteady, but one of the others can work with him individually to get him acclimated. I would suggest Abby or Emma for that task. After lunch, have the experienced ones work on the dormitory again."

Layla absorbed his words before responding, "You sound as if you won't be there."

"I will be working with Brigid today."

The female warden frowned, "She is still weak from her ordeal. Shouldn't she rest another day or two?"

The irony of a warden suggesting leniency almost made him laugh, but he suppressed the urge. "She won't be doing much. You'll understand later."

Layla had questions, but she kept them to herself, which was a quality that he often wished Kate and the others from Colne would cultivate. Leaving her behind, he made for the house, but Ryan Carter ran up to him before he could get to the door.

"Sir," said the boy.

"Call me Tyrion," he told Ryan. "Or, if you're feeling formal 'Lord'," he paused then before adding, "Or if you want to be formal and familiar at the same time, I will even accept 'Father', but only if you are willing to accept the burden of being an heir of my blackened heart."

Ryan stared at him, mouth half open, unsure how to respond. Tyrion sounded as though he was making a joke, but he had learned to never assume such things where the older man was concerned. Mistakes could have painful consequences.

Tyrion took pity on him, "Tell me what you needed to say."

"Uh—my lord, the dormitory is progressing, but we need other materials to finish it properly," said the boy at last.

"What materials?"

"Iron. Simple pig-iron will do, and the shape doesn't matter. We can shape it ourselves, but we can't make hinges and door fittings with only wood and stone," answered the teen. "Well, we *could,* but it would be much better if we could make them from iron. I've seen the fittings in your house, but I don't know where you obtained the metal."

Chapter 26

Tyrion nodded, "How much do you need?"

"A hundred pounds at least," said Ryan immediately. "But we can use as much as you can provide. I can find a use for a lot more than that, if it's available."

As much as I can provide, eh? thought Tyrion. *Somehow I doubt that.*

"It will be in the yard by the lumber pile in the morning," he told the skinny lad.

Ryan's brows knitted together in confusion, "Where will you get it?"

Tyrion graced him with a genial smile and wordlessly left him, entering the house and closing the door behind himself. Once inside he almost stumbled directly into Kate, and there was an awkward silence as the two of them stepped clumsily around one another.

The others were all outside now, except for Brigid who still occupied his bedroom, so the two of them were completely alone. Tyrion spoke first, "I didn't intend for you to hear that yesterday."

Kate frowned, unsure why he would apologize for kind words. "I shouldn't have been listening."

Another pause ensued while he tried to figure out where to go from there. "I know coming here has been hard for you, and I made things worse by interfering with you and Layla, but that was just my frustration coming out. She only did what I forced her to do. You shouldn't hold it against her." He knew the two of them hadn't been intimate since he had 'borrowed' Layla, and he thought it would be good if they could smooth out their differences. It was all the more important now that he didn't expect to be around much longer, not that he could tell Kate that.

"What?"

He repeated himself.

She gave him a look that seemed less than flattering, "You think I'm angry with you for what happened with the two of you?"

Tyrion laughed, trying to cover a sudden feeling of uncertainty. "No, you have plenty of other reasons to be angry with me. I just don't want you to hold it against her. Friends are rare in this place, and you'll need her in…"

Kate held up her hand, "Just shut up a second. You had sex with yet *another* woman, and you are worried that I might be angry with her? Do I have it right this time?"

His uncertain footing was making him irritable. He felt vulnerable talking to Kate, and over time he had come to truly hate feeling vulnerable. "Yeah, that's about it," he said. "I was angry, jealous, tired, and horny, and I took it out on you and Layla the only way I knew how, so don't hold it against her."

Her eyes narrowed, "I gave up *everything* to follow you here, my family, my *son,* everything, just so I could keep an eye on Brigid, and maybe, just maybe, help you. And now you suggest that I am jealous of yet another of your conquests? After fifteen years in Colne, after all the women you impregnated, you think I'm upset about Layla?"

He lightened his tone, "You certainly sound angry."

Her eyes flashed with green fire, "I'm angry because you are a complete *ass!*"

Chapter 26

The challenge was thrown now, and he was more than glad to take it up. Anger he understood, anger was his close companion. It was certainly more comfortable to him than vague feelings and uncertainty. "No," he insisted, "you're jealous. The only real question is, were you jealous because I fucked your girlfriend, or were you jealous because your girlfriend fucked me?"

Kate's face went through a remarkable transformation. Furious, she struggled to restrain her temper as her hands clenched and unclenched. She could feel her lip starting to tremble so she bit down on it and closed her eyes before taking a deep breath. "I have other things to do," she replied in an even tone.

Tyrion watched her walk away. His anger was draining away, and he mentally reviewed his remarks. It was clear that he hadn't made the best use of his words, not if his intentions were to make peace with Kate. *I seem to be the world's worst apologist. The next time I think about saying 'I'm sorry' to someone, I should just walk up and slap them. It will be faster, and the same thing will be accomplished.*

He went into his bedroom, closing the door behind him. After a second thought, he uttered the word to seal it as well. It wouldn't do for them to be interrupted. Facing the bed, he found Brigid sitting on the side, spooning something from a small bowl into her mouth.

"How are you feeling?" he asked.

"It doesn't hurt to move anymore," she replied, "but my head feels delicate. No pain, but I'm being careful with it."

Tyrion nodded, "You won't need to do anything today but listen, watch, and remember."

Brigid set the bowl aside, giving him her full attention. Her face was clear today, empty of the strong emotions he had witnessed the day before. It was unsettling to see her looking at him with such an earnest expression, as if her true feelings were not so dark.

He pushed those thoughts aside and began, "We are going to tattoo your arms with symbols similar to these. I call them 'runes', and it will probably take us two or three days to finish. While we work on that, I will explain what they do and how they work." Moving to one side of the room, he opened a small box he kept in a drawer there. Inside it were several small bottles. They contained alcohol, water, and pigments, along with a small bowl to mix them in.

There was no needle, that part was performed more precisely with his aythar. "The magic you have used until now, is what I think of as 'natural' magic. It is raw, unrefined, unrestricted, but it also lacks permanence and strength. I've shown you how to use lines and circles drawn in the dirt to improve your shields, and how words can improve your results as well. This is an extension of that.

"Using runes you can create effects that last much longer and with greater potency, but you must understand the meaning of each symbol for it to work properly." Using his finger he drew a line of blue fire in the air, creating a triangle with a wavy line inside of it. "This is the rune for water."

He began showing her runes one after another in careful succession until at one point she held up her hand. "Where did the runes come from?" she asked.

"I made them up."

"What, just like that? You just decided, 'this is water', 'this is air'? Why do they work then?"

"Because I've ingrained the symbol and the concept with one another in my mind. Just like words, the meaning your mind assigns to a symbol is what is important."

"Why do they all have triangles then?" asked Brigid.

He smiled, "I made each within a triangle so that I can fit them together easily when drawing. You'll understand that part better when I explain enchanting."

"This isn't enchanting?"

"No, this is just runes. An enchantment is built from them, but if they aren't balanced against each other with proper geometric precision, they won't last. You wind up with something that's just a very strong, long lasting spell, something I call a 'ward', but if they are fitted properly, they become permanent, and much more powerful. That's an enchantment," he explained.

She thought about his statement for a minute, her eyes taking in the tattoos on his arms. "So those are wards then, since they aren't permanent?"

He shook his head, "Not exactly. These are incomplete enchantments. Since I don't want to be stuck with force blades permanently around my arms and hands, or shields around my entire body, I kept them unfinished. I activate them by creating the final symbols just like I drew this one in the air. I can turn them off by removing the final rune when I no longer want them to be active."

The dark haired girl's eyes showed uncommon understanding. He could almost see her mind working as she sorted through the concepts he was explaining. It made him proud, but he kept that thought to himself.

"It doesn't have to be on your skin does it?" she wondered aloud.

"No, it could be on an object, like I've done with the stones in this house, or the doors. In those cases you can usually make it complete and permanent," he answered.

"Then why not put your shield enchantment on your armor, or your blade enchantment on the sword?" she asked.

Tyrion nodded, "I would, but when I made these I was a normal slave, as you are. The She'Har don't allow anything into the arena but your body, no weapons, no possessions, nothing external to yourself."

Brigid thought about it for a moment before pointing at his lower left leg, "So what's that one do then?"

He frowned, "Those are just part of the shield enchantment that covers my body."

She shook her head, "No, not the ones on the skin, the ones inside, on the bone."

Tyrion struggled to mask his surprise. He hadn't expected her to look so deeply. The runes engraved on his shin bone were inactive and difficult to see unless one was looking for them deliberately. He kept his voice calm, "An experiment. Something I never used. Why were you looking beneath the skin?"

Brigid's face was smooth as she answered honestly, "Don't you study your enemies? That's what you taught us. 'Study your foe, examine them completely in order to find their weaknesses or hidden strengths'."

The words sent a faint shiver down his spine. She studied him to kill him. He gazed at the beautiful girl, *there's no denying she's my daughter.*

"Let's get back to the topic at hand," he insisted. "We need to start the tattooing. I'll explain the other runes as we go."

She nodded.

"I can block the nerve in your shoulder to stop the pain…"

"No," she answered, "Don't do that."

"Why not?"

"The pain is my own," she replied. "It will help remind me of everything you are owed."

The Silent Tempest

Chapter 27

The tattoos took two and a half days. Despite her resolve, Brigid still hissed at the pain as they worked and occasionally let out a yell. She swore and said things that he knew wouldn't have been allowed if she were still at home, but in Albamarl he couldn't see any reason to censor her language.

Why bother trying to make her talk like a lady when she was being trained to be a killer?

Brigid's strength returned as they worked, but he knew she still wouldn't be fully recovered by the time the arena day had arrived. He hoped the arm blades would be enough, for they didn't have nearly enough time to do the shield tattoos.

They developed a semblance of closeness while he worked on her arms, a bond born of pain and shared time together. Once or twice he saw her smile again, in between grimaces, as she made light of her own gasps and occasional yelps. It was as if she sometimes forgot to be angry.

The smiles were the worst, for they reminded him of the happy girl she had once been.

At one point she caught herself laughing at some dark joke he had made. Bright eyes and a flash of white teeth complimented the light sound of her laughter, but she stopped abruptly, closing her mouth and looking down, as though she had forgotten something.

"You don't have to do that," he told her. "It won't hurt you to relax a little. You can think about the dark stuff when the time comes."

"I don't understand you," she said without preamble.

He nodded sympathetically.

"When I came here, you were everything she said you were. Everything you did fit perfectly with her description, but you seem different now," she declared.

"Whose description?"

"Mother's."

Brenda Sayer, it made perfect sense now. *Brenda 'Tolburn'*, he mentally corrected himself. He could only imagine what she had told her daughter about the circumstances of her conception and birth.

"She said you were disturbed, violent, and bloodthirsty," added the dark haired girl.

"That's certainly true," he agreed.

"None of the others know what to think. Some of them never learned anything about what you did from their parents. They kept it hidden from them like some dark mystery. Some of their mothers lied, like Emma and Abby's mothers. They told them they were born from secret romances, but Mother told me the truth." Brigid spoke as if she were reciting something from a story, something she had repeated to herself many times.

"Go ahead," he told her. "Say it."

"You hurt her, beat her until she let you have what you wanted. Didn't you?"

The words were more painful than he had expected. It was ironic that she had told Brigid that, since Brenda was the one woman he *hadn't* raped. He supposed the lie was an easy one for her, almost necessary, to keep her daughter's respect. Brenda was dead now, though.

Chapter 27

What would she do if I told her the truth? he wondered. He doubted she would believe him. She couldn't; the thought would undermine everything else she believed, and if she did, she might no longer have what it would take to kill Haley. *Better to let her have the lie,* he thought. *No one should hate their own mother.*

He nodded, accepting her words.

"Why did you do it?" she asked.

The memory of those days flooded his mind, Brenda's coercion, his weakness, and eventually her extortion. He could still see the look on Kate's face when he had been forced to tell her he didn't really love her. The guilt, the sickness of it, and later the anger, they all were bound together and unbidden tears sprang from his eyes. "Because I could," he said simply.

"It doesn't make sense, though," she said, confused by his sudden sadness. "If you're really that selfish, that evil, why are you doing this?"

"Doing what?" he asked.

"I thought you wanted to kill me, but you didn't, instead you kept me alive…"

"Only so you can kill Haley for me," he corrected.

"To protect the others," she added. "None of it makes sense. Why would you agree to let me kill you?"

He finished the last rune, ignoring the sudden intake of breath as he pierced the skin more deeply than was strictly necessary. "Perhaps I'm remorseful now. I'm older, and the guilt of my crimes weighs heavily on me. Or perhaps I'm too selfish. My life has become nothing but suffering, but I'm too proud to let the products of my labors be ruined one by one. *You,* and your brothers and sisters, are my legacy to the world."

Brigid watched his face, as though trying to see behind the mask. She shook her head in disbelief.

"Does it matter?" he added. "You're getting what you wanted."

"So are you," she replied, "that's what bothers me." Her aythar flickered with suppressed emotion, a not quite slumbering fury.

If Tyrion could have seen himself, he would have realized that her aythar almost perfectly reflected his own. In his inner core he still saw visions of burning trees, forests ablaze with the flames of vengeance. What he really wanted, as much, or possibly more than protecting his children, was revenge on the She'Har for what they had done to him, what they had done to all mankind. He would be giving that up in exchange for Haley's death, for a short term reprieve, to save some of his children.

"I'm not getting everything I want," he told her. "Content yourself with that."

***

Two days had passed, and it was time once more to leave for the arena. Kate, Layla, and those of his children who were required to go, waited in the front yard, except for Brigid, who had yet to emerge.

Tyrion turned to Byovar, "I have a favor to ask."

"Name it," said the lore-warden.

"Will you restore Layla's collar? I can't take her to the arena like this."

Byovar frowned, "What happened to it?"

Chapter 27

"I took it off," said Tyrion flatly.

Surprise showed in the Illeniel She'Har's face, but he kept his thoughts to himself. "If I put the collar on her she will belong to me."

Tyrion answered frankly, "I'll just remove it when Lyralliantha returns and have her put a new one on then."

Byovar sighed, but said nothing more as he began the task. Brigid chose that moment to walk out and join the others.

She had recovered most of her strength, but not all. He would have preferred for her to have another week to be certain, but as with most things in life, there was no mercy or leniency to be had with the She'Har.

When Tyrion stepped back out, it was with Brigid close beside him, uncommonly close. Kate watched the two of them with interest. She knew that of all the youths gathered there, Brigid was the one who hated him the most. Ian was a close second and more verbal about it, but her dark haired sister harbored a quiet hatred that eclipsed even his. Of the other teens, she doubted any of them truly hated him anymore.

So why is she standing so close to him? wondered Kate. Brigid looked almost happy to be next to her father. *They must have talked a lot over the past few days, but I can't imagine she would change her opinion so completely.*

That didn't make sense either. Daniel was terrible with words. After two days alone together almost anyone would want to kill him. She still hadn't quite forgiven him for her own last conversation with him.

"It's time," said Tyrion, leading the way.

Brigid remained close, even going so far as to put her hand on his arm, resting it close to the elbow. She walked beside him as though he were escorting her to a dance. Tyrion, for his part, looked uncomfortable with the familiarity, but he held his tongue, keeping his features a study in practiced indifference.

Kate caught up to them, giving her younger sister a strange look, "What are you doing?"

Brigid glanced at her casually, "Father is giving me a present today. I'm just showing my gratitude." Something akin to madness hid behind her smile.

Tyrion merely nodded, and they both continued to walk.

Kate let them draw ahead, falling back to walk next to Layla. *Father? She's never called him that before. What's going on here?* She looked at the female warden, "Doesn't that seem strange to you?"

Layla nodded, "In Ellentrea no one has family, but it turns my stomach to see them touching like that. She's his *daughter.* Isn't that wrong among your people?"

Kate frowned, "Isn't what wrong?"

"For fathers and daughters, or mothers and sons, to trade *favors*," elaborated the warden.

Kate shook her head. Just when she thought she couldn't be surprised anymore, Layla said something so obviously ridiculous that it amazed her. She knew the meaning the wardens had for the word 'favors'. "That's not it, Layla. There's something strange here, but it isn't *that.* Our people often hold hands, especially parents and children, as a sign of caring, not of sexual intimacy."

Chapter 27

Layla's brows went up, "Oh. It still seems unnatural, though. I don't think I'll ever get used to your customs. People shouldn't touch, unless they're about to trade favors."

"What is strange is that she would walk arm in arm with him," said Kate. "I don't really understand why, but she hates him more than any of the others."

"He is a very strange man," agreed Layla, not really understanding at all. "After we had sex, he tried to lay with his arms around me." The tall woman shuddered slightly at the memory.

Kate didn't say anything in response to that. The thought of the two of them together that day still irritated her, but she didn't expect Layla to understand. The statement also made her feel a little sad for him. She already knew for herself how standoffish the female warden could be once her physical needs were met. Daniel had been among these people for over fifteen years now.

How long has it been since someone held him?

The Silent Tempest

Chapter 28

Thillmarius almost looked pleased to see him when they arrived at the arena. The Prathion lore-warden walked toward them rather than wait, and he had a faint smile on his face.

"Tyrion, Byovar," said the Prathion, nodding in their direction.

He even said my name first, noted Tyrion. The world had grown strange and unfamiliar. In the past, he could have never expected such a thing from one of the She'Har, much less from his old tormentor.

"You seem cheerful," observed Tyrion.

"Things have gone well for me lately, and perhaps for you also," said Thillmarius.

Byovar frowned, "You go too far. Nothing has been decided yet."

Tyrion looked at the Illeniel She'Har, "What hasn't been decided?"

"We are forbidden to speak of it," responded the Byovar impassively.

"Am I not a child of the grove now?" reminded Tyrion, deciding to push his luck.

Thillmarius put a friendly hand on his shoulder, an almost alien gesture for the She'Har. "Let it go for now, Tyrion. You will be informed once the elders are done, and personally I believe you will be pleased."

"I would rather know now…"

"Enough," ordered Byovar, brusquely. Normally the Illeniel lore-warden was the more gregarious of the two She'Har. Things were definitely afoot.

Tyrion closed his mouth, frustrated, but Thillmarius stepped in to fill the awkward stop in the conversation.

"Lyralliantha emerged from her meeting with the elders yesterday. I spoke with her," informed Thillmarius.

"She did?" said Tyrion. "I have not seen her yet."

"She gave me a message for you, before being summoned back," said the dark skinned lore-warden.

"Summoned back?"

"The elders still debate. She was sent to give notice to the lore-wardens before returning to them," explained Thillmarius.

"And her message?"

"She told me to tell you to do nothing rash until she is done," said the Prathion.

Tyrion's heart skipped a beat, disturbing the calm he had worked hard to cultivate that day. *Does she know somehow?* He had told no one of his bargain with Brigid. There was no way for Lyralliantha to have any inkling of his terminal plans for the day. Unless there was a spy in Albamarl.

He quickly dismissed that notion. None of his children would know enough to give him away, even if they wanted to. It was technically possible that a Prathion might have sneaked into his home, though. What if one of them had been in his room?

They would have had to wait days, risking discovery the entire time, just to overhear that one conversation. It simply wasn't possible, but he still stared at Thillmarius with suspicion. "Why would she say that, I wonder?"

Chapter 28

The Prathion lore-warden almost laughed, "You have led an exciting life, Tyrion. Perhaps she knows you too well."

Koralltis' voice rose above the noise of the many She'Har talking in the treetop balconies that ringed the arena. The murmur of the crowd gradually disappeared, and Tyrion noticed that the number of Illeniel She'Har attending the event was even higher than usual.

When he had first begun fighting in the arena, the Illeniels never came. They hadn't been represented since they had no slaves of their own, and their elders were philosophically opposed to the practice, but he had changed that. Over time, his unmatched record of victories slowly drew more of them to witness his battles. Now the Illeniel Grove had a much larger group of new humans entering the matches, and their interest had returned anew.

"Win for us, Tyrion," said Byovar, standing next to him. "The entire grove stands behind you."

He glanced at the lore-warden. *Us?* "I am not fighting today."

"They are," said the Illeniel She'Har, pointing at the holding cells where the teens from Colne were being held. Almost all of them were inside a cell now, except for Piper and Blake, the only two whose abilities had yet to manifest.

Tyrion turned away in irritation, heading for David's cell first, since he had just been named. "They will do what they must," he replied. *But only to survive, not for yours, or any other She'Har's amusement.*

Opening David's door, he found the boy within shaking with fear and adrenaline. "Are you ready?" he asked.

David nodded, but almost stumbled as he stepped out.

"Deep breaths, boy. Too much adrenaline will get you killed. Clear your head," he cautioned, leading his son to the edge.

David's fight was against a Mordan slave, one who had already won several bouts in the past. His opponent began teleporting at random, making it difficult for the young man to attack him. After a few minutes of cat and mouse though, David drew a wide circle around himself some seven feet across before using it to create an especially potent shield. Then he straightened his arms at his side, closing his eyes as if in meditation.

Thillmarius clapped, "I remember you doing that once."

"The shield is too big," noted Byovar. "His opponent can just teleport inside it."

"That's the point," said Thillmarius, glancing at Tyrion knowingly. "He doesn't have your special tattoos, though."

"He won't need them," Tyrion answered the lore-warden. "His opponent isn't a She'Har, nor does he have the strength to protect himself from my son's close assault."

It was a good trick, although if the slaves had been permitted to watch the matches in the past, it would have soon become useless. Since they were kept in the dark, unable to watch the fights, none of them had ever

Chapter 28

caught on. It made it difficult for them to learn from other's mistakes.

David's opponent was cautious, and he continued to move about outside the shield, testing it now and then, but eventually he realized that it was far too strong for him to break, nor was it causing David any difficulty to maintain it.

He should attempt to disrupt the ground, or starve David for air, thought Tyrion, but the Mordan mage did neither.

Instead he began to teleport more quickly, attempting to disorient the young man standing inside the fortified shield. Tyrion smiled. David had already won.

Seconds later the outcome arrived, violent and bloody. The Mordan slave teleported within the circle, hoping to surprise the boy from Colne. David's arm blade destroyed his opponent's shield and continued on to nearly bisect the other man.

I need to put some lines on their arms, or go ahead and give them tattoos, thought Tyrion. *He almost didn't have enough to finish him in one shot after breaking the shield.*

David roared, lifting his arms toward the sky as the shock and relief of winning washed over him. It was a feeling that Tyrion was well acquainted with, and for a split second he found himself jealous. He missed the thrill of it, seeing the blood and knowing it was not his own, knowing he would live another day.

Seeing the look on David's face turned his stomach, though. The boy's triumph had flooded him with joy, and yet as it faded he was faced with the realization that he had just butchered another human being. Tyrion could read his son's feelings moment by moment as excitement slowly turned to disgust and remorse. He had lived it too many times himself.

The remorse fades though, and eventually the blood won't disgust him anymore, thought Tyrion. *The thrill of victory is a drug, and it will start to call to him in his dreams, until life outside the arena begins to seem dull and lifeless.*

"Until he's a dead husk inside, like me," muttered Tyrion to himself.

"Pardon?" asked Byovar, standing next to him. "Did you say something?"

Tyrion shook his head, "No, nothing." He met David at the edge of the field and escorted him back to his cell. "Good work."

The boy looked up at him, guilt in his eyes. He was vulnerable then, at his lowest point, ready to grasp at anything that would lessen the self-loathing. "Really?"

Tyrion nodded, "It was you or him, and you gave your enemy the gift of a swift death. Keep your head up, there is no shame in that."

Emma was next, and her match was decisive, clear-cut from the beginning. She was fighting a Centyr mage. Marching forward, she closed the gap quickly while her opponent summoned her first spellbeast. Drawing lines in the dirt, Emma hemmed her enemy in quickly, separating her from her magical ally and keeping the beast at bay until she was close enough to finish the mage. At twenty yards it was over. Two rapid-fire lances of power ended it, one to break the shield and the other to drive a hole straight through the other mage's forehead.

Chapter 28

Tyrion was impressed by her speed and precision. The girl walked back toward him with a face carved of stone. She had turned her back on the whole thing the second it was over, a sure sign, to his eyes, of what she was feeling, despite her taciturn expression. She didn't quite make it to the sidelines before she stopped, doubling over and vomiting onto the dry earth.

He stopped Emma at the field's edge, giving her an approving look and then wiping the corner of her mouth for her. She searched his face with desperate eyes, looking for answers for the pain she felt.

Tyrion had none, so instead he smoothed her hair, pushing aside a loose strand that had fallen across her forehead. "You did well," he told her. "You did as you must. She felt nothing."

She nodded and let him lead her back to her cell, but he could feel Kate's eyes on them the entire time. He brought Abby out next.

Kate leaned close after the girl had entered the field, "That was nice."

"What was?" he asked, looking at her in surprise.

"What you did for Emma."

Tyrion shook his head, "No, I was just doing what was necessary. They're vulnerable now. They've learned to kill, but it still makes them sick. They need validation, reassurance, someone to tell them it's alright, someone to make them feel better about what they've done. I'm just telling them what they want to hear—to make them better killers."

Kate reached up, tugging at his ear painfully, "Stop it, Daniel. You always see the worst in everything, most particularly yourself. Whatever reason you're claiming, the kindness is still your own. Don't forget that."

He looked at her in surprise, unsure how to respond and once again found himself caught in her emerald eyes. "I'm sorry," he said.

Her expression turned curious, "For which thing exactly?"

"Take your pick," he said.

Abby's match began, and their attention turned again to the arena. Her opponent was a Prathion, and from the beginning things didn't go well. The Prathion mage vanished, but never reappeared.

Unsure how to respond, Abby drew a tight circle around herself before creating a powerful shield.

"No!" growled Tyrion to himself.

"What's wrong?" asked Kate.

"She should use the mist to equalize things, or use the ground to find her opponent, instead she's locked herself into one position," he explained. "It's exactly the wrong thing to do now."

"The Prathion can't see her anyway," said Layla from his other side. "He hasn't lowered his invisibility once."

"Don't be so sure," said Tyrion. "Some of them have tricks you might not expect. I've fought Prathions before who could remove only a tiny part of their veil, allowing them to see while being very hard to detect themselves. Since he hasn't come out once, I would assume this mage is one of them."

Layla was a Prathion herself, and it was her turn to be surprised. "I did not know that was possible."

Because none of your people learn from one another. The only reason I know is because I've fought

Chapter 28

hundreds and hundreds of fights and survived, thought
Tyrion, but he didn't say it. There was no point.

"I don't see anything," complained Kate. "She's
just standing there."

Tyrion and Layla both felt the earth move then,
directly beneath Abby's location.

"He's underneath her," said Layla.

Tyrion had seen more, however, a tiny flash of
aythar almost too small to detect. "No, he's—shit!"

Abby had felt the earth shifting as well, directly
beneath her shield. Releasing it, she stepped to the
right, directly toward the tiny flash Tyrion had seen,
and in her haste she neglected to replace the fixed
shield with a more mobile personal one.

A grinning man appeared directly in front of her,
his hand sweeping up and out, sheathed in razor sharp
aythar, aythar he used to punch through Abby's
unprotected abdomen before ripping sideways, tearing
through her liver and one lung. She fell back, her eyes
wide with surprise. There was blood everywhere.

The Prathion leaned over her, his shield still
protecting him. "Stupid bitch," he said, right before
his head exploded.

He hadn't counted on Abby's strength. Still
conscious and at close range, she had destroyed his
shield and obliterated his head and neck with a single
retributive strike. His headless corpse collapsed on the
ground beside her, arms and legs twitching reflexively.
Abby looked at him once before her eyes closed as she
lost consciousness.

Tyrion was barely aware of Kate screaming beside
him as he watched Koralltis walk onto the field. *Why
was the She'Har so slow?* There was no time. Abby

was dying, and rapidly. He started to run forward, but Thillmarius grabbed his arm.

"No, Tyrion. No one may enter until Koralltis has called it."

The master of the arena did call it, long seconds after, a victory for Illeniel. Then he knelt over the fallen girl while Tyrion ran from the sidelines. The She'Har was spellweaving, wrapping Abby's body in wide swathes of vine-like magic.

"She's not dead!" cried Tyrion, trying to get the She'Har's attention. "You can save her."

Koralltis looked at him in annoyance, "This is a stasis-weave. It will preserve her until we can get her to a better location. She will be returned to you later— unharmed."

Tyrion stopped short of them, watching the spellweave enfold Abby. He had never seen a stasis-weave before, but he supposed it must have been used on him in the past since he had been mortally wounded more than once. Entranced, he sharpened his magesight, trying to resolve the individual She'Har symbols that empowered the spellweave.

Years past, while attempting to learn spellweaving, he had learned that his magesight was considerably better than most mages, or She'Har; not only was his range greater, but he was able to see far finer details. Very few She'Har could see the fine detail of their own spellweaving, which was something that was handled in an unconscious fashion by the seed-mind they carried within.

Unfortunately, even though he could see the minuscule hexagonal symbols that they used for spellweaving, he was unable to replicate them. That was why he had developed his own system, the larger triangular runes that he used for enchanting. Functionally, his enchantments were the same as spellweaving, it just took much longer for him to produce them.

The time factor involved in creating enchantments was a disadvantage in many ways, but it could also be an advantage. It simply meant he always had to plan carefully, keeping his thoughts on the future. The She'Har failure to recognize this was a blind spot of their own. They always assumed they would have time to produce whatever spellweave was needed.

If he could understand the principle behind the stasis-weave, he could undoubtedly produce an enchantment to replicate its effect.

Ru, Eolhi, Frem, Lyer, Thal, Sharra… deep in concentration, he tried to memorize the pattern. Like most spellweaves, it began to repeat at a certain point, if he could just reach the end of the pattern and remember the order and geometric placement before…

Abby's body was lifted, and the spellweave began to move, blurring the symbols as he tried to read them. *Dammit!*

He knew better than to try to delay Koralltis, so he turned away, heading back to the sidelines, a look of disappointment and frustration on his features. Caught up in his thoughts, he walked back slowly, his eyes on the ground.

Kate was tearful when he got there. She couldn't understand Erollith, of course, and the look on his face had been discouraging. She thought they were taking Abby's lifeless body from the field. "She was the kindest, the most compassionate one of them all," she said, her voice breaking as she spoke.

"She's fine," said Tyrion.

"What? They just carried her away," said Kate.

Frustration ate at him as he tried to remember what he had seen. "Dammit, just be sil...," he paused. He had lost it. There was no way to figure it out from the little he could recall. Not that it mattered, he would be dead before the day was over.

Something more important was happening in front of him. Kate was upset, and he had been about to order her to silence. He caught her eyes with his own, seeing the hurt there. She had only just learned that Abby was still alive, and she still had no idea how good the She'Har healers were. Softening his features, he reached out, pulling her into his arms.

"They can heal her, Cat. I'm sorry, I wasn't thinking. You don't have to worry. Abby will be fine," he squeezed her tightly.

Kate tensed in his arms. It was the first time he had held her since... almost ten years before, when they had last parted. She was still angry with him, she was still worried about Abby, she didn't want... *I can't do this, not again,* she thought, and then she relaxed despite herself and let herself sink deeper into his embrace.

"It's time for the next match, Tyrion," said Byovar from beside him.

He didn't want to let go. *This is probably the last time.* Looking around, he could see Layla standing a few feet away with a nauseated expression of disapproval on her face.

Chapter 28

Kate pushed him away, "Later." Her eyes were soft, with a light in them he had thought he would never see again.

I don't want to die, came the sudden thought, but he pushed it aside. Duty called. He went to fetch Ryan from his holding cell.

The Silent Tempest

Chapter 29

Ryan's fight went smoothly, as did Tad and Sarah's, and after that came the blooding fights. This was the first week for Ashley, Ian, Violet, and Anthony. Tyrion had worried that Brigid's fight might be called before that, but apparently the She'Har wanted to save the most dramatic matchup for last.

Of the four first time matches, none were particularly elegant or well executed, Ashley and Violet won their fights reluctantly but without incident. Anthony's was short, his opponent was already wounded, probably from a fight in the pens before he had been brought to the arena. It wound up being almost a mercy killing, and the boy was clearly distraught afterward. Tyrion tried to console him with kind words, but there was obviously little honor to be had in such a one-sided slaughter.

Ian's fight was disturbing. He had been matched up against a young girl, probably no more than fourteen years of age, if that. It was hard to tell for sure, children in the pens of Ellentrea were usually malnourished and underweight, so their ages were difficult to judge.

She had curly brown hair, and despite her small size, she was energetic and clever. A Prathion, she went invisible shortly after the lights changed and attempted to get closer to her opponent.

Ian, for his part, attempted to cover the ground in a sensing net that would show him her location, but his powers were too new, and he had had too little practice at it. His pattern was filled with large holes and gaps.

Somehow, whether by skill or by chance, the Prathion girl managed to avoid stepping on any of the active areas, thus evading his detection.

One thing Ian had learned well, though, was how to shield himself. His embarrassing fight with Ryan had shown him the importance of that skill. When the girl appeared close beside him and attempted to pierce his shield with a surprise attack, she failed. His return stroke shattered her defense and sent her reeling to the ground, nearly unconscious from the feedback.

Rather than kill her immediately, however, Ian knelt and then pulled her upright yanking painfully on her hair.

"What is he doing?" asked Kate, but Tyrion was looking down, his eyes closed and his jaw clenched.

Ian, like the girl he fought, was naked. He brought his head close, biting her neck as his hands fondled her small breasts.

"That's against the rules, right? That can't be allowed, can it?" demanded Kate, outraged.

Layla was laughing too hard to answer, so finally Tyrion spoke up, "It's stupid, but the She'Har don't care what happens, so long as one of them dies."

Ian had the girl's back on the ground now, spreading her legs as he brought his member forward to press against her tender regions. Seconds later his body convulsed in pain as the slave collar punished him for attempting to enter the girl.

Layla's laughter grew louder, "Is the child addled? Didn't you tell them, Tyrion? I know you told him."

Kate stared at her in shock, "This isn't funny! He's trying to rape her."

Chapter 29

The female warden snorted, "If he lives through this, he'll never forget which door to use again, the collar is unforgiving."

Tyrion's face was red with fury and embarrassment. Some of the spectators laughed at the sight of the boy convulsing as he fell away and to one side. While the pain had stunned Ian, it seemed to have roused his opponent. The girl rose to one knee, her eyes finding her assailant.

Her first attack was a fiery lance that burned a hole through Ian's right thigh, close to his manhood. She had missed. He screamed in pain, but adrenaline and fear brought him back to his senses. Desperately he shielded himself before her next attack could land.

Seeing her advantage had vanished, the Prathion mage vanished, but Ian knew her location. Sending forth a broad blast of force, he sent her sprawling, and she reappeared rolling across the dirt a mere ten feet away. His next attack rendered her unconscious, but she was still breathing.

"He was lucky," commented Layla. "She should have aimed for his chest. She let her anger get the better of her."

The burn through his leg made it impossible for him to walk, so Ian half crawled, half pulled himself toward her. The boy was in a rage from the pain, and rather than use his power to finish the girl, he began pummeling her, driving his fists into her head and stomach.

Whether she regained consciousness or not was hard to tell, for while her body flinched and curled in on itself during his assault, she never managed anything resembling an organized defense. After several more blows, her body went limp, but her heart still beat.

Ian continued to pound on her for a minute or more until he gradually came to realize she wasn't dying. Switching tactics, he choked her, throttling her flaccid body until her face turned purple, and her faltering heart finally stopped.

Watching his son strangle the girl was eerily reminiscent of his first fight in the arena, and Tyrion found the bile rising in his throat. He fought the urge to retch as he entered the field, moving to reclaim Ian after Koralltis had declared him the winner.

He let his anger push the nausea aside.

"One moment Tyrion," said the She'Har. "You can have him after I have restored his leg." After a few minutes the arena master helped Ian to his feet. "He may have a limp after this, burns are difficult to heal, even for us."

"I don't care," said Tyrion, pointing to the sidelines, indicating the direction Ian should walk. "Move."

The teen began to walk, limping heavily while Tyrion followed silently behind him.

"What's the matter? Did I shame you?" asked Ian with an audible sneer.

Tyrion was fighting the urge to kill the boy already. "Do you know what the She'Har call us? What their term for humans is?"

Ian held his tongue.

"They call us 'baratt', which means 'animal' in their language," he said, continuing. "Until now I believed that they were wrong, except in the case of those that they raised to be animals, the people that came out of the pens. But today you just proved their point, trying to rut in the dirt like a pig. Is killing not enough for you? Are you so starved for sex that you would try to rape your opponent? You didn't even give her a clean death!"

Ian stopped before entering his cell, "Isn't that what you did, *Father*? Isn't that how I came to be? Should you be so surprised that I turned out like *you*?"

Tyrion snapped then, punching the unshielded boy hard in the nose. Blood erupted from Ian's face as he fell backward. He started to scramble when he landed, but his father's hand caught his hair, pulling hard to jerk his head back. Tyrion's other hand rose toward Ian's throat, encased in its enchanted blade of aythar.

Byovar shouted from behind him, "Tyrion, no! Not here, wait until later. They are calling for the next one."

He froze, feeling the boy's heart pounding in his chest, thumping in time with his own. "I was about to kill you, boy," he whispered. "Don't forget that." Releasing Ian, he stepped back, slamming the door to the cell closed.

Taking a deep breath, he moved down several doors until he was outside the cell that held Brigid. *This is it.* The door opened at his touch, and Brigid looked up at him from beneath shadowed brows, "You look upset, Father." She stood and extended her hand to him.

"I've had better days," he told her, staring at her hand. She lifted one brow, smiling at his hesitation until finally he offered her his arm.

"You aren't having second thoughts about our deal are you?" she asked, her voice shifting tone oddly. Her features radiated calm confidence, but her aura was uncertain.

A dozen things passed through his mind at her question, but it was Ian's recent disgrace that remained when everything else was done. *I'm no better.* "No," he answered surely. "Nothing has changed." An unusual feeling of peace settled over him as he said the words. *Let it be over.*

Brigid's hand tightened on his arm, "I don't want to do this."

"She doesn't either, but none of us have any choice," he replied. "You understand the reasons, and I think she does as well."

"We've always been friends..." Brigid was looking across the arena now, seeing her sister stepping out on the other side.

Tyrion put his hand over hers on his arm, pulling her along when her steps became reluctant. "This isn't your fault, Brigid. It isn't Haley's either. The blame falls squarely on my shoulders. Remember that. Make sure you win. You can avenge her after it's over."

"No, please," Brigid looked up at him, her eyes pleading. "Can't you do it? I shouldn't have to, it shouldn't be me—it—I can't."

"You're right," he agreed, untangling her arm from his, "but 'right' doesn't matter a damn in this cursed world. Remember what I told you, focus on your defense. Don't let her see the blades until it's too late, until she's too close."

Her face twisted as he walked away, red eyes and swollen lids spoiling her beautiful features. Brigid's shoulders hunched inward as she fought to control her grief. Grief for a sister not yet dead, grief for a murder not yet done. She kept her eyes on Tyrion's back, though. He could feel them there as he withdrew.

"You're next," she said softly, and then the lights changed and the chime sounded.

Haley had been watching them from across the field. She had been too far to hear their words, but her hungry eyes had taken in every detail. Seeing her sister and closest friend, Brigid, enter the field as her opponent had filled her with despair.

For an unknown time the field was silent as the two girls stared at one another. Haley's hair was a dark brown, a shade lighter than Brigid's raven locks, but in every other respect they almost appeared to be twins. But where Brigid's face was marred by grief and anger, Haley's was filled with deadly resolve. She began advancing on her sister, taking careful steps.

She's too strong, observed Tyrion, watching from beyond the arena barrier. Both of his daughters shone with brilliant, powerful aythar, but Brigid was still recovering from her injury. He could see that Haley held a small but distinct edge as they were at present.

At fifty yards, the peaceful air was split with actinic light as Haley struck, sending a bolt of pure lightning racing toward her sister. It struck with sizzling power, but there was no chance it would penetrate the shield Brigid had prepared.

That wasn't its purpose, however. The light and sound were disorienting, making it difficult for Brigid to react properly to the following attack, a lance of pure force, focused and deadly. That was the attack meant to crack her shield.

The speed of Haley's assault was breathtaking, and Brigid's response was just as fast. Acting on a level that had to be almost pure instinct, she contracted her shield and sidestepped, letting the shieldbreaker pass without making contact. She sent a return stroke of her own in the space of the same breath, sweeping low to try and force Haley to move before she was ready.

The progress of the battle over the next seconds was almost too rapid to follow as the sisters traded blows at speeds that were almost inhuman. The crowd of spectators grew hushed as they tried to follow the course of the combat. *This* was the fight they had hoped to see. Gabriel had been a disappointment, but Tyrion's daughters were delivering the kind of fight they hadn't seen since Tyrion himself had retired from the arena.

Naturally, Kate was unable to see much of what was happening beyond the occasional flash of light and the thunderous sound of invisible forces battering against one another, but as she glanced to her side, she could see that Layla's mouth had fallen slightly agape. The female warden watched the battle with what could only be described as awe.

Of all those watching, only Tyrion possessed the acuity of magesight and enough combat experience to truly follow their movements, and even he was impressed by the sheer ferocity of their blindingly fast struggle for dominance. And Tyrion was worried.

Don't fight her at range, you're already at a disadvantage. You can't keep it up as long as she can.

A sound like thunder rolled across the arena as Brigid's latest battering blow connected directly with Haley's defense. It was a solid hit, and in that moment there was no subtlety or cunning in Haley's opposition.

Chapter 29

Brigid's best had failed to crack her sister's shield. She was the weaker of the two, and she was tiring already.

Haley's counterstroke was a hammer blow that might have broken Brigid's shield and killed her outright, but the raven haired girl met it with an angled plane that diverted much of Haley's attack to one side, where it struck the ground. The vibrations of that shock could be felt far beyond the arena itself.

A flurry of attacks followed, each as powerful as the last, each striking from a different direction as Haley accelerated her attacks against her sister, attempting to pulverize her with unadulterated power. The earth began to roil at her feet, kicking up in fits and starts as the wind churned. Haley was whipping the air into a storm, even as she bombarded Brigid with earth shattering attacks.

The combination of attacks was bewildering. Layla was squinting beside Kate, as if scrunching up her eyes would somehow help her magesight to better discern what was happening.

"What's going on?" asked Kate.

"Your sister is losing," said Layla uncertainly. "No one could survive that."

Tyrion was holding the hilt of his sheathed sword, his knuckles white as he concentrated on the battle, his emotions indiscernible. "She's still fighting," was all he said. Within the storm of wind and dirt he could see Brigid's skillful defense.

Kate's dark haired sister hadn't yet learned to use the wind and soil as a weapon the way Haley had, but she had practiced for more than two weeks now with the most accomplished survivor of the arena in its entire history. Brigid met each attack with unbelievable precision, deflecting them with the minimum angle necessary to avoid taking the full brunt of them. She conserved her waning strength with careful efficiency.

That was why Haley had chosen to add the windstorm. The area attack tore at Brigid whenever she shifted her defense to deflect one of her sister's powerful blows. Brigid had stopped using a personal shield entirely, relying on reflexes and balanced precision to divert only Haley's most deadly strikes.

Brigid's body was covered with tiny cuts and tears. She bled from more than a dozen wounds, but none of them were serious. Even as Tyrion watched, she deflected a flying stone that threatened to decapitate her, while ignoring several smaller ones that battered her thighs.

Unable to see through the gale, Kate watched Tyrion's face instead. Strangely, he was smiling even as a tear made a slow track down one cheek.

"Daniel?" she asked worriedly.

"They're beautiful, Cat," he answered, his voice thick with pride. "My daughters are beautiful. Trained and untrained, they're the most incredible things I have ever seen, on or off of the arena field."

The wind was dying now, as Haley began to pay the price for her overzealous use of aythar. The dirt began to settle, and as the air cleared, Brigid walked toward her half-sister, her childhood friend. She still had some strength left in her, but she didn't waste it on a shield.

Haley watched her approach with sad eyes. She still had her shield, and her face was unmarked by the wind and grit that had scoured the area, unlike Brigid, who was covered in blood and grime.

"I'm sorry Briddy," she told the wounded girl, using an old familiar name. "I wanted to let you win, but I just couldn't help myself. I couldn't let you have it that easy."

"I haven't won, Haley," replied the raven haired girl, blinking as blood dripped into her right eye. A cut in her scalp had covered her right cheek in a crimson wash.

"I saw the tattoos from the very start," said Haley. "I've seen them before."

Brigid shook her head, taking another step, "I don't think I've got enough strength left to even activate them."

Haley smiled sadly, "Liar. I know you better than that."

"I can't even make a shield," replied Brigid. "You've got more than enough to finish me."

Haley took the final step, bringing them face to face, less than a foot and a half apart, her shield still shining vibrantly. "Show me his gift, Brigid. I want to see it before we finish this."

"I'm tired, Haley. I don't think I can," said Kate's sister. "Just make it quick—please."

"Show me, Briddy," said Haley, calling her by her nickname again.

Brigid nodded her head weakly. "I might be able to manage, just the hand, though." Frowning, she concentrated, and the enchanted blade sputtered to life, sheathing her open palm and fingers in knife-like force.

In the space of a heartbeat, Haley released her shield and stepped in, grabbing her sister's arm by the elbow. Brigid's hand sank deep into her abdomen, and the brown haired girl let out a painful gasp.

Brigid shrieked in denial of what her eyes were showing her, what her hand was feeling. Her power exhausted, the enchantment flickered out, and her hand came away covered in warm blood and bile. Her cry rose, growing louder as it changed pitch and then slowly lowered into a sorrowful wail.

"Damn," said Haley, sinking to her knees. "That hurt more than I thought."

"Why, Haley? Why?!" cried Brigid, dropping down beside her friend.

"I couldn't do it anymore—not after Gabriel. I never wanted to be a killer. I wanted to let you win at the start, but I just couldn't do it. Not until I had worn myself down, not until I had seen what I had done to you. I was never as strong as you Briddy."

Haley's face grew pale, and she used one arm to ease herself down, wincing as the tear in her stomach pulled.

"No, no, no, no, no," moaned Brigid. "I don't want this Haley. They can stop this, we can heal your wound. Maybe I can close it…"

"Don't be stupid, Briddy. One of us has to die, and I'm already mostly there. Let me be a hero this time, you always made me play the bad guy when we were kids," said Haley, her voice growing weaker.

Desperate, Brigid knelt, bringing her head closer and speaking earnestly into Haley's ear. "He's going to pay for this Haley. I swear it."

Haley's eyes were closed now, but she was still listening. "You'll get revenge for us, Briddy, but not him. Don't hurt him. He loves us. I knew it when I saw your tattoos. Kill them…"

"Who?" asked Brigid, confused. "What are you talking about?"

"I had a dream, Briddy, but it wasn't sweet. It was terrible…"

"What dream, Haley?" said Brigid. "What dream?"

But Haley didn't answer again. Her consciousness had slipped away, leaving Brigid to watch her sister's breathing gradually slow, until it seemed to stop altogether. Her heart still beat though, and death was not kind. Haley's body gasped again and again, waiting longer between each desperate draw of air. It was minutes before it was done, and her aythar faded away at last.

Brigid was alone, and she sat and cried until Tyrion came, dragging her to her feet before lifting her into his arms to carry her away.

The Silent Tempest

Chapter 30

She felt light in his arms. Brigid had gone still and quiet as he lifted her. She buried her face against his shoulder to shut out the sights around her, although he knew her magesight would not be so easily stopped. He was certain her focus was on the same place his eyes were staring—Haley's motionless form.

She had been beautiful, but only rapidly cooling flesh remained, his throat tightened, and he turned away. *She deserved better.*

The clear sky began to cloud as he walked back, but he had expected that. The voices in the air were filled with sorrow, though whether it was of their own accord, or because of his feelings, he couldn't be sure.

The sight of the others waiting for them as he stepped outside the arena made his chest hurt, but he took solace in the slow beat of the earth beneath his feet. *I feel nothing.*

Kate and Layla were watching him closely, but it was Byovar who spoke first, "There is one more match coming."

Tyrion's face grew worried, "Surely they are done with us?"

"Not us, it's a Prathion match with Gaelyn, two long time veterans. The winner may be retired and made a warden," explained the She'Har. "We can't take them out until it's over," he added, indicating the holding cells.

"I need to take her back. She needs tending," said Tyrion, glancing down at his daughter.

He looked at the others. He had been speaking to Byovar in Erollith, so only Layla had understood their conversation. Kate's eyes were full of worry and questions.

"I'm going to take her back and clean her up," he said to her, hoping it would be enough to satisfy her.

Kate nodded, "I'll come with you."

He shook his head, "No, I want you to stay here with Layla. She'll bring you back in a little while."

"Bring me back?" asked Kate. "I still have legs. Let me help you."

"I'm sorry, Cat," he told her.

She frowned, "What are you sorry for this time?"

He showed his teeth, but the smile didn't quite reach his eyes, "Take your pick."

Kate studied his face, and what she saw there worried her. There was something deeper, something behind the casual words. "What are you thin…"

Tyrion's will wrapped itself around her mind, smoothing out the turbulence of her thoughts and pressing her awareness down, into the darkness. She felt his lips touch her forehead once, just before oblivion took her away. "Sleep…," he murmured softly.

Layla caught her as she sagged and began to fall. She looked at Tyrion, "What was that for?"

"I didn't feel like arguing with her," he said simply. "Will you obey me, Layla?"

"Of course, my lord."

"Even in death?"

The female warden frowned, "Yours or mine? I cannot obey anyone if I am dead."

Her practicality made him smile faintly. Trust a warden to ask such a question. "Mine."

"I do not think there is anyone alive who could kill you, my lord," she replied proudly before lowering her voice, "but death aside, I think I have become a 'fool' for you."

Her statement was the last thing he had expected to hear. It was probably the closest a warden could come to professing love or friendship. It was also the sort of thing they despised admitting, since such feelings were considered a sign of weakness among the slaves of the She'Har.

He looked away, unable to respond for a moment. Kate would have understood his emotion as gratitude, but Layla would take it as embarrassment. The warden was already turning red as she realized what she had said. "When you return, I want you to take care of Kate for me," he told her. "She will be understandably upset. You may also need to protect Brigid from her, or the others. Make sure none of them hurt one another."

Layla's voice turned serious, "What are you planning?"

"I will be going away for a while," he said, as drops of rain began to fall. Fat drops that seemed swollen with all the regrets that even something as large as the sky could no longer contain.

"Where will you go?" asked the warden, but he ignored her question.

Carrying his daughter carefully, he made his way through to the trees of the Illeniel Grove, for they bordered the Prathion Grove near the arena, and from there he began the hour long trek back toward Albamarl.

Once they were among the massive god-trees, the rain seemed to vanish, for it would take a while before the great limbs and leaves above them had taken on enough water to begin to drop the excess to the ground below.

"I can walk," said Brigid, stirring in his arms.

"I know," he returned, reluctant to let her go. He wanted to pretend, if only for a short while longer.

"Let me down," she added.

They walked together in silence, separated by only a few feet. A few feet that represented an impossible gulf between them. The rain found them again as they emerged from the forest and began to cross the rocky field that led to Albamarl.

He warmed the rain and funneled more of it toward her as they went, using it to wash the blood and dirt from her skin.

Brigid looked a question at him.

"You have to clean the cuts before sealing them. Even so, you may develop a fever over the next few days," he told her. "Don't push yourself before you finish recovering."

"Has this happened to you before?" she asked.

He nodded, "Similar things."

"Is this your kindness?" suggested Brigid.

Tyrion shrugged, "I have been among the She'Har too long. I am not sure I know the meaning of that word anymore."

"I won't forgive you," she told him. "I know the She'Har are to blame for today, and for so much more, but I can't forgive you. The hurt runs too deeply."

"I would never ask for that," he replied before stopping. They stood outside the house now, in the empty yard near what had become a permanent fire pit after Ryan had worked on it. He reached out to her, but she flinched away at his touch now, suddenly shy of contact.

"Don't."

"Let me close the wound," he said. Touching her scalp, he used his magic to draw the torn edges together, sealing them shut.

She hissed at the pain, and fresh tears began to roll down her cheeks, but he didn't stop. Instead, he reached down, tracing the ripped skin along her ribs, the cut on her hip, and then her thigh, closing each in turn. Those were the worst of her lacerations, and after that he drew back.

Brigid looked up at him with wet, swollen eyes that seemed to mirror completely the rage and agony that had filled his heart over the years.

He knelt in front of her.

"I don't think I have enough strength left," she lied, holding up her tattooed arm.

He could see quite well how much she had recovered already, but instead he told her, "I wouldn't make you do that." Reaching across his body, he drew the wooden sword before handing it to her, hilt first. "Use this."

The sword shook in her grasp, but it wasn't just her arm that was shaking, it was her entire body that had begun trembling. "I'm too tired," she told him. "If you changed your mind, I couldn't hope to kill you right now."

"I want you to do it, Brigid. I want your face to be the last I see. You deserve this more than anyone," he replied, taking the point of the blade and setting it to his chest so that it rested against the 'x' scar he had created there previously. In the distance he sensed the others. They had come within the range of his magesight. They would reach them within minutes.

"We don't have much time," he added, creating a shield around the two of them to prevent interference.

Brigid looked straight into his eyes. "I hate you Daniel Tennick," she said, using his birth name. "I hate what you did to my mother, what you did to the people of Colne. I hate you for what you did to so many women. I curse you for bringing me here!" As she spoke, her voice rose, gaining volume and vehemence.

She was pressing forward now, leaning against the sword, its tip cutting through the skin of his chest. Razor sharp, it would only take a bit more pressure to drive it home, to slip betwixt his ribs and pierce his beating heart. Brigid's voice was ragged now as she yelled the last, "Most of all I hate you for choosing *me* to kill Haley! Damn you!"

Kate, Layla, and the others were running toward the house now. They could see the scene in the yard, and while none of them understood what was happening, Kate knew they needed to stop it. Her voice split the air as she ran, but whatever she was saying was incomprehensible.

Brigid took another breath and gave forth a deep guttural growl that rose from the depths of her belly and echoed the frustration that ran to her very core. Her hands gripped the sword tightly as the sound

376

climbed in pitch and turned into a wretched sob, her belly clenching so hard, she could scarcely draw breath.

She wept tears of anger as blood ran from the cut in his chest, but she found herself unable to thrust the blade home. Staring into her father's mournful, cerulean eyes she saw herself there, a soul ravaged by anger and fury.

In the back of her mind, she could still hear Haley's words, *"Don't hurt him. He loves us."*

Her hands opened, and the weapon fell from her nerveless fingers. Furious with her own weakness, she struck him hard in the chest, her fist slipping across the blood there. "I hate you so much," she sobbed, dropping to her knees in front of him. "I hate you, I hate the She'Har, I hate everyone!"

Tyrion's arms went out, pulling her toward him while she fought, twisting and clawing. "It's too late for that. You should have killed me when you had the chance," he whispered, drawing her in against her will.

"I hate you…," she said again, and then with a wracking cry she added, "…and I hate Mother! She lied to me."

He said nothing to that. There was nothing he could say.

"She lied! Didn't she?"

He held her close against his bleeding chest, skin to skin, and the blood from their mutual wounds mingled while she cried. The rain ran down them, carrying away their tears in sanguine rivulets. He had released the shield around them, but the others didn't approach, they stood around the two in a silent circle, heads down as they joined in their sorrow.

"You are my true daughter," he said softly, just loudly enough for all of them to hear, "my daughter in flesh and spirit." Raising his head, he looked at the others, "And this is my family; sons and daughters born of misery and forged in the fires of our shared pain. I bear the sin that made you, and I can offer only one consolation."

His aythar flashed in time with the angry beat of his heart. "Together we will have our vengeance, for Gabriel, for Jack, and for Haley. Together we will destroy the She'Har."

The youths gathered around him nodded, murmuring, "…for Haley." Even Ian joined in their response.

Kate found herself alone, surrounded by them, like a tiny spark of sanity adrift in a sea of madness.

Tyrion stood and slowly released her, letting Emma pull Brigid away to console her. One by one, each of the others passed by him, giving him a touch on the shoulder, or sometimes just a meaningful look. Eventually they moved away, into the recently roofed, though still unfinished, dormitory.

Layla had already gone inside the main house, and he found himself standing in the waning light, staring at Kate. She met his gaze evenly.

"And what am I?" she asked. "I am no mage or fighter, and I am not your kin." She rubbed her shoulders, warming them against a cool breeze.

He walked toward her, closing the distance, "You are my wife."

Kate was stunned. "I'm married alr…," she began to protest.

"No," he interrupted. "That was another world, another life. That life is done. You belong to me. I am your husband, and this is your family now."

"But Seth…"

"…is divorced," he concluded for her.

"I have a son."

He paused at that, "Do you want him to live here?" He gestured toward the great trees of the Illeniel Grove.

"No."

He took her by the hand, leading her toward the house.

"There hasn't been a ceremony. Daniel, people can't just say something like that and make it true."

"I can."

"Where are we going?" she asked, but she already knew. She could sense it so strongly she wondered why she bothered to say the words.

"To consummate our marriage."

Kate's heart was pounding as he pulled her inexorably along. His rough hand was like a force of nature, and the heat from it seemed to radiate up her arm. *I should stop this,* she thought, but the words floated through her mind like tissue on the wind, all form and no substance.

She rallied at the bedroom door, pulling back. "What if I don't want—this?" she said, indicating the doorway.

He released her hand, "Then this is going to be a very boring marriage. You can sleep in the other room, if that's what you prefer." His voice was calm, as if he had resigned himself already.

"No," she corrected, "What if I don't want to be married to you?"

His hands came up, and he said a faint word. There was a dangerous look in his eyes as he set them carefully on her shoulders. "Hold very still."

She froze as his fingers reached her throat, and then there was a moment of quiet resistance followed by an odd popping noise. The collar at her throat fell apart and faded into non-existence.

"If you want to leave, you can," he told her. "None of the She'Har will pursue a nameless slave. You never had to come here at all. You're free. A day's walk will see you home again."

Her eyes widened.

"I love you, Kate. You were right about that, fifteen years ago, ten years ago, and even now, but I'm a very bad person. I've done terrible things. I tried to keep you away from this, then and again when we brought the children from here, but you wouldn't stay out of it. You've seen what my life is like."

"What are you trying to say?" she asked.

"This is your last chance."

She looked away. "Daniel this has to be the worst proposal in the history of the world."

"That's exactly why you should go," he told her. "I'm not inviting you to share a life of love, laughter, and children. I'm inviting you to share my damnation. My morals have become so degraded that I'm finally willing to drag you down with me."

She moved closer, "You aren't lying."

"Does that surprise you?"

Kate narrowed her eyes, "Frankly, yes. Every time we came close to this in the past, you lied and pushed me away. For once you've told the unvarnished truth."

He watched her, trying to figure out what she was about to decide. Her aura had taken on an ambiguous appearance, but it resolved rapidly as she made her choice.

She lifted her chin, "Very well, damn me then." Her hand rose to the back of his head, and she pulled his face closer, kissing him at last. It was several breathless minutes before they separated again. "I have one condition," she added.

"What is it?" he asked as he lifted her, preparing to carry her to the bedroom.

"You have to play your cittern every evening—for all of us."

"And if I refuse?"

"Too bad," she replied. "You shouldn't have married *me* then."

The Silent Tempest

Chapter 31

Abby returned the next morning. She had a long, faint scar across her abdomen, and she was noticeably paler, but she was otherwise unharmed. As Tyrion had discovered in the past, She'Har healers were unmatched in their ability to restore health to the wounded.

Life went on.

Tyrion had them continue their practices during the mornings, but he gave them more leeway now. Almost all of them were blooded, and most had fought twice now, so he let them practice with one another, usually under Layla's watchful eye. Occasionally their ideas were unexpectedly dangerous, and it helped to have someone more experienced on hand to dissuade them.

Ian kept his distance from Tyrion most of the time, but when they did cross paths, he was deferential, dipping his head respectfully. Tyrion hadn't repeated the details of Ian's match to the others, something the boy had noticed and was perhaps grateful for, now that the shame of his actions had sunk into his thick head.

Even so, Tyrion kept a wary eye on Ian. Now that his blood had cooled, he no longer felt he had the right to judge him for his actions, but he worried about the future. The world of the She'Har was no place for idiots.

Brigid was the most changed. Where before she had been openly hostile toward Tyrion, she now hovered by his side whenever the opportunity was present. She became more distant from her siblings, choosing to focus more of her attention on her father.

He worried that killing Haley had broken something within her, something that could never be repaired. The madness and rage that had before seemed to hover just beneath the surface was still present, but it was more controlled now. The air seemed cooler when Brigid was nearby. She kept her words to a minimum, and when she did speak, it was never about trivia.

Her eyes were continually on her father.

She was standing next to him a few days later when Ryan walked up, his face thoughtful and earnest.

"May I talk to you?" he asked, looking at Brigid briefly before focusing on Tyrion.

"Certainly," he told his son.

"Alone?"

Brigid glared at him, but said nothing.

"I don't mind," said Tyrion. "Let's walk."

After a minute, Ryan began, "It's about the building."

"You needed to be alone to discuss that?"

Ryan gave him a sheepish look. "Not really, but she creeps me out."

Tyrion raised his brow, "Brigid?"

The young man nodded, "Yes. She's so intense. Sometimes it feels like her eyes are going to burn a hole through me, and it isn't just me either. Most of the others feel the same way."

"She's been through a lot," suggested Tyrion.

"We all have," reminded Ryan, "but she's different. She reminds me of...," he stopped suddenly.

"Reminds you of what exactly?" prompted his father.

"I mean no disrespect, sir," said Ryan, "but she reminds me of you. She's a little scary."

Tyrion laughed, "I will remember that. Scary can be useful now and then. So, what was it you wanted to talk about?"

The young man rubbed his hands together, this was a subject he was more comfortable with. "Well, as you know the dormitory is essentially finished, other than for minor details, and Violet is more interested in managing those."

Violet had turned out to have a penchant for artistic pursuits. While the others had spent their time and labors hauling, fitting, and cutting stone with their magic, she had preferred the finishing work. It had started with smoothing the interior surfaces, adding rounded curves to wooden features and doors and had progressed to scrollwork, carving, and delicate reliefs.

The girl had an absolute obsession with beautiful designs, and the others chose not to complain if it took her away from the heavier work, for her efforts were turning their living space and rooms into something lovely to behold.

"Are you worried about having too much time on your hands?" asked Tyrion.

"Yes and no," said Ryan. "I have some ideas, if you will permit."

"What would you like to do?"

"Well, we could use a storage building. The pantry in your house is large, but for as many people as we have, it would be nice to have a place to keep more than just that. It would also be nice to have a place for the horses, and Abby suggested it would be good to have a place to work that isn't constantly exposed to the elements…"

"A workshop?"

"Several," said Ryan with a nod. "It's best not to work with metal in a place where others are doing more delicate work or dealing with food, or cloth, or pottery." Using his aythar, he created a flat plane of green in the air between them. "This is Albamarl."

Ryan's fingers sketched the outline of Tyrion's house, then added a larger rectangle next to it, "And this is the dormitory. Now, I was thinking we could put a large storehouse here, and a barn and stables back here. Workshops would be along this area, and we could leave the central area open…"

"What are these lines on the outside?"

"If you think it's a good idea, those would be exterior walls…"

"Defensive walls?"

Ryan shrugged, "Well, if something happens with the She'Har, I don't think they would do much good, but they would keep wolves away from the chickens."

"Chickens?"

He pointed at the far corner of his diagram, "Back here, so we would have eggs."

"There are no chickens in the Illeniel Grove," said Tyrion. "Where will you find them?"

"Can't you send someone to Colne?" suggested Ryan. "There are a great many things there we could use here."

Tyrion rubbed his chin. He had never given it thought before. In the past, it simply hadn't been an option, but with his new status it might be possible to do many things that had been inconceivable before.

"That's an interesting suggestion," he said slowly, "but we don't have anything to trade."

Tyrion's face grew stern as he considered taking what they needed. He had already forced the Hayes' family to provide them with a wagon and some goods, and years ago he had forced them to give his parents a considerable amount of lumber. *How much can they afford, though? Or should we force some sort of tribute to be given by the entire town?*

Ryan could see the wheels turning in his father's head. "Wait," he said hurriedly, "Tad thinks we do have something to trade."

He paused, looking at his son.

"Iron," said Ryan, answering his unspoken question, "or granite, or even lumber. We've gotten very good at quarrying. We can produce a lot of materials in a short time span, compared to what they're used to."

Cut stone was a rarity in Colne. Most people used wood for building. It was far easier to work with and moving it in quantity was easier. The only stone masons that Tyrion had ever heard of worked in Lincoln and it was too far to transport much stone there.

"Lumber has to cure, and that takes time," said Tyrion. "Stone is too much work to transport that far. I can't have all of you traveling to Colne. I'm not even sure I can let *any* of you go yet. Iron would be easier. I can produce as much as you might wish, and a single wagonload would be of considerable value."

Ryan smiled. "I hoped you would say that."

"Talk to Tad. Draw up a list and figure out what you need the most and then sort your needs out. You'll want to create a timeline. We can't do everything at once, so you need a plan—what to do first and what you need for it."

"Yes sir!" Ryan was positively beaming.

Tyrion watched him walking back, newfound purpose in his steps. *He smiled at me.* A lump formed in his throat.

***

The next day he had an unexpected visitor. Thillmarius appeared at the front door and politely knocked, which surprised Kate, no one ever knocked. Tyrion's children came and went, usually wanting to know what would be served at lunch or dinner. She opened the door without giving it a thought.

She stared at the ebon hued man standing on the doorstep. Gold eyes stared back at her with unsettling intensity. "Err…, can I help you?" She stepped back to let him enter.

Thillmarius reached out, touching her hair almost fondly. "Where is your collar, child?"

Kate's mouth opened and then closed again. She had no answer for him. She knew there were dire consequences for a human found without one, the least of them, being claimed by the first of the She'Har to find them. The worst didn't bear thinking about. *What would he do if he knew it was Daniel who removed it?*

She lifted her chin, "That is not for me to say." She had no believable lie, so delay was her best option.

"I found it inconvenient," said Tyrion, stepping out from the hall, "so I got rid of it."

Chapter 31

Thillmarius turned his attention to him as he entered, "How fascinating! How did you do it?" He hadn't bothered to close the door.

"Get the door, would you, Kate?" suggested Tyrion. His mind was racing. Depending upon the lore-warden's motivations he might have to do something drastic. Closing the door would make it more difficult for an invisible opponent to escape, and Thillmarius was a Prathion after all.

The She'Har turned his head, watching the red haired woman shut the door with something approaching delight in his features. Looking back at Tyrion, he exclaimed, "How remarkable. Are you thinking to kill me?"

Tyrion smiled, fighting to suppress the fear he always felt when he heard Thillmarius' voice. Despite the years and his experiences, his time under the trainer's 'care' had left an indelible scar on his soul. He hoped he could fight effectively despite it. "Of course not," he answered, hoping the She'Har didn't notice the sweat that had begun to bead on his forehead. "I just prefer to keep the bugs outside now that spring is here."

"Relax," chuckled Thillmarius. "My purpose here is not so dire, nor do I plan to claim your female. I have another reason for coming."

"I would offer you a seat, but we haven't had time to produce many chairs yet," replied Tyrion, trying to slow his heart.

"We can soon remedy that," said the lore-warden, lifting his hands and readying his aythar. He paused for a second, "Will you permit me?" He didn't want to startle Tyrion with sudden spellweaving. The human was quite obviously feeling anxious, and an anxious man might react badly to unannounced magic.

Tyrion nodded, "Go ahead."

Thillmarius did, and a half a minute later there were two comfortable chairs in the front room. He gestured to Tyrion to take a seat. "Before I say anything else, I would like to apologize to you, Tyrion."

Tyrion's eyes widened, of all the things the She'Har might have said, that was the most unlikely.

"When you first came to us, I was ignorant of a great many things, but with patience I have learned from my mistakes, primarily by watching you," said the lore-warden.

Tyrion opened his mouth temporarily, but he couldn't decide what to say.

"I have studied your kind for most of my life, but it wasn't until you arrived that I began to see that much of what I thought I knew was wrong," continued the Prathion. "It was your startling successes in the arena that got my attention initially. At first I attributed that to your excessive strength, but over time it became apparent that it was much more than that. You adapted and changed much faster than any of our baratti. Eventually we placed you in situations that were far beyond your ability to survive on strength alone, but your cleverness saved you over and over again, despite our best efforts to push you beyond your limits."

"To kill me," corrected Tyrion.

Thillmarius nodded, "Just so, and even after you fought the krytek, demonstrating abilities that we believed impossible for a human, I still remained ignorant. It was not until your children were brought here that I began to see properly."

"To see what?"

"You must understand, that to my people, humans appear to be children. We do not even place much value on ourselves. To us, maturity, adulthood, these are things we attribute to the elders. Humans, with their inability to spellweave, and with their low intelligence, did not seem worthy of much respect."

Tyrion found himself bristling at the She'Har's words.

Thillmarius held up a hand, "I do not mean to offend. Seeing you and seeing your children, has changed my views. Your intellect is far greater than that of our slaves, and watching your children, I can see that it is not a rare event. The conclusion that I have arrived at, is that our methods of raising humans is stunting their mental development."

"What are you getting at?"

"I would like to make amends. When you came to us, I treated you just as I would any difficult animal. I fed you, I watered you, and when it seemed necessary, I punished you. My intention was to train you, as I had so many others, but I now understand that I was doing you a great harm. My efforts were not only ineffective, they may have made it more difficult for you to succeed.

"Watching you interact with your offspring has also made me realize that what happened in the arena a few days ago was a terrible wrong. I do not expect you to believe me, but I campaigned against that match, even though I had no control over the Mordan or the Illeniels."

Tyrion was stunned. It was difficult for him to decide what to feel. He still feared, no *hated*, the She'Har, Thillmarius more than any of them, but now he was hearing something he had never expected. *Is he mocking me?* That was unlikely, though. The She'Har were notoriously honest. They could lie if necessary, but a fake apology was far too subtle for them. The She'Har really was trying to apologize.

"Lyralliantha's pronouncement," added Thillmarius, "that you were her kianthi, changed your status, but the debate has gone far beyond that."

"The debate among your elders?"

The lore-warden nodded, "Not just among mine, but the elders of all the groves. Last month I proposed that my people change their definitions of both baratti and She'Har to create a new category for your people."

"Please explain, Thillmarius," said Tyrion. "Nothing has changed, why this sudden change of heart?"

"Our understanding has changed, Tyrion. When we first came to this world, we had only three major categories for defining life. The first category was inhabited by just ourselves, living, intelligent, self-aware life that can manipulate and control aythar. We considered this to be the highest form of life, the only sort of life with what your ancestors would have called a 'soul'. The second category was all other life, the baratti, animals, living things that possessed aythar but could not manipulate it. Humans fit neatly within this category when we first arrived, therefore we had no qualms about taking this world for our own."

"You saw their cities, you've studied their science," Tyrion pointed out. "How could you think them animals?"

Thillmarius nodded, "We knew they were intelligent, but we did not believe your kind to be truly alive in the same way that we are. We thought of you as living machines."

Tyrion found himself grinding his teeth and consciously forced himself to relax. "What was the third category?"

"The Great Enemy that pursues us across the stars, across the dimensions," answered Thillmarius, "but they are not pertinent to this discussion."

"Could they come here?"

The Prathion smiled, "No. We are safe here. The Illeniel and Mordan elders devised an unbreakable defense for this dimension before we came to this world. The Mordan and Centyr were able to make it work as the Illeniel elders planned. There will be no more pursuit."

Tyrion had about a dozen questions, but he focused on the most basic first, "Why are they a different category? What's different about them?"

"That is not something I am at liberty to discuss," Thillmarius informed him, "nor is it pertinent to this conversation. What is important here, is that we now believe your species is truly self-aware, truly alive."

Tyrion shook his head, "How could that take you so long to figure out? Anyone could have told you that."

The lore-warden pursed his lips, thinking carefully. After a brief pause, he continued, "This is difficult to explain. Did you know that it is possible to create a machine that can think?"

His experience with machines didn't go much past wagons and looms, but he remembered the ancient human city that Thillmarius had once shown him, along with the descriptions of the fantastic things they had devised. It still seemed strange, though. "That doesn't really make sense."

"Nevertheless, it is true," said Thillmarius. "Your people had already done so when we arrived. The main point is that it is possible to create a machine from simple materials—metal, stone, glass. One can create a machine that can think and converse, but it is not alive, it is not truly self-aware. It may have the 'seeming' of a She'Har, or in your case, of a human. It can be made so perfectly that it would be impossible for you or me to tell the difference, but it is still just a machine."

Tyrion imagined a doll that could talk, and the idea gave him chills. "That's just—disturbing."

"Just so," agreed Thillmarius. "That is how we thought of your people."

"What?! How could you mistake us for machines?"

"But you are, dear human. You are a fantastic, naturally occurring machine, but instead of metal and gears you are built of blood and bone," said Thillmarius. The look on Tyrion's face made him hurry to add, "And so are the She'Har, whether you are talking about our elders, or our children, such as myself. We are fantastic biological machines."

It felt as if he was mentally drowning. The concept that Thillmarius was trying to convey had twisted his mind into knots. "Your argument is circular, Thillmarius. There is no way to know whether your kind or mine are truly alive according to what you say."

"But there is," said Thillmarius. "Awareness is a property of aythar, even the grass at your feet possesses it in some small quantity. Animals and such things possess it in even greater amounts. The humans we first encountered on this world had it as well, but they were unable to manipulate it. They were unable even to sense its presence. That is why we thought them to be animals, or in the words we just discussed, minimally aware biological machines. Creatures possessing intelligence but no true self-awareness, no real soul. Therefore we saw fit to do with you as we wished."

"That's inane. I have much more aythar than you," reminded Tyrion, "but I would not be so foolish as to think you were not truly intelligent."

Thillmarius nodded, "Intelligence isn't the point, though. We thought there was some threshold of true awareness. Intelligence can be produced even in a true machine without any aythar. The criteria that we thought pivotal was the ability to manipulate aythar at a high level, what we call spellweaving.

"After we produced our first 'human' children, She'Har adapted to this world, we proceeded to experiment with true humans. The result was the human slaves you see today in Ellentrea and the other slave cities. They were identical to the wild humans we first fought, but with the addition of a few genetic changes they were able to perceive and manipulate aythar. We had made them mages, just as you are. At that time, we thought that might make them truly self-aware and sentient," continued the lore-warden.

"But they were cruel and savage brutes. Their intelligence was lower than that of your distant ancestors, and they had no inkling of compassion or empathy. We decided that they must be animals still, albeit intelligent ones. At that point we conjectured that spellweaving must be the crucial difference."

"We still cannot spellweave," noted Tyrion. "Has something changed your mind?"

"You, Tyrion," said Thillmarius. "You changed my mind. Your suffering was apparent from the beginning, but I thought it no different from our other slaves at first. But then you began to show signs of something deeper, your music for one thing, although others debated that the ancient humans had that as well. Your compassion and concern for you children and their empathy for one another were also strong factors in the debate. Even that was not enough to convince many of the elders, though.

"Your success in the arena is what first restarted the debate. Your children's success is pushing it to the point at which few of the elders will be able to deny it," said Thillmarius.

"Why would violence and killing change their minds? Your slaves have been doing that for centuries now."

"It was also your primitive spellweaving," said the lore-warden. "This 'enchanting' as you call it. That was pivotal, but the obvious superiority of your wild upbringing, and the superiority of your children, who were similarly raised, has made the difference. Now my people can no longer ignore what has been in front of them for so long. Not only are your kind aware, but it is the actions of my people that have made them seem so primitive. We have not just taken your world, but in our attempt to create a sentient, self-aware human race, we were actually making you worse. We have not been experimenting with animals, we have been torturing a fellow sentient race."

Thillmarius stared deeply into his eyes, "This is what I believe, although I was ignorant at first. The Illeniels believed this all along, but my grove, and the others, did not. Now they are starting to change their minds. I am trying to make them see, but some do not want to listen."

"Why is that so hard for them to believe?"

The Prathion looked at the ground, "Because changing that perception, paints my people as tyrants and monsters. If they accept the notion that your kind are like us, then we have perpetrated a great crime against another truly self-aware species. We have been murderers, torturers, and violators of the worst kind.

"I would ask for your forgiveness, Tyrion. I have harmed you, and I continued to harm you even after I began to have doubts. I cannot make up for the wrongs I have done, but I will do my best to create a better world for your children."

The anger that had simmered for so long beneath the surface in Tyrion began to rise once more. Thillmarius' admission of guilt did nothing to assuage it, in fact, it only seemed to fan the flames. "The hatred I feel for you and your people goes far beyond what a word like 'forgiveness' could ever hope to cure," he told the lore-warden.

Thillmarius bowed his head, "I can only accept that, Tyrion, for I believe you have good cause to feel that way, but I should tell you, that it is your 'love' that has brought the greatest change."

"Love?!" He hadn't even thought the Prathion knew the word.

"Yes, love. When Lyralliantha declared that you were her kianthi, she was invoking love. Our people have never been highly emotional, but once, in our distant past, we knew the meaning of love. The kianthi were our partners, and we felt love. They were responsible for the expansion of our race when we were struggling just to stay alive. The elders know this, and the lore-wardens know this, but Lyralliantha did not. We remember what once was, even though it is no longer present in our people. One reason she was chosen to take the loshti, was because the elders suspected she had rediscovered this. If she becomes a lore-warden, she will be able to compare the past to what she has found with you in the present."

Tyrion shook his head, caught between anger and confusion, but Thillmarius went on, "I reopened the debate about your kind some years ago, but it was going nowhere. When Lyralliantha said that you were her kianthi, her words set fire to the elders' thoughts. The other groves could no longer ignore my protests, they could no longer ignore the philosophy of the Illeniel Grove. They had to open their eyes."

"So what happens now?" asked Tyrion.

"Nothing," said the Prathion. "The debate still goes on. Some refuse to be convinced, but with each victory your children produce, they demonstrate their superiority to our slaves. That is proof that our